PROLOGUE

THE ASTEROID BELT, 53.000 YEARS AGO.

Huge and impossibly ancient, the object slowly tumbled end over end through space. Out here, more than 500 million kilometres from Earth, between the orbits of Mars and Jupiter, it had remained for millions of years. It had first arrived during the formation of the Solar System, when it slipped into orbit around the young star, along with billions upon billions of other objects that were already here.

There it had traversed space silently, while life arose from the primordial soup on Earth. It had seen Mars transform from a blue watery world, into its dead frozen orange form. It had become part of the Sun's asteroid belt, but it was not originally from this place. It was merely a visitor.

The Asteroid Belt contains trillions of objects, but the distances between them are so enormous that collisions at this stage in the life of the Solar System are rare. Spacecrafts from Earth have passed straight through the belt, without bumping into so much as a speck of dust.

4.5 billion years ago, during the early days of the Solar System, when the accretion disc around the newly formed star was still dense with material, it was a very different story. Objects as small as tiny pebbles, and metallic rocks as large as mountains, would constantly slam into each other at speeds of thousands or even tens of thousands of kilometres per hour, releasing huge amounts of energy, mainly in the form of intense heat. The heat would turn the metallic rocks into liquids in an instant, after which the debris would scatter, cool and then coalesce into more and ever-larger bodies, finally resulting in the planets we know today. However, around 3 AU from the Sun, which is three times the distance between the Earth and its parent star, a number of objects were to end up never quite captured by any of the planets. This motley collection of left-over debris from the formation of the planets and the moons, is what is now known as the Asteroid Belt.

Silent and majestic, the giant metallic rock had traversed space alone for eons, but now, directly in front of it loomed another body. Both were the size of large buildings, and they were now on a collision course. The seemingly huge distance between them closed in just a few seconds. The impact was forceful, but not enough to break the two objects apart. They merely crashed hard into each other, sheering large amounts of rock and metal from each other. Then they separated again, leaving a huge volume of space between them full of rock and dust that had been ripped off their respective surfaces during the impact.

The enormous amounts of kinetic energy that had been converted into thermal energy during the impact, left a long luminescent scar on the rock. But in addition to the warm orange light of molten metals, there was something else. A strange blue glow shimmered on the impact surface.

The giant rock's destiny was now sealed. It had finally acquired the kinetic energy it needed to leave the Asteroid Belt, and was now on a trajectory that would take it towards the inner Solar System. A trajectory eventually resulting in the rock entering an elliptical orbit around the sun, where it would remain for tens of thousands of years, circling the sun until finally, its orbit intersected that of the Earth.

★   ★   ★

THE NILE DELTA - EGYPT, 2572 BCE

Hepu had decided to spend the night with his herd, rather than walk home in the dark. He had been held up by a lambing sheep, and was now forced to bed down in the grass next to the river. This was not at all an unusual occurrence, but as he lowered himself wearily onto the soft grass next to the fire, he lamented not being able to see his children until morning.

Still, the full moon was out, and it was pleasant here. The only sounds he could hear were the sheep chewing the grass, and the gentle sound of trickling water. The river was flowing slowly and gently along, winding its way to the Nile to which it was a tributary. The meadow where he would spend the night was next to a large irrigated area of farmland, where crops were planted every year. It was a peaceful setting to go to sleep, except for the mosquitos that were lurking in the darkness, waiting to pounce on him should he stray too far from the fire.

The Nile was the lifeblood of the land. Every year, the river would flood its banks and submerge the surrounding plains in muddy, silty river water that was full of nutrients. The regularity with which this happened, had meant that a few centuries earlier, the Pharaoh *Djer*, had instituted a new type of calendar year, comprised of 365 days and divided into three seasons; Inundation, Emergence, and Low Water. This cycle governed everything in the kingdom, and along the Nile, the young king had ordered the construction of dozens of nilometers. These were stone buildings erected around deep wells, some large enough to have stairwells built on their inside, for easy access to the water table. At their centre were tall stone columns, against which the water level of the Nile was regularly measured and recorded. Careful analysis of the change in the water level through the seasons and at multiple locations along the Nile, allowed the priesthood remarkable success in predicting the water levels, and thus the scale of the summer floods. This in turn determined the taxes that the Pharaoh would be able to levy on his subjects for that year.

Looking up at the twinkling stars in the night sky, the shepherd remembered how his father, Manetho, had told him about the rising of *Sopdet*, the Pole Star, and how it signalled the beginning of the annual inundation.

Sopdet was also the goddess of fertility of the soil, brought about by flooding. She was represented by a five-pointed star, and this symbol was chiselled neatly into the limestone over the doorway of every nilometer.

As a child, Hepu had sometimes been allowed to join his father outside their hut after sunset, marvelling at the night sky and the seemingly endless number of tiny lights. Manetho has explained to him how the gods lived in the region of the sky where the constellations Orion and Sirius rise just ahead of the sun at dawn on the day of the summer solstice. He also told him how, far away in Giza, they were building three great pyramids in honour of Pharaoh Khufu's eventual death, and how these pyramids were placed perfectly in accordance with the positions of the three adjacent stars in the belt of Orion.

Hepu's father had died of old age a few years ago, and as the shepherd lay down to admire what seemed like a vast river of stars flowing overhead, he pondered where his father's soul would be now. Upon death, it would have entered *Duat*, the underworld, where it would have been moving through a corridor full of statues of deities until it reached *Osiris*, the god of the afterlife. Here, Osiris would have determined the virtue of his father's soul. Had he lived his life 'elegantly'? Had he been a moral man? Had he acted justly? Had he adhered to the Egyptian creed? This would decide if his soul would be allowed a peaceful afterlife.

Hepu felt calm and content that the gods would look kindly upon his father's soul. He had been a gentle and compassionate man, and he had raised his five children to be the same. He had been a good father, and Hepu felt a pang of sadness at his loss.

One day, we will meet again, thought Hepu.

*   *   *

When the meteor hit, Hepu had only a few seconds warning. He had sat back up and was tearing a piece of bread from the loaf he a brought with him that morning when he noticed something strange. He could hear nothing since the meteor was travelling at several times the speed of sound, but upon entering the Earth's atmosphere, friction heated it up to a point where it was ablating large amounts of material, which stretched out behind it in a trail of fire and smoke. At first, he noticed the terrain around him gradually becoming illuminated, almost as if the sun was coming up very quickly. He thought his mind was playing tricks on him, or that somehow the fire had started burning more brightly.

He quickly stood up, and immediately noticed his shadow on the ground in front of him growing more defined, and then becoming shorter and shorter. Confused, he stared at it for a few seconds, and then slowly turned around to see what was creating this light behind and above him. Instantly, his confused frown turned into wide-eyed fear. There, in the sky over the distant mountains, a new sun seemed to have appeared. It shone brightly, but unlike the sun, it seemed to be rapidly getting bigger. Hepu barely had time to process what happened next.

It took the meteor only a few seconds to close the distance between the mountains over which it had entered the atmosphere, and the meadow where he was standing, watching this terrifying apparition approach him.

As it slammed into the ground, it instantly vapourised the first few meters of wet soil in a bright flash, and a powerful shockwave raced out in all directions, flattening everything in its path.

The impact happened far enough away for the shepherd to remain uninjured, yet close enough for the shockwave to knock him off his feet.

As mud, bits of plants and a few fish came clattering down around him, he stumbled to his feet and peered through the haze that had been left by the searing hot meteor. It had smashed into the wet soil, right next to the river about two hundred meters away.

His ears were ringing, and his vision was blurred as he tried to steady himself. He noticed a strange warm sensation on the side of his head. He touched his right ear, and as he brought his hand back out in front of his face, he realised that it was covered in blood. The shockwave had been so powerful, it had ruptured his eardrums.

Hepu looked around, trying to see if he could spot anyone else, but it seemed like the whole world had shrunk to this tiny area next to the river, where only he and the fireball now existed.

Feeling dazed, he nervously staggered closer to the impact site, trying to see what could have created such carnage. And that is when he spotted it. There was steam rising from the impact site, but that was not was unnerved him. He stopped dead in his tracks and simply stared. Then he took another few steps forward and squinted. Were his eyes deceiving him? It was as if the steam was being lit up. He could not see by what, but amidst the roiling steam, the faint light was unlike anything he had ever seen before. It was blue.

Once again, he turned around to see if he could spot any of his sheep, but they had all vanished as if plucked from the ground by the hand of a giant. Perhaps they had fled. Perhaps they were unharmed because they were lying on the ground, whereas he had been standing. Had he been unconscious for a few moments after the impact, while they had made their escape?

He decided to ignore the sheep and instead turned his attention back to the glowing impact crater. As he stumbled closer, he began to hear a strange hissing sound, as if the river water was boiling off something extremely hot.

Now, no more than fifty meters away, he suddenly felt strangely unsteady on his feet, but he continued forward, unable to resist the urge to look. What was this thing? He had never laid eyes on anything that looked even remotely similar to this. It was like seeing lightning or snow for the first time. He simply had to get closer.

The impact had left a crater around 20 meters wide and 5 meters deep. The rim of the crater was pushed up a couple of meters above the surrounding meadowland, and as he crested it to look down into the crater, he was met with a sight that took his breath away. In the middle of the crater, was an indentation, inside which lay a dark object, like a rock the size of a large cow. But this was no living thing.

Its surface was covered in small glowing patches of orange molten metal, and it hissed as it evaporated the water that was in the ground underneath it. Steam and smoke were billowing angrily away from it as if from a sword heated by the village metalworkers and then plunged into water to cool it off. But this was different. The dull light emanating from it was unmistakably blue.

Hepu had never seen a colour like this. It was intense and radiant, and yet at the same time calm and mesmerising. He did not so much decide to walk down into the crater towards the rock, as he simply found himself doing it. It was as if some strange force was drawing him in. At this point, he did not think of his safety, his wife, his children or anything else. He was utterly spellbound by the object in front of him, and nothing but him and the object now existed in his mind.

As he closed the final distance of around five meters between himself and the rock, he could feel the heat radiating off it. But that was not all he could feel. He suddenly felt the skin on his face tingling, and a few seconds later his vision became blurred, and it seemed as if tiny shooting stars were whizzing back and forth in front of him. Then a sudden urge to vomit came over him, and he doubled over and threw up on the ground in front of him. He fell to his knees, eyes watering, as he retched violently.

Steadying himself with his hands on the wet sandy ground, he suddenly noticed a strange discolouration of his skin, visible even in the dim light of the moon. Dark patches, like bruising, seemed to be appearing on his hands even as he was watching them. He attempted to brush the sand from his hands and then realised that they were swollen. Horrified, he violently swiped some more sand away, and suddenly a small piece of skin came loose and folded over onto his hand. The pain was excruciating. It was as if his tissue was disintegrating.

Horrified, he touched his face and immediately felt strange watery bulges protruding from his forehead, his cheeks and his neck. It felt as if his face was melting. Now in insufferable agony, and utterly terrified, he brought himself to his feet, only to immediately collapse onto his knees again. His legs could not support him, he was becoming delirious, and pain, like he had never experienced before, was spreading throughout his entire body.

Gods help me, he thought, as he mustered one final effort to escape the cursed rock. Sweating profusely and barely able to see, he began crawling frantically back towards the edge of the crater, away from the rock. Whatever it was, it was possessed of evil powers, and he needed to get as far away from it as possible. Living beings have evolved to sense when their lives are truly in peril, and he was now in a full panic. He clawed at the soil and kicked his legs to try to get over the crater rim, but his body was failing him. His bloodied fingers were cramping up into tight fists, causing him to cry out in anguish, and his legs no longer obeyed his commands.

As he inched forward, his breathing became laboured, and after a few seconds, he started coughing. He tried to clear his throat, but that only resulted in a coughing fit, and through the pain, he was able to taste the blood. He spat, and a big blob of pink blood fell onto the sand, where it was slowly absorbed. His lungs were bleeding. His insides were coming apart.

In a final desperate attempt to escape, he brought his knees up under his body and tried to push himself forward, but it was no use. He only managed to roll onto his side, gasping for air, and producing an unsettling gurgling sound as the blood-filled his lungs and his windpipe.

Hepu finally rolled onto his back, his head, arms and legs splayed out in the shape of a five-pointed star, and there he exhaled for the final time, his eyes fixed on the stars above. His heart had stopped beating, but his brain still had a few seconds of consciousness left before it was deprived of oxygen. Enough time for Hepu to understand that this was the end. Enough time to say goodbye to his children. Enough time to hope that Osiris might grant him a peaceful afterlife, and that he would see those that had gone before him again.

Father.

★   ★   ★

Aswan - Egypt, 1268 BCE

The makeshift torch lit easily, and the flame quickly found the oil that had been infused into the cloth wrapped around the long stick. As the orange flames enveloped the torch, the man could now clearly see the small entrance at the back of the cave. As he approached, the flickering light made the cave walls seem to come alive with movement, as if the cave itself was waking up from a long slumber.

He reached the small doorway and pushed with his shoulder against the slab of rock that he had cleared of sand a few hours earlier. The doorway had no markings on it, except for a small disc at the top, with what seemed like rays coming out in all directions.

Despite its size, the huge slab slid back easily, and the man marvelled at the precision of whatever balancing mechanism was holding it in place and allowing it to move after only a firm push.

He looked down to his left hand to check that the mouse was still in its small metal cage. The little animal was sitting still, shifting its head slightly from left to right, sniffing the air and trying to figure out what was happening. It did not seem frightened.

The man bent down and headed through the doorway into a corridor that sloped downwards. Moving through it, he could see that the walls had been built using limestone expertly cut into square pieces, but there were no markings on any of them.

Because of the narrowness of the corridor, he had to hold the torch uncomfortably close to his face as he went through. This meant that he was unable to see very far ahead of himself, but he pushed on. The scroll had described this entry, and as he moved further downward, he knew that he was now approaching a chamber.

Sure enough, a short distance later, the corridor ended, and he stepped out into a large round chamber, which became lit up as he brought his torch through. He wondered how long it had been since any light had fallen on these walls.

In the middle of the chamber was what appeared to be a huge square rock. He cautiously approached it, trying to guess its size and whether it fit with what the scroll had described. The only sound was of the gentle flickering of the torch's flame, the soft sound of sand under his sandals, and the occasional timid squeak of the mouse in the cage.

As he came nearer, he realised that what he was seeing was not a rock. It was a giant box, perhaps 3 cubits long and almost as wide, and just over 2 cubits tall. It was square, but most astonishingly it seemed to be reflecting the light from the torch.

He stepped close to it, leaned forward slightly, and then extended his arm to wipe some dust from its side. HHer eyes widened as he realised that what he was looking at was gold. The whole box was made of gold, just as the scroll had foretold.

Now feeling confident that this was indeed what they had been searching for during all of those long years, he lifted his gaze to see a small protrusion in the middle of the box's perfectly flat top. It had a small handle. It was a round hinged lid the size of an egg.

He immediately knew what to do, and leaned in to adeptly open the lid. He flipped it open, and let it drop onto the top of the box. It was surprisingly heavy, and the sound as the lid hit the top of the box told him that the entire box was made of thick plates of gold. He paused for a moment and looked at the opening. For a brief moment, he thought he saw a faint blue light emanating from it, but the torch made it difficult for him to see clearly. He squinted to see better, but there seemed to be nothing there now.

Leaning in over the top of the box, he quickly plonked the small cage with the mouse over the opening.

'Sorry little friend,' he said quietly, and then took a step back.

At first, nothing happened. The mouse was sitting calmly, sniffing the air. But after just a few seconds it twitched, clearly sensing that something was wrong. It tried to scurry over to one side of the tiny cage but then ran to the other. The cage wobbled as the mouse threw itself with increasing desperation at its sides. Then it started squeaking loudly, clearly in distress.

After less than a minute, the man thought he could see blood trickling out of its eyes and nose. It was now running and jumping as much as the small space would allow it, and as it clawed frantically at the cage, the nails and skin on its feet started to come off. The body of the mouse was literally beginning to fall apart in front of his eyes.

The man stood dumbfounded at the sight, on the one hand feeling guilty for having done this to this little creature, but on the other sensing the significance of what he was witnessing.

Mercifully it was soon over. After a last desperate attempt to break free, the mouse collapsed on the metal floor of the cage, blood oozing from every orifice, and from the cuts it had inflicted on itself. It coughed blood a few times but then did not move again. As the man watched it lie there, he could have sworn that its body seemed to flatten, almost as if it was liquifying.

Not sure why, he found himself lifting the torch high over his head, and then bashing the small cage so that it flew off the gold box and ended up tumbling across the floor until it came to a stop next to the far wall. Then he used the torch to flip the small lid closed again. This moment, as shocking as it was, meant that he had to leave immediately. He had to tell his master.

A few hours later, the man was racing through the dark streets of the small worker's village. There were only a few people still out, and soldiers were patrolling the streets to make sure the slaves did not get up to mischief in the night after their work shifts had come to an end.

In the dim moonlight, the man weaved his way adeptly left and right through the narrow streets and back alleys, until he finally bolted through a door at the end of an alleyway. Here he was stopped by two burly men, who took a moment to realise who he was. Then they let him proceed through to the next room. Here an old man was sitting in a large but simple wooden chair, that was raised slightly off the floor. He was wearing a thick grey beard, a dark brown robe, and in his hand was a worn wooden staff.

'Moshe,' said the man and fell to his knees in front of the old man.

'What is it, my son,' said the old man calmly, leaning forward in his chair, his kind eyes gleaming in the light from the candles.

'It is there,' whispered the man breathlessly, tears welling up in his eyes. 'It is there, just like the scroll said it would be. This is our way out. Our way home.'

The old man sat up and then leaned back slowly in his chair, his gaze rising slowly towards some distant horizon that only he could see.

'If you are right,' he said slowly. 'This will allow us to return to our homeland. Tell the others, we must prepare to leave.'

The man rose off the floor, took two measured steps backwards while bowing to the old man, and then he turned around and hurried out of the house.

The old man sat motionless for a few moments.

'Home,' he said slowly, as if tasting the words for the first time. 'After all these years, our people can finally return.'

One

CAIRO, 2ND OF MAY – PRESENT DAY

Doctor Bahir Mansour was getting ready to leave for home. A short rotund man in his late fifties, he had short black hair, a small beard and spectacles. He always wore a neatly pressed shirt and a vest, and only ever wore light coloured linen trousers. The air-conditioning in the offices of the museum were notoriously unreliable, so he had to dress accordingly.

Mansour had spent all day at his desk in the Coptic Museum in Cairo, poring over copies of texts related to the origin of a metal book casket. Holding a PhD in archaeology, he was now the curator of the museum's metal artefact collection, and as such oversaw all research into artefacts like tin and copper pots, various tools, weapons and other relics.

The originals of the texts he was examining were hermetically sealed inside airtight containers in the vault in the basement under the museum. The containers were filled with the inert gas argon, so as to eliminate oxidisation of the paper upon which the text had been written centuries ago. Many of them were in such a fragile state, that Mansour considered it indefensible to take them out and bring them upstairs just to read them. Both physical and digital copies had been made more than a decade ago, and as far as he was concerned, they were more than adequate for his research. Similarly, the metal relics themselves had been photographed extensively, and some were even in the process of being 3D scanned, in order to preserve a record of those items indefinitely, even if the physical object were to be lost, stolen, damaged or simply end up degrading over the decades and centuries to come.

For a moment, Mansour absentmindedly imagined actually bringing one of the texts upstairs, and then accidentally spilling coffee all over it. He quite literally shuddered at the thought, and then found himself glancing at his coffee cup, just to make sure it wasn't about to be knocked over.

He had been at his desk in the museum all day, and his back was telling him it was time to stop. He had suffered from back problems since he was a young man, but he considered himself lucky that he had been able to attend university and become a scholar. At least this way, his livelihood did not depend on the health of his body.

The museum was directly opposite the Mar Girgis Metro Station in Cairo's Coptic district, and every day hundreds of tourists would visit to see the now large and ever-expanding collection of manuscripts, stone carvings, metalware, and even textiles. Most items were centuries old. The oldest manuscript was from the 4th century. The oldest textile was a tapestry from the 5th century, and some of the metal artefacts were several thousand years old.

Construction of the museum had begun in 1908, after the Egyptian Coptic leader Marcus Simaika Pasha had obtained permission, along with a large number of artefacts, from Patriarch Cyril V. Since its opening in 1910, it had held and exhibited thousands of artefacts, and Mansour was proud to be the curator of the metals department. He thoroughly enjoyed his work, and he joked with his colleagues that, unlike them, he never felt stressed. The reason was that manuscripts and textiles are fragile and prone to degradation over as little as a single human life span. Metal objects, on the other hand, degrade so slowly that he never felt in a rush to do anything.

His office was on the first floor on one side of the main building, with a window out to the alley through which the tourists would swarm throughout most days, except when it was raining. He did not mind the throngs of people. He liked people, especially interesting people who knew interesting things, but he also took pleasure in the fact that the Coptic Museum was a popular place to visit for tourists, foreigners as well as Egyptians. He took that as a sign that he and his colleagues were doing a good job bringing the ancient history of Egypt to the people.

Every day he would take breaks from sitting at his desk, get himself a cup of coffee, and wander over to the window to look down into the alley where the museum's visitors were moving slowly from the ticket gate and along the building towards the main entrance. Wearing sunhats, backpacks, and carrying cameras and guidebooks, he could spot them easily anywhere in the city. So could the unsavoury underbelly of Cairo, and pickpocketing was a significant problem throughout the city. The museum, however, had installed CCTV throughout the sprawling complex, and along with lots of signs pointing to their existence, the cameras seemed to have made a difference. Reports of theft were now much reduced compared with a couple of years ago.

I guess word spreads fast among cockroaches, thought Mansour.

He carefully took another sip of his coffee and leaned in over the picture of the casket. Made of several types of metal, most likely bronze and iron, it had once contained a manuscript, but the pages had disintegrated long before the casket came into the possession of the museum. Its provenance was still unknown, and it was this problem Mansour was now trying to solve.

Caskets like this one, also called *treasure bindings*, were essentially book covers, made of three hinged and interlocking metal plates, which wrapped around the whole book, and they typically had extravagant ornaments and sometimes some text describing the book's content. This casket, however, was unusual. There were no glyphs or any other kind of writing on the cover, except for a single small word stencilled neatly into the metal plate below the main motif. It was written in glyphs that roughly translated to 'Heat', but there was nothing else to put that word into any context.

The motif itself was of a mountain, which seemed to have two rounded peaks, almost like the humps on a camel. Centred above the two peaks, was the sun, complete with rays shining out of it. This overt depiction of the rays of the sun was found on many limestone reliefs from as early as the 25th century BCE, during the 5th Dynasty, when the sun god Ra was becoming one of the most prominent ancient Egyptian deities. Usually, the sun was depicted at the top, with its rays coming down towards the main motif in the middle of the image. The number of rays was normally between 12 and 18, and they only ever came out of the bottom third of the sun.

What was unusual about the motif on the casket, was that the rays were radiating out from the sun in all directions. Mansour had never seen this before in any of the other metal artefacts, wall paintings or limestone reliefs he had ever come across. He had seen and examined hundreds of artefacts, and as far as he knew this was completely unique.

He wondered what the artist's motivation for this deviation from the norm had been. The sun god Ra was among the most powerful of all the Gods, and Mansour had to think that breaking from convention in the depiction of the Sun in this manner, must have required a very good reason.

This, however, was not the only strange thing about the casket. As far as anyone knew, there was exactly no clue at all as to its provenance. It had apparently been one of the original pieces gifted to and moved into the museum during the period 1908 to 1910 when the Coptic leader Marcus Simaika Pasha had urged the Coptic community in Cairo to donate any items they believed to have significant historical value. But as for the original owner, where the casket had been kept, which book or manuscript it might have contained, and when and where it could have been made, there was absolutely no information. It was almost as if it had simply popped into existence in 1910.

But Mansour knew full well that this could not be true. The art style on the front of it bore a clear relation to that of the Old Kingdom, circa 2700 to 2200 BCE, and yet they did not match exactly. There was little to no relation to any prominent art styles observed in subsequent dynastic epochs. This left Mansour wondering if it might have been made even earlier, possibly around 3000 BCE, more than 5000 years ago. Metallurgy, which involves separating metals from their ores, was not invented in ancient Egypt, but its use was widespread from the 4th millennium BCE. Various copper tools and trinkets have been found from that period.

Gold and copper ore, often found together in quartz veins, was the foundation of ancient Egyptian metallurgy. The ancient prospectors were highly skilled at discovering new sources of ore, and many of the modern sites known today were also known to the ancient Egyptians. Copper and gold were both mined from quartz veins, and in the case of copper, ancient Egyptians knew how to extract it from oxide and sulphide ores. They also understood how to repeatedly smelt the ore, to get ever purer metal. Copper was mixed with arsenic, to create a copper alloy that was harder and more durable.

Eventually, copper tools were replaced by bronze tools, which were themselves replaced by iron tools. Sources of iron ore were not very rich in Egypt, unlike in Nubia further to the south, so they relied on trade for raw materials. There is, however, evidence that ancient Egyptians used iron from meteorites for making beads for jewellery more than 5000 years ago.

The mystery of the casket had puzzled Mansour for weeks now, and he often found himself pondering what the original content of the pages that used to sit inside it, might have been. He was not the only person to have attempted to penetrate the mystery of the casket. His predecessor Jabari Omran, who had held the job of curator for almost two decades during which time Mansour had been deputy curator, had seemed obsessed with the casket. He had spent many months examining it, writing about it, and simply staring at it, as if by sheer force of will that might somehow solve the enigma. Omran had been convinced that the now crumbled pages of the casket had been the repository of ancient wisdom, and that if he could only decipher the meaning of the motif on its front, he would find clues to some long-forgotten secret. Even when he was not actively studying the casket, he had kept it on his desk, or on a shelf behind his chair in his office.

To his colleagues, Omran had been seen as somewhat eccentric, which was not exactly unusual in this business. In fact, Mansour suspected that the man knew full well what was being said about him, and that he rather took pride in his singular focus and effort to unlock mysteries of the past.

Sadly, Omran had died a few years earlier, following a short but dreadful battle with cancer. He had left a letter to the Director of the Coptic Museum, Professor Sadiki, urging him to appoint Mansour as his successor. The old man had apparently appreciated Mansour's work ethic and his attention to detail, and when offered the position, Mansour had not hesitated. Not long after taking over the role, he had decided to attempt to pick up where Omran had left off, and continue the study of the casket. This was partly because he was as intrigued as Omran had been, and partly because he wanted to honour the memory of a deceased colleague, who had also become a friend.

Unlike Omran, however, he preferred to leave the casket in the vault in the cellar. He had spent a fair amount of time looking at it himself over the years, and there were plenty of photos to base his work on. There were also many texts, both old and new, which he employed in the process of trying to address all the unanswered questions the casket presented. Finally, he had at his fingertips the wealth of research that Omran had produced over the years. Surely, the answers were here somewhere.

And yet, here he sat, once again staring vacantly at the picture of Marcus Simaika Pasha, which hung on the wall in every office in the museum complex. He did not like to admit it, but he had made no progress at all. He had gone over the same photos and the same notes several times, and he had found himself unable to contribute anything that Omran had not already discovered or deduced.

Perhaps he was wrong in thinking that he could do this work just sitting in his office, looking at pixels on a screen, or re-reading Omran's notes. Perhaps he really did need the physical specimen in his hands, in order to have a chance at solving the riddle.

After a few moments of hesitation, he resolutely got up and walked out into the corridor towards the stairs leading down to the cellar. On both sides of the corridor hung photos of previous curators of the museum's various departments, as well as photos of all the previous Egyptian presidents and rulers, seemingly as far back as photos existed. This was a country steeped in its history, and immensely proud of the role it had played in the evolution of civilisation. Clearly, this had carried over into the way the museum had been decorated. Mansour looked at the pictures of some of the presidents and shuddered. Far from all of them seemed to him to have been role models.

He entered the four-digit code on the keypad, and immediately the door to the cellar stairwell unlocked and began to open. He made his way down the winding staircase and found himself outside the vault. Entry inside required another code on a different keypad, which he dutifully supplied.

Once inside the vault, he knew exactly where he was going. The casket was on the top shelf at the very back of the aisle containing metal artefacts. He had been down here plenty of times, although never to retrieve the casket. It had remained down here since Omran's death, and for a brief period afterwards, he had wondered if the casket was somehow cursed. Not that he would ever admit that to anyone.

He pulled the large wooden box down from the shelf and carried it towards the stairwell. It was remarkable heavy. Once back upstairs in his office, he sat down at his desk with the box in front of him. Laying eyes on the artefact was a strangely poignant moment for him since it had become so entwined with his memories of Omran.

After a few moments, he opened the lid of the box, extracted the casket, and set it down gently on his desk. He did not know where to begin. If he had harboured any hope that seeing it again would somehow produce some eureka moment, then that hope was quickly extinguished. His mind was as empty as his coffee cup.

Inside the wooden box next to the casket, was a small clear plastic container. Mansour had almost forgotten that it was in there, but he now recalled how two tiny metal fragments from the casket had come off many years ago when the casket had been examined by a heavy-handed PhD student.

Deciding that there was nothing more he could do today, he got up and picked up his bag and his coat. For a moment he considered carrying the artefact back downstairs to the vault but decided to leave it on his desk. After all, he would be back in less than eight hours.

As he turned out the lights, he glanced back at his desk to make sure he had not forgotten anything, and that is when he saw it. The cold moonlight was reflecting off the metal casket, but that was not all. Were his eyes playing tricks on him, or did the casket seem to have an extremely faint blue glow? He strained his eyes to look, but suddenly could not see it anymore.

After turning the lights back on, and then off again, he walked slowly back towards his desk. The casket looked just as it always had done. Dull and slightly worn metal, with the motif depicting the dual peak mountain with the sun above it.

It must have been the moonlight, he thought to himself. *And I really need some sleep now.*

Working hard and being sleep deprived was one thing, but if he was beginning to see things that were not actually there, then that was quite another and much more serious issue. Perhaps he needed a holiday.

As he stood on the platform at Mar Girgis Metro Station waiting for the train home, he could hear the distant screeching of metal train wheels against the iron rail tracks. And that is when it occurred to him, that perhaps the metal itself held some clues that might help him determine its provenance. He almost turned around to make his way back to his office in the museum, but then he stopped himself in his tracks.

No more, he thought to himself. *Sleep is what you need now.*

Two

LONDON, 23ʳᴰ OF MAY

Andrew Sterling was watching the news on the wall-mounted TV in his kitchen while preparing himself some breakfast. He had just switched it on, to learn that a meteorite had streaked across the sky in Australia during the previous evening, and impacted somewhere in the outback next to a road. Luckily, no one had been injured, as there was seldom any traffic to speak of.

He was standing next to the island in the middle of the spacious kitchen, where the morning sunlight was bathing the dark wood floor in its golden light. The kettle had just finished boiling, and as he poured the hot water into his teacup, the familiar aroma of English Breakfast Tea made it to his nose.

Grabbing a jug of milk, pouring it over his cornflakes, and adding a bit to his tea, he glanced over at the TV again. The news networks were showing footage of the event from multiple angles, shot by a whole host of people who had been going about their normal business when the sky had suddenly lit up. It was fascinating to watch. In one video, which must have been shot by someone with a high-quality camera and a steady hand, the meteor could be seen travelling across the sky whilst leaving a long trail of glowing fragments as the air friction in the atmosphere tore it apart.

From the ground, it seemed at first to be travelling slowly, but that was an illusion caused by the fact that the meteor was around 80 kilometres up when it was first spotted. Another piece of footage, however, showed the meteor much closer to the ground and appearing to travel significantly faster as it shot across the sky from the perspective of whoever was filming it. The video tracked the bright ball of fire as it raced overhead, and disappeared from view behind some trees. It then apparently slammed into the red dirt of the Australian outback with a blindingly bright flash that caused the person holding the camera to recoil, and the image to jump around as the person ran for cover.

At that point, the news show cut back to the presenter in the studio. She was a blond, pretty and excitable young lady with a thick Australian accent.

'Welcome back to Seven News at Breakfast,' she said in that broad Australian drawl that Andrew had always found attractive. 'I'd like to go now to our guest, Professor Williams from the Institute for Astronomy at the University of Sydney. Thank you very much for joining us this morning.'

The professor was sitting in what appeared to be his faculty office, with a wall of books behind him, including one placed prominently with its cover visible over his right shoulder, which very obviously had him as the author. He jolted to attention at the sudden introduction and cleared his throat.

'Uh. Hello! Good morning, Vivian. Nice to see you.'

'Professor, what did we just see on our screens?', asked Vivian.

'Uhm, well,' said the professor, shifting in his chair, suddenly feeling very self-conscious. 'What we just saw was basically a large chunk of metal falling to earth."

'There are reports of windows being broken along the path of the meteor,' interrupted Vivian in an almost conspiratorial voice, whilst pretending to read something on a piece of paper in front of her. 'How worried should the ordinary Australian be about something like this?'

The professor smiled benignly. 'The average person should not worry about this. Of course, meteors enter our atmosphere every day, but it is important to remember that humans have only urbanised roughly three percent of the Earth's landmass, and since two-thirds of the planet is covered by oceans, that means that any given meteorite has less than a one percent chance of coming down in one of those urban areas. Regarding the broken windows, they are not caused by the meteorite itself, but by the shockwave that is generated as the object is travelling through the atmosphere at supersonic speeds. None of those houses were anywhere near the impact site.'

'You have used the terms meteor and meteorite,' said Vivian, appearing confused. 'Could you explain to our viewers what the difference is?'

'Certainly,' replied Professor Williams cheerfully. 'Simply put, a meteor is an object from the asteroid belt that enters the Earth's atmosphere and burns up before it reaches the surface. A meteorite is a meteor that is large enough to make it all the way down, without burning up. And that is what we saw last night.'

'I see,' said Vivian, looking mildly annoyed at the unwelcome complexity. Still sounding like she thought that perhaps her audience ought to worry at least a little bit about being hit by a meteorite, she pressed on. 'But, isn't it true that the Earth is hit by thousands of meteorites every day?'

Here it comes, thought Andrew and smiled wryly.

'Yes,' said the professor hesitantly, clearly sensing where this was going. 'We estimate that between 50 and 100 tons of meteorites fail to burn up on atmospheric entry, and therefore end up falling onto the Earth's surface each year. But most of that material is made up of tiny fragments, so-called metallic globules, that are ripped off the meteors because of friction during entry. The meteors are typically travelling at anywhere between twenty-five thousand and one-hundred-and-fifty thousand miles per hour, so the fragments from the surface of the meteorite melt, are ripped off the surface, and then cool down again, all within a few seconds as the meteor makes its way through the atmosphere. Most of the material that comes down is in the form of so-called micrometeorites, which are perhaps a millimetre across or even a lot smaller.'

'One hundred tons?' interjected Vivian suspiciously. 'That sounds like an awful lot of material, professor.'

'It might sound like a lot,' replied Williams. 'But the Earth is a pretty big place. We estimate that each square meter on earth receives around 1 micrometeorite each year. So yes, you could say that there are a lot of them, but they are just so small that we don't notice them.

'Ok, so you're saying it definitely is a risk,' said Vivian, clearly pleased with her line of interrogation. 'Professor, we'll have to leave it there. Thank you for coming on the show this morning.'

The professor's lips moved again, but his audio had clearly been cut and a split second later the image cut back to Vivian in full-screen mode, looking like the reluctant bearer of bad news.

'Well, there you have it, folks. Meteors might look pretty, but they at least have the potential to be pretty darn dangerous.'

Andrew chuckled. He had to admire her skill in perpetuating the permanent state of fear and anxiety that tabloids and so-called news networks work so hard to cultivate. The spectre of some external threat had been a great motivator throughout history, whether it was to get people to go to war, vote for a particular political party, buy a particular newspaper, or all of the above.

'Wonderful', he mumbled to himself, sardonically.

He was just finishing his cornflakes when his mobile phone started ringing and vibrating, making it appear to dance and move slowly across the white marble countertop on the kitchen island. He finished chewing and picked it up.

'Andrew here,' he said, whilst trying to remove a piece of cornflake that had become lodged between his teeth.

'Andy,' said a pleasant female voice. 'Are you alright? You sound funny.'

'Yes, I am fine thanks, Fiona. Just having breakfast. If you had taken me up on my offer last night, you could have been here too. The cornflakes here are to die for.'

Fiona laughed. It was one of the things he liked best about her. Whenever it happened, which was quite often, it always felt uplifting to him, as if somehow the world became a slightly better place whenever she laughed.

She could be feisty when things weren't going her way, but she never stewed on things, and always apologised if she had crossed the line.

After their adventures in Central America and Antarctica, chasing after the lost continent of Atlantis and the origin of a secret Nazi weapons program, the two had naturally bonded. And then, one day whilst walking together in Hyde Park, she had suddenly taken his hand in hers, and before they knew it, they were kissing. It had all felt a bit awkward, but they quickly agreed that they were both adults, and perfectly able to manage their own relationships without needing approval from anyone else.

Andrew had, however, told his boss, Colonel Gordon Strickland, about it, in the interest of full disclosure. Gordon had been almost dismissive and told him to go right ahead. He liked Fiona and respected her immensely after her contributions in the hunt for the Nazi pathogen. He had even invited Andrew and her to a barbeque in his garden in Fulham the previous summer. He probably wasn't expecting to ever have to work with the two of them in a professional capacity again. But that was about to change.

'Right,' said Fiona. 'I have got to run. I am attending a conference in an hour, and I don't want to be late.'

'Alright,' replied Andrew. 'I will call you this evening if that's alright?'

'Of course,' she said, smiling. 'Later Andy. Bye'

★ ★ ★

The next morning, Doctor Mansour had barely sat down at his desk, before he picked up the phone to a friend at the Faculty of Archaeology at Cairo University. He had enjoyed a long night's sleep and felt full of energy, ready to push ahead with his research. On the way to his office, he had called his friend Professor Khalil Amer at Cairo University, to arrange an informal meeting later that day. They were to meet at the fountain in the small park next to the Faculty of Archaeology.

As he got up to leave, he glanced into the wooden box where the casket lay and then reached out for the small plastic container with the two fragments. His hand hovered over the container for a couple of seconds as he hesitated, but then he decided that there was no harm in bringing the fragments along, so he picked the container up and slipped it into the inside pocket of his beige suit jacket.

Khalil and Mansour knew each other from many moons ago when they both attended the University of Cairo as young students. They had stayed in touch, even as their careers had taken different paths. Khalil had continued on at the university, first as a PhD, and then as a Professor of Archaeology. Mansour had decided to pursue a career in the less formal research sphere that existed in museums. Whereas Mansour had always been attracted to traditional methods of archaeology and study, Khalil had embraced any new technology that could help further his research, and Mansour had to admit that he sometimes felt slightly left behind by all the new technological progress, both in archaeology and in society in general.

Over the past decade, Khalil had become one of Egypt's foremost experts in the application of radiocarbon dating and ion-chromatography to the field of archaeology. Both methods are designed to tap into the presence of organic molecules in different kinds of matter, in order to extract information about the age of that object.

Khalil had always been the more flamboyant of the two, whereas Mansour was the quiet somewhat shy type. But for some reason, the two had bonded, and become good friends.

The trip by metro train to the University was swift, and soon he was walking up towards the fountain where his friend was waiting. Khalil was a tall, clean-shaven man with mid-length black hair that was swept back and held in place with a pair of Aviator sunglasses. He was wearing a light shirt, dark brown linen trousers and light beige shoes. Broad-shouldered and with an easy smile, he exuded self-confidence.

Suave as always, smiled Mansour to himself. Khalil had always had a certain playboy air about him. But he was as solid a character as they come.

It was mid-morning but the sun was already inundating the city with heat from its rays. The fountain would be a pleasantly cool place to sit and talk.

As he spotted Mansour, Khalil's face lit up. 'Bahir!' he shouted and started walking towards Mansour with his hand outstretched and a big grin on his face. 'So good to see you. How are you, my friend? And how is work?'

'Very well, thank you,' said Mansour. 'Yourself?'

'Not too bad,' smiled Khalil. 'Busy as always. Every time I manage to turn a class of students into knowledgeable researchers, they leave me, and then a new bunch turns up.'

Mansour laughed. 'I guess that's what you're here for.'

'I know,' replied Khalil. 'It's alright. I enjoy it. What can I do for you?'

They both sat down on the edge of the large basin surrounding the fountain.

'Well,' began Mansour. 'I am in the middle of researching a metal casket of unknown provenance, without much luck I might add, and it occurred to me that perhaps there is a way to analyse and date the metal it was made from. Is that something you could help me with?'

'I am sure we can think of something,' replied Khalil with a winning smile. 'The most reliable method remains the tried-and-tested radiocarbon dating method, but there are a few new techniques that are showing a lot of promise.'

'Would you mind reminding me how carbon dating works?' asked Mansour. 'It has been a while since I sat on those benches over there in the auditorium,' he smiled sheepishly and pointed towards a large circular building in the middle of the campus.

'Of course,' said Khalil. 'But before I do, I should probably go over what exactly atoms are, and what they are made of. This will help me explain radiocarbon dating.'

'Alright. I am all ears,' said Mansour.

Khalil rolled up his sleeves as if he was about to engage in some activity that required physical strength. 'Ok,' he said. 'As you know, everything in the universe is made up of different types of molecules, and molecules are made from atoms. Atoms themselves are made from a small number of building blocks; Protons, that have a positive electrical charge. Neutrons, that have no charge. And electrons, that have a negative charge. The core of an atom, also called the nucleus, is where the protons and neutrons both sit all clumped together. They are held together by something called the 'strong nuclear force', which is the strongest force we know of, and the basis for nuclear fusion and fission. With me so far?'

'Yes, I think so,' said Mansour, now feeling every bit the eager student.

'Good,' continued Khalil. 'What this means is that the nucleus has a net positive charge. The electrons, on the other hand, are negatively charged particles that orbit the nucleus. Most atoms have a net neutral charge, since all atoms seek out a stable and balanced state as they interact with their surroundings.'

'As for their mass or weight, protons and neutrons both have a mass of 1 atomic mass unit, which is absolutely tiny. Off the top of my head, the number is 1.66×10^{-24} grams.'

Mansour blinked a couple of times, trying to find a way to put that number into context. '1.66, with twenty-four zeroes in front of it?' he said, smiling at the thought of trying to write that on a piece of paper.

'Yes,' laughed Khalil, seeing the bemused look on his friend's face. 'It is quite difficult to wrap your head around such a tiny number. In order to get a single gram of neutrons, you would need around 600 thousand, billion, billion of them.'

'Isn't there some intuitive way of thinking about this?' asked Mansour inquisitively.

Khalil held up his index finger and smiled. 'Of course, there is, and you are not the first student to ask this question,' he said and winked at his friend. 'So here is an answer I like to give during lectures. We know that the earth weighs around 6×10^{27} grams, so on that scale, the weight of a single proton or neutron would equate to just under ten kilos. Ten kilos, versus the weight of the entire Earth. That's the weight of a neutron or a proton, relative to a single gram.'

'And electrons?' asked Mansour hesitantly.

'About 2000 times smaller,' replied Khalil matter-of-factly.

'Right,' replied Mansour, not quite sure where that left him. 'My head already hurts. How does radiocarbon dating fit into this?'

'Well,' said Khalil, and clasped his hands together, taking a moment to think of the simplest way to explain it. 'The way traditional radiocarbon dating works is by exploiting the natural decay of carbon atoms over time. The most common carbon atoms on our planet have six protons and six neutrons. This is called Carbon-12 because its atomic mass is twelve. However, there is also a form of carbon called Carbon-14, which is created high up in the upper atmosphere, when cosmic radiation, in the form of neutrons from the sun, hits Nitrogen-14 atoms, causing them to lose a proton and gain a neutron. A neutron from the Sun effectively bounces a proton out of the nitrogen atom's nucleus and takes its place. These newly created Carbon-14 atoms mostly have the same properties as Carbon-12, in terms of how they combine with other atoms to form molecules, including how they serve as building blocks for amino acids, proteins, cells, plants, animals and humans. So, we all carry around lots of Carbon-14 atoms inside our bodies, along with the much more common Carbon-12 atoms. In addition, Carbon-14 atoms are formed at a very steady rate, so the ratio between Carbon-12 and Carbon-14 is very stable and predictable. If my memory serves me, the ratio between the two, both in the atmosphere and down here on Earth, is something like 1 to 1 trillion.'

'I think I am starting to remember how this works,' said Mansour. 'But do go on.' He was enjoying this refresher on organic chemistry.

'Right,' continued Khalil. 'Carbon-14 is different from Carbon-12 in one important respect. It is unstable and decays over time, which is to say that it is ever so slightly radioactive. The process is called beta decay because it involves the loss of a beta particle, which is either an electron or a so-called positron, which you can think of as a positively charged electron. The key here is that all living carbon-based things constantly replenish both their Carbon-12 and Carbon-14 as they breathe and eat, so the ratio between the two carbon atoms inside plants and animals remains constant and the same as in the atmosphere. But when something dies, this replenishment process stops, and so the ratio between Carbon-12 and Carbon-14 begins to change. This is because the number of stable Carbon-12 atoms remains the same, while the number of unstable Carbon-14 atoms starts to fall due to beta decay. Because we know how quickly Carbon-14 decays, by taking a sample of organic material and determining the current ratio between the two carbons, we can calculate when the carbon replenishment stopped.'

'This decay time period is what is called Half-Life, isn't it?' asked Mansour.

'Correct,' smiled Khalil. 'And the half-life of Carbon-14 is known to be 5,730 years, so if the ratio of Carbon-14 to Carbon-12 in a sample is exactly half of what it is in the atmosphere, then we know that the replenishment process stopped very close to 5,730 ago. Similarly, if it is a quarter of the normal atmospheric ratio, then the sample must be 11,460 years old.'

'Beautiful,' smiled Mansour.

'It is, isn't it?' smiled Khalil. 'It is one the most useful tools we have in modern archaeology. It does have one important limitation though. You see, in order for us to be able to use radiocarbon dating, the sample in question needs to be carbonaceous, that is to say, it must contain molecules with carbon atoms. This is usually associated with living or other organic matter, which is why carbon dating is difficult to apply to metals. However, artefacts made from metals like iron or copper often have traces of slag embedded in them, from the firepits where they were made. And since that slag was created by burning wood or coals made from wood, we can sometimes apply radiocarbon dating to certain ancient metal artefacts.'

Mansour picked this moment to reach into his jacket pocket, and pull out the small clear plastic container.

'These are two small fragments of the casket I have been working on,' said Mansour and handed it to Khalil. 'I would very much like to try to date them. Both myself and my predecessor Jabari Omran have been unable to make any progress whatsoever in identifying and dating the casket. Is that something you could help with?'

'I am sure we can handle that,' said Khalil while slowly turning the container over in front of his face, trying to peer inside. 'It might take a couple of days, but we should be able to do it.'

'Excellent,' smiled Mansour. 'If this doesn't yield any results, then I am not sure what else to do.'

'Don't worry, my friend,' smiled Khalil and rose. 'I will do my best, but I must get back to work now. I have a lecture in 10 minutes, and I need some coffee first.'

Mansour stood and gave Khalil his hand. 'Thank you. I really appreciate this.'

'No trouble at all,' replied Khalil and grinned. 'Just remember to mention me when you solve the mystery and become famous on archaeology TV shows.'

The two men parted ways, and Mansour ambled slowly through the park towards the exit, while pondering what Khalil had just told him.

Perhaps I should start taking more of an interest in the latest technological advances in archaeology, he thought to himself. *They really can be very powerful tools. They just don't have the same romance as delicately excavating an artefact from the soil, using a small brush.*

Three

Two days later, Khalil had finished his analysis, and he had offered to come by Mansour's office to tell him about the results. Mansour came to meet him at the main entrance and buzzed him through a small metal gate away from the tourist entrance. The two of them walked upstairs to Mansour's office, and as soon as Khalil saw the casket lying on Mansour's desk, his face changed.

'You probably should not have that sitting right there in front of you,' he said, sounding uncharacteristically worried.

'Why not?' asked Mansour perplexed.

'It is radioactive.'

'It's what!?' exclaimed Mansour.

'I mean,' continued Khalil, 'Almost everything in the universe is radioactive, simply due to cosmic background radiation, but the amounts that surround us every day are so tiny that they are exceedingly unlikely to do any harm. But this thing is something else entirely. I ran the analysis on the fragments you gave me, and they are giving off significantly higher amounts of alpha-radiation than you would ever expect from a metal like this.'

'I don't understand,' mumbled Mansour confused.

'Look,' said Khalil. 'Let's talk later, but for now, you should bring that casket back down to the vault and leave it there until we have decided what to do with it.'

'But isn't it dangerous?' asked Mansour, his eyes darting nervously back and forth between Khalil and his desk.

'In theory yes, as far as I understand it. But only with prolonged exposure, over several days or weeks.'

Omran, thought Mansour and shuddered. *Perhaps this is what made him ill and eventually took his life.*

'Right,' said Mansour decisively. 'Let's do it now.'

He walked over, snapped the lid of the wooden box shut, and carried it resolutely down the corridor into the vault and back to its usual spot on the top shelf at the back. Walking out of the vault and away from the box, he already felt calmer, until he realised that Khalil was still carrying the two metal fragments.

'Khalil', he called as he walked briskly down the corridor and back towards his office. 'Khalil. Have you got the…'

'These?' smiled Khalil as his head appeared through the doorway. He was holding up another plastic box, but this one was black and significantly larger than the small container Mansour had handed him the day before. 'The fragments are in here.' He said and placed his hand on his friend's shoulder.

'We're quite safe. This box is lined with lead on the inside. The radiation can't penetrate that.'

'Oh, good,' sighed Mansour. This was all becoming a bit more dramatic than he would have liked. 'What on Earth is going on? And how did you discover that the fragments are radioactive?'

'Quite by accident, I am ashamed to say,' replied Khalil. 'I had just completed the radiocarbon dating process in the main building of the Faculty of Chemistry when I walked behind a colleague who was in the middle of using a Geiger counter. This device measures ionised radiation, and as I walked past him, it suddenly chirped loudly. This colleague of mine turned and looked at me suspiciously, and asked me what I was carrying. When I showed it to him, he pointed the Geiger counter at it, and the meter instantly shot into the red on the gauge. We just looked at each other, and I think he could see how surprised I looked. Without a word, he jumped up, walked to a cabinet and rummaged around for a few seconds. Before I knew it, he had returned, snatched the fragments out of my hand, and placed them in this black box, which he promptly snapped shut.'

'What a story,' said Mansour. 'Did he say anything else?'

'Just that I should be a bit more careful, and that perhaps I should have those metal fragments analysed. He couldn't tell me if the radiation type was alpha, beta or gamma, but since all of these are the product of the same decay process, they are usually observed together, so it is probably best to assume that all three types were present.'

'What do you mean by type?' asked Mansour.

'Well,' replied Khalil, 'I am no expert on this, but as I understand it, there are different particles and waves that are produced by radioactive materials at different points in the decay process. Perhaps we should call in some assistance on this. I am starting to feel a bit out of my depth.'

Usually a very self-confident man, Khalil was beginning to look slightly unsure of himself.

'What did your analysis say?' asked Mansour. He had almost forgotten what this was all about.

'In short: 1500 BCE. But I don't have a lot of faith in the result. For some reason, the readings were very inconsistent, and I only had a small amount of material to work with.'

'1500 BCE? That's much older than I ever would have guessed,' said Mansour pensively. 'Do you have anyone in mind that can help us push this further?'

'I do know of one person that might be able to help,' but it is going to take a bit of work to make it happen.

'Why is that?' asked Mansour.

'Well,' said Khalil. 'He works at the Nuclear Research Center in Inshas. It's about 60 kilometres northeast of Cairo. I am not sure he could be allowed to allocate research facility resources to something like this. But who knows? It might pique his interest.'

'Nuclear Research Center?" said Mansour. 'I wasn't aware Egypt had one of those.'

Khalil chuckled. 'It's a fairly low-key facility for obvious reasons. It is run by the Egyptian Atomic Energy Authority, and functions as a research and testing facility.'

'Any weapons research?' asked Mansour, eyebrows raised.

'I am pretty sure all that goes on in that facility is civilian research, but I don't know for sure. Anyway, his name is Dr Ibrahim Zaki. I met him at a conference a few years ago, where he was part of a panel discussion about the application of radio-isotope analysis to the field of archaeology. Isotopes are basically just variants of the same atom, but with different numbers of neutrons in the nucleus.'

'Right,' said Mansour. 'Well, let's get on with it. Do you have his number?'

'I am sure I have it somewhere,' replied Khalil.

Less than an hour later, the meeting had been set up. It was to take place the next day at 10 am, at the research facility in Inchas, roughly a ninety-minute drive north of Cairo. Dr Zaki had been very accommodating of their request, and he sounded like he was genuinely interested in helping solve the mystery of the casket.

★   ★   ★

When Khalil and Mansour arrived at the nuclear research facility the following day, they were struck by its appearance. Comprised of several smaller buildings and one main building, the complex was smaller than Mansour had expected, but it looked imposing nonetheless. They had to enter through a gate in the three-meter-tall fence that surrounded the entire complex, where five heavily armed guards wearing black uniforms and surly frowns took their time to check their IDs.

Stretching back to 1954, when the first nuclear reactor was acquired from the Soviet Union, the Egyptian nuclear research program had from the outset had the goal of migrating Egypt's energy consumption away from fossil fuels towards nuclear energy. However, after the loss to Israel in the Six-Day War in 1967, and the resultant heavy blow to the Egyptian economy, the program was deemed too expensive and then scrapped. The following year, President Gamal Abdel Nasser signed the Nuclear Non-Proliferation Treaty, but the treaty was never ratified since the Egyptian government claimed that Israel had undertaken its own nuclear weapons research program. The Egyptian nuclear research program was eventually revived in 1992 when the second research reactor was bought from Argentina. The reactor was installed and brought online near the village of Inchas.

The main building resembled a modern prison, with a cubist design, solid-looking walls and very few windows. As they pulled up at the main entrance, a tall thin man in a lab coat came out to greet them. He had a short beard, a large nose and keen eyes. Around his neck hung a security badge with his photo and name on it. Ibrahim Zaki.

Khalil strode towards him and stretched out his hand. 'Doctor Zaki. So good to see you again. This is my friend Professor Mansour.'

'Good to meet you, Doctor,' said Mansour. 'And thank you for taking the time to see us.'

'It is my pleasure,' said Doctor Zaki in a calm baritone voice. 'Please. Come this way.'

A few minutes later they were seated in Doctor Zaki's office, with the small black plastic box placed in the middle of the table between them. Despite the dour exterior of the building, Doctor Zaki's office felt light and welcoming. It was sparsely furnished and seemed very serene as the morning sun lit it up through the heavily tinted windows.

'So, this is it then?' asked Dr Zaki and nodded at the box. 'I understand you have run a radiocarbon analysis on it already?' he said and looked at Khalil.

'Yes, I did,' replied Khalil. 'But the results were inconclusive. That is to say, the analysis found small traces of carbonaceous material. Best guess is that the metal was last in a liquid state 1500 BCE, so around 3600 years ago. But the confidence level is rather low, since I was only able to take a small sample, and that included only tiny amounts of slag remnants trapped in the metal.'

'I see,' said Dr Zaki. 'Well, we might be able to corroborate your findings. I have been working on several new techniques that utilise the same radioactive decay methodology you have already used when you did your radiocarbon analysis.'

He then clasped his hands together, and with a furrowed brow he leaned in over the table, looking as if he was trying to choose his words carefully. 'As for the radioactivity of the fragments, what can you tell me about that?'

Khalil recounted his experience at the Faculty of Chemistry, and Doctor Zaki nodded along sagely, appearing to consider every bit of information carefully as it was presented to him.

After Khalil had finished his story, Doctor Zaki sat back silently for a few moments. 'Very strange,' he finally said. 'I think we can already conclude that what the Geiger counter picked up was probably gamma-radiation.'

Mansour and Khalil looked at each other, and from the expression on their faces, Doctor Zaki concluded that he would need to bring them up to speed on the general topic of radiation.

'Ok,' he simply said and smiled. 'Most of the radioactive materials in existence today was created during the Big Bang 14.5 billion years ago. They are all inherently imbalanced and therefore unstable, which is why they decay over time as they try to bring themselves into a balanced state. When radioactive materials such as uranium decay they give off three different types of radiation, and each of these types have very different properties, and represent very different health risks.'

'What do you mean by *balanced*?' asked Mansour.

Doctor Zaki smiled and nodded, and then he rose and walked over to a whiteboard on the wall opposite the windows, where he picked up a pen and started drawing.

'This is a Uranium atom,' he began, drawing an atomic nucleus with a large number of particles at its centre. 'Uranium-238, the most common uranium isotope in nature, has 92 protons and 146 neutrons for a total of 238 particles in its nucleus. With me so far?'

They both nodded, and Mansour was feeling rather pleased with himself. Perhaps he would be able to understand these things after all.

'When Uranium-238 starts to decay, the first thing that happens is that it loses a so-called alpha-particle, which consists of two neutrons and two protons. The process is naturally called Alpha-decay, and it turns the uranium atom into thorium-234, which has 90 protons and 144 neutrons, for a total of 234 particles in the nucleus. So, the nucleus now has four fewer particles than before.'

'Incidentally,' continued Doctor Zaki with a conspiratorial smile, 'The half-life of Uranium-238 is 4.5 billion years.'

Mansour's mouth nearly fell open. '4.5 billion years?' he said incredulously. 'You mean, this metal loses only half of its radioactivity in the time it took for our solar system to form?'

'That's right,' chuckled Doctor Zaki, clearly enjoying the impact his words were having. 'The uranium-238 that was present when our planet first formed, is now only half as radioactive as it was back then. Amazing, isn't it?'

'Sure is,' said Khalil. He was clearly thoroughly enjoying this private lecture.

'Anyway,' continued Doctor Zaki. 'Alpha particles emitted from uranium-238 atoms are relatively heavy, weighing four atomic unit masses, and because they have a positive charge of 2, stemming from the two protons, and because of their relatively low speed, only around 5 percent of the speed of light, they are very likely to interact with other atoms as they exit the uranium nucleus. In practice, this means that they will usually be stopped by air molecules after just a few centimetres, and will certainly be blocked by something as simple as a piece of paper.'

'So,' began Mansour, and shifted in his chair. 'You're saying that if our two metal fragments were emitting alpha particles, then they would never have been harmful to me or my colleagues?' His thoughts returned to Jabari Omran.

'That is correct,' replied Doctor Zaki and nodded emphatically. 'The only way in which alpha particles can represent a danger to human health is if they are ingested or find their way into the body through some other means. I am sure you both remember the case of the Russian dissident Alexander Litvinenko, who was poisoned with polonium-210 in a London restaurant in 2006.'

'Yes,' nodded Khalil. 'Dreadful business. That was alpha-particles?'

'Yes, it was,' replied Doctor Zaki. 'Once ingested, they can do terrible damage to internal organs, due to their weight and electrical charge.'

He continued. 'Anyway, you might think that alpha-decay simply continues like this ad infinitum, but that is not what happens. Thorium-234 has a half-life of just 27 days, and it decays through a process called beta-decay, through which a neutron in the nucleus of a thorium atom transforms into a proton, and in the process emits several particles. One of these particles is the beta particle, which can be either positively or negatively charged. These particles are fast, travelling at 98 percent of the speed of light, and so are highly energetic, which is why they have the potential to do serious harm.'

Doctor Zaki opened a bottle of water and took a quick swig. Then he continued.

'This decay chain continues with another beta-particle emission, which turns the thorium atom into a protactinium-234 atom with a half-life of another 27 days, which then decays into uranium-234 which has a half-life of 245 thousand years. And so it goes on through consecutive decays and so-called *daughter-products* with varying half-lives until you get to things like lead-206, which is stable. It is a rather complicated process, and its progression depends on which radioactive isotope you begin with.'

'You mentioned one more type of radiation, didn't you?' asked Khalil.

'Yes,' nodded Doctor Zaki. 'The third type is called gamma radiation, and it is by far the most dangerous, because it is in the form of a high energy electromagnetic wave, as opposed to a particle. This means that it can penetrate most materials. In order for an atom's nucleus to undergo gamma decay, it must be in some sort of excited energetic state. Protons and neutrons can achieve such an excited state following the emission of an alpha- or a beta particle. When this happens, the new nucleus must somehow release energy to allow the proton or neutron to relax back down to a more stable state. This happens through the emission of a gamma-ray, which is essentially just a highly energetic photon. The key thing to note here is that gamma radiation is contingent on alpha or beta radiation having already happened, so they are always observed together.'

Doctor Zaki cleared his throat and took another sip of water. Then he continued.

'As I mentioned, and as the name implies, gamma rays are not particles, but electromagnetic radiation, like microwaves, but orders of magnitude more energetic. This makes them extremely harmful to living tissue. Like alpha and beta particles, they are a type of ionising radiation, which means they have enough energy to detach electrons from atoms, which can in turn damage the DNA inside living cells because DNA is simply a long strand of molecules. Unlike those two other types of radiation, however, gamma rays pass easily through even dense materials, so effective shielding against it requires things like gold, or this,' he said and leaned in to tap his finger on the black plastic box.

'Lead lining contains the radiation completely?' asked Mansour.

'If it is thick enough,' replied Dr Zaki and sat down in his chair again. 'Now, regarding the reason we're here today, let me say that I would be happy to have a look at your samples, and run some tests on them.'

'That would be great,' said Khalil. 'Which tests are they? You mentioned some new technological advances you were intending to make use of.'

'Yes,' smiled Doctor Zaki, and pointed to the whiteboard, which by now was full of diagrams, and where he had also written out the entire uranium-238 decay chain. 'As I showed you on the board, there exists a very specific and well-understood decay chain for radioactive materials like uranium-238. The decay processes are highly predictable, and so are the ratios between materials like uranium-238 and thorium-232 in a sample. In addition, the half-lives are very accurately mapped out, and as you saw, some half-lives are many orders of magnitude shorter than others. Using certain assumptions about an initial state of a metal found in say an ancient artefact, we can use this information about the ratios to first determine the extent to which there exists any so-called *disequilibria* in the decay chain. This is a complicated way of saying that certain events can create deviations from the expected ratios between different radioactive materials in a sample, and one of the events that can cause this is smelting. In other words, we can use data on deviations in the ratios between different radioactive materials, to infer when a metal might have been melted and reshaped, possibly by human hand. It is not an exact science, but it is pretty good, and it obviously has the potential to extend well beyond the roughly 60-thousand year effective limit of radiocarbon dating, because the half-lives of some of these isotopes are tens or even hundreds of thousands of years.'

'Remarkable,' said Mansour, whose head was now swimming with all the information he had been absorbing over the past few days. 'I would be very grateful if you would run your tests on those fragments.'

'Ok,' replied Doctor Zaki. 'I can't guarantee that those tests will be completely non-destructive, but I will do my best to only use as much of the metal as I absolutely need to.'

'That would be much appreciated,' said Mansour. 'I am sure you understand the historical value of this artefact.'

'Oh, I think I understand that better than most,' said Doctor Zaki cryptically. 'Anyway,' he exclaimed, as if eager to move on. 'My tests should take no more than a day or two, so I will get back to you as soon as I have something.'

He was about to get out of his chair when Mansour held up his hand apologetically.

'I am sorry,' he said 'But I have a few final questions about the toxicity of these radioactive metals,' said Mansour.

'Certainly,' said Doctor Zaki and sat back down, with a curious look on his face.

'A few years ago,' continued Mansour, 'my predecessor at the museum became seriously ill with cancer over a very short period of time. He spent an inordinate amount of time with the metal casket from which these two fragments came. Could this have been caused by radiation exposure?'

'It is conceivable,' said Dr Zaki. 'As I said, exposure over a prolonged period of time could be quite harmful, depending on the level of radioactivity. Usually, when people think of radiation poisoning, they are really referring to what is called ARS, or Acute Radiation Syndrome. This is what happens after massive radiation exposure over a short period of time. It is a ghastly thing, involving vomiting, bodily functions shutting down, seizures, burns of the skin and internal bleeding. This is what happened to many of the workers at Chernobyl in 1986.'

'Sounds horrific,' said Mansour and glanced at the black plastic box. 'I hope the lead in that box is sufficient protection.'

'I am sure it is,' said Doctor Zaki. 'The fragments are very small, so there is no need to worry.'

'Alright,' smiled Mansour and rose. 'We'll take your word for it.'

Doctor Zaki escorted the two men out to their waiting car, and they bid each other farewell. After Mansour and Khalil had left, Doctor Zaki was making his way back towards the laboratory building, when one of his younger colleagues, Tarek Osman, came jogging along the corridor behind him, trying to catch up.

Tarek was the resident computer wiz, currently working on the application of neural networks to isotope characterisation. It was all beyond Doctor Zaki, who was much more comfortable with real analysis of actual physical samples, as opposed to inference using computer algorithms. He also did not like the young man very much. Always poking his nose in other people's business.

'Ibrahim. Wait up,' called Tarek, as he came up alongside Doctor Zaki. 'Who was that?' he asked casually.

'Just two researchers from Cairo,' replied Doctor Zaki dismissively. 'They have an artefact they have had trouble dating, so I am going to try the uranium-238, radium-226 method I have been working on.'

'Can I join you?' asked Tarek.

Here we go, thought Doctor Zaki to himself. 'No thanks, Tarek. I would prefer to do this on my own,' he replied in as friendly a tone as he could manage.

'Alright,' said Tarek and peeled off down another corridor, apparently unperturbed.

Why is he always in my business? thought Doctor Zaki. *And why does he always call me by my first name?*

Originally being of Jewish heritage on his father's side, Doctor Zaki's name was indeed Ibrahim, which is the Arab version of the name Abraham. His parents had given it to him in honour of the Old Testament prophet Abraham, the 'father of many nations'. The progenitor of the Jews. The first Jew.

Doctor Zaki might be a man of modern science, but his roots were firmly anchored in the ancient Jewish traditions and Jewish history. Abraham had become the patriarch of the Jewish nation, after passing ten gruelling tests set for him by Yahweh. Ibrahim merely hoped that he himself would be able to pass his test, which was now surely coming.

When he was alone in the lab, he fished out his phone from the pocket in his lab coat and dialled a number that was not pre-programmed into the phone's address book. It rang only twice before it was picked up.

'How did it go, my son?' said the voice of an old man.

'It went well,' replied Doctor Zaki. 'We spent most of our time talking about how we might analyse the fragments. I think they were happy with that.'

'Good,' said the voice. 'And now?'

'I have the fragments here in my possession. I will carry out the tests and report back.'

'Could this be the real thing?' asked the voice calmly.

'It is possible,' replied Doctor Zaki hesitantly. 'It certainly seems like it, but I will need to complete the test first."

'Ok,' said the voice. 'Report back when you have the results. Take care, my son. Moshe is with us.'

'Moshe is with us,' repeated Doctor Zaki, and ended the call.

Four

Doctor Zaki leaned back in the chair in his office, and sat motionless for a few seconds, contemplating what he had just read. He had run the test twice, on two small samples of each of the two metal fragments, and the results on the print-outs were puzzling.

Can this really be true? he wondered.

The fragments seemed to be made of an alloy, which meant that its constituent metals had at some point been melted and mixed in order to obtain the desired properties. What was surprising, was its composition. It contained all the usual suspects like copper, tin and small amounts of iron, as well as miniscule trace amounts of various radioactive isotopes, including uranium-238 and radium-226 as he expected. In fact, these isotopes were what he had used to arrive at an estimate of its age.

But the results also showed a significant amount of what appeared to be a type of thorium, but it was an isotope he had never seen before. In fact, he was sure he had never even read about anything like this, and its characteristics did not match anything in the periodic table. Because of the ambiguous readings, the analysis machine, when arriving at a designation, had defaulted to thorium. But it was definitely not thorium. It was much too heavy for that, and it was much more radioactive than it should have been. The gamma-radiation was extremely high for such small samples, and had tripped a caution alert on his PC after the analysis was done.

He would have concluded that somehow an error had crept into the testing or measuring process, except the results were the same for both samples, which were processed separately on two different machines on two separate days.

The samples were also surprisingly pure for an object this ancient, which hinted at the fact that whoever made it would have been an exceptionally skilled metallurgist.

Somehow, this highly radioactive metal had been melted down and mixed in with an otherwise standard copper alloy more than four thousand years ago. Considering the unknown isotope's half-life, which his testing equipment had estimated at twenty-three thousand years, the metal was now only slightly less radioactive than it had been back then.

Could this really be from the Source? thought Doctor Zaki.

★ ★ ★

The next day, Mansour came into the office at his usual time. He took off his beige suit jacket and sat down at his desk while loosening his tie. It was going to be a hot day again.

As he did so, he was eyeing the spot on his desk where the casket had sat a couple of days earlier. The whole affair had unsettled him, not least because it almost put beyond doubt that his friend and colleague Jabari Omran had succumbed to the destructive powers of the casket. It was as if a curse had been placed on it, and it made him wonder if somehow this was connected to the fact that the casket had found its way into the possession of the museum more than a hundred years ago, yet no one knew who donated it.

As he switched on his computer, he poured himself the first cup of coffee of the day. As always, he checked his emails first thing in the morning, and today at the top of the pile in his inbox was a message from Doctor Zaki at the Nuclear Research Centre.

Mansour clicked on it immediately, and read the contents.

'More than four thousand years?' he muttered to himself incredulously. 'Surely that can't be right.' This would mean that it was made during the time of Khufu, or Cheops, as he is often known throughout the world.

If these test results were accurate, then this metal artefact was by far the oldest of this type he had ever heard of. It was well established that papyrus was produced as far back as the 4th millennium BCE, so the now disintegrated pages of the casket could conceivably have been made during the 3rd

millennium, around 2500 BCE. But for the casket to have been made during that same period would have required metallurgical and artisanal expertise far beyond what was generally accepted to be present at that time.

Mansour continued reading the email and had to read the section from Doctor Zaki about the radioactivity of the metal fragments twice. He felt that he had understood most of what the nuclear research scientist had explained to himself and Khalil, but now he wasn't sure what to make of it all.

'Highly radioactive,' he slowly read aloud. 'Abnormal gamma-ray output. Inconclusive analysis of radioactive trace metal type. Indeterminate source of gamma radiation.'

He wasn't quite sure exactly what that meant, but it sounded distinctly bad, and the implication was clear. The casket was dangerous, and Khalil had been right to ask him to move it back down into the vault. The other obvious implication was that Jabari Omran had almost certainly succumbed to its deadly effects.

Mansour spent the next few minutes replying to Doctor Zaki's email and thanking him for his help. He was now in two minds about what to do next. On the one hand, his gut told him to back off and focus on something else. After all, there were plenty of other artefacts in the museum's collection that needed to be studied and written about. On the other hand, he now felt invested in this mystery, and he had the distinct feeling that something very interesting lay at the end of this path. In addition, part of him could not shake the feeling that quitting now would be an abandonment of Jabari Omran's legacy. As if somehow his death had been for nothing.

Closing his eyes and leaning back in his chair, Mansour spent a few minutes meditating on this, until finally, he had made his decision. He would press ahead. Perhaps Khalil would continue to assist him, and perhaps the two of them could solve the mystery together.

Mansour then spent a couple of hours brushing up on 4th-millennium metallurgy, while also finding time to arrange for several pieces of lead to be delivered to his office. It was surprisingly easy to find since moderately thick yet relatively malleable lead sheets are often used for roofing. They would be arriving the next day. He would sleep better at night, knowing that the wooden box in the vault had a proper radiation insulation lining on the inside.

As he was walking down the corridor on his way from the coffee machine, Mansour stopped outside what used to be Jabari Omran's office. It now belonged to the curator of the ancient pottery collection. This was often referred to as the least glamourous collection, even if it often provided some of the richest detail on how ordinary people lived several millennia ago.

The office had been left virtually unchanged since Omran's death. Same furniture. Same paintings on the walls. Omran had been particularly fond of a large painting of the outside of the Tomb of Nefertari, which hung directly opposite where his desk had been. It was still there, and as Mansour stepped into the office, he felt himself being drawn to it. He walked closer and inspected the scene. Giant granite statues of the queen, side by side and cut into the rockface of a promontory in southern Egypt.

As he was about to turn and walk back to his own office, he noticed something odd that had never occurred to him before. The painting seemed to be jutting out slightly from the wall on the left side. He stepped closer and peered behind it.

'A safe', muttered Mansour surprised.

He hesitated for a few seconds, but unable to resist his own curiosity, he put down his coffee cup on the mahogany console table under the painting and gently lifted the painting off the wall. It was a very small safe, which looked like it had been there for a long time. The wallpaper, which probably had not changed for many decades, was fraying slightly around the edges of the safe, and the metal lock wheel looked grimy and well worn.

Mansour knew immediately what the combination must be. He had known Omran for most of his career, and he knew that the old man had always been captivated by the reign of Pharaoh Djoser, whose reign ended with his burial in the famous step pyramid at Saqqara, roughly six kilometres south-east of the Giza Necropolis.

Mansour reached up and held the wheel between his fingertips.

2649 BCE. The year of Djoser's death.

The lock made a single firm click, and he opened the door to find an empty safe, except for a single item. A notebook. For the next hour, Mansour perched on the back of a chesterfield sofa, leafing through the pages and feeling quite stunned by what he was reading.

Omran had chronicled some of his research in this notebook. He never got comfortable with writing on a computer and had always preferred his own handwritten notes. But this research concerned something much bigger than the casket. In fact, it made even the pyramids pale in comparison.

This can't be, whispered Mansour.

After an hour of studying Omran's notes, his head was beginning to spin with the implications of what he had read. He decided to place the notebook back inside the safe, and once more conceal the safe behind the painting. He knew that he ought to inform the museum's director, but decided he would need to sleep on it, before he made up his mind about what to do. This was too important for him to make a snap decision.

★   ★   ★

In the early afternoon, the young man sat down at a table outside a coffee shop on Gezira Street in Cairo. Wearing trainers, jeans, a light blue shirt and a baseball cap with an 'NY' badge at the front, he looked every bit the young cosmopolitan. A waiter came out of the shop and took his order, and a few minutes later he was sipping a Latte.

He had sat down with his back to the wall, then pulled out his laptop and placed it in front of him. He opened it up and connected to the café's WiFi network. Then he typed in a series of passwords, after which he accessed the encrypted Virtual Private Network, which would allow him to trick servers on the internet to think he was somewhere else. He was in Cairo, but he could choose to appear to be in Beijing, Dallas, or any other location on Earth. Today he went for Oslo.

As soon as his VPN connection was established, he opened a command prompt and pinged an IP address northeast of Cairo. The server in that location responded, and he sent the tailored electronic handshake that would tell the server to allow him access to its computer network. Within seconds he was in.

He smiled and shook his head ever so slightly, not quite able to believe that this actually worked. In his experience, cyber-security in most of the government agencies in Egypt was woefully inadequate, but he would still have expected it to be significantly harder to hack into the computer network at a nuclear research centre. Especially so when that research centre was run by the government through the Egyptian Atomic Energy Authority, and as such was a quasi-military entity.

He quickly navigated his way through the network, using the fake administrator account he had set up several years earlier. At this point, everything he did was routine, but today was special. Today the backdoor into the system that he and his accomplice had set up, looked like it was finally going to yield a tangible result.

A few minutes later he had accessed the encrypted email server, found his intended target, and downloaded all the correspondence he was looking for. He had received clear instructions about what to retrieve, so he ignored everything else. After that, he used his administrator privileges to access the database containing all the files pertaining to internal research at the facility. Helpfully, all the research results were stored in one location on the network. A few seconds later, it was all sitting on the hard drive of his laptop. He typed in a couple of commands, which altered the log files on the server, in order to delete any record of him ever having been inside the system. Then he logged off and closed the connection to the server.

A few minutes later he had finished his latte and got out his wallet. He fished out a few banknotes. He didn't bother to count them. It would be more than enough to pay for the latte, and there was plenty where that came from.

As he walked away, he smiled to himself. His paymaster would be pleased. Casting his net wide across a large number of government and military server networks, he had finally got his hands on something big. This would be worth a lot of money. Today was payday.

★ ★ ★

The black Range Rover drove swiftly up the ramp and left the parking garage under the expensive townhouse in the upmarket Zamalek district in the centre of Cairo. It had heavily tinted windows and diplomatic license plates, and as it swung out into the wide tree-lined boulevard and drove south towards the 15th of May Bridge across the Nile, no one looked twice at it. This was the embassy district, and people here were used to seeing cars with tinted windows being escorted back and forth by the special diplomatic protection service of the Cairo Police Department.

Having crossed the river, the powerful car got off the bridge and turned south towards the Old Cairo neighbourhood a few kilometres further along the river and across from the Giza district. After approximately ten minutes, it did a u-turn and pulled over on Kasr Al Shame'e Street, where it parked up with its engine still running. It was almost 7 pm. The sun had sunk beneath the horizon behind the Giza district to the west, and darkness was quickly closing in.

The rear passenger door behind the driver's seat opened, and a burly man in a dark brown suit stepped out onto the pavement. He closed the car door, adjusted his clothes, and then walked calmly along Mari Gerges Street towards the entrance to the Coptic Museum. The museum had closed several hours ago, and the gates were locked. There were several office windows with the lights still on inside the complex, but the exterior was dark, except for one small light bulb mounted above the metal gate that served as the staff entrance.

The man ambled over to the gate and turned around to lean against the wall. Here he lit a cigarette, and casually glanced down the street to his left where the Range Rover was parked, and then to his right. All was quiet. The only people he could see were a couple of elderly men who were standing on the train platform at the Mar Girgis Metro station on the opposite side of the street, but they were facing away from him and seemed deep in conversation.

As he brought his cigarette up to his mouth again, he casually stepped out from the wall, turned and reached up to grab the light bulb above him. He gave it a firm quarter turn counter-clockwise, and instantly the bulb went out and the area in front of the staff gate was now in darkness. All that was visible was the orange glow from his cigarette. He let it drop to the ground and then he extinguished the ember by stepping on it with his shoe.

A couple of minutes later, at his usual time, a short man in his fifties exited the museum's main building and made his way across the grounds towards the staff gate. He noticed the light above the gate not working, but he could not see the man in the suit leaning against the wall a couple of meters away from it. When the short man was halfway along the path from the main building to the staff gate, the black Range Rover started crawling forward along Mari Gerges at walking pace. Its headlights were off and its engine was growling softly, giving only a vague hint of its power.

There was a metallic-sounding snap when the lock on the staff gate released, and as the small bespectacled man walked through it, the Range Rover began to pick up speed.

In what seemed like a carefully choreographed sequence, the burly man in the suit stepped out from the wall only a few paces away, and at the same time, the Range Rover's engine roared as it accelerated towards the museum. The man in the suit came up behind his unsuspecting victim, placed his heavy muscular arm around his chest while pushing a hypodermic needle into his neck.

Almost instantaneously, the short man's legs gave way underneath him. As quickly as it had gone in, the needle was pulled back out again, and the man in the suit easily held the weight of the ragdoll that was now in his arms.

Within a few seconds, the Range Rover had closed the distance to the two men, and as it braked hard, the passenger door sprang open and another man jumped out. The driver kept the engine revved up, ready to get away. The two men bundled the short bespectacled man into the back seat of the car and jumped in after him. Even before the passenger doors had closed completely, the Range Rover leapt forward, swerved out into the street and accelerated away from the museum, its engine roaring angrily.

The whole thing had taken less than a minute, and now the street was empty and quiet again. Almost as if it had never happened.

On the train platform, one of the elderly men had heard the sound of the Range Rover's engine, and as he turned with a frown on his face, he saw its red taillights disappearing towards the north along Mari Gerges.

Damn those foreign diplomats, he thought. *They think they own the city.*

Five

HEREFORD, UK – 2 DAYS LATER

It was raining in Hereford, and the heavy grey clouds hung low over the green landscape. Shielded from view and far from public roads and villages, the special forces training compound sat behind barbed wire fences, watched over by CCTV. Inside building C were even more cameras, that would allow the teams to review their simulated assault, and hopefully improve on anything that could have been done better or more effectively.

As Andrew walked towards the building, he could see the breach team getting ready by the entrance.

'Andy,' said Colonel Strickland, and started walking towards him, his right hand stretched out to greet him. The head of the SAS unit specialising in chemical and biological and nuclear terrorism threats looked happy to be out of the office for the day.

'Gordon, sir!' smiled Andrew. 'I see you're keeping the boys busy?'

'Got to make sure they're sharp,' replied Strickland.

'Absolutely, sir' said Andrew, and continued in a voice loud enough for him to be overhead by the team. 'We can't have chaps like McGregor get all fat and lazy now, can we?'

McGregor, who was preparing to lead the team into the training complex turned slowly and glared at Andrew with mock disdain. 'Why don't you lose the suit and join us, Andy?' He said in his broad Scottish accent. 'If anybody is getting fat these days, it's you.'

That elicited a subdued chorus of laughter among the men. Most of them had been on the teams that went into Syria and Sudan in pursuit of the Antarctic pathogen, and they knew better than to underestimate Sterling. But they would never say no to a chance to laugh at him for sitting behind a desk most of his time these days.

'Alright lads, that's enough,' said McGregor in an authoritative voice, and instantly the team snapped back into complete professionalism. 'Line up on me!'

The team filed in behind him, checking their weapons and equipment. They were all carrying silenced 9 mm Heckler & Kock MP5K-PDW submachineguns, and wearing body armour that was light and flexible enough to allow them to move in tight spaces, yet strong enough to stop most small calibre bullets.

McGregor ran a final comms check and then signalled for the explosives expert to advance.

'Dunn, you're up,' said McGregor and made a hand gesture over his shoulder.

Immediately, the man behind him stepped out of the stack and approached the door with a breaching charge. In just a few seconds, he had fixed the charge to the door of the training complex and filed in at the back of the stack behind Wilks, the team's sniper who had joined the breach team on this exercise. He was usually several hundred meters away on overwatch, but McGregor had decided to have him join the team today. He might need to assist in close quarters combat at some point.

Seconds later, the directional breach charge detonated with a deafening dry crack, and the door was blown in. Before the debris had finished falling, the stack, led by McGregor, filed swiftly through the door and into the first room of the training compound. The interior of the building was made of wall sections that could be moved around, allowing the instructors to change the room layout, and give the teams a new and different challenge every so often.

As the team swept through the building, using their endlessly rehearsed Close Quarter Combat, or CQC tactics, they called out "Clear!" as they worked their way through all the rooms, using flashbangs and firing at dummy targets. There was a lot of noise and yelling and shouting as the raid took place, which might have made it seem chaotic to an outsider. However, to Andrew that just meant that the team had injected the right amount of aggression into the exercise and that they were communicating well as they progressed through the building.

The whole thing was over in just a couple of minutes, and as they filed out of the exit at the other end of the building, the instructors started walking towards the compound's main building, where they would be going over the footage of the exercise with the team.

'Good job,' said Andrew looking content with what he had witnessed. 'Seems like they nailed it. Good speed. Good aggression. Nice efficiency of movement.'

'Yes, I think that was spot on,' replied Colonel Strickland. 'These chaps know their stuff, Andy. That business in Syria and Sudan was top-notch, by the way. The instructors are already using it as a case study for new recruits.'

'I am not surprised,' replied Andrew, reflecting for a moment on the potential impact on humanity this small group of men had already had, when they assaulted and neutralised the pathogen production facility in Syria several months earlier. 'I saw the recordings from their body cams. Bloody good work.'

'It was indeed,' said Strickland as they started walking back towards the main building. 'Anyway, I would like you to come by my office tomorrow morning, if you don't mind.'

'Certainly, sir. What about?'

'We've received intelligence that there are things afoot in Egypt that we might need to take an interest in. But I will give you the details tomorrow. It is currently classified, so I am technically not at liberty to discuss it outside the HQ.'

'No problem, sir. I'll be there tomorrow morning. Say 9 o'clock?'

'Perfect,' said Strickland. 'Now let's go and watch the footage. I am sure there's something McGregor was unhappy about.'

Andrew smiled. 'There always is, sir. That's why he's so bloody good at this.'

★　　★　　★

Halima Omran had been visiting a friend in Cairo's Abdeen district in the east of the city and was now returning home to her flat in the Al Manial district on Rhoda Island in central Cairo. After the death of her husband Jabari a few years earlier, her female friends from her youth had seemingly come out of the woodwork and rallied around her. Every week they would arrange for her to join some gathering or activity, which she hated doing at first. But slowly, she began to enjoy them, and eventually, she could feel herself healing inside and slowly finding her feet again.

Her friends' efforts had been sorely needed, especially in the beginning, since Jabari's death had taken a terrible toll on her. Watching her soulmate crushed by cancer had been a shocking experience, and as much as she felt shame to admit it, when he finally passed, she had experienced a strange sensation of relief, mixed with sadness and loss. But now his suffering was over.

The journey on the public transportation system back to her small flat on the 2nd floor of an apartment complex on Refaat Street was long and arduous for a woman in her seventies, but it had all been worth it. She felt invigorated and cheerful as she opened the door to the stairwell and began walking the two flights of stairs up to her front door. Approaching the landing on the 2nd floor, while fishing her keys out of her pocket, she noticed that something felt out of place.

She looked up to see her front door open. Hesitating for a few moments, she then walked slowly forward to peek inside. There was nobody there and no sound of anyone being in the apartment. But the sight that met her as she entered the apartment shocked her. It had been ransacked, and the contents of all the cupboards and drawers lay strewn across the floor. All the paintings had been torn off the walls, and all the books she and her husband had collected over the years had been ripped from the shelves.

Her tired legs trembled as she stood there, trying to decide what to do. Then she slowly walked over to the telephone and dialled the number for the police.

* * *

The next morning, Andrew arrived well rested at the London offices of the SAS's chemical, biological and nuclear anti-terrorism unit at Sheldrake Place. From the outside, it looked like any other sleek corporate headquarters, but past the revolving doors, the lobby provided the first hint that this was no ordinary office building. There was a reception desk with a friendly-looking receptionist, polished black marble floors and two security guards, who carried themselves in a way that was instantly recognisable to someone like Andrew. These two were not just a pair of rent-a-cops. They had clearly seen combat.

Andrew greeted the receptionist and nodded towards the two guards, who responded in kind. No need for small talk.

Exiting the lift of the 3rd floor, Andrew swung by his office where his secretary Catherine was talking on the phone. He quickly dove into his office to put down his bag and take off his suit jacket, and then he headed towards Gordon Strickland's office.

'Gordon. Morning sir,' he said and knocked on the door frame of the open door.

'Ah! Andy. Come in,' replied the colonel, and got up from behind his desk. 'Do sit,' he continued and gestured towards a dark brown leather chesterfield sofa with a small coffee table in front of it.

Andrew sat down on the sofa, and Gordon placed himself in a matching leather armchair.

'Right,' said Strickland and clasped his hands together. 'I will come straight to the point. As you know, we have a close intelligence-sharing program with the US, Canada, Australia and New Zealand.'

'Yes,' nodded Andrew. '5 Eyes.'

'Correct. The program is highly active, and there are quite significant amounts of information being exchanged on a daily basis about individuals, organisations and general trends in what we each observe. This is especially true regarding online activity and topics being discussed in private forums and even several encrypted messaging services. Occasionally, we invite other countries to join us on certain efforts, and one of the intelligence services that we have had a close but unofficial relationship with for several years now, is Egypt. That country has significant extremist elements, especially in particular regions of the country.'

'Yes. The Sinai Peninsula, if I am not mistaken,' said Andrew and leaned forward.

'That is correct. An insurgency sprang up after the removal of President Hosni Mubarak in 2011, and it has been going on ever since. It mainly targets military installations, but there have been several instances of attacks on civilians. I am sure you remember the downing of the Russian Metrojet airliner in 2015. 224 civilian lives were lost. They also attacked a Sufist mosque in 2017, killing 300 civilians, including 23 children.'

'Bastards,' said Andrew through gritted teeth whilst shaking his head.

'Indeed,' nodded Strickland gravely. 'For this reason, we have assisted the Egyptians with anything we have been able to pick up here in the UK, where a sizeable proportion of the Egyptian diaspora lives. A small minority of those have extremist leanings.'

'Ok,' said Andrew, furrowing his brow. 'So, what have we come up with?'

'Actually, the question is: What have *they* come up with? You see, Egyptian intelligence got in touch two days ago, regarding a missing person. A certain archaeologist named Doctor Bahir Mansour, who works for the Coptic Museum in Cairo.'

'Sorry sir,' said Andrew confused. 'I don't quite follow. An Egyptian archaeologist at some museum in Cairo disappears for a few days. What does that have to do with us? I bet he just ran off with his mistress.'

'If only it was that simple,' replied Strickland. 'Somehow, the Coptic Museum got its hands on an old metal artefact over a hundred years ago, and apparently it had been sitting in storage there for most of that time. However, the good Doctor Mansour had taken an interest in it lately and had even had the metal analysed. And would you believe, it turned out the be radioactive.'

'Crikey,' said Andrew surprised. 'Really? Just how radioactive was it?'

'Well,' said Strickland, shifting in his armchair. 'We don't have the full picture yet of course, but the short answer seems to be *very*. The reason Egyptian intelligence decided to come to us, is that Mansour and a friend of his took samples of the item to a nuclear research facility not far from Cairo. After one of their scientists, a certain Doctor Zaki, performed a series of tests and uncovered exactly how dangerous this radioactive material was, that facility's computer network was hacked, and the test results stolen.'

'That does sound rather suspect,' said Andrew, looking concerned.

'It does indeed,' replied Strickland. 'The intruder apparently made an effort to hide his presence in the network, but there were still some traces of his activities that Egyptian intelligence was able to find. He had set up a backdoor to the network a long time ago. When and how, we don't know. But he had become sloppy and missed a couple of registry keys on the server when he deleted the logs of his activity.'

Strickland looked at Andrew with a sober expression. 'The bottom line here is that an archaeologist who was unwittingly in possession of radioactive material has disappeared, and the facility that analysed his samples has been hacked. Add to this, that our joint 5 Eyes efforts to scan encrypted messages and phone conversations between suspected terrorist sympathisers, has seen a clear uptick in references to nuclear material. This might be a coincidence but taken together it all points to this being the result of some form of organised activity. By whom, and for what purpose, we simply don't know, but we can only speculate that a terrorist group may be trying to acquire radioactive material for some purpose. And that is where you come in.'

'Let me guess,' smiled Andrew. 'You want me to take quick a trip to Cairo, look into this business about radioactive material, and try to find out what happened to Doctor Mansour?'

'I do,' said Strickland. 'But I would like you to bring Fiona along. She's exactly the right sort of resource for a mission like this.'

Andrew's eyes narrowed, and he hesitated for a moment. After a couple of seconds, he realised that he definitely did not like the name "Fiona" in the same sentence as the word "mission". In his experience, the latter often involved extreme danger and sometimes loss of life, and after having had a gun pointed at the two of them in a cave in Mexico, whilst investigating ancient Inca ruins, he wasn't in a hurry to put her in harm's way again.

'Look, Andy,' said Strickland. 'I know what you're thinking. But rest assured, you two will only be there in an investigatory capacity. You have to admit that she is an extremely capable archaeologist, and if we want to make progress in this matter, we are going to need someone like her.'

Yes, thought Andrew reluctantly. *Someone like her. Not necessarily actually her.*

'But listen,' continued Strickland. 'It is entirely up to the two of you to decide. I can't order her to do anything, and quite frankly, neither can you.'

'I have a feeling that would be a grave mistake anyway', smirked Andrew.

'Indeed,' smiled Strickland knowingly. 'She's a feisty one. Anyway, the fact remains, that she is bound to be a huge asset in exactly this sort of situation. So, if you wouldn't mind letting her know that I would be very grateful if she would consider joining you. In the event that she agrees, you would both be leaving on a flight tomorrow morning.'

Andrew sat motionless for a few moments until he realised that regardless of how he felt about it, it simply was not up to him to decide.

'Right,' he finally said. 'I will have a chat with her later today.'

★ ★ ★

'Absolutely not, mister' said Fiona indignantly. 'You don't get to tell me whether I can come along. I am not some precious little thing that you can decide whether to take with you or not. Frankly, you should be grateful that I want to join you at all. How are you going to make sense of anything to do with archaeology?'

'Alright. Alright,' smiled Andrew, and held up his hands defensively. He should have known not to think that he could have any say in the matter. 'Fine. We're both going. Ok?'

'Yes, we are.' asserted Fiona sternly.

'Look, I know you are a brilliant archaeologist,' said Andrew. 'I am just trying to make sure nothing bad happens to you, ok?' he said sheepishly.

'And that's very sweet,' she replied in a slightly calmer voice. 'And I do appreciate that, but I am a big girl, and I don't need you to protect me.'

'Right,' said Andrew, nodding affirmatively. 'Ok. Big girl. Got it. Now let's get packing.'

★   ★   ★

It was just after 2 am in Cairo, and the Coptic Museum was dark and quiet. There were no lights in any of the office windows, but someone had screwed the light bulb above the staff entrance back in, casting a dim light on the immediate area around the gate's exterior.

The hooded figure, however, did not come in from the street. He had crawled over the rooftops behind the museum and dropped down into a courtyard, from where he was now silently making his way to a side entrance in the main office building. The whole compound was closed and locked during Sundays like today, and all the doors required a code to be entered on a keypad, and then a subsequent alarm deactivation code to be entered on a different keypad inside the building.

The figure, who was wearing all black and carrying a small rucksack, stopped at the door, flicked open the keypad housing, and quickly tapped the correct sequence. The lock disengaged, and as he pushed the door open to enter, he quickly turned his head to check behind him. There was no sign of anyone being in the museum complex, except for him.

Holding a dim flashlight and moving in a calm and deliberate manner down the corridor, the CCTV cameras captured him entering Doctor Bahir Mansour's office. There were no cameras inside individual offices, so the CCTV system did not capture what he was doing. It did however record light and movement inside the office, which suggested that things were being moved around in there.

Several minutes later, the hooded figure re-emerged and walked purposefully towards the stairwell to the vault. Here, it stopped, entered the access code on the keypad, and descended into the basement.

A different camera mounted under the ceiling in the corner of the underground storage unit, captured the figure making his way to the very back of one of the aisles, and reaching up to grab a box sitting on a shelf. He carried the box out of the field of view of the camera, but a couple of minutes later, he re-emerged at the top of the vault's stairwell, carrying a large bag that he must have had inside his rucksack. The bag was clearly heavy, and the figure waddled slightly from side to side, as he made his way towards the door that he had entered through just a few minutes earlier. Once outside, he quickly made his way towards a back entrance to the museum complex and slipped out into the street where a car picked him up. It was now just before 2.30 am, and the museum was quiet again.

Six

The next morning, Andrew and Fiona boarded a Royal Airforce BAe 146-200, at RAF Northolt in the western part of the Greater London area. The small passenger jet belonged to the No. 32 Squadron, which serves as a passenger transport service for royals and UK government VIPs. The trip out from central London had been swift, and barely two hours after getting out of bed, the two of them were seated comfortably in plush seats inside the cabin, barrelling down the runway and then lifting off into the clear pale blue sky. They took off from runway 25, which meant they were going almost due west when the wheels lifted from the runway. As the aircraft banked to the left, Andrew could see Wembley Stadium just a few kilometres away to the east.

Cairo was at the very limit of the small aircraft's maximum range of 3000km, but wind direction and overall flying weather was expected to be good, and so the pilots had calculated an expected travel time of just 4 hours and 20 minutes.

They were expected to land at Almaza Airforce Base in north-eastern Cairo at just after 2 pm local time, where they would be met by Major Bahman Elsayed from Egyptian Military Intelligence. He would then brief them at the airport, and arrange for transport to a hotel in central Cairo.

Colonel Strickland had provided them both with a short but concise write-up, produced by the UK's Government Communications Headquarters, also known as GCHQ. This agency is responsible for so-called SIGINT, or signals intelligence. In practice, this means that GCHQ is in charge of electronic interception of information that might have a bearing on the UK's national security.

The document detailed most of what the Egyptian intelligence agencies had uncovered so far, regarding the security breach at the Inchas Nuclear Research Facility, and also what they had managed to piece together about the disappearance of Doctor Mansour, which was not very much. There was also a section by British intelligence, mapping the so-called general 'chatter' on the internet originating from hundreds of intercepts of phone conversations and encrypted messaging apps. Andrew found this particularly concerning. There was no obviously discernible pattern to the data, but somehow his gut told him that something sinister was percolating beneath the surface of this digital sea of voices, thoughts and emotions.

All of this information was technically classified and as such should not be provided to civilians like

Fiona Keane, but Colonel Strickland had secured her a temporary and conditional clearance, which would allow her to view all the information that was available to Andrew. This would obviously be a requirement for them to be able to work as a team during this trip.

'Did you know that most people in the UK have never heard of the Suez Crisis?' said Fiona, looking at Andrew enquiringly.

Andrew slowly shifted his gaze to Fiona, whilst trying to extract himself from his musings about the intelligence report he had just read. 'Uhm, no I did not know that,' he finally replied.

'It's true,' Fiona continued. 'Quite surprising, considering it is unquestionably a watershed moment in Britain's post-war history. It is not difficult to argue that 1956 was the effective end of Britain as a global superpower.'

'How do you mean?' asked Andrew, knowing that there was no stopping Fiona now.

'Well,' she said and shifted in her seat, clearly preparing to deliver a minor monologue.

'It is actually a really interesting story. After the Second World War, Britain was technically victorious, even if the country was utterly bankrupt and economically broken. But having effectively been able to tag along with the United States in the Allied invasion of Europe, and claim victory in front of the British people, there was a renewed sense of imperial clout and confidence in the corridors of power in London. When Egyptian president Nasser suddenly nationalised the Suez Canal in 1956, effectively kicking out Britain and France, who had controlled it jointly since its opening in 1869, Israel saw that as a national security threat and decided to invade the Sinai Peninsula. Nasser had already tried to establish himself as the leader of the Arab world, and the focal point of Arab opposition to continued British influence in the Middle-East, so the nationalisation of the canal was just the culmination of that process.'

Andrew leaned back in his chair, got himself comfortable and glanced at his wristwatch. 'Good thing we've got another 3 hours until we land,' he smirked. 'Carry on.'

Fiona slapped him playfully on the arm and laughed. She knew she could get a bit carried away, but she kept going.

'As I am sure you're aware, she continued. 'The state of Israel was largely a construct created by the British government in 1948, and president Nasser objected to this, as did the vast majority of Egyptians and other Arabs. The then prime minister of Britain, Anthony Eden, was hell-bent on ousting Nasser, at one point apparently calling him 'Hitler on the Nile', so when Egyptian forces took over the canal, this was Eden's excuse to act.'

'Sounds like it got personal,' said Andrew.

'It certainly did,' nodded Fiona. 'In genuine cloak-and-dagger fashion, Nasser held a speech in July 1956, where he specifically mentioned the name Ferdinand de Lesseps, who was the French builder of the Suez Canal. This was actually a code word for the Egyptian military to seize control of the canal. On the same day, the canal was closed to Israeli shipping, and Egypt instituted a blockade of the Gulf of Aqaba, which is the gulf between the Sinai Peninsula and the

Arabian Peninsula, effectively closing down the Israeli port of Eilat. In both Britain and France, the seizure was seen as completely unacceptable, and as a humiliation of those two colonial powers, and so there was support in both countries for military action. Nasser was seen in London as a threat to British influence in the Middle-East in general and Israel in particular, and the government in Paris held Nasser responsible for the anti-colonial rebellion in French-controlled Algeria which began in 1954.'

'What about the United States,' asked Andrew. 'Surely they would have had a say in this?'

'The US actually opposed any kind of military intervention, because they were concerned that it would push the Arab world into the arms of the Soviet Union. This all happened as the Cold War was beginning to take shape, so the US was more concerned with the nuclear arms race and the rivalry with the communists than with anything else.'

Andrew nodded. 'That makes sense.'

'It was a very complicated affair,' said Fiona pensively. 'Anyway, in October 1956, after a couple of failed attempts at a diplomatic solution, Britain, France and Israel initiated a rather underhanded plan, whereby Israel would invade and take the Sinai Peninsula, and once that had been secured, Britain and France would then publicly argue for a truce and a peaceful solution. Before that though, British marines performed an amphibious landing at Port Said, where the Suez Canal meets the Mediterranean Sea. At the same time, French paratroopers dropped into other parts of the city, and before long Egypt had lost control of the canal.'

'So, was that the end of it then?' asked Andrew and helped himself to some peanuts.

'Far from it,' replied Fiona. 'The reaction to the British and French heavy-handedness, and to their conspiracy with Israel to stage an excuse for an invasion, was universally scathing. British interests were attacked throughout the Middle East, and Saudi Arabia imposed a complete oil embargo on Britain and France, which I don't think any of those two countries had anticipated. Soviet First Secretary Khrushchev actually threatened direct strikes on Britain, France and Israel. But worst of all, the US applied serious financial pressure to Britain.'

'Really? How?' asked Andrew, looking surprised. This all sounded quite far removed from the so-called special relationship, that now exists between the UK and the US.

'Well,' said Fiona. 'The British economy was still barely recovering after the Second World War, and having been cut off from its otherwise reliable oil supply by the closure of the Suez Canal, Britain was suffering economically. Exploiting this pressure point, the US threatened to dump its holdings of British government debt on the market. This debt had obviously ballooned during the Second World War, and because much of it was held by the US, it effectively left completely Britain beholden to whims of Washington.'

'Wow,' said Andrew. 'This is hard core'.

'It got worse,' said Fiona. 'The US basically told Britain, that the country would not be able to deal with the devaluation of the Pound that would surely follow an oil embargo along with an inevitable economic collapse. Furthermore, the US would refuse to plug the gap in oil supplies left by Saudi Arabia's embargo, and it would also block Britain from obtaining a loan from the International Monetary Fund in order to rescue its fragile finances unless Britain withdrew its forces from Egypt. In the end, Britain backed down and complied.'

'Crikey!' exclaimed Andrew. 'I am surprised the Egyptians are prepared to have anything to do with us, even today.'

'Well,' said Fiona. 'It's a long time ago now, and ultimately, mutual economic interests win out as the decades pass.'

'I guess so,' conceded Andrew. 'And here I was thinking I knew something about the Suez Crisis, but I don't remember ever being told any these details.'

'Well, it was obviously extremely humiliating for the former empire, so I am not surprised if it is not something that is taught in schools in much detail in England.'

'Well, you're Irish, so how come you know all this stuff?' grinned Andrew.

Fiona held up a book that had been tucked down next to her seat. 'I like to read history books. I am an archaeologist, remember?'

'Smart arse,' he said, shaking his head and smiling.

Fiona leaned back in her seat and shrugged. 'I just thought I would read up on a bit of history before we arrived. I also brought some books on ancient Egypt. And a bible.'

'Excuse me? You brought a bible?' asked Andrew, looking at her sceptically.

'You never know what might come in handy,' said Fiona.

★   ★   ★

Coming in directly from the north towards runway 18 at Almaza Airforce Base, Andrew could just make out Port Said around 60 kilometres away to the West, as they passed over Egypt's Mediterranean coastline. After another few minutes, the landing gear was lowered, and at 2.08 pm the BAe 146-200 touched down on the baking hot runway. The dry heat hit them like a wall as soon as the aircraft had taxied to its parking spot and the door opened.

'Drink plenty of water,' said Andrew and looked at Fiona admonishingly.

Fiona nodded and saluted. 'Yes, sir.'

On the tarmac, a car had already pulled up, and a driver was now standing by the open passenger door. They hopped in the back, and a few minutes later they were being shown to a corporate meeting room inside the terminal.

They did not have to wait long before Major Bahman Elsayed appeared, flanked by two junior officers, who looked like they were more interested in avoiding upsetting the major than anything else.

Major Elsayed, who looked like he was in his late fifties, appeared toned and strong but had the leathery face of someone who had spent most of his career outside as opposed to sitting behind a desk, which is what he probably did now. He had short black hair and was wearing an olive-green uniform, with a veritable fruit salad of military decorations on the left side of his chest. Andrew guessed that despite his current job with the intelligence services, he could probably be found on a shooting range or even an assault course from time to time.

'Mr Sterling,' said Elsayed in a baritone voice as he greeted him. His handshake was short and firm.

'Major Elsayed,' said Andrew. 'Thank you for seeing us. This is my assistant, Miss Keane.'

The major nodded politely towards Fiona, and then returned his attention to Andrew. 'Please sit down,' he said and gestured at the meeting room table in the middle of the room.

'As you know,' said Elsayed after they had arranged themselves on opposite sides of the table. 'We have had one of our nuclear research facilities compromised, and subsequently, the archaeologist who brought a sample of radioactive material in for analysis at the facility has disappeared.'

'Is there any progress on this?' asked Fiona.

The major looked at her and hesitated as if surprised to hear an assistant speaking. The two junior officers looked unsure as to how to react. The major then smiled benignly and replied. 'There is.'

He snapped his fingers, and the junior officer to his right swiftly brought a small laptop up onto the desk, typed in a password, and then swivelled the laptop around so that the screen was facing Andrew and Fiona.

'This is footage from a CCTV camera mounted on the Coptic Museum where the missing Doctor Mansour works.'

Andrew and Fiona leaned in, studying the recording intently. It was a grainy black-and-white recording of what appeared to be the museum grounds, with date and time information in the top right corner.

'As you can see,' continued Elsayed. 'Doctor Mansour was last seen leaving the museum just a few days ago. This is the only camera mounted on the front of the building, and if you look closely, you can see him walking along the path to the staff gate.'

The image quality was poor, but they could clearly see a short man in a badly fitted suit shuffle along the path in the darkness. As he reached the gate, he appeared to enter a code on a keypad, and as the gate swung open, he exited. There was nothing unusual about any of it, except that just after he had walked through the gate, a scuffle seemed to be happening. The view from the camera was partly blocked by the long leaves of a palm tree, and the image was blurry in that sector of the screen, but they could just make out several pairs of shoes shifting around rapidly on the pavement. Then, as if out of nowhere, the wheels of a car appeared. Then there seemed to be another scuffle, and a few seconds later the car sped off again, seemingly leaving no one left on the pavement.

Andrew and Fiona both leaned back in their chairs, exchanging a quick glance at each other.

'A kidnapping?' asked Andrew, now looking concerned.

'We believe so,' replied Elsayed. 'Doctor Mansour has not been seen since that recording was made. We were unable to track the car after it left the museum. There is a camera on the façade of the train station opposite the museum, but it is out of order, so at the moment we have no leads.'

Andrew nodded sagely. 'Except that all these events are probably related somehow.'

'I believe you are correct,' replied Elsayed, placing his palms flat on the table, and then seeming to pause for a moment. Then he continued. 'There is one other thing you should be aware of,' he said. 'Early this morning around 2 am, the Coptic Museum was broken into, and Doctor Mansour's office was raided.'

'Really?' said Andrew, looking shocked. 'I guess they managed to squeeze him for information, and then came back looking for whatever it was he gave them.'

'That is our assessment as well,' said Elsayed. 'Using Doctor Mansour's passkey, the intruder also accessed the underground vault, and escaped with the item the radioactive fragments had been taken from.'

'Seems like they knew exactly what they were looking for then?' asked Fiona.

'Possibly,' said Elsayed and shrugged, whilst tilting his head to one side. 'The intruder clearly knew what he wanted from the vault, but he left Doctor Mansour's office completely ransacked. It was as if he was looking for something specific, but couldn't find it.'

'I see. Alright,' said Andrew and sat upright in his chair. 'Well, I believe you spoke to Colonel Strickland yesterday, is that correct?'

'Correct,' nodded the Major. 'As requested, I have arranged for you to be taken to your hotel, and then on to the museum to meet its director, Professor Sadiki. I have asked him to tell you everything he knows about what happened, and provide any details about Doctor Mansour's work. He will be expecting you at 4.30 pm.'

'Excellent,' smiled Andrew. 'If there's nothing further, I guess we had better get going then.'

'Very well,' said the major, and rose. His two companions, who had so far not said a word, mirrored him and stood up.

'I will walk you back to the car,' said Elsayed.

Soon after, Andrew and Fiona were in the back of the chauffeur-driven black Audi, heading for the Fairmont Nile City Hotel, which was sitting on the riverbank in central Cairo, facing west and overlooking Zamalek Island in the middle of the Nile.

The hotel was an impressive five-star colossus with twenty-five floors and a host of restaurants, pools, gyms and other entertainment. Guests would not need to leave the hotel, as everything was provided there, except a view of the pyramids. For that, they would have to take one of the many tour buses over the river and through the bustling city.

Fiona flung herself on the bed in the upmarket hotel room on the 10th floor and smiled, looking up at the ceiling. 'I could get used to this. Is this how you SAS people like to travel?'

Andrew shrugged and smiled. 'I am not really sure. I don't do this sort of thing very often. This is probably the nicest hotel I have been in. But I would be just as happy camping out under the stars. I believe it is a balmy 25 degrees during the night at this time of year.'

'Well,' said Fiona. 'Perhaps we can do that too as soon as we get to the bottom of this mystery.'

'Yes,' mumbled Andrew. He had a feeling this was about to get a whole lot more challenging and complicated than he had initially thought.

Half an hour later, Andrew and Fiona got back into their car and were taken south along the riverbank towards Old Cairo and the Coptic Museum. It was a quick 15-minute journey, and as they stepped out of the car on Mar Gerges by the metro station, Andrew was struck by how calm everything seemed, belying the sinister plot that was unfolding around them.

Inside the museum, they were greeted by Director Sadiki, who was an elderly gentleman, dressed smartly in a grey pinstriped suit and wearing a bowtie. He was clearly not particularly comfortable speaking English, and he did not seem overly enthusiastic about them turning up, but he dutifully showed them to Doctor Mansour's office.

As they walked along a corridor on the first floor, he gestured to an office. 'Here it is,' he said. 'Bad mess.'

Andrew and Fiona walked inside the office cautiously. The director was not exaggerating. The whole office looked as if a hand grenade had gone off inside it, with pieces of paper, books and items from Doctor Mansour's desk strewn all over the floor.

'Do you have any idea what they might have been looking for?' asked Andrew politely. He was keen not to ruffle the director's feathers, coming in as they had with little advance notice and asking him to account for something that he was probably somewhat embarrassed about.

'No,' replied Sadiki, and shook his head. 'No ideas.'

Fiona was walking slowly around the room, looking for anything that might provide a clue. As she carefully moved behind Doctor Mansour's desk where his office chair lay toppled over, she suddenly stopped. 'Andy?' she said. 'Over here.'

Andrew came over and stood next to her. 'What?'

'Look at that,' said Fiona, and pointed at the PC, which appeared to be at least fifteen years old.

The front panel of the PC case had been removed, letting them see inside. Andrew leaned down to peer inside it. As far as he could see everything looked normal, except for one thing. The hard drive was missing, and the cables that should have connected it to the motherboard were sticking up inside the case.

'Crap,' mumbled Andrew. 'The drive is gone. The intruder must have ripped it out.'

'Damn,' said Fiona, looking concerned. 'That is going to make things a lot more difficult. I was hoping to find out precisely what he was working on.'

'Yes,' said Andrew, pressing his lips together. 'Seems like your thief got at least some of what he came for.'

'Excuse me, Professor Sadiki,' said Fiona, slowly approaching the director. 'Doctor Mansour was working on identifying a metal casket, is that correct?'

'Yes, Madam,' said Sadiki. 'He was working on that for very long time. He seem crazy with it. Just like Omran.'

'Just like who?' she asked, probingly.

'Jabari Omran. He was curator before Dr Mansour.'

'And he was also trying to find out about the casket?' asked Fiona.

'Yes,' said the director ruefully. 'For years he just staring and thinking about that thing. Never find anything.'

'Was this also his office?' asked Andrew.

'No, no,' said Sadiki. 'Omran's office just over there.' The director was pointing behind him along the corridor.

'Could we see it,' asked Fiona.

'Fiona, I am not sure we should…' began Andrew.

She turned and raised his eyebrows at him. 'Let's just have a look. You never know,' she said, trying to sound persuasive. Then she turned back to the professor with a winning smile.

'Ok,' said Sadiki and shrugged. 'Follow please.'

Omran's former office was unremarkable, and it was clear that the intruder had not been in here. Nothing was disturbed, and everything seemed neat and tidy.

Andrew went straight for the PC but found no evidence of it having been tampered with. Fiona made her way around the chesterfield sofa to the back wall, where a large painting of the Tomb of Nefertari hung.

'Eew,' she suddenly said. 'That's gross.'

'What?' asked Andrew and joined her.

'Look at that,' she said and pointed to a coffee cup that seemed to have been left there several days ago. The milk in the coffee had collected on top of the coffee as it had cooled, and was now a thriving blue-green fungus colony.

'Remind you of anything,' she said and looked at Andrew knowingly.

'Only too well,' replied Andrew solemnly. It did look remarkably like the pathogen the two of them had been instrumental in hunting down and containing not long ago.

'Oh!' exclaimed Professor Sadiki, who had now joined them. 'This is… Doctor Mansour's coffee cup.'

'Are you sure?' said Andrew curiously.

'Absolutely,' replied Sadiki. 'He always drink coffee. Always that cup.'

Andrew and Fiona looked at each other, thinking the same thing.

What is it doing in here?

'Why would it be here?' said Fiona to no one in particular. 'And why would *he* have been in here on the night he disappeared?'

Andrew felt his senses sharpen, and his eyes started scanning the cup, the console table it was sitting on, the wall next to it, the painting above it.

The painting.

Without a word, he reached out with his left hand and gently gripped the painting's gilded frame. Pulling ever so gently, he instantly felt that, rather than pulling the bottom of the painting away from the wall, he was moving the entire painting out and away, like the door on a cupboard.

'Wow,' said Fiona when she saw the safe.

Both she and Andrew turned to look at Professor Sadiki, who looked from Andrew to Fiona and back to Andrew. 'I did not know this,' he said, clearly also taken aback by the revelation. 'I work here twenty-six years, and I never see this.'

Andrew turned his attention back to the safe and placed his hand on the handle next to the combination wheel.

'It is unlocked,' he said surprised, and gently pulled the safe open.

Inside lay a small notebook. It looked well worn, but otherwise in good condition.

'Do you suppose this might have been Omran's notebook?' asked Fiona.

'Yes,' replied Sadiki, and nodded. 'Could be. He did not like computers.'

'Do you mind?' asked Fiona and reached towards the notebook.

'Please,' said Sadiki, gesturing for her to continue.

Fiona carefully picked up the notebook and lifted it out of the safe. She held it in her hands as if it were made of glass and could splinter at any moment. Ever so carefully she opened it onto the first page. Her eyes skimmed down the page, then the next, and then another.

'You read Arabic?' asked Sadiki, clearly surprised.

'A little,' replied Fiona, without taking her eyes off the notebook. 'Comes with the territory for some archaeologists, and I am one of them.'

'Professor,' said Andrew, turning to Sadiki. 'We are going to have to ask you to let us take this notebook with us. It might help us find out what is going on here. It might help us find Dr Mansour.'

Sadiki hesitated for a moment, but then nodded vigorously. 'Of course. You will take it to police?'

'We are going to have a look at it ourselves, and then decide what to do,' replied Andrew.

'Ok. Very good,' said Sadiki, nodding again.

'If you have any photographs of the casket that Doctor Mansour and this gentleman Omran were working on, I would be most grateful if I could borrow them,' said Fiona imploringly. 'I promise, I will give them back to you.'

'We do,' said Sadiki. 'I will find them.' Then he disappeared down the corridor.

'Can you read all of this,' asked Andrew once they were alone. 'I am just wondering if we might need some assistance.'

'I can get the gist of what is going on, but there might be some tricky part where we may need to call on someone else. I will try to think of someone we can trust.'

'Good,' said Andrew. 'I guess we can conclude that Doctor Mansour has read the contents of this notebook?'

'I would assume so, yes,' replied Fiona, still engrossed in the notebook's yellowing pages, that seemed full to the brim of handwritten notes, sketches, and what appeared to be several maps.

'Given the break-in here,' pondered Andrew. 'And given the ransacking of Doctor Mansour's office, and the theft of the casket, I think it is safe to say that whoever is behind this, has managed to squeeze Doctor Mansour for information about this place. But Mansour clearly has not told them anything about this notebook. I wonder if they have managed to get anything out of him about this Jabari Omran.'

A couple of minutes later, Sadiki returned with an envelope containing a set of photos that Doctor Mansour had taken of the metal casket. They thanked the professor and made their way back out into the heat of the afternoon. Half an hour later they were sitting on the sofa in their hotel room, sipping gin and tonics.

Seven

'Hello?' said Andrew, and sat down on the chair next to the desk where the hotel room's phone was placed. 'Ah, Major Elsayed,' he exclaimed, and turned to make eye contact with Fiona. 'What can I do for you?'

Andrew nodded a few times. 'Oh. Really? That's terrible. Ok. I see. Is she alright? Any trace of the culprit.'

Fiona looked at Andrew intently, as if trying to divine what was being said on the other end of the line.

'Oh, great. Thank you. Tomorrow at 9 am in the lobby. Got it. We will be there.' He nodded again and sighed. 'Alright, thank you for keeping us updated. Yes. Ok. Thanks again. Goodbye.'

He stood up and walked slowly back towards the sofa. 'Seems Omran's widow had her flat burgled.'

'Poor old woman,' said Fiona sympathetically. 'No prizes for guessing who did it.'

'I guess that answers the question as to whether Doctor Mansour has handed over information about Jabari Omran. And no prizes for guessing what they were looking for,' replied Andrew.

Fiona held up the notebook. 'He must have withheld what he knew about the safe in Omran's office. Whatever is in here must be really important.'

'Yes, I guess so,' replied Andrew. 'Major Elsayed has arranged for us to meet Doctor Zaki from the nuclear research facility. He will be meeting us here at the hotel tomorrow morning. It might be useful for us to try to glean what his conversations with Doctor Mansour were about.'

'Ok,' said Fiona. 'Sounds good. Now, I want to get to work on this notebook. It has to be the key to this whole thing.'

Then she leaned forward, placed the notebook on the coffee table to her left, and her laptop on the right. Soon she was completely engrossed in Jabari Omran's notes.

'Right,' said Andrew. He knew that it was best to leave her completely alone, and let her concentrate, so he walked over to the bed and lay down. He had borrowed Fiona's book about the Suez Crisis. Never too late to learn something interesting.

★ ★ ★

The townhouse in Zamalek had been on the market for only a couple of days when it was snapped up by a foreign buyer the previous year. The real estate agent had never met the buyer, and the property was never even viewed before an offer was placed. During the whole process, which took less than two weeks, the agent dealt only with what he assumed to be some sort of shell company located in Panama. Like most countries, Egypt has anti-money laundering regulations in place, to ensure that proceeds from criminal activity cannot re-enter the legal economy. However, these laws are lax, to say the least, and everyone in the industry has a direct personal incentive to disregard them. Unless the agent secured a signature on the dotted line, he would get no sales commission.

After the deed and the contract for the sale of the townhouse arrived back in his office with a valid e-signature, it took less than ten minutes before he could confirm that the money had hit the account of the seller's solicitor.

At that point, all he would normally have to do was to meet the buyer at the property and hand over the keys. In this case, however, it had been arranged for a courier to turn up at his office, to then bring the keys to the buyer, whoever that really was.

The agent, however, did not mind. It saved him a trip to the property, and as long as he got paid, he was more than happy to accommodate this particular client's idiosyncrasies.

From the outside, the townhouse appeared to be occupied by a well-dressed gentleman who could occasionally be seen leaving or arriving at the house. This man, however, was just one of several people who currently occupied the house. The others only ever left the house out of sight of the local residents, hidden behind the heavily tinted windows of a black Range Rover.

Since purchasing the townhouse, the new owner had installed security cameras in several locations on the outside of the building, as well as throughout the interior. The old front door had been swapped out for a steel-reinforced multi-lock door made of solid oak and thus appearing like any of the doors on the other buildings in the neighbourhood. The parking garage under the building had been sealed off by an automatic steel gate, and hydraulically operated extendable bollards had been installed in front of the entrance, effectively blocking any vehicle that did not have permission to enter.

But the most significant alteration to the property was the construction of a new basement complex next to the parking garage, consisting of a small self-contained apartment, which had everything a person might need for a protracted stay, except for natural light.

The work had been carried out strictly within normal working hours, so as not to attract undue attention, and the new underground space could only be accessed from a concealed door behind a false wall in a downstairs guest bathroom.

The hidden apartment had initially been intended as a safehouse, where one or two people could remain hidden for several weeks if they were ever to find themselves wanted by the authorities. However, as of the previous week, the safehouse had been used for a different purpose.

Locked inside the safehouse, confused, afraid, and unable to communicate with the outside world, was a short middle-aged man, who until the previous week had lived an unremarkable and peaceful life as a curator of a well-known museum in Cairo. Never in his most terrible nightmares, had he imagined ending up in this situation. A few days earlier, he would have sworn that this sort of thing only happened in the movies, and yet here he was, nursing a deep cut on his head, a black eye, and genuinely wondering whether he would ever make it out of here alive.

Suddenly, he heard the multiple locks and bolts on the only door into the safehouse snap and click. A couple of seconds later, one of the suited captors, who would not have looked out of place in an investment bank, entered the room. He was carrying a pistol, and behind him was another man, similarly dressed and also holding a gun. Once the two of them had satisfied themselves that their prisoner was not attempting an escape, they holstered their weapons and stood on either side of the door. At that moment, it dawned on Doctor Mansour that the two men in expensive suits were identical twins. Even their guns were the same.

After a few seconds, another figure appeared. He was older, with a moustache, and was wearing an elegant pin-striped suit. He carried himself in a calm and supremely self-assured manner, and as he strode into the room, Doctor Mansour could sense that it would be in his best interest to comply with whatever he wanted, and he was beginning to have a very clear idea about what exactly that was.

This was the second time the older man had paid Doctor Mansour a visit, and upon seeing him again, he broke out in a cold sweat. He had tried to tell him what he thought he wanted to know, whilst not revealing what he had found behind the painting in

Jabari Omran's office. But right now, he was regretting not telling the man everything.

Doctor Mansour steadied himself by holding on to the back of a chair next to the dining table, his legs beginning to tremble. He was now sweating profusely, and he looked terrified.

'Please,' he stammered imploringly.

★   ★   ★

When Andrew woke up, the late afternoon sun was pouring in through the west-facing floor to ceiling windows of the hotel room. He had dropped off in the middle of reading about how in 1956, when Egypt's then-president Nasser had learned of the invasion of Sinai by Israel, and of the forces of Britain and France landing in Port Said, he had ordered all ships present in the Suez Canal to be sunk, and used as physical barriers in the canal.

Andrew sat up, rubbed his eyes, and looked at his wristwatch. He had been asleep for over two hours. He glanced over at Fiona, who seemed to not have moved a muscle since he lay down on the bed.

'How's it going?' he mumbled, still feeling drowsy.

There was no reply.

'Hello?' he said and smiled. She was clearly still completely engrossed in Omran's notebook. On the coffee table was an open water bottle, and an empty packet of peanuts.

Finally, she lifted her head, and slowly directed her gaze in Andrew's direction. 'Sorry?'

'I asked you how you are doing,' he repeated. 'Any progress with the notebook?'

Fiona hesitated, and then seemed to make an effort to extract herself from her state of deep concentration. She leaned back in the sofa, closed her tired eyes for a few moments, and took a deep breath.

'I am not sure where to start,' she said, sounding slightly overwhelmed. 'There's a lot here, and it is probably going to sound quite far-fetched to you.'

'Try me,' said Andrew, and swung his legs off the bed. He then stretched his back and walked over to sit down next to her on the sofa.

'Alright,' said Fiona, looking like she was taking a moment to organise her thoughts. 'It seems the good Doctor Omran spent a lot of his time on research that he never shared with anyone else.'

'You mean, the metal casket?' asked Andrew.

'Well, not just that,' replied Fiona. 'In fact, it seems like the casket was only the starting point for him. He must have spent years on this, and I am not surprised if he did not share this with anyone. Academic research can be very dogmatic at times, speaking from personal experience, and I think it is fair to say that if he had gone around talking openly about even half of the stuff that is in here, he would have run the risk of either being called crazy or perhaps even ended up being harassed by religious fundamentalists.'

'Really?' said Andrew, looking sceptical. 'How crazy could it possibly be? It's just an old piece of metal.'

Fiona shook her head and frowned. 'It is so much more than that, Andy. But let me lay it out for you as best I can. Some of my translation is definitely not perfect, but I am confident that I have got a good handle on the main thrust of his research. Just try not to interrupt too much, please. Ok?"

Andrew nodded, put his thumb against his index finger and ran the two across his mouth, pretending to be zipping it.

'Right,' said Fiona. 'Doctor Omran appears to have uncovered an ancient Egyptian legend about a rock that fell from the sky to spread death and destruction. He was convinced that somehow the metal casket he was working on was connected to this legend, and once you know about the legend, the motif on the casket becomes obvious. Look here,' she said and showed him one of the photographs of the casket that professor Sadiki had given them.

The front of the casket had a frame a few centimetres wide, which was covered in intricate ornamental metalwork. Inside the frame was a motif stencilled into the metal of a mountain with two distinct peaks. Above it was a disc that appeared to show the sun, with rays shining out in all directions.

'According to Omran's notes,' said Fiona. 'This image on the front of the casket, is a depiction, not of the sun, but of a meteorite coming down from the heavens. He was never able to deduce the location of this event, or which mountain is depicted on the casket.'

'A meteorite impact in ancient Egypt,' said Andrew. 'I guess that sounds plausible. As I understand it, these things happen all the time.'

'They do, but this one was different. And frankly, part of me is hoping it was all just a story, because the rest of the legend is disconcerting, to say the least.'

'How do you mean?' asked Andrew, now genuinely interested.

'The legend holds that this "rock" fell during the night and that the villagers that came to investigate all died a horrible death, along with all the livestock nearby. And it wasn't the impact that killed them. Apparently the "Rock from Heaven" was possessed of evil powers, that drained the life from anyone who came near it, and made them collapse, covered in burns, bleeding and convulsing.'

'Crikey,' said Andrew. 'That is quite some legend. It obviously can't be true, can it?'

'Well,' said Fiona tilting her head slightly to one side. 'That is where Omran's theory gets really interesting. He was convinced that this "rock" was indeed a meteorite, but that it was essentially entirely metallic, and extremely radioactive.'

Fiona could tell from Andrew's face that the penny was starting to drop and that he was beginning to connect the dots.

'Holy crap,' he finally breathed. 'Could this be true? I mean, is it even physically possible for a meteorite to be radioactive.'

'I honestly don't know,' said Fiona and shrugged. 'Perhaps. But is it likely that it could be as lethal as what is described in the legend? I am not sure about that. We would need to speak to someone who really understands these things.'

'So did Omran think the casket was made from part of the meteorite?' asked Andrew.

'Apparently, he never made that connection himself, as far as I can tell. It seems that Doctor Mansour was the first person to realize this. Omran's focus was on something else entirely, which could be infinitely more significant if it was ever found to be true.'

'Really?' asked Andrew, inquisitively. 'It already sounds quite legendary. What could be more significant than this?'

'Well,' said Fiona and put a hand flat onto the notebook, and turned to look at Andrew. 'This is the big one, so hold on to your hat please.'

Then she cleared her throat. 'Apparently, Jabari Omran had convinced himself that the Ark of the Covenant carried a large chunk of that radioactive meteorite inside it.'

She paused to allow Andrew to absorb what she had just said.

He just looked at her, dumbfounded for a few seconds.

'The Ark of the Covenant?' he finally said, sounding incredulous. 'You mean the actual Ark of the Covenant? As in, the ark that carried the Ten Commandments, that were given to Moses by God?'

'The very same,' nodded Fiona.

A tiny hint of an uncertain smile flickered across Andrew's face, but he wasn't quite sure what to say, so he just stared at her.

'Sorry,' he finally said. 'Can we just back up a bit? If this meteorite, which supposedly was a big lump of metal, was so highly radioactive, how did they manage to move it, not to mention, cut it into pieces?'

'According to Omran's notes,' continued Fiona, 'The legend tells the story of how dozens of workers perished in the attempt to move the "rock". However, it then also recounts how the ancient Egyptian priesthood chanced upon gold as a near-perfect insulating material for the evils of the "rock". This is one of the central pillars of Omran's research, for two reasons. Firstly, it is well established that gold played an important role in ancient Egypt, and that it was in plentiful supply due to dozens of open mines across the whole region at that time. It was also believed to have divine properties since it was intricately connected to the sun god Ra. Secondly, gold, along with other heavy metals like lead, is very good at absorbing radiation. Remember the workers at the site of the reactor explosion in Chernobyl in 1986? They were wearing protective clothing lined with lead plates, in an attempt to try to protect them from the radiation. An attempt, by the way, which largely failed, due to the extreme levels of radiation they were surrounded by.'

'How big was this thing supposed to have been?'

'The meteorite? It was large. Possibly as much as four *cubits* long. A cubit was a unit of length employed by the ancient Egyptians, and it equates to around half a meter. So, this meteorite would have been about two meters long, and almost as wide.'

'It must have been heavy,' said Andrew.

'Well,' said Fiona, looking at the screen of her laptop. 'According to my back-of-the-envelope calculations, and assuming it was made of something heavy like lead, it would have weighed at least 15 tons.'

'Wow,' replied Andrew. 'Could they even have moved something that heavy?'

'Are you kidding?' chuckled Fiona. 'This was ancient Egypt at the beginning of the pyramid-building age. Some of the blocks for the Pyramid of Khufu near Giza, are estimated to weigh between 50 and 80 tons. So, this would have been a piece of cake, provided they could protect themselves from radiation.'

'Ok,' said Andrew, clearly struggling to fit all the pieces together in his head. 'Even if this legend about a meteorite impacting here in Egypt in ancient times is true, what on earth does it have to do with the Ark of the Covenant?'

'Well, a lot of it is conjecture, mixed with historical accounts and also various segments from the Bible. Some of these Biblical accounts concur with other contemporaneous historical accounts and later scientific research, and some do not. But according to Omran's research, the "rock" was removed by the Egyptian priesthood, who believed that they would be able to harness its power. But apparently, they must have failed somehow, because the meteorite, which they now understood was made of metal, was kept hidden somewhere in a secret place, and pretty soon it disappeared from any known records.'

'How can something like that just disappear?' asked Andrew sceptically.

'Well, Omran seemed to think that its secret, including its location, was guarded by a very small group of Egyptian priests. We know from other historical sources that these priests often guarded their secrets zealously, and Omran contends that they could all have died from radiation exposure. They might have survived initial contact with the meteorite, using gold as an insulator, but they could still have suffered long term damage, which might have eventually led to their deaths. This is consistent with modern cases of radiation exposure. Omran's theory is that they died soon after hiding the meteorite, and that they took their secret with them to their graves.'

'Alright, but how did it make it into the Ark of the Covenant?' asked Andrew, beginning to sound impatient.

'I am going to assume you have some idea of the story of Exodus?' said Fiona, and looked dubiously at Andrew.

'Exodus. Sure,' he said, suddenly feeling like he was taking an exam. 'The Bible story about the Jews leaving Egypt.'

'That's right,' nodded Fiona. 'According to the Book of Exodus, a large number of Jews, also called the Israelites, had lived in Egypt for hundreds of years. This supposedly happened around 1300 BCE, although the historicity of the Bible is disputed, to put it mildly. Up until that time they had lived peacefully, and were apparently well integrated into Egyptian society. However, a new pharaoh, King Rameses II enslaved the Jews. When a prophecy foretold that a new leader of the Israelites would be born and that this leader would liberate the Jews and lead them out of Egypt, Rameses II decreed that all newborn Hebrew babies should be killed. As you may know, one of these babies was Moses. Now, Moses was supposedly a direct descendent of Abraham, who to this day is regarded as the father of the Jewish nation. Abraham had fled the Jewish homeland of Canaan after a famine around 2000 BCE, depending on which source text you think is most credible.

'Canaan?' said Andrew. 'Not sure I have heard of it. Where was that?'

'Canaan was a large area in the southern Levant, so more or less present-day Israel, but also Lebanon, and Gaza, as well as parts of Jordan and Syria.'

'Right,' said Andrew, looking sceptical. 'And was that actually a real place, or just a Bible story?'

'Oh, Canaan was very real,' said Fiona. 'There are huge amounts of written evidence from that time, from all the major surrounding empires like the Hittites, the Assyrians, the Babylonians and the Egyptians. All of them refer to that particular area of what we now call the Middle East.

'I see,' said Andrew, and sipped some water from a glass.

'Anyway,' continued Fiona. 'Most people probably know the story about how baby Moses was placed in a reed basket, and sent adrift on the Nile River, in order to escape being killed by the pharaoh's soldiers. He was then supposedly rescued by the pharaoh's daughter, who raised him as a prince and her own son. A prince of Egypt.'

'It rings a very faint bell somewhere,' said Andrew grudgingly.

'Well,' continued Fiona. 'According to Exodus, Moses temporarily flees Egypt to go to Midian on the Arabian Peninsula, after having killed an Egyptian man who was beating a Jew. When he returns, it is with the aim of freeing the enslaved Jews, and taking them back to Canaan.'

Andrew sighed impatiently. 'I am sorry, but I'm failing to see how any of this is relevant.'

'Just hang on for a bit,' replied Fiona, clearly not appreciating being interrupted mid-monologue. 'The story goes, that Moses led the Israelites out into the desert, chased by the pharaoh's army. You probably remember how he supposedly parted the seas and allowed the Israelites to escape.

'Yes, I remember seeing that in a movie. Obviously didn't happen.'

'Eventually,' continued Fiona in an overbearing tone of voice. 'They arrived at Mount Sinai. Here Moses walked up alone to the peak of the mountain, and this is where he received the Ten Commandments on two stone tablets. At this point, God supposedly provided very detailed instructions about how to construct an Ark for the Ten Commandments, since they are quite literally the physical embodiment of God, or Yahweh, here on Earth.'

'What, like a blueprint?' asked Andrew.

'Pretty much,' replied Fiona affirmatively and nodded. 'Listen to this,' she said and picked up the Bible she had brought. 'This is what the Book of Exodus says God supposedly said to the Israelites. *"Have them make an Ark of acacia wood - two and a half cubits long, a cubit and a half wide, and a cubit and a half high. Overlay it with pure gold, both inside and out, and make a gold moulding around it."* That's pretty specific, wouldn't you say?'

'I guess so,' said Andrew grudgingly.

'Now,' said Fiona, pausing for breath. 'Let's assume that this story is actually loosely true, except of course for all the divine, or superstitious, elements, depending on what you prefer to call them. Let's assume that sometime around the 13th century BCE, the resident Israelites fled Egypt, intending to return to Canaan. They would have needed some way to protect themselves on what would have been a long and dangerous journey. What if somehow in the months or years leading up to the exodus, they had obtained the secret knowledge of the meteorite that the Egyptian priesthood was guarding. At that point, it would have been at least a thousand years since the meteor impacted somewhere in Egypt. But it is conceivable that some record of it was preserved, which the Israelites then discovered. They would have understood this to be a weapon that they could use to protect themselves on their journey back to their homeland. In addition, it would have served as a powerful tool, physical and metaphorical, to establish themselves once they reached Canaan. The bottom line here, according to Omran's research, is that if the Israelites somehow managed to carry a portion of the highly radioactive meteorite with them out of Egypt, then that would explain an awful lot of the stories about the Ark, that can be found in many different places in the Bible.'

'Such as?' asked Andrew, sounding unconvinced.

'Gosh. Where do I start?' asked Fiona, and turned both of her palms upwards. 'How about the period mentioned in the Book of Samuel, when the Ark was taken by the Philistines after a battle with the Israelites at a place called Ebenezer. People in all the towns where the Ark was subsequently kept, were supposedly afflicted with tumours, burns and other sicknesses.'

Fiona grabbed her Bible again, and flicked through it until she found what she was looking for. Then she sat up straight, holding the Bible in one hand while raising the index finger of the other.

'In the First Book of Samuel, chapter 5, it goes into detail about how God struck the inhabitants of Ashdod with tumours. Next, he sent tumours upon the men of Gath. Then, in Ekron, *"there was a deadly destruction throughout all the city. The hand of God was very heavy there. And the men who did not die, were stricken with the tumours."* Sounds a lot like radiation poisoning, doesn't it?'

'Possibly,' admitted Andrew reluctantly.

Fiona continued. 'The Philistines finally decided they'd had enough and sent the Ark back to Israel on a cart pulled by two cows. Without a driver to direct them, the cows went straight for the Israelite town of Beth-Shemesh. Not long after its arrival, the men of the town *"looked into the ark"* and God *"struck the Israelites with a great slaughter."* Apparently, seventy Israelites were struck down, suffering burns and plague-like symptoms.'

'You know,' smiled Andrew teasingly. 'You could have had an incredible career as a televangelist.'

'Shut up,' she smirked. 'Just try to take this vaguely seriously for a few minutes, will you?'

'Ok,' said Andrew reluctantly. 'I noticed that the instructions for how to make the Ark mention gold. I suppose that that would fit with needing a way to protect the bearers of the Ark from radiation.'

'Exactly,' exclaimed Fiona. 'Gold, both on the inside and on the outside of the Ark. The very thing that the Egyptians found could protect them against the deadly power of the meteorite. And assuming Omran's theory about the Jews in Egypt is correct, then whatever the Egyptians knew about gold as an insulator, the Israelites would have known as well.'

Andrew sat still for a moment and stared blankly ahead. He had to admit that much of what she was saying did fit quite nicely together. Then he shook his head as if resisting being drawn into Fiona's train of thought.

'Alright,' said Andrew and rose. 'I think this is the part where I throw up my hands and tell you that this is completely bonkers and that we need to focus on the job at hand.'

Fiona smiled. 'Actually, this is the part where I tell you to be open-minded. It is also the part where I remind you that stranger things have happened, as we both experienced when we found an entrance to Atlantis, remember? As in, the actual Atlantis from Plato's dialogues. And besides, as far as I am concerned, this *is* the job at hand.'

Andrew rose and slowly began pacing in front of the windows.

'Let me guess,' he said. 'You think Omran's theory is sound, and that we should try to solve this particular mystery? Pick up where he left off?'

'Right again,' said Fiona, not quite being able to resist taking a small amount of pleasure from watching Andrew struggle to open his mind to something that, on the face of it, sounded completely outlandish.

'You have to admit,' said Fiona, 'As unlikely as all of this sounds, it is at least plausible that it could have happened. According to Omran, the story is recorded in ancient Egyptian writings from around 3000 BCE. It is depicted on this ancient casket, that both Omran and Doctor Mansour were captivated by. The stories about the horrific effects of going near the "rock" match the sorts of acute effects that you would expect from exposure to a highly radioactive material. It also makes sense that the ancient Egyptians could conceivably have used the abundant supply of gold as insulation when cutting and moving the meteorite. If a large chunk of the meteorite had been placed inside a gold-lined box, such as the Ark of the Covenant, it could have been a terrible weapon, and that is exactly what is recorded in the Bible.'

'You don't actually believe that the Bible is an accurate historical account, do you?' said Andrew with a frown.

'Of course not,' replied Fiona. 'But all of those stories or legends, or whatever you want to call them, originated somewhere at some point in time, and who's to say how much of it actually happened. You have to admit, that if you just look at it from a purely scientific perspective, you might conclude that these afflictions mentioned in the Bible were caused by exposure to heavy doses of radiation. If you strip away all the stuff about divine or magical powers, then what is left is a perfectly credible story about how a radioactive meteorite was employed by a group of people as a weapon against another group of people. I mean, it's pretty much the first thing human beings do whenever they come across something new and dangerous. Just look at the Manhattan Project and the atomic bomb.'

'Look,' she continued. 'I am no weapons expert, but imagine if the Israelites had worked out how to use gold to shield themselves from the radiation, then they could have placed part of the meteorite inside a box made of gold, and if one of the sides of that box were to be removed, the radiation would effectively be shooting out in that direction only, right?'

'I guess so,' said Andrew, pondering the idea for a few moments. He had to admit that something like that could have happened. 'So, where is the Ark now?' he finally asked. 'What happened to it?'

'If I knew that, I would probably win the Nobel prize in Archaeology if such a thing existed. No one knows what happened to it. There are lots of theories, but the last time it is mentioned in the Bible, is just before the fall of Jerusalem to the armies of the Babylonian king Nebuchadnezzar II, in 587 BCE. Up until that time, the Ark was supposedly kept in the Temple of Solomon in Jerusalem. After that date, however, there is no mention of it anywhere. It simply vanishes from the Bible.'

'I don't know,' said Andrew wearily. 'I am having trouble separating fact from fiction.'

'Welcome to my world,' shrugged Fiona. 'But just go with me on this for a moment,' she continued, holding up the palms of her hands as if to placate him. 'If this legend really is true, then this would have represented incredible power, at a time when the most effective weapons were spears, bows and arrows.'

'I suppose you're right.' said Andrew and rubbed his temples with his fingertips. 'Anyway, if we just back up a bit, and remember why we are actually here in Egypt. Even in this day and age, a highly radioactive source like that would represent a huge prize for any would-be terrorist. Can you imagine it being placed in a densely populated area? Or if it was carved up and distributed. Or if it was ground into powder, and fed to the water supply of a major city. The threat of that alone would be bound to give a terror group the PR platform they always seem to crave.'

'Bingo,' said Fiona. 'The casket. The meteorite. Doctor Mansour. The kidnappers, who are probably really some kind of terrorist group. All of those things are connected, and the Ark of the Covenant is the key to this whole thing. Find the Ark, and we find the origin of the radioactive material. That could be our best chance of heading off whoever is looking for the radioactive source. Put differently, if Omran's theory is correct, then the only guaranteed way of finding the radioactive source is to find the Ark.'

'Well,' said Andrew ironically. 'Of course, it's only the Ark of the Covenant we're talking about here. I mean, how hard can it be?'

Fiona laughed, fully appreciating the magnitude of what she was proposing. 'I know,' she said. 'I understand better than most people what the Ark is, and what it represents. And I know full well that people have been looking for it ever since it disappeared more than two-thousand five-hundred years ago.'

'Oh boy,' smiled Andrew. 'I feel like I need to lie down again.'

'Yes, I can have that effect on people,' smirked Fiona, and winked at him.

'I can't believe you got this far in just a couple of hours, while I was asleep' he said, incredulously. He was genuinely impressed with Fiona's analytical abilities.

Fiona smiled coyly, evidently pleased with herself. 'Contrary to popular belief,' she said. 'Archaeology is 95 percent research, and only 4 percent digging.'

'And what's the last 1 percent?' asked Andrew, instantly regretting it.

'Answering questions from people who don't like it when they have their pre-existing ideas challenged,' smiled Fiona.

'Alright Sherlock,' said Andrew and smiled. 'Let's go downstairs and pick a restaurant where we can have dinner, preferably before they close. We don't want to miss that.'

Eight

The next morning, Fiona was in the bathroom having a shower, and Andrew was still lying on the bed watching TV. There were more than fifty channels to choose from, but only a few of them were in English. Most were in Arabic, which meant that Andrew could only guess at what was being said. He had always found it fascinating to watch TV in other countries, not just because they spoke different languages, but because he felt like a part of their culture and national character came across in the way people spoke to each other and interacted, and in the way things such as the news was being presented. Everything was the same as at home, yet at the same time, everything was almost imperceptibly different in almost every respect.

When Fiona emerged, she was dressed in smart casual khaki trousers and a white short-sleeved shirt. On her head was a light beige straw sunhat.

'You look like the female version of Indiana Jones,' chuckled Andrew.

Fiona just shook her head. 'It is going to be a hot day. I hope you have brought appropriate clothes.'

'I'll be fine,' said Andrew, and hopped off the bed, still only wearing underpants.

It was no secret that Fiona found him a very attractive man, with his athletic physique and confident demeanour, but she pretended not to notice him as he walked towards her.

'Or you could just go like that,' she laughed.

Andrew shook his head and smiled.

'I don't want to get myself arrested,' he said and went into the bathroom.

An hour later they had finished their breakfast and were sitting in one of the plush and generous seating areas in the lobby of the hotel. They had picked a corner away from the main throng of people passing through the lobby on their way to and from their hotel rooms. It was busy, but everyone seemed to be minding their own business.

In the group of sofas next to them were a family of French tourists with two small children, who seemed determined to escape their parents and run off and explore. Andrew could have sworn that they were coordinating their efforts, with one of them creating a distraction, while the other made a run for it.

Past the entrance, on the other side of the large open lobby area, sat a couple of businessmen in smart suits, who looked like they were about to attend a conference in one of the hotel's events rooms.

Right on time at 9 am, Andrew spotted a man walking through the entrance to the lobby. He was tall, with a short black beard, and he looked like he was uncomfortable in the light grey suit he was wearing. Poking an index finger down the front of his shirt collar and trying to loosen his tie, it was obvious that he preferred less formal attire. He stopped only a few paces inside the lobby and glanced around, unsure of where to go next.

'I think that's our guy,' said Andrew to Fiona and rose. He quickly strode to the man in the light grey suit, flashing a friendly smile at him. 'Doctor Zaki?' he said and stretched out his hand.

The doctor turned, hesitated momentarily, and then returned the smile. 'Yes. Are you Mr Sterling?'

'I am indeed,' replied Andrew as they shook hands. There was something about the man's demeanour that Andrew immediately warmed to.

'Please join us?' said Andrew and motioned for Doctor Zaki to follow him. 'My colleague is sitting just over there.' Fiona was looking in their direction with a smile.

'Of course,' said Doctor Zaki.

'Hello Doctor Zaki, my name is Ms Keane. I am an archaeologist, currently assisting Mr Sterling. Thank you for coming. How are you?'

'Very well. Thank you,' said Doctor Zaki.

'Excellent,' said Andrew and sat down. 'Now, I know this meeting was set up with very short notice, but we could really use your assistance.'

'I understand,' replied Doctor Zaki. 'Major Elsayed was most insistent that I meet you and offer any assistance you might need,' he said, his eyes revealing that he would have had very little choice in whether to attend or not.

'Right,' said Andrew in a hushed voice. 'I will come straight to the point. We understand that Doctor Mansour of the Coptic Museum in Cairo met with you a couple of weeks ago.'

'Yes. That is correct,' said Doctor Zaki, shifting uncomfortably in his seat.

'And as you know, Doctor Mansour has gone missing. So, let me ask you a fairly straightforward question. Why did he ask to see you, and what did you talk about?'

'Well,' said the doctor, and put the fingertips of both hands together. 'I met Doctor Mansour, when he and professor Khalil Amer, contacted me. They told me that he had an artefact that they were struggling to date. He and Professor Khalil had attempted carbon dating, but they did not trust the result, so they came to me. I have been working on a new technique for dating metals, using radioactive decays of different types of isotopes, and professor Khalil thought I might be able to help.'

'And was he right?' asked Fiona. 'Did you manage to arrive at a reliable estimate?'

'I did,' said Doctor Zaki. 'I believe the metal fragments that I was given, stem from a metal alloy that was manufactured some 3.600 years ago, around 1500 BCE.'

Fiona nodded. 'I see,' she said. 'And did Doctor Mansour ever tell you precisely where the fragments came from?'

'Not in any detail, no,' replied Doctor Zaki and shook his head slightly.

'But you did ascertain that it was radioactive, correct?' asked Andrew.

'Yes,' said Doctor Zaki and nodded. 'In fact, it was very radioactive, and I was unable to arrive at a definitive conclusion as to exactly which radioactive isotopes were contained within the fragment.'

'And would you say that was unusual?' asked Fiona.

'Yes,' said Doctor Zaki, now sounding more animated, and a bit more relaxed. 'My equipment is extremely sensitive, and should have been able to determine the composition of the alloy, as well as the exact isotopes that were present, but this did not happen.'

Doctor Zaki shifted, and suddenly looked slightly nervous again. 'I believe Major Elsayed forwarded my analysis results to your people in London?'

'That is correct,' replied Andrew. 'I have only skimmed their report, but am I correct in saying that you were forced to speculate about its nature?'

'Well. As I stated in my notes,' said Doctor Zaki, now wishing he had never written those notes, 'It was as if I was presenting the sensors with an entirely new type of radioactive isotope.'

'But that is not possible. It is?' asked Andrew. 'Don't we know of all the elements in the periodic table by now? Haven't we mapped out all the different radioactive isotopes a long time ago?'

'We have,' said Doctor Zaki and cocked his head, whilst gently wringing his hands. 'However, that doesn't mean that we have necessarily discovered all the elements in the universe.'

Fiona looked confused and briefly glanced at Andrew, and then returned her gaze to Doctor Zaki. 'I am sorry, but how it is possible that we have mapped out all the known isotopes, and yet there might still be things we haven't discovered?'

'We have mapped out all the naturally occurring radioactive isotopes on Earth,' said Doctor Zaki. 'But there is no guarantee that we have encountered all the elements and isotopes that exist in the entire universe. You might even say that it would be a bit presumptuous of us humans to believe that every element that has ever existed in the universe, is also present here on Earth right now.'

Fiona was clearly persuaded by the underlying sentiment of that statement. 'I think that is a very valid point,' she said. 'One of the most predictable things about human beings is their capacity for self-centeredness. Just remember that it took us thousands of years of observations, to finally accept what should have been obvious from the outset, which is that the Earth revolves around the Sun and not the other way round.'

'Exactly,' nodded Doctor Zaki vigorously. 'We should not presume to know or understand everything around us, or expect it to make sense strictly in accordance with our perception of reality. We humans have existed for a very short time, compared with the age of this planet, and we should be careful not to think of ourselves as more than just ants, crawling all over the place, trying to make sense of it. The universe does not care about us, or whether we understand how it all works. The universe just is.'

Andrew glanced hesitantly from Doctor Zaki to Fiona, and back again. He was not quite following this little philosophical detour, and the two of them were clearly on the same page, but he was keen to get the meeting back on track.

'I am sorry, Doctor Zaki,' he said. 'Getting back to your analysis results. Is there any evidence that more elements and radioactive isotopes could exist?'

'As a matter of fact, there is,' replied Doctor Zaki, and looked at Fiona, having realised that she was the more receptive audience. He seemed like he had come into the meeting trying to talk as little as possible, but now his natural enthusiasm for his field of research was evidently winning out.

'There is a famous laboratory in Russia called the Flerov Laboratory of Nuclear Reactions,' he said. 'It is about 50 kilometres north of Moscow, and I have been lucky enough to visit there once. It was set up in 1956 under General Secretary of the Soviet Union, Nikita Khrushchev, and since then it has produced nine completely new elements, including the five heaviest elements known to man.'

'Really?' said Andrew surprised. 'I have never even heard of that place, and I work in this field.'

'Not many people have,' replied Doctor Zaki. 'But they are at the very leading edge of research in nuclear physics. As you may know, the heaviest element occurring naturally is uranium, which has atomic number 92. This means it has 92 protons in its nucleus. So, you can imagine what a leap it is to get to number 118, which is the latest element they have produced there.'

'How exactly do they do this?' asked Fiona, clearly captivated by what the scientist was saying.

'They have six particle accelerators, which they use to smash lighter known elements into heavier atoms.

Every so often, the nuclei of the light and heavy atoms fuse, and a new element is born. Slamming neon which is element 10, into uranium, for example, yields nobelium, which is element 102.'

'That's incredible,' said Fiona, and looked excitedly at Andrew, who wasn't quite sure of what to make of yet another detour.

'If those elements are that much heavier than anything in nature,' asked Andrew. 'Why haven't we heard about any commercial or military applications for them? I would have thought that there would be all sorts of uses for new elements like that.'

'Well,' smiled Doctor Zaki. 'The thing about these new artificially manufactured elements is that they are incredibly unstable. That is to say, they only exist for a fraction of a second, and then they decay via an extremely fast process of alpha decay. So, element 118, called Oganesson, which by the way is named after the research centre's founder, Yuri Oganessian, becomes element 116, which then becomes element 114 and so on, until it reaches a stable nucleus. All of this happens in a split second, so it has not been possible to actually use these new elements for anything. At least not yet.'

'What do you mean by "not yet"?' asked Fiona.

'Who knows what might happen?' replied Doctor Zaki and shrugged. 'One day they might be able to make an element that is both heavy, and also somewhat stable.'

'But if that ever happened,' asked Fiona, with a concerned look on her face. 'If they ever ended up with a super-heavy but also relatively stable element, then that would effectively be a new and very potent radioactive material, right? Something that would decay over a longer period of time.'

'That is correct,' replied Doctor Zaki. 'And there is every reason to believe that it would then be employed as a weapon. That is what history tells us.'

Fiona looked pointedly at Andrew. This was exactly the point she had been trying to make to him the day before.

Andrew cleared his throat. 'Doctor Zaki, do you believe that the fragments brought to you by Doctor Mansour were from a radioactive source that could be called *weapons-grade* material?'

The doctor pressed his lips together and shook his head slowly. 'No. The fragments were certainly from a very radioactive piece of metal, but that metal was itself an alloy. This means that the radioactive material had been mixed in with other metals during a smelting process. And it is that process that I estimate took place around 3.600 years ago in roughly 1500 BCE.'

Doctor Zaki suddenly looked like a person that had just realised that he might have said too much. 'Anyway, it is all in the report that Major Elsayed has given you,' he said and took a sip of water from his glass.

Fiona moved out to sit on the edge of the sofa opposite Doctor Zaki, leaned forward and looked at him intently. 'Doctor Zaki, what I am about to tell you, might sound strange. But we have reason to believe that this radioactive metal came from a meteorite, and that it may be connected to an ancient artefact.'

Doctor Zaki's face changed visibly as if several emotions flashed across it in a split second. Fiona noticed him suddenly sitting up rigid in his seat, and she thought she could see him sweating ever so slightly from his forehead. He was clearly uncomfortable and looked like he was searching for an appropriate response.

'Uhm, well,' he mumbled and swallowed nervously. 'This is not something I have any expertise in. Perhaps you should talk to a physicist or historian about this.'

'We understand,' said Andrew, and looked at Fiona. 'What we are actually interested in, is the issue of the extent to which something like gold might be an effective insulator against radiation. Can you tell us anything about that?'

'Sure,' said Doctor Zaki, now seeming slightly more relaxed. 'Just like lead and other stable heavy metals, gold is an excellent insulator against gamma radiation, which is by far the most dangerous form of radiation. I am sure you are both familiar with the concept of half-life?'

Andrew and Fiona both nodded.

'Ok,' continued Doctor Zaki. 'There is a similar concept called Half-Value-Layer. This is simply a measure of the required thickness of a material, in order to reduce the power of a given radiation source by 50 percent. So, for example, the isotope called radium-226 is a highly radioactive isotope, which by the way has a half-life of 1600 years. In order to reduce the radiation from a sample of radium-226 by 50 percent, you would need 16 millimetres of lead. In order to reduce it by 99 percent, you would need 110 millimetres of lead. Gold is even more effective, so you would need less of that, but of course lead is extremely cheap, so that is the preferred option in industrial radiation shielding.'

'But if you had an abundance of gold and if cost was no issue, would you then choose gold over lead?' asked Fiona.

'Well, yes,' said Doctor Zaki, looking uncomfortable. 'Of course. I just don't know why you would, since it is so much more difficult and expensive to obtain.'

'Ok. Thank you, Doctor Zaki,' said Andrew. I think that is all we needed. We're very grateful that you would come and see us here at such short notice. I am sure you have plenty of things to do back at the research centre.'

'May I ask,' said Doctor Zaki, clearly trying to sound as casual as he could. 'What sort of artefact do you think this metal might be connected to?'

'We're not really in a position to be specific,' said Andrew. 'But we are looking into whether a meteorite could potentially be used as a weapon. This is basically the whole reason we have been sent here.'

'Oh. I see,' said Doctor Zaki. 'Well, I wish you the best of luck in your endeavours. And I hope you find out who is holding Doctor Mansour. He seemed like a nice man. I can't imagine why anyone would wish him ill.'

'Thank you,' said Andrew and rose. 'We are doing our best, as are Egyptian officials, I am sure.'

'Thank you again,' said Fiona and stood up, offering Doctor Zaki her hand.

He smiled, took her hand and bowed slightly. 'Very nice to meet you both. I hope I was of some small assistance to you.'

'You have been very helpful,' said Andrew. 'Thank you again. Have a nice day.'

Doctor Zaki then left the hotel lobby and got into a taxi for the drive north to the nuclear research facility.

'Did you notice how he reacted when I mentioned that this might be connected to an ancient artefact?' asked Fiona, after they had walked back up to their hotel room.

'I did,' replied Andrew, rubbing his chin. 'What was that all about?'

'I am not sure,' replied Fiona. 'But he also seemed to become nervous whenever we talked about the meteorite. Almost like he knew what it was about.'

'How could he know?' asked Andrew. 'Unless he is somehow connected to the people who kidnapped Doctor Mansour.'

'I do not believe that is the case,' said Fiona. 'I think I am an excellent judge of character, and I do not for a second believe that Doctor Zaki could be involved in the kidnapping.'

'I have to say, I agree,' replied Andrew. 'He just doesn't seem like he would be capable of something like that. We also have to assume that military intelligence is on top of all the employees at the country's main nuclear research facility. If they are anything like MI5, then there is no chance that someone like him could be involved with a terrorist group and not get found out.'

'What do you make of what he said about this Half-Value-Layer that he mentioned?' asked Fiona. 'I thought it sounded pretty compelling, in the context of gold as a radiation insulator for the Ark.'

'Yes, I agree,' said Andrew. 'Even if most of that story is a myth, the idea that gold could have been used as a container to transport a radioactive meteorite is clearly a plausible one.'

'Good,' beamed Fiona. 'We finally agree on something.'

'What do you mean?' exclaimed Andrew in mock affront. 'We agree on lots of things.'

'Well, let's see if that is still true once this trip is over,' Fiona replied and winked at him.

★ ★ ★

Having watched the two Europeans leave for their room, the man in the dark blue pinstriped suit, stopped the recording software and disconnected the long-distance microphone that was disguised as a packet of cigarettes.

Within a few seconds, the audio file had been uploaded and emailed to an account that only he and a handful of other people had access to. He could have just brought it back with him to the townhouse in Zamalek, but his boss would appreciate receiving it without delay.

He had suggested following Doctor Zaki but had been told not to. The doctor was on company time, and would almost certainly return to the nuclear research facility, so there was no point in tailing him.

If anything, he might realise that he was being followed, and that would create problems.

The man closed the lid on his laptop and shoved it into its padded pouch. Then he rose, adjusted his suit and left the hotel, looking like any other corporate slave having just finished a meeting.

Nine

Later that evening, Andrew and Fiona had just finished dining in the hotel's L'Uliveto restaurant. They both wanted to try the local cuisine at some point but decided to play it safe with a nice Italian restaurant, and then perhaps explore local options in the area around the hotel over the following days.

They had just sat down in a cosy booth inside the Champagne Bar for a quick after-dinner cocktail when a concierge from the front desk approached them.

'Excuse me, sir,' said the concierge apologetically, and with a pained expression on his face. 'Are you Mr Sterling?'

'I am,' replied Andrew. 'Is there a problem?'

'No sir. No problem,' said the concierge. 'It is just that there is a gentleman here to see you. He is waiting in the lobby. Are you expecting him?'

Andrew and Fiona looked at each other, puzzled by this odd turn of events. None of them had arranged for anyone else to come and see them today. Could it be that Doctor Zaki had returned to discuss something else with them?

'We're not expecting anyone,' said Andrew, turning back to the concierge. 'What does he say his name is?'

'He says he is Khalil Amer. He says you have a mutual acquaintance.'

'Khalil Amer,' repeated Fiona, and placed a hand on Andrew's arm. 'That was who Doctor Zaki mentioned. He is a friend of Doctor Mansour, right?'

'Could you ask him to join us please,' Andrew asked the concierge.

'Certainly, sir,' said the concierge and bowed his head. 'I will ask him right away. Sorry to disturb you.'

'Not a problem,' smiled Andrew.

'What do you suppose he wants?' asked Fiona confused. 'And how does he know who we are and where we are staying?'

'No idea,' replied Andrew and shrugged. 'We're about to find out.'

At the other end of the Champagne Bar, Andrew spotted the concierge, accompanied by a tall athletic man in a smart but casual suit. The concierge pointed in their direction, and the tall man started walking towards them. As he walked past the bar, Andrew noticed how he had drawn the attention of two young women sitting there. They did their best to make themselves noticed, by flicking their hair and giggling, but the tall man stared straight ahead as if he had not even noticed them. As he arrived at their booth, Andrew and Fiona both rose to introduce themselves.

'Hello, Mr. Amer,' said Andrew, and offered his hand.

'Mr. Sterling,' said Khalil, in a deep voice that no doubt engendered respect amongst his students. He gave Andrew a short but firm handshake.

'This is Ms. Fiona Keane. She and I are working together in this matter.'

Khalil shook her hand and bowed chivalrously. 'A pleasure to meet you Miss. May I sit?' he said and gestured at a chair by their table.

'Of course,' said Andrew. 'Please.'

The three of them sat down, while Fiona and Andrew exchanged a quick glance. Their guest possessed a strong physical presence, but his eyes and face betrayed a man burdened by worries. As tall and handsome as he might have looked from a distance, Khalil now seemed like someone who was weighed down by worries. He looked gaunt and seemed to have a permanently pained expression on his face as if he was desperate to get something off his chest.

'Seems like you already have a fan club at this hotel,' attempted Andrew cheerfully, nodding his head in the direction of the two women at the bar.

Khalil looked perplexed at Andrew and then turned slightly to his right to see what he was referring to. Then, completely ignoring the women as well as Andrew's remark, he turned back to face the two.

'I am sorry to disturb you,' he said in a subdued voice, looking down at his hands. 'You must be wondering why I am here.'

'You are Doctor Mansour's friend, aren't you?' asked Fiona gently. She could sense Khalil's anguish, as if a cold grey fog had enveloped their booth.

'I am,' said Khalil and looked up at her.

Fiona thought he looked like someone who had barely slept for a week. Perhaps that was true.

'Apologies,' said Khalil. 'Doctor Zaki who you met this morning, told me that you were here and that you are looking into the disappearance of my friend.'

'I see,' said Andrew and looked briefly at Fiona. There was something about his presence in a foreign country being telegraphed all over town that felt highly disconcerting to him. Probably because it ran against everything he had ever trained for in the SAS.

'You must understand,' said Khalil. 'To me, he is Bahir. To him, I am Khalil. We have known each other since we were young men, perhaps eighteen years old. He is a dear friend. He is also one of the most decent people I have ever met, and I am shocked to find that he may have been kidnapped. This is what Major Elsayed has told me.'

'We understand,' said Andrew. He knew better than anyone what it was like to have a comrade go missing in action.

'But what is worse,' sighed Khalil, seeming to steel himself for what he was about to say. 'What is much worse, is the thought that I may have been responsible for what has happened to him. At least indirectly.'

'What do you mean,' asked Fiona, clearly perplexed and sounding full of empathy.

'Well,' continued Khalil. 'This whole business about the radioactive fragments.' he said, and then took a moment to see if anyone was standing within earshot of him. 'I was the one who suggested we visit Doctor Zaki.'

'Mr Amer,' said Fiona. 'We have both had access to Major Elsayed's report, as well as intelligence on both Doctor Mansour and Doctor Zaki, and as far as we can see there is absolutely no way any of you could have known that something like this would happen. It was a perfectly reasonable and legitimate thing to do, given the ambiguity you were facing in dating those fragments. None of you had any suspicions that either of you or indeed Doctor Zaki, were being watched, right?'

Khalil shook his head vigorously. 'No, none at all. As far as we were concerned, we were just looking for the best way to get a precise answer. But if I had never called Doctor Zaki, then Bahir would be in his home right now, probably reading a book and drinking coffee.'

'Doctor Amer,' said Andrew.

'Please just call me Khalil.'

'Alright Khalil,' continued Andrew. 'There is no way you could have seen this coming. You should not blame yourself. The best thing you can do right now is to help us find him. We don't have much to go on so far, but with your help, we might be able to make some progress.'

Khalil's face seemed to brighten slightly. 'I hope so. I will help you in any way I can. I don't care about those fragments or about the casket. I just want to find my friend.'

'Alright,' said Andrew, and found himself placing a hand on one of the tall man's shoulders. Somehow, he had developed empathy for this tortured man in just a few minutes. His anguish was undeniable, and Andrew felt an urge to try to help him.

Suddenly, Andrew had an idea. 'Khalil, would you mind if I have a quick word with Ms Keane in private please?'

Khalil hesitated for a brief moment, but then shook his head. 'Not at all,' he said. 'I will just go to the restroom. Excuse me.'

'Thank you very much,' said Andrew.

After Khalil had walked out of earshot, Andrew turned to Fiona.

'What's going on?' asked Fiona, looking mystified.

'Well,' he said in a hushed voice. 'I have an idea, but I needed to see if you were alright with it.'

'Ok,' said Fiona intrigued. 'What is it?'

'Khalil already knows what Doctor Mansour was working on. He also already understands the possible implications of this being connected to some sort of radioactive source. And he must have connected the dots sufficiently to guess that whoever is holding Doctor Mansour is after whatever radioactive source the casket was made from.'

Fiona nodded. 'I am sure all of that is correct,' she said. 'So, what's your plan then?'

'We give him the notebook,' said Andrew, and watched Fiona blink a few times as she was trying to process what he had said.

'We what?' she blurted out.

'I know,' said Andrew, holding up his hands as if to placate her. 'I know it seems mad, but what I mean to say is that we provide him with copies of all the pages in the entire notebook. And then we ask him to have a look and tell us what he makes of them.'

Fiona pondered the idea for a few moments. 'Perhaps that's actually a really good idea,' she said.

'He already knows a lot about what has happened and why. He might as well be told about Omran's research. After all, that is what set this whole thing in motion.'

'And,' said Andrew. 'He is a researcher himself. And he is highly motivated to get results, whatever they might be, and where ever they might be found.'

'And he is an archaeologist,' added Fiona, now sounding like she was fully on board with the idea. 'I think this could work.'

'One more thing,' said Andrew. 'Do we trust him though? What does your gut tell you?'

Fiona looked at him resolutely. 'My gut tells me that this man is in real pain and that the only thing he is interested in is finding his old friend. I don't think there is any reason to think that what we just saw was not completely genuine.'

'I agree,' nodded Andrew. 'My feeling is that he is trustworthy, and I think that he could really help us move this investigation along.'

'Alright then,' said Fiona and got up. 'Let me just run up to the room and get the notebook.'

'No, I will do that,' said Andrew and rose. 'I am just the hired help here. This is your show. And besides, you need to explain to Khalil what we have in mind. I am sure you will be much better at that than I would.'

'Alright, fine,' said Fiona and sat back down.

'I'll take the notebook to the reception, and see if I can borrow their photocopier,' said Andrew. 'You did remember to put it in the safe, right?'

'Of course,' said Fiona and rolled her eyes. 'Of the two of us, I am the clever one, remember?' Then she flashed him a smile, as he walked out of the bar towards the elevators.

When Khalil returned, he seemed momentarily confused by Andrew's absence. Fiona explained to him where he had gone, and what they were proposing.

'I will be more than happy to assist you in any way I can,' said Khalil solemnly.

'Great,' said Fiona. 'Now, let me begin by telling you what I have been able to glean from Jabari Omran's notebook myself. My Arabic is not perfect, so I am sure there are several nuances that you could help me with. But as I said, we would really like you to read the whole thing yourself, and tell us what you make of it all.'

Fiona then went on to provide Khalil with a summary of everything she had discovered in the notebook so far, including Omran's theory about the meteorite being radioactive, and that part of it might have ended up in the Ark of the Covenant. She also laid out the idea that the best chance they had of solving the mystery, preventing highly radioactive material from falling into the hands of terrorists, and also of finding Doctor Mansour, would be to find the Ark or the meteorite, or possibly both.

As she did so, she suddenly felt very self-conscious, realising that in some respects this was his history she was talking about, or at least the history of his country and his ancestors. Modern Egyptians rightly take great pride in their ancient history, and the story of Exodus is riddled with notions of strife, division and repression of the Jewish people. For this reason, it is a sensitive issue in Egypt, but also because it is based on a Hebrew biblical account, that it is difficult to claim is an accurate historical record.'

But Fiona was gratified to discover that Khalil seemed sanguine about those aspects of the contents of the notebook. As a professor of archaeology, cultural and religious undertones of research efforts was just part and parcel of the job. Whenever something new of that nature was uncovered or speculated to have existed, there was always some group of people somewhere who didn't like the implications for their particular special interest.

After Fiona had finished presenting her findings, Khalil sat back in his seat, with a sombre look on his face. The connection to the Israelite Ark of the Covenant did not seem to faze him. In fact, when Fiona told him about Omran's notes on that particular point, it had seemed like he was momentarily lost in his own thoughts as if he was recollecting something from the back of his mind.

After a minute or so, Khalil sat up straight and placed both hands flat on the small table next to them.

'Miss Keane,' he finally said, speaking slowly and deliberately. 'I am sure that you appreciate the possible implications of this theory of Omran's. But I have no reason to doubt that his research was very serious and very diligent. He would not have produced lots of conjecture without any basis, so I have to believe that he might have been on to something.'

'That's interesting to hear,' said Fiona. 'My own sense of this was also that, as outlandish as it might sound when first hearing about it, there is a real sense that this is the result of proper research.'

Khalil nodded. 'I must confess, I have sometimes been struck by certain aspects of ancient Egyptian culture and imagery. There seems to me to be a close link between that and Hebrew culture and imagery. I have noticed it several times over the years, but only now that you have explained Omran's research, does it seem undeniable that there is a link.'

'What do you mean, specifically?' asked Fiona, looking intrigued.

Khalil paused for a moment as if to organise his thoughts. 'Miss Keane. I should very much like to accompany you both to Luxor. There is something there that I believe will be extremely interesting to you, and you really must see it with your own eye. I think it would help cement some of the things we have been discussing, and possibly give us a clue about how to proceed.'

Fiona hesitated for a moment, but then a smile spread across her face. 'That sounds perfect,' she finally said. 'I think Andy and I need to get out of this hotel anyway.'

Just then Andrew appeared at the other end of the bar. When he returned, he thought Khalil looked appreciably better. The deep furrows in his brow were gone, and his eyes seemed clearer and more confident.

'Got it,' said Andrew and held up an envelope. 'All pages have been copied, and the notebook is back in the safe.'

'Great,' said Fiona. 'I have explained everything I have discovered so far to Mr. Amer. I mean, to

Khalil,' she corrected herself and smiled apologetically.

Khalil nodded and smiled.

Andrew handed him the envelope and sat down again. 'Please do take your time,' he said. 'We're more interested in accuracy than in speed on this one.'

'Actually,' said Fiona with a smile, and sounding slightly hesitant. 'There has been a change of plan.'

'There has?' asked Andrew and gave her a surprised but good-natured look.

'We are going to Luxor,' she beamed.

Andrew looked at her for a few seconds, about to ask for reasons, but then simply bowed his head slightly and smiled. 'Alright, Miss Keane. You're the boss.'

★   ★   ★

Doctor Mansour opened his eyes. He had been asleep for several hours, and it took him a few seconds to realise where he was. Then the crushing realisation hit him yet again, followed by the pain in his hands. He was still in a windowless room somewhere, being held and interrogated by people he had never met and did not know who he was. The only thing he knew was what they wanted. Everything he knew about Jabari Omran's research. Even if he did not know precisely who they were, it was evident from their questions that what they wanted was to find the source of the radioactive material that had been found in the alloy that the metal casket was made from.

Doctor Mansour had been able to deflect their questions and avoid providing them with the location of the notebook, up until the point when they started breaking his fingers. At that point, he had found himself helplessly surrendering everything he knew. He was no hero. That much was clear. But then, he had never pretended to be one. All he had ever wanted to do was read, learn and understand the history of the world around him. He simply was not cut out for this, and his captors had been very efficient in establishing that fact.

Now he was filled with shame at his failure to protect Omran's work. He was also worried about his friends and colleagues. Who else might his captors attempt to snatch off the streets of Cairo?

Another question kept coming back to him again and again. How was he supposed to get out of here? Even if he told them everything, would they not eventually kill him? After all, if they simply dumped him by the side of the road somewhere, he would then have to reappear at the museum, and then the police would need to get involved. Surely, this was the last thing these people wanted.

Any way he looked at it, all he could conclude was that he was never going to leave this place alive. This realisation had robbed him of his appetite, and for several days now he had only eaten a bit of bread.

He was powerless, at the mercy of his captors, whoever they were, and he felt like a dead man walking.

★ ★ ★

Late in the afternoon, Andrew and Fiona were sitting in the bar at the roof-top pool of the Fairmont Nile City Hotel. They were seated comfortably in reclining chairs under a parasol, and the breeze high up on the top of the hotel made for a pleasantly balmy experience, even if the temperature was in the red.

The sun was moving lower in the sky, bathing the land in its warm light as it had done since the days when this area around the Nile was known as Memphis, and had served as the seat of power for the early pharaonic kingdoms.

Around them, other hotel guests were lounging near the pool, or standing by the chest-high glass barriers, looking out over the Nile and the city of Cairo. Next to them was a family of three, including a six-year-old girl who was busy asking her parents about the pyramids and who built them, and whether they were made of giant Lego blocks. Sitting by himself at the bar next to them was a young man wearing a baseball cap, black jeans and white trainers. He was busy typing away on his laptop and sipping a Diet Coke.

'Andrew,' said Fiona. 'I have had a thought.'

'Ok,' said Andrew and extracted himself from his work. 'Let's hear it.'

'I have been thinking that one possible way of at least starting to look for the Ark, would be by finding out as much as possible about the people who made it.'

'What do you mean exactly?' asked Andrew. 'Provided it actually ever really existed, does anyone know anything factual about who made it?'

'First of all, there are so many references to the Ark in the Bible, and so many actual historical sites where the Ark is supposed to have been kept, that it is beyond reasonable doubt that it was an actual physical object that existed. Secondly, there are quite a few references to the individuals responsible for actually building it.'

'Didn't you say that the Bible can't be trusted as a historical record?' asked Andrew.

'I did,' conceded Fiona. 'But I also said that all of these stories and legends originated from somewhere, within a cultural context, and much if not all of that cultural context is known. For example, the Temple of Solomon in Jerusalem was undeniably there in 957 BCE, and its only purpose was as a place to keep the Ark of the Covenant safe. There are several other places where the Ark is supposed to have been kept in the years leading up to that point, where archaeologists have found the remains of temples, whose designs hint at them being locations where the Ark could have been kept.'

'Alright,' said Andrew. 'I yield. So, tell me what we know about the people who built it then.'

'Well, there are only a couple of people mentioned by name in the Bible. They are Bezalel and Aholiab, and as I told you the other day, they received incredibly precise instructions about how to make it.'

'Wait. Instructions from whom?' asked Andrew curiously.

Fiona smiled, raised her eyebrows and slowly pointed skywards.

'Oh. Right,' said Andrew and smiled. 'I see.'

'Anyway,' continued Fiona. 'The main architect of the Ark was Bezalel. He was apparently a grand-nephew of Moses and was supposed to have been only thirteen years of age when he accomplished this great work. At least, this is what the Rabbinical literature says. He was said to be highly gifted, showing great skill and originality in engraving precious metals and stones and in wood-carving.'

'Bright young chap,' said Andrew and sipped at his Mojito cocktail.

'In other words,' continued Fiona. 'He would have been able to construct a containment vessel out of gold, designed to hold something like a radioactive meteorite.'

'I suppose that is a reasonable assumption,' said Andrew. 'Is there anything else in these very precise instructions that hint at the possibility of the Ark actually being such a vessel?'

'Not specifically,' replied Fiona. 'But there are additional details that are worth noting. For example, the Ark was designed to be carried on staffs, thereby ensuring that it was always kept at a relatively safe distance from the Levites, who were the only tribe who ever carried the Ark on its journey from Egypt to Jerusalem. Both the staffs and the Ark itself were covered in gold, which also makes sense from that perspective.'

'I seem to remember something about an ornate lid,' said Andrew. 'I am no history buff, but I have seen images of reconstructions of the Ark, with bird-like creatures sitting on top of it.'

'Yes,' said Fiona. 'Those are the Cherubim. They are two-winged human-like beings, conceived in the

Hebrew Bible as guardians of Eden, and protectors of Yahweh here on Earth. They sit at either end of the Ark's lid, facing each other, and their wings are swept forward in a protective pose over the so-called Seat of God, which is at the centre of the Ark.'

'They sound a bit like angels, don't they?' asked Andrew.

'They do, and that is sometimes what they are equated with, depending on which of the major religions you consult. In the Hebrew Bible, God is described as 'The Lord of Hosts', which just means the lord of armies. But in all three of these monotheistic religions, they are just one type of angel.'

'I see,' said Andrew. 'Forgive me, but how does all this help us in locating the Ark of the Covenant?'

'It is just useful background information,' replied Fiona. 'Anyway, if we are ever going to have any chance of figuring out where the Ark might be, we will need to talk to someone who has researched its history in-depth. I have taken the liberty of contacting a couple of people about that already.'

'Ok,' said Andrew. 'Who do you think we should see?'

'Actually, I have already arranged a meeting with a Professor Ari Finkelstein at the Hebrew University of Jerusalem.'

'Oh,' said Andrew, sounding surprised. 'When?'

'In two days,' replied Fiona. 'He is a renowned expert in this field, and has focused his research on historical validation of the Torah.'

'That's the Jewish Bible, right?' asked Andrew.

'That's right. The Torah is also called 'Torat Moshe', which means the Law of Moses.'

'Sounds like the perfect guy,' nodded Andrew.

'I am hoping he can help us shed some light on the historical accuracy of the story of Exodus. There has never been a shortage of disagreement amongst academics about this particular issue, but hopefully, he can help point us in the right direction, or at least steer us away from obvious dead ends.'

'Are you planning to tell him that we are looking for the Ark?' asked Andrew. 'It might be a slightly sensitive issue.'

'I have thought about that already,' replied Fiona. 'And you are right. But I don't think there is any point in talking to him if we are not being honest about what we are trying to do.'

'I agree,' said Andrew. 'I will schedule the flight for us after our return from Luxor. I just need to get in touch with Gordon back in London.'

'Great,' said Fiona and took a swig at her drink. 'You know, I could get used to this life. Visiting interesting places in our own jet, looking for ancient artefacts, and having cocktails in expensive hotels. I am glad I met you,' she giggled and winked at him.

'Gee, thanks.' He responded in mock outrage.

'Plus, you're also nice company,' she continued, in her best attempt at sounding placating.

Andrew grunted, and decided to leave it there. He always lost when they engaged in banter like this, and this time would be no different.

Ten

Early the next day, Andrew had been in touch with Colonel Strickland in London, firstly to update him on their progress so far, and secondly to arrange for the BAe 146-200 to take them from Almaza Airforce Base near Cairo to Luxor International Airport. The famous ancient temple ruins of Luxor, are among the most visited by tourists travelling to Egypt. Andrew had arranged for Khalil to be picked up from Cairo University and brought to Almaza Airforce Base by 10 am. He had initially thought that going all the way to Luxor to look at a temple ruin, seemed like a bit of an arduous journey for something that could probably be achieved by Googling the place. But he had deferred to Fiona who was very enthusiastic, and also to the professor who seemed to genuinely think that seeing the ruins in person would somehow impart some sort of insight that would be helpful in their search for the meteorite and possibly for the Ark as well. Khalil had asked them both to be patient regarding the exact purpose of their visit to Luxor.

It would take just under an hour to reach Luxor International Airport, so Andrew had got himself comfortable with a drink and a book about Luxor and the Valley of Kings, where several pharaohs were buried.

Fiona and Khalil had been deep in conversation most of the way so far. Khalil had been studying Omran's notes well into the night, and Fiona was keen to hear what his thoughts were.

'I am no expert on meteorites,' said Khalil. 'But it is clear that ancient Egyptians had experiences with these things. It is also worth noting that there is a sizable number of scholars who believe that the black stone that is set into the eastern corner of the Kaaba in Mecca in Saudi Arabia, is of meteoric origins.'

Fiona nodded. 'Yes, I have read that too. What is definitely clear, is that the heavens and the stars have always played a central role in all the various belief systems that have sprung up in the Middle East and North Africa. The connection to celestial powers is fairly ubiquitous.'

'Indeed,' replied Khalil. 'As you might already know, all the different gods in ancient Egypt had their place among the stars in the night sky. And one of the most powerful gods was the sun-god Ra.'

'What are the oldest references to the stars that have been uncovered in Egypt?' asked Fiona.

'Well,' said Khalil. 'Initially, there are no references as such, since no written language has been found to accompany the oldest archaeological sites. But there is very clear evidence of a connection between the people of this region and the heavens, at sites like Nabta Playa.'

'Oh, I think I might have heard of that place before,' said Fiona. 'Could you remind me again?'

'Of course,' replied Khalil. 'Nabta Playa is in the Nubian Desert, about 800 kilometres south of Cairo. There are several interesting archaeological sites there, but probably the most significant is one which consists of a large stone circle. This circle is believed to be aligned so that it could track the summer solstice, and thereby help forecast the annual floods.'

'And how old is that site,' asked Fiona.

'Our best estimates say that it is about 7500 years old.'

'Wow,' said Fiona, clearly impressed. 'That would make it much older than Stonehenge. By several thousand years, in fact.'

'Oh yes,' nodded Khalil. 'We believe it to be the oldest astronomy site in the world. This was during the so-called pre-dynastic period, during the 5th millennium BCE when the foundations of later Egyptian belief systems were just beginning to take form.'

'Is it true that the pyramids near Giza are aligned with the stars?'

'Absolutely,' replied Khalil. 'All the pyramids are aligned with the pole star, and the three main pyramids at Giza are positioned almost perfectly in accordance with the positions of the three stars in Orion's Belt, relative to each other.'

'That is quite amazing,' smiled Fiona, clearly excited by the implications of this. 'It is easy to forget just how advanced this part of the world was in those days. And there is so much more to discover.'

Khalil nodded in agreement. 'There is plenty of work for archaeologists in this country for many centuries to come.'

'Alright, you two,' said Andrew. 'Ten minutes until we land. Better strap in.'

Fifteen minutes later, the plane rolled to a stop at a parking spot near the terminal for private civilian aircraft. There were no security checks since the plane had arrived from Cairo, and within just a few minutes of landing, they were walking through the Arrivals Hall, where Khalil motioned to the taxi stand outside.

'I will ask our driver to take us to Medinet Habu,' he said. 'It is one of the most impressive temples built during the so-called New Kingdom in ancient Egypt. It was built as a mortuary temple for Ramesses III, who reigned from 1186 to 1155 BCE, and many parts of it are extremely well preserved. In fact, there are more than 7000 square metres of wall art there, all depicting or describing with hieroglyphs events that happened during his reign. As you can imagine, they are mostly about conquests of foreign lands and peoples.'

'No surprise there,' smirked Fiona.

Khalil laughed. 'Like most men of great power through the ages, Ramesses III was keen to ensure that his subjects never doubted his might, even after he had died.'

'I believe it is called "imposter syndrome",' said Fiona. 'You know, when deep down people have doubts about whether they are deserving of the way in which other people see them. Mind you, if I had pyramids and temples built in my honour, I think there is a chance I might suffer from that too. I mean, who wouldn't?'

'Plenty of people,' smiled Khalil ruefully. 'The entire area around Luxor is full of mortuary temples for the great pharaohs. All of those temples were built when the pharaohs were still alive, so they were very much involved in the designs of the structures that were meant to honour them after their deaths. And I think we all know of certain leaders these days who would quite like to rule like pharaohs. Modern Egypt has certainly had its fair share of those people.'

'Right,' said Andrew and smiled. 'Let's just keep our eye on the ball here, and not get caught up in contemporary politics. This is much more interesting anyway.'

They all got into a taxi, where Khalil exchanged a few words with the driver, and then they were off. Driving out of the airport complex and southwest towards the Luxor Bridge across the Nile, they could see the city of Luxor in the distance to their right.

Khalil turned to his two companions while gesturing out of the window. 'This area was once called Thebes, and it has been populated since around 3200 BCE. Almost five and a half thousand years. At its peak in ancient times, it is believed that more than one hundred thousand people lived here on this bend in the Nile. Over there on the other side of the Nile is the Theban Necropolis, where most of the pharaohs were buried, including Ramesses III. That's where we are going.'

Their taxi crossed the Luxor Bridge and then peeled off to the right towards the village of Ad

Dabiyyah. As it did, Andrew glanced through the rear window to see another taxi also turning off the main road.

'Everything alright?' asked Fiona.

'Sure,' smiled Andrew. 'Just looking around. Old habits die hard.'

After twenty minutes, and another two sleepy villages, they arrived at the tiny hamlet of Qasr al-Aguz. Their driver navigated through a couple of narrow streets until they arrived on the far side of the village by the entrance to the temple complex.

Medinet Habu is a large sprawling complex, but only the central temple is still standing. Over the centuries, the necropolis has been looted and used for various other purposes, so much of the building materials that were initially there have been removed or destroyed. Large blocks of limestone and remnants of structures can be seen dotted across a much larger area surrounding the main temple. About 5 kilometres behind the complex, Andrew could see the sand-coloured mountains rising up. This was where another necropolis, the Valley of Kings, was located, but they would have no time for that today.

'Wow,' said Fiona, putting on a straw hat as they got out of the taxi. It was now close to mid-day, and the sun was beating down on them. 'This place is absolutely huge.'

'Yes,' smiled Khalil, looking for a brief moment as if the dark clouds that had been hanging over him when they first met, were beginning to clear. 'The Medinet Habu temple complex is some 400 by 200 meters in size, with the temple itself measuring around 150 meters in length.'

Andrew pulled out a bottle of water he was carrying in a shoulder bag. Staying hydrated was important on a day like today. As he took a swig, he turned slightly to look behind them. There were a couple of tour buses parked to the side of the entrance, and another taxi was just arriving. A man in a light beige suit, who looked like he was Egyptian, got out and paid the taxi driver. Then he pulled out what appeared to be a guidebook, and started leafing through the pages.

'Please,' said Khalil and gestured towards a limestone structure at least twenty-five meters tall, that appeared to be the main gate into the temple. It looked like a giant wall, with a doorway in the middle of it. Its wall sloped inward ever so slightly, and it looked to be at least ten meters thick.

'This is the Great Pylon,' said Khalil, gesturing to the huge structure. 'It is the main entrance to the temple itself. As you can see, it is covered in relief carvings and hieroglyphs. On the other side of it, is the First Courtyard.'

They proceeded through the gate, which was as ornately decorated as the exterior of the structure. In fact, it seemed as if every single square centimetre of the entire complex was covered in either hieroglyphs, stone relief carvings or wall paintings.

'This is incredible,' said Fiona. She looked like a kid in a candy store.

'It is a spectacular place,' agreed Khalil, as they entered into the First Courtyard. 'I like to imagine what this would have looked like more than three thousand years ago when it was in pristine condition, and there would have been people walking around here, carrying out various temple duties.'

The courtyard was around 50 by 50 meters, and on both the left and the right sides were colonnades lined with statues of ancient Egyptian royals, each some ten meters tall.

'How is anyone able to read these hieroglyphs?' asked Andrew. 'They look nothing like any recognisable alphabet I have ever seen.'

Khalil and Fiona both smiled and exchanged a look that said they both wanted to tell this particular story. Fiona bowed he head slightly, and gestured for Khalil to proceed. 'This is your country,' she said. 'I am sure you can do a much better job of it than I can. And besides, it is such a good story that I don't think I can do it justice.'

'Ok,' said Khalil and walked over to a column with hieroglyphs wrapping all the way around it, and covering it from the ground to its top around ten meters above them.

'Technically, hieroglyphs are not letters, and so calling it an alphabet is actually inaccurate. It is a way of writing that is based on symbols, and in that respect, it is read in quite a literal sense. The only reason we are able to read it is because of a happy accident that occurred just over two hundred years ago. Up until that point, hieroglyphs had been lost to time, and no one had been able to read them in the way we can all read texts today using less than 30 Greek characters.'

'Imagine the frustration,' interjected Fiona. 'An entire region, full of ancient structures from an advanced civilisation, covered in writing, and absolutely no ability to read any of it. It must have been maddening for archaeologists in those days.'

'Indeed,' smiled Khalil and continued. 'Then, in 1798, during Napoleon's campaign in Egypt, the French army was strengthening the defences of Fort Julien a few kilometres north-east of the port city of Rosetta, which today is called Rashid. A French lieutenant by the name Menou spotted a large slab of stone that the soldiers had dug up, intending to use it as building material. It was covered in writing on one of its sides, and as it turned out later, the writing constituted a decree from Memphis at the coronation of the Egyptian King Ptolemy V in 196 BCE, pronouncing him as the new supreme ruler. But the most amazing thing was that it was written in three different scripts. The top and middle texts are in Ancient Egyptian using hieroglyphic and Demotic scripts respectively, while the bottom is in Ancient Greek. This enabled archaeologists to decipher the hieroglyphs, based mainly on the Greek but also the Demotic scripts. The slab had been broken into several pieces, but enough of the decree in all three languages remained on this one piece, to allow for a complete deciphering. And of course, more importantly, it suddenly allowed for all the hieroglyphs that were all over ancient Egyptian structures to be read and interpreted.'

'That really is amazing,' said Andrew, clearly impressed. 'Happy accident indeed.'

The three of them stood in the middle of the courtyard and admired the sight. Behind them, another group of tourists were passing through the entrance to the courtyard. The man in the beige suit was at the back of the group.

Opposite the main entrance where they had entered, was another large wall that rose up as high as the first one, and similarly to the first, it had a doorway that led deeper still into the temple.

'This is the Second Pylon,' said Khalil and gestured towards it. 'This is believed to be a monument to Ramesses III's father Amon-Re. 'And just beyond this is the Second Courtyard, which is what I have been so keen to show you.'

Andrew and Fiona followed Khalil through the enormous doorway and into the second courtyard, which was approximately the same size as the first. On either side were colonnades, each with five intricately decorated columns. Opposite the entrance was another doorway, that led into what used to be the covered part of the temple. The limestone blocks that had once made up the temple roof had all fallen down, and many had been plundered and used as building materials in the local area.

Andrew and Fiona took a moment to admire the art, which would have taken many skilled craftsmen thousands of hours to make. Behind them, on either side of the entrance they had just passed through, were colonnades with more statues of royals from the New Kingdom period, which spanned around 700 years, between the 16th century BCE and the 11th century BCE.

'This is the true court of the temple,' said Khalil. 'Over here on this wall behind the statues is what I have wanted to show you all along.'

He motioned for them to join him as he made his way into the shade between two massive columns.

'Here,' he said and gestured towards the wall, which was at least ten meters tall, and covered in several detailed relief carvings. 'This is known as the East Wall of the Second Courtyard. Please, tell me what you see. And remember, this was created more than 3000 years ago, around 1150 BCE, or roughly within 100 years of the consensus estimates for the exodus of Moses and the Hebrews from Egypt.'

Fiona slowly stepped closer to the wall, her gaze locked on the various motifs towering above her. Khalil remained silent, now leaning against a column with his arms crossed, and an expectant smile on his face, as if he was a teacher waiting for his student to solve a riddle.

To their right, some ten meters away, the man in the beige suit was seemingly inspecting a detail on the wall in front of him. He looked as if he was comparing the carving in front of him with what was shown in his guidebook. Andrew noticed he had earphones in his ears, so he was presumably listening to an audio tour of the complex.

Fiona walked slowly back and forth along the enormous wall a couple of times, inspecting the motifs, before stopping and turning to Khalil. Then she suddenly stopped.

'This was in Omran's notebook,' she said breathlessly and pointed to a motif above her.

Khalil stepped away from the column and joined her with a contented smile.

'Indeed,' he said. 'What you see here is an image of a procession of priests, carrying a divine artefact, also called a reliquary. We find them in many places in different temples and mausoleums, and they appear at many different times through the various dynasties of ancient Egypt. There is nothing particularly unusual about this stone carving unless you look at it in the context of Exodus in the Hebrew Bible, or the Old Testament. Then you suddenly realise that this is a depiction of something that looks almost identical to the stories about the Ark of the Covenant.'

'Yes. You are right,' exclaimed Fiona. 'There's clearly a procession of priests, and they are carrying what appears to be a box on long staves, which must be the reliquary. This looks remarkably like the depictions of the Ark of the Covenant that I have seen.'

'That's right,' smiled Khalil. 'Now look above the reliquary. What do you see there?'

Fiona peered upwards and moved her head to the side as if to get a better angle. 'Those look like little winged creatures,' she said, trying to get a good look. She suddenly spun around to face Khalil. 'Cherubim!' she exclaimed. 'The winged cherubim that were placed on the lid of the Ark.'

Khalil raised both hands in front of himself as if to calm her down. 'Perhaps. Perhaps not. There are many winged creatures that show up in ancient art from this period. We know from the tomb of Tutankhamun, that his shrine was shaped much like the Ark is supposed to have been shaped, and that it is covered in gold, just like the Ark, and that it has depictions of two cherubim facing each other on its sides.'

'I am no archaeologist,' said Andrew. 'But I think I know when things stop looking like coincidences and start looking like a pattern, and I feel like I am looking at a pattern here.'

'I agree,' said Khalil and gestured to the wall relief. 'Please understand that this does not mean that the Ark of the Covenant, if it ever existed, was actually in Egypt at the time of this procession during Ramesses III's reign. It just means that carrying an important reliquary in this manner was common at that time.'

'Oh, I think I know where you are going with this,' said Fiona, sounding as if a lightbulb had switched on inside her head.

'In fact,' continued Khalil. 'You might argue that the very reason the Ark was designed the way it was, and ended up being carried the way it was, is simply a continuation of religious traditions and practices that were already an integral part of ancient Egyptian religious practices, and had been so for hundreds of years. Remember, according to Exodus, the Israelites had lived in Egypt for centuries, so there is every reason to believe that they had adopted some of the local religious practices and iconography. At the very least, it seems reasonable to argue that because they had been enmeshed in Egyptian society and culture for several centuries, they would naturally look to Egyptian practices and designs at the point in time when the Ark was eventually constructed.'

'That makes a lot of sense,' nodded Fiona. 'You are saying that the cultural context was Egyptian, and that this was partially adopted by the Hebrews after such a long period in Egypt.'

'Yes, exactly,' said Khalil. 'There is no compelling reason to believe that what we are looking at here is the actual Ark of the Covenant, but it is clear that things that were remarkably similar to the Ark as it was described in Exodus, already existed in ancient Egypt during those days. At this point, the Israelites had lived in Egypt for perhaps as much as 10 or 15 generations. They were well integrated into the local culture, and none of them had ever seen anything different. Moses himself never set foot outside Egypt until he was a grown man, so it is perfectly conceivable that when they needed to build some sort of vessel to carry the Ten Commandments in, they ended up making something that they were already familiar with, and that someone clearly knew how to build.'

'The Ten commandments, or possibly an ancient radioactive meteorite,' smiled Fiona.

Khalil bowed his head. 'That is not for me to say,' he smiled. 'Although clearly, Jabari Omran thought that this was highly likely. His notebook makes that quite clear, and I must admit that I can find no logical inconsistencies in his work.'

'I have to say,' said Fiona. 'This is a brilliant piece of deduction. Excellent work.'

'Thank you.' said Khalil. 'Since reading Omran's notebook, I was able to spend a couple of hours looking into this particular aspect of his research. It turns out that there have been several academics and scholars who have devoted time and effort to the connection between ancient Egyptian religious practices and those of the Hebrews in Egypt. Clearly, the best non-Israelite parallel to the Ark of the

Covenant comes from Egypt in the form of the sacred barque.'

'You mean a type of boat?' asked Fiona.

'Yes,' replied Khalil. 'The barque was a ritual object deeply embedded in the ancient Egyptian mythological landscape. It was carried aloft in processions or pulled on a wagon, and its purpose was to transport a god or a mummy. The Israelite conception of the Ark probably originated under Egyptian influence in the 12th century BCE. This particular connection between the ancient Egyptian barque and the Ark of the Covenant was first noticed by the 19th-century French theologian, Fulcran Vigouroux.'

'It is obvious, once it has been pointed out,' said Fiona and looked up at the limestone relief again.

'Like most things,' smiled Khalil.

Andrew had been listening to their conversation while keeping an eye on the man in the beige suit to their right. He could not put his finger on it, but there was something about him that seemed off. He decided to stop being paranoid, and simply walked over and stood next to him, looking at the same bit of wall. The man barely seemed to notice, but when Andrew took another step towards him, Andrew saw him turn his head slightly to the left and take half a step away. But he still did not actually look at Andrew.

This was not normal behaviour. If someone comes into their personal space, most people will turn towards the interloper, and look at them. This man almost seemed like he was trying to resist that reflex, and just stared straight ahead at the wall in front of him.

Andrew's instincts were now telling him that there was definitely something wrong here. He glanced down at the man's guidebook, and noticed that it was a book about the Sphinx in Giza, 800 kilometres to the north.

Andrew looked from the book up to the man's face in surprise, and somehow the man must have felt the change in Andrew's demeanour. His head snapped to the left, and for an instant, they locked eyes. In that moment, Andrew knew that this man was no tourist. He was here on a mission. He had been watching them and listening in on their conversations, and he was clearly trained in how to shadow people in a public space.

Andrew's eyes shot back down to the guide book, and there on the back of the book, he could see a small circular hole with a black reflective lens. Next to it was a smaller hole. The guidebook was not a book. It was a camera with a microphone.

The man instantly registered what Andrew had deduced, and in one smooth motion that betrayed his training, the man took one short but fast step towards Andrew and slightly to his right, and as he did so his right elbow came up and slammed into Andrew's jaw.

Andrew staggered backwards, momentarily dazed by the man's lightning-fast attack, but then quickly regained his balance. Behind him, he could hear a shriek from Fiona, who must have caught what had happened out of the corner of her eye. He steadied himself with a hand against a column and looked up to catch a final glimpse of the man as he sprinted through the doorway from the second courtyard into the first courtyard and headed towards the exit of the temple complex.

The next thing he knew, Fiona and Khalil were next to him, shouting and confused.

'What happened?' yelled Fiona. 'Are you alright?'

'Yes, I am fine. I need to get the bastard,' said Andrew and started moving unsteadily towards the courtyard exit where the man had disappeared a few seconds earlier.

'No, you don't,' proclaimed Fiona, trying to hold him back by grabbing on to one of his arms. 'You're in no state to go chasing after that guy. You have no idea what he is capable of.'

'Oh, I have a pretty bloody good idea,' replied Andrew, looking determined. 'He's just like me.'

'Can I help?' asked Khalil, with a hard edge to his voice.

Andrew looked at Khalil, and he could see that the offer to help was genuine. Khalil had a steely look in his eyes, and Andrew suddenly remembered how this whole thing was very personal to him.

'No,' said Andrew and started walking towards the courtyard exit, but still facing Fiona and Khalil. Then he pointed to Fiona. 'But you can stay here and look after her.'

Then he spun around and bolted through the doorway to the first courtyard. There he could see the figure of the man in the beige suit, sprinting through the doorway opposite, out through the main gate and towards the parking lot.

Andrew's legs were pumping as he raced past confused onlookers, most of them having spotted him and now busily trying to get out of the way. Then Andrew had an idea.

'Stop thief,' he yelled, hoping that someone would tackle the man, but nobody seemed to register him, or perhaps they thought it best to stay out of this, whatever it was.

He didn't blame them. From the smooth and efficient way in which he had moved during his attack, to the way he ran across the courtyard, Andrew could tell that whoever he was, he had received training in the use of force, and he was clearly extremely fit.

Andrew was passing through the middle of the first courtyard when he suddenly started to feel the effects of the heat and the impact on his jaw, combining to make him less than steady on his feet. As much as he hated surrendering to that feeling, he knew that if he ignored it, he might well pass out right there on the stone slabs.

As he passed through the main gate into the open area in front of the Great Pylon, he just caught sight of the man jumping into the taxi that had brought him there half an hour earlier. He must have asked for it to stay and wait for him.

'Clever bastard,' panted Andrew and stopped, placing his hands on his hips and bending forward, trying to catch his breath.

A few moments later, he heard the sound of running feet behind him. Fiona and Khalil had caught up with him.

'What the hell is wrong with you?' yelled Fiona. 'You could have got yourself killed. There could have been more like him out here. You wouldn't have stood a chance.'

Andrew had not thought of that. Once he had started running after the man, he had been like a heat-seeking missile, or a greyhound dog on a racecourse, chasing a rag. Able to focus only on one thing. Still panting, he looked up to see a seething Fiona, with Khalil standing behind her with his hands spread out, as if to say *"I couldn't stop her"*. Andrew couldn't help but grin through the pain. Fiona was always going to be Fiona.

'Hello?' she continued angrily. 'I bloody hate it when you men push women like me out of the way and treat us like little damsels in distress.'

'I was trying to protect you,' replied Andrew defensively as he slowly straightened up, still clutching his sides.

'I know,' she erupted. 'That's exactly the problem. Because as far as I could tell, you were the one who needed help. So let me help you.'

'Alright, listen,' he said and held up his hands. 'It's over now anyway. That guy is long gone, so let's all just calm down.'

'Did he get into a car?' asked Khalil.

'Taxi,' winced Andrew. 'He must have asked it to wait for him.'

'Are you alright? You muppet.' asked Fiona, now sounding more conciliatory. She ran her hand gently across his jaw, which was slightly swollen and red on the left side.

'I'm fine,' said Andrew dismissively. 'Barely a scratch. Nice punch though. Elbow to the face. Super quick.'

'Well, I am glad you can at least admire his handiwork,' replied Fiona incredulously. 'What on earth happened?'

'There was just something about that guy that rubbed me the wrong way,' said Andrew. 'As I went over to him, I spotted a camera and a microphone disguised as a book, pointing at us. He must have been recording us the whole time we were here.'

'What?' exclaimed Fiona. 'What is that supposed to mean? Why? Who was he?'

'Well, if I had to guess I would say he is with the outfit that is holding Doctor Mansour. They are clearly after the same thing we are, and they thought they could snoop on our conversations to try to get ahead of us. Anyway, he realised I was on to him, so he rammed his elbow into my face and ran off.'

'Bloody hell,' said Fiona.

'This is serious,' said Khalil hesitantly, suddenly looking slightly out of his depth.

'Anyway, it was my stupid fault,' said Andrew, sounding bitter. 'I am so used to looking out for bad guys dressed in rags and military equipment, and holding AK47s. The suit lulled me into a false sense of security. I should have been on to that guy from the very beginning.'

'No use blaming yourself,' said Fiona. 'Let's focus on what we do now. They clearly know who we are and what we are doing. The question is how?'

'Perhaps they have been following me?' said Khalil sounding uncomfortable but looking nothing like a man about to back out. 'After all, I am one of Bahir's oldest friends. Who knows for how long they might have been spying on me?'

Andrew shook his head and then instantly regretted it as pain shot through his forehead. 'How is it possible that this sneaky bastard was here, just after we arrived?' said Andrew and rubbed his jaw, wincing. 'He couldn't possibly have followed us from Cairo. We even flew out of a military airport.'

'Good question,' said Fiona, looking concerned.

'So,' continued Andrew. 'If they didn't follow us, how the hell did they know we would be here today? Are our communications compromised?'

'Hard to say,' said Fiona. 'But we have to assume that they are. Perhaps you should have a word with Strickland when we get back to Cairo.'

'Yes,' nodded Andrew. 'I will definitely need to do that.'

'Right,' said Khalil. 'I know this is your show, but I think we should head back. We have seen what we came here to see, and if there is any other information we need, I can provide it to you after we get back.'

'I agree,' said Andrew. 'I feel like we have outstayed our welcome already.'

Fiona hesitated, looking for a brief moment like a child that had just been told that the amusement park was about to close. But then she bowed her head in acceptance.

'Alright boys,' she sighed. 'You've caused enough trouble for one day. Let's get back to the airport.'

Eleven

Doctor Zaki was sitting by himself in a cosy outside space at a coffee house, locally known as an *ahwas*. He had walked here from his apartment in the affluent Mohandessin district of Cairo. The area had all the usual trappings of a modern international metropolis, and yet it was easy to find a traditional *ahwas* where one could relax, drink coffee and smoke a water pipe. The sun was out, and the temperature was already climbing, but Doctor Zaki was sitting comfortably in the shade of the building on the other side of the street. Next to his table, groups of middle-aged men were chatting, laughing and playing backgammon, which is a descendent of the ancient Egyptian game *Senet*.

Doctor Zaki sipped at his coffee again and pulled up his left shirt sleeve to check his wristwatch. As he did so, a man placed a hand on his shoulder.

'Do not be so impatient, my friend,' said a voice, which sounded like that of an old man.

Recognising the voice, Doctor Zaki smiled and looked up to see the familiar face of a man whose real name he had never learned, despite having known him for over a decade.

'Malpannah,' said Zaki, using the Aramaic word for *teacher*. He rose and clasped both hands around the old man's hand, whilst bowing his head in respect. 'Thank you for seeing me.'

'Not to worry, my son.' said the old man, slowly sitting down next to Doctor Zaki.

His physical health was clearly not what it had once been, but his bright blue eyes were those of a person with wisdom and a sharp mind.

'Tell me what is on your mind,' he said.

Doctor Zaki nodded, and then looked like he was pondering something for a few moments. 'As you know, Doctor Mansour has disappeared, and the Nuclear Research Centre was hacked somehow. We're still trying to work out exactly how that could have happened.'

'Yes, I know,' replied the old man gravely. 'You are concerned that we may have been exposed.'

'I am,' said Doctor Zaki, looking troubled. 'But it is not just that. Today, at Major Elsayed's request, I met with two people from the UK who are here to investigate the disappearance of Doctor Mansour, and any link it may have to radioactive materials. They are clearly concerned that this material might fall into the hands of terrorists.'

'And so they should be,' said the old man, stroking his beard.

Doctor Zaki nodded gravely. 'One of them is with an anti-terror unit of the SAS, and the other is an archaeologist.'

'An unusual pair,' observed the old man.

'Indeed,' replied Doctor Zaki. 'They seem like they know a lot already. It is very disconcerting one day to feel that everything is under control and safe, and then the next day it seems like people we have never heard of are closing in on us.'

'I know,' said the old man. 'This has happened to many a member of the brotherhood over the centuries. Do not worry. We will find a way to deal with this too. If it wasn't for you and your position at the nuclear research facility, we would not even have discovered this whole thing.'

'Well,' said Doctor Zaki. 'It is part of the reason I am there at all.'

'Indeed,' replied the old man. 'And you have served the Brotherhood well in that regard.'

Doctor Zaki sighed. 'They are already digging in the right places, even if they don't yet know what it is they are digging for. I was trying to hold back, but everything I said was already in the report that Major Elsayed had demanded, so they know all those things anyway. And I couldn't falsify the test results. Those are all logged in the computer system at the facility and shared on the network.'

'I understand,' said the old man calmly.

'And,' continued Doctor Zaki. 'If the people who are holding Doctor Mansour manage to connect the right dots, we in the Brotherhood may find ourselves in a situation where we will need to actively pick sides here.'

The old man nodded sagely. 'I know, my son' he said. 'I have reached the same conclusion. But we must not make any hasty decisions just yet. Let us sit back and watch for a while longer, and see how they progress. If need be, we may have to intervene. Ultimately, the safety of the Source is the only thing that matters.'

'I understand,' said Doctor Zaki. 'What shall I do then?'

'Simply offer your assistance whenever possible,' replied the old man. 'And keep an eye on them as much as you can.'

'Ok, I will do that. Thank you, Malpannah.'

The old man placed his hand on Doctor Zaki's shoulder again, leaned in and whispered. 'Moshe is with us, my son.'

'Moshe is with us,' repeated Doctor Zaki.

Then, gently tapping Doctor Zaki on the shoulder with the palm of his hand, the old man rose, walked past him and then left the *ahwas*.

Doctor Zaki did not turn around to look. It was better if he knew as little as possible about the Malpannah.

* * *

It was now late afternoon in Cairo. Having returned from Luxor to their hotel, Andrew and Fiona spent the rest of the day in their room, discussing the events that had transpired in Luxor. They both agreed that, although there was no way of knowing precisely who had been behind the attempted snooping on their visit to Medinet Habu, or indeed what those individuals might be prepared to do, they had no choice but to push forward and continue their investigation. According to Colonel Strickland back in London, the Egyptian police and intelligence services had turned up nothing in the search for Doctor Mansour, and they were equally stumped when it came to who might be behind the attempt to obtain Omran's notebook.

Just as Andrew was getting up from the sofa, and about to make his way to the outside terrace, his phone rang.

'Andrew?' said a voice.

'Yes. Colonel Strickland, sir.'

'How are you two? I got your message about the incident in Luxor.'

'We're ok, sir,' sighed Andrew. 'My ego hurts a lot more than my jaw, to be honest.'

'Don't worry old chap,' replied Strickland. 'You can't blame yourself for that. Short of grabbing a complete stranger in the middle of Medinet Habu, and then interrogating him right there on the spot, you simply couldn't have known that he was spying on you.'

'I suppose,' grumbled Andrew reluctantly. He didn't like shirking responsibility when something went wrong, but Strickland did have a point. There is vigilance, and then there is paranoia.

'Anyway Andrew,' said Strickland. 'I have taken the liberty of setting up a video call for the two of you tomorrow with a chap from the Kavli Institute for Cosmology at Cambridge University. His name is Professor Harold Lazenby, and he is a highly respected cosmologist specialising in asteroids and comets. Given what you have told me about this chap Jabari Omran and his theories, I thought you two needed to speak to a scientist who can answer any questions you might have about things falling out of the sky.'

'That sounds excellent, sir,' said Andrew. 'When is the meeting scheduled for?'

'Tomorrow morning at 10 am your local time.'

'Great,' said Andrew. 'We will look forward to it.'

'Oh,' said Strickland. 'The trip to Jerusalem that you asked about has now been arranged, and the flight plan has been approved by both the Egyptian and the Israeli authorities.'

'Brilliant,' said Andrew. 'Sorry about the short notice. Fiona likes to take charge of things.'

'That's no problem at all,' replied Strickland. 'It is a good thing that she does. She's very capable.'

'She is indeed,' said Andrew. 'I would have been stuck more than once already if it had not been for her.'

'Glad to see you working so well as a team,' said Strickland. 'If I had to work with my own wife, we'd probably end up killing each other.'

Andrew laughed. 'Well, it's still early days. And also, we're not married.'

'I know,' chuckled Strickland. 'Perhaps that's the secret.'

'I might well be,' said Andrew and glanced over at Fiona who was sitting on the sofa reading a book. The conversation had made her peek over the top of it, and raise her eyebrows at Andrew.

'Anyway,' said Strickland. 'There's one other thing I need to discuss with you.'

'Certainly, sir,' said Andrew, now taking on a more serious demeanour.

'Following your little incident in Luxor yesterday, I have sought and obtained from the Egyptian security services permission for you to carry a concealed firearm.'

'Right,' said Andrew, subconsciously glancing in the direction of the safe, where his service pistol was locked away.

'The thing is,' said Strickland. 'There's just no knowing what these people are up to. If they really are behind the disappearance of Doctor Mansour, there is no reason why they would not try to interfere further in our investigation.'

'I agree, sir,' replied Andrew. 'We probably can't be too careful.'

'Precisely,' said the colonel. 'So as of this moment, you have permission to carry your firearm on you at all times, and to use it if necessary, in order to protect life.'

'Got it,' nodded Andrew gravely. 'I hope I won't need it, but I would rather have it and not need it than need it and not have it.'

'That was exactly my thinking as well,' replied Strickland. 'I have also asked that Egyptian police maintain a presence outside Professor Khalil Amer's house and at his faculty at Cairo University. Both Major Elsayed and I think he might become a target if his affiliation with Doctor Mansour becomes known to these people, whoever they are.'

'Sounds sensible,' replied Andrew. 'He's a good man.'

'He is,' said Strickland. 'And with that, I will let you get on with your evening. My regards to Fiona.'

'Great,' said Andrew. 'We will keep you posted on any progress we make.'

'Marvellous. Speak to you soon.'

★ ★ ★

Doctor Mansour was paralysed with fear. He was strapped to a chair at the dinner table in the safehouse under the Zamalek townhouse, sweating profusely even though the room was kept at normal room temperature. He had no idea what day it was, or whether it was morning or noon or the middle of the night.

As he was sitting there, he was unable to take his eyes off it. It was lying there on the table in front of him, and yet his brain was unable to process what it was seeing. But it was real. The blood on it was real. The way the light reflected off of its still wet surface was real, and the fly that was sitting on it was real. It was a section of his finger. A couple of minutes earlier, it had been part of his body. But now it was there on the table, looking so familiar, and yet at the same time so alien.

An hour earlier, he had been lying on the bed, having just had a meal that had been brought to him by one of the twins in suits. He had never heard any of them speak a single word, and he had almost allowed himself to become comfortable with their presence. That was to change.

As usual, the older man with the moustache and the pin-striped suit had come in and sat down across from him. But this time, his calm demeanour seemed different somehow, and when one of the twins had suddenly grabbed his arms, while the other tied them to the arms of the chair with duct tape, Doctor Mansour had panicked, realising that today was not going to be like the previous days.

'Safiya,' said the man calmly but sternly.

'What?' said Doctor Mansour confused. 'Who?'

'At the Coptic Museum. You have a colleague there called Safiya. She worked for Omran.'

Doctor Mansour had instantly felt the hairs on the back of his neck stand up. What was he saying? What were they planning to do to her?

'Please don't hurt her,' Doctor Mansour had whispered.

'We spoke to her in her home early this morning,' the man had continued calmly, his cold dark eyes locked onto Doctor Mansour's. 'Using the combination you gave us, she very kindly agreed to go to Jabari Omran's old office, and open the safe behind the painting of Queen Nefertari's tomb.'

Doctor Mansour had allowed himself to relax for a moment. At least they had not harmed her, or worse still, brought her here to the safehouse.

'As you can imagine,' the old man had continued. 'Both she and I were somewhat disappointed when it turned out that the safe was empty.'

Doctor Mansour's eyes had widened at this revelation, and his heart rate had increased so much that he could feel the pounding in his neck and his temples.

'What you told us was not true,' the old man had said, his previously calm voice now revealing a hard edge of seething anger.

'I swear,' Doctor Mansour had blurted out. 'It was there. It was there when I opened the safe, and I don't know who else could have…'

He suddenly trailed off, as the realisation hit him.

'Someone else knows,' he whispered.

The old man had nodded slowly, pressing his lips together and looking menacingly at him. 'Someone else knows,' he repeated. 'Now,' he had continued. 'We need to make sure that you are completely focused on the task at hand, so in order to do this, we are going to demonstrate to you just how serious we are about finding the radioactive source.'

The old man had then snapped his fingers, and one of the twins had grabbed his arm in a vice-like grip, while the other twin had produced a syringe. With the efficiency of people who had done this sort of thing many times before, they had quickly injected the contents of the syringe into Doctor Mansour's left index finger. A few seconds later, he had felt how a numb sensation had spread through most of his hand. Then, to his horror, he had watched as one of the twins retrieved a scalpel from a drawer in a nearby console table.

Without hesitating, and helped by his brother, the twin with the scalpel had grabbed Doctor Mansour's hand, held it down onto the table, and then deftly severed the outer-most section of the finger, complete with the nail still attached.

'It is called the Distal Phalanx,' the old man had said dispassionately, pointing to the severed part on the table, and then looking intently into Doctor Mansour's eyes. 'You have nine more.'

Doctor Mansour had been in such a state of shock, that he never even noticed the other twin quickly bandaging up the stump to stop the bleeding.

Despite his almost paralysed state, he was still lucid enough to suddenly feel foolish for having spent so much time worrying about whether they might kill him. He now realised that these men were capable of doing things to him that were much worse than death.

'Now,' said the old man ominously, and produced the smile of a praying mantis about to eat its mate. 'Let's get to work again. Why do you think your friend Khalil and the two brits went to Luxor? What were they looking for?'

The fly twitched and began sucking up the nutrients in the blood that was slowly seeping out of the severed finger.

Twelve

The laptop powered up, and a few minutes later Andrew had established a secure VPN connection to the University of Cambridge, through which the video call would be made. Fiona joined him on the sofa with two cups of coffee and sat down next to him. Out of the corner of his eye, Andrew noticed her adjusting her clothes and flicking her hair back. He turned slightly and smirked.

'You're not going on a date, you know,' he said.

Fiona stopped what she was doing and shot him daggers with her eyes, pretending to be upset.

'Who knows,' she said cheekily. 'He might be even more handsome than you.'

Andrew smiled, shook his head and was about to retort when the call from Cambridge came in. They both snapped to attention and focused on the laptop's screen.

'Here he is. Ready?' asked Andrew.

'Yep,' replied Fiona. 'Let's do this.'

'Mr Lazenby?' said Andrew as the screen came alive, and an image of a well-groomed, middle-aged man appeared. He was smartly dressed with short greying hair cut neatly, a shirt and tie, and he did not look anything like what Andrew had expected from a cosmologist.

'Yes,' exclaimed the man and smiled. 'Can you see me alright?'

'Yes, we can,' replied Andrew. 'Thank you, Professor. My name is Andrew Sterling, and this is my colleague, Fiona Keane. Nice to meet you. I take it Colonel Strickland has provided you with some background on both of us, and what we are investigating?'

'He briefly outlined what you are looking into, yes. Not in any great detail though. It all seems a bit hush-hush, doesn't it?'

'Yes, well,' said Andrew. 'There are limits to what we're at liberty to divulge at this point. However, I think I can safely say that we are looking into whether a terrorist group might have been able to get their hands on radioactive material, so any help you can provide would be greatly appreciated.'

Professor Lazenby nodded gravely. 'Certainly. Anything I can do to help. What would you like to discuss?'

'Well,' said Andrew, furrowing his brow and taking a few seconds to make sure he phrased his question precisely. 'We have indications, that the original source of the radioactive material we're looking for may have been a meteorite.'

Professor Lazenby nodded but did not respond. He seemed to be waiting for more detail.

'So,' continued Andrew. 'This material is supposedly highly radioactive, although we have not been able to secure a sample of it at this point.'

Fiona leaned in towards the screen. 'The only thing we have samples of are small fragments of an alloy that may have been created using part of this original radioactive source. But we can't determine its provenance with any certainty.'

'I see,' nodded Professor Lazenby sagely.

'In a nutshell,' said Andrew. 'We're trying to understand the extent to which something like that is even possible. Has anything like this ever been found, and can such a highly radioactive meteorite even exist?"

Professor Lazenby had been scribbling notes on a piece of paper in front of him and took his time to finish them. He sat for a moment, clearly pondering the question, and then looked up at the camera again.

'Well, nothing like that has been observed in the modern era, as far as I am aware. But I wouldn't rule out that it could happen. Anyway, perhaps I should start by giving you some general background information on this whole topic. It can be quite involved."

'That would be great,' said Fiona. 'I admit, I was not the best student in physics classes in school, so we probably need a little refresher. Right, Andy?'

'Sure,' smiled Andy. 'Can't say I have ever needed to be an expert on things falling from the sky that weren't made by human beings.'

It took a moment for the Professor to understand what Andrew was implying, and then he smiled. 'Ah. Yes, I see what you mean. Anyway, let me just break down the difference between comets, asteroids, meteoroids, meteors and meteorites. A lot of people find this confusing, and I don't blame them, given this nomenclature. I know it might seem pedantic, but I am a bit of a stickler for these things, and it will help us have a more focused conversation.'

'Great,' said Fiona. 'That would be useful.'

'Alright,' said Lazenby and sat up in his chair, clearing his throat.

'Let me just zoom out a little bit and explain what asteroids and comets are. They are basically bodies in space that orbit the sun, either in the Asteroid Belt between Mars and Jupiter, the Kuiper Belt which is beyond the orbit of Neptune, or the Oort Cloud, which is much further out. All three of these consist of extremely large numbers of icy, rocky and metallic bodies. Comets are primarily made of ice, which is why they have a tail that is streaming away from them as they get hit by the Sun's rays. Asteroids on the other hand are mainly rocky and metallic, and those that consist of metals are mainly made of iron and nickel. As far as we know, all of the material in these bodies is as old as our solar system, and essentially just left-over matter that ended up never becoming part of the sun, the planets or the moons.'

Fiona and Andrew were listening attentively, and Fiona was taking notes on a small notepad. Andrew decided that he would be able to remember what the professor said if it was important enough. In any event, the video call was recorded, so they could play it back later if need be.

'A meteoroid is a smaller rocky object that is not part of say the Asteroid Belt, but which is travelling through space on some trajectory. It could be orbiting the sun, or one of the other planets, or it could potentially even be passing through our solar system from another star.'

'From another star?' asked Fiona intrigued.

'Yes, we have observed something like that several times, but it likely happens very regularly. We just don't notice it, because the meteoroids are relatively small and hard to spot.'

'Amazing,' said Fiona.

'It is, isn't it?' said Lazenby. 'Anyway, a meteor is any meteoroid that enters Earth's atmosphere and burns up. This is what people used to call *shooting stars* before we understood what they really are. Lastly, a meteorite is a meteoroid that has made it to the Earth's surface without burning up completely.'

'Ok,' nodded Fiona. 'Meteoroid. Meteor. Meteorite. Got it. So, if we use the term *meteorite* about this possibly radioactive metallic object which we believe fell to the Earth's surface, then we would be using the correct noun?'

'You would,' smiled the professor apologetically. 'Sorry to drag you through this tedious exercise.'

'No, no,' said Fiona. 'It's great to understand these things properly. I am an archaeologist, so I like to think that I adhere to proper scientific processes, including accurate nomenclature.'

Andrew was starting to feel like a third wheel, so he shifted slightly and cleared his throat. 'Sorry,' he said and smiled. 'I guess the Asteroid Belt is the most likely source of these space rocks?'

'Ah, yes,' said the Professor. 'The Asteroid Belt is probably something most people are familiar with. It begins just beyond Mars' orbit and extends roughly halfway out to Jupiter's orbit, so it is between 2 and 3 AU.'

'AU?' said Fiona, looking perplexed.

'Sorry,' exclaimed Lazenby. 'An AU is a so-called Astronomical Unit, which is basically just the average distance from the Earth to the Sun. About 150 million kilometres.'

'I see,' said Fiona, and scribbled away in her notebook.

'So,' continued Lazenby. 'Although there are probably trillions of individual objects in the Asteroid Belt, its combined mass is estimated to be only three or four percent that of the Earth's moon. Surveys have estimated that there are more than 200 asteroids larger than 100 kilometres across, and as many as 2 million that are larger than 1 kilometre. The average size seems to be around 16 kilometres. This may seem like irrelevant information, but it is worth noting that any one of the larger asteroids would be big enough to cause a catastrophic event on this planet if one of them were to impact here.'

'I think we have all watched disaster movies about asteroids,' said Fiona. 'I suppose they carry a huge amount of energy.'

'That's right,' said Lazenby. 'You might remember the meteorite impact over Chelyabinsk in southern Russia a few years ago? We estimate its size to have been no more than 20 meters in diameter, and yet because of its speed of roughly 70,000 kilometres per hour, it released energy equivalent to as much as 500 kilotons of TNT. The atomic bomb over Hiroshima was only 15 kilotons.'

'That's frightening,' said Fiona.

'Indeed,' replied Lazenby. 'The only reason meteorites like that don't create the same amount of destruction as an atomic bomb, is because they almost always come in at a shallow angle, and so they lose a lot of that energy through friction with the atmosphere. This friction also causes ablation, which is essentially the outer layers of the meteorite melting and being ripped off or turned into gas as it tears through the atmosphere. Anyway, you can perhaps imagine the amount of energy that would be released if a very large asteroid were to impact Earth again. An asteroid roughly 10 by 10 kilometres, which would still be smaller than the average asteroid, would release the equivalent of 50 million megatons of TNT. This is more than 3000 times the energy released by the bomb over Hiroshima. As I am sure you're aware, this type of event happened several hundred million years ago, and it ended the reign of the dinosaurs within a few months.'

'How often does a really destructive meteorite hit the Earth?' asked Fiona.

'Well, by their very nature they are impossible to predict since their orbits depend on a multitude of gravitational forces, and most of the time we don't see them until they are here. But in terms of the observed historical frequencies, as a rule of thumb, one 1 metre meteorite hits the earth every year. Roughly one 100-metre meteorite hits the Earth every 10,000 years, and a 10-kilometre meteorite will tend to hit the Earth every 100,000 years. The latter would of course be completely devastating. But these numbers are in no way predictive. It is simply an estimate of the frequency of these events when looked at over millions of years.'

'Still, said Andrew, and rubbed his chin. 'Sobering stuff, and not exactly the sort of threat we are looking into right now though.'

'No,' said Lazenby, and smiled apologetically. 'I tend to get carried away. I'm sorry.'

'It's fine,' said Fiona and nudged Andrew's knee, whilst smiling disarmingly at the professor. 'The more background information we can get the better.'

'Right,' replied Lazenby. 'Anyway, moving on to the Kuiper Belt, this is similar to the Asteroid Belt, but it starts just beyond the orbit of Neptune at roughly 30 AU, and extends to about 50 AU. Unlike the Asteroid Belt, the objects here consist mainly of water ice, methane and ammonia, and it is much more massive. Best estimates are that it is 200 times more massive than the Asteroid Belt. It is thought that there are more than 100,000 objects in the Kuiper Belt that are larger than 100 kilometres across.'

'More objects that could potentially hit the Earth?' said Fiona with an uncertain look on her face.

'In theory, yes,' said Lazenby. 'The likelihood is tiny though. Objects do get ejected out of the Kuiper Belt due to collisions between objects and gravitational influences from planets, but the vast majority get hoovered up again by the much stronger gravitational fields of Jupiter and Saturn.'

'And the Oort Cloud?' asked Fiona.

'The Oort cloud is a bit different, in that it is thought to consists of both a disc that reaches all the way around the Sun, and a sphere of material that envelops the whole solar system. It also consists of mainly icy objects. But it is located at a quite extreme distance from the sun, at least compared with the Asteroid Belt and the Kuiper Belt. Our estimates at the moment, are that it sits in the range of 2,000 to 50,000 AU from the Sun. To put that into perspective, it takes light from the Sun more than 9 months to reach the outer edge of the Oort Cloud.'

'Wow,' smiled Fiona. 'That is amazing. But that doesn't really make it less of a threat, does it?'

'Only in so far as it produces mainly comets, rather than metallic meteoroids, but it could theoretically eject a rocky object that would be able to cause real problems for us here on Earth if it were to ever hit us.'

'I guess that's the next question,' said Andrew. 'What are the chances of something being ejected from one of these three bodies, and sent in the direction of Earth?'

'Well,' replied Lazenby. 'The many objects in the asteroid belt actually makes for a very active environment. Collisions between asteroids probably occur quite frequently on astronomical time scales. We estimate that collisions between bodies with a radius of 10 km happen about once every 10 million years.'

'10 million years is frequent?' asked Andrew sceptically.

'On a time-scale of 4.5 billion years since the creation of the solar system and the asteroid belt, then yes, that is quite frequent.'

'Alright,' said Andrew pensively. 'But what are the actual chances of this happening, and it resulting in an impact here on Earth?'

'Actually,' said Lazenby, spreading out his hands and pressing his lips together. 'Calculating the chance of something specific like that happening is next to impossible. But just in terms of actual observations, we know that it is overwhelmingly likely that anything that falls on Earth comes from the Asteroid Belt. Of the 50,000 meteorites found on Earth to date, 99.8 percent of them are believed to have originated in the Asteroid Belt.'

'In other words, anything falling here on Earth is highly likely to be metallic?' asked Fiona.

'Correct,' said Lazenby. 'As I said, mainly iron and nickel, but there could be lots of different metals and isotopes contained within them, not least gold.'

'Gold?' asked Fiona.

'Yes,' chuckled Lazenby. 'Gold is quite literally one of the by-products of exploding stars, or so-called supernovae. And when the remnants of such former stars eventually start to clump together to form new stars and planets, that gold is included in the mix of materials. This is why we find it all over the Earth in small amounts.'

'So gold is forged inside stars as they explode?' asked Fiona.

'Yes. When stars shine, they do so because of continuous nuclear fusion. Initially, a star is just a giant ball of burning hydrogen. It then fuses hydrogen into helium, which it then burns, and then these turn into things like carbon, silicon and oxygen. And this process continues, in a manner not dissimilar to a decay chain for radioactive materials, except in this case it revolves around nuclear fusion. Anyway, this process goes on until the star has an iron core, which it can't fuse into anything heavier. The fusion process then fizzles out, and at that point, the outward pressure from the nuclear fusion in the star's core weakens and is no longer enough to keep the star inflated, and it then collapses in on itself in a giant explosion, which is what we observe as a supernova. And it is in that moment that very heavy elements like gold and lead and uranium and many others are created. Nothing else in the universe can create those elements.'

'That is really fascinating,' said Fiona excitedly. 'So, if I am wearing gold jewellery, all that gold must necessarily have come from inside a supernova?'

'That's right,' smiled Lazenby. 'Every single atom in that piece of jewellery would have been formed that way. Most likely several billion years ago.'

'Professor Lazenby,' began Andrew.

'Please call me Harold.'

'Ok. Harold,' continued Andrew. 'Getting back to our theory that a radioactive object was ejected from the asteroid belt, and sent on a collision course with Earth. What would your thoughts about that be?'

'Well,' said Lazenby. 'As I said, virtually all of the meteorites that land on Earth, are from the Asteroid Belt, but whether one of them could be radioactive, that is a different question altogether.'

'How do you mean?' asked Andrew.

'Well, most metallic meteorites have very faint traces of radioactive isotopes, and as I am sure you already know, there is the ever-present cosmic background radiation, which is simply the radioactive afterglow of the Big Bang. There are plenty of naturally occurring radioactive isotopes on earth, all of them also from supernovae. But for us to reach sufficiently high concentrations, in order for us to be able to use them for energy production or weapons, they need to go through an enrichment process, which I am sure Andrew is very familiar with. It is quite literally the gateway to weapons-grade uranium and plutonium.'

Andrew nodded. 'Yes. Only too familiar.'

'So, wait.' asked Fiona, almost sounding dejected. 'Are you saying that highly radioactive meteorites are simply not possible?'

'Not exactly,' replied Lazenby hesitantly, clearly pondering the issue as he spoke. 'If we are talking about highly radioactive metals sitting in the Asteroid Belt, and then being ejected at some point and impacting on Earth, then I would say that is very unlikely, and not something we have ever seen before. Radioactive materials typically only exist in very low concentrations naturally, simply because they constitute a very tiny percentage of the matter that ends up forming new stars and planets, and they tend to be distributed fairly evenly in a so-called accretion disc around a newly forming star.'

'So, how is it possible then?' asked Fiona perplexed. 'I am sure you said that it definitely wasn't *im*-possible.'

'Well,' said Lazenby, and shifted in his chair, with a smile on his face that told the story of him having had this conversation a few times before.

'This is somewhat controversial,' he began. 'But I and a few other colleagues have been working on a new theoretical concept that we are currently performing computer simulations on. We call it ECRIC, and it is a rather a novel idea in cosmology.'

'What an acronym,' smiled Fiona.

'Yes,' chuckled Lazenby. 'We realise that, but at least it is catchy. Anyway, it is short for Extreme Cosmogenic Radioactive Isotope Creation.'

'Lovely,' said Fiona, and laughed. 'Sounds like a Nobel prize to me.'

Lazenby laughed out loud and waved defensively with his hands. 'Let's not get ahead of ourselves. This is still very much in the theoretical phase.'

'So, what is it then,' asked Fiona, clearly excited by this discussion with a fellow academic.

'As the name implies,' said Lazenby, 'our framework describes the creation of highly radioactive isotopes, typically inside asteroids, while they are in space. The basic idea is that high energy particles like protons, or similarly high energy electromagnetic waves, hit an object like an asteroid. Because of the extreme levels of energy being imparted on the asteroid, it basically becomes radioactive.'

'Sounds complicated. How exactly does that work?' asked Fiona.

'Some scientists are actually using it already in the field of geochronology here on Earth, which is the science of dating the formation of certain geological features like volcanoes. Here's how it works. When cosmic rays hit the earth, radioactive isotopes like Beryllium-10 are created through a process called spallation, whereby cosmic radiation ejects a number of protons and neutrons from an atom, leaving it unstable and therefore radioactive. Since we know that the half-life of Beryllium-10 is 1.6 million years, and since only the first few centimetres of rock is ever exposed to the radiation, the concentration of Beryllium-10 on a rock's surface, versus the concentration in its interior, lets us calculate how long a particular piece of rock has been irradiated. In principle, there is no reason why this same process could not happen in space as well, quite possibly producing radiation levels that are orders of magnitude more powerful.'

Fiona narrowed her eyes, trying to grapple with the concept. 'But for a material to become extremely highly radioactive, you would need correspondingly high levels of energy, wouldn't you?

'Precisely,' replied Lazenby. 'Simple background radiation is not enough, and the energy from the Sun, as impressive as it is, is also not nearly enough.'

'So, are there any such sources of very high energy in the cosmos?' asked Fiona.

Lazenby nodded affirmatively. 'That is exactly what our research has been focussing on. The one thing in the universe that emits more energy than anything else, is a so-called gamma-ray burst.'

'I think I have heard of those,' said Fiona. 'They are pretty dangerous, right?'

'That is probably the understatement of the year,' smiled Lazenby. 'I think perhaps Andrew might appreciate the back-story, given his line of work.'

'Oh?' said Andrew. 'How do you mean?'

'Well, you see,' said Lazenby. 'They were first discovered by accident in 1967, by two satellites called Vela 3 and Vela 4, which had been launched by the United States. The US and the USSR had signed the Nuclear Test Ban Treaty in 1963, but the US was concerned that the USSR would not adhere to the treaty. They therefore launched a number of satellites that had been designed to detect gamma rays from nuclear explosions deep inside Soviet territory.'

Andrew nodded. 'Yes. That is something that is still carried out on a continuous basis.'

'Indeed,' said Lazenby. 'Anyway, in July 1967 two of them picked up a gamma-ray signal, but it turned out to have a different signature than expected, and it seemed to be coming from deep space.'

'How intriguing,' said Fiona. 'So, what was it?'

'It was our old friend the supernova,' said Lazenby. 'When a sufficiently large star reaches the end of its life and implodes in a supernova event, it becomes a so-called neutron star. And when two of those collide, that is enough to produce one of these extremely energetic gamma-ray bursts.'

'How often do these things happen?' asked Andrew.

'Our best estimates are that it happens roughly once per day somewhere in the universe.'

'Wow, that is a lot,' exclaimed Fiona. 'But you mentioned that no gamma-ray bursts have been observed in our galaxy. Surely that is just an accident.'

'That is correct,' said Lazenby. 'There is no reason why it couldn't happen in our galaxy too. In fact, it probably has happened thousands of times since humans first walked the Earth. The closest gamma-ray burst that we have observed was outside of our galaxy some 1.3 billion light-years away, so that is an immense distance. This is also the reason we haven't suffered any ill effects from something like that yet. At least not as far as we know.'

'But I suppose it could be considered an existential threat to the planet?' asked Andrew.

'That's right,' replied Lazenby. 'It could probably more or less sterilise a planet like ours if it happened sufficiently close to us. By this I mean, it would more or less wipe out all life. Gamma rays are so-called ionising radiation, which means they carry extremely high levels of energy and can ionise atoms, which essentially means they can add or remove electrons from atoms, including those inside our cells and our DNA. This in turn makes them lethal, because ionised atoms in the molecules that make up our cells and DNA can behave very differently from non-ionised atoms. Their chemical properties simply change, and this renders our normal biochemistry altered and effectively non-functioning. At a molecular level, this is what radiation sickness stems from. And once the damage is done, it is very difficult for the body to repair itself.'

Andrew and Fiona looked at each other with grim faces.

'This is something we have heard about already,' said Fiona. 'It is horrid business.'

'In addition,' continued Lazenby. 'For reasons that are poorly understood at the moment, the bursts seem to be directional. This means that the majority of the gamma radiation is released in a narrow cone, like around the axis of rotation of the burst, making it even more perilous to be in the way of that barrage of radiation.'

'So precisely how does that tie into the notion of radioactive meteorites?' asked Andrew, who was starting to feel overwhelmed by the volume of information the professor was throwing at them.

'Well, gamma-ray bursts are only one component of our theory. Another crucial piece is the notion of interstellar objects. As I have explained, there are trillions of objects orbiting the sun in addition to all the planets and moons. Sometimes a star will pass close enough to another star for objects in one star's orbit to become perturbed and end up being pulled out of orbit and flung into interstellar space. This is a well-established phenomenon. There is even quite solid science suggesting that entire planets could be pulled out of their orbits around their local star.'

'That sounds terrifying,' said Fiona, and looked at Andrew.

'It is a slightly chilling prospect, I agree,' said Lazenby. 'But this is thought to happen very rarely, and we would definitely see it coming. Anyway, what certainly happens all the time is that asteroids are ejected from a star system, and end up flying through interstellar space for millions or even billions of years before being captured by the gravitational pull of another star. And this, combined with gamma-ray bursts, is the key to our theory.'

'Oh, I think I see where this is going,' smiled Fiona.

The professor nodded approvingly and smiled. 'Yes. What we propose is that such an interstellar object, like a metallic meteoroid, could find itself exposed to not just one, but multiple gamma-ray bursts as it traverses interstellar space over the course of millions of years. Theoretically, such an object could end up becoming exceptionally highly irradiated. It is also perfectly conceivable that such an object could be captured by the gravitational pull of a star like ours, and end up slamming into Earth at some point. Given that some radioactive elements have half-lives of millions of years, it could then still be highly radioactive as it impacted our planet, and for a long period thereafter.'

'But,' interjected Fiona. 'Is it actually possible that an interstellar object like that could get hit by multiple gamma-ray bursts?'

'Yes, of course.' said Lazenby emphatically. 'It may seem like one gamma-ray burst per day in the entire universe is not very much. And granted, on the scale of a human lifetime, the creation of supernovae and neutron stars are somewhat rare occurrences. However, on a galactic time scale, gamma-ray bursts are an almost continuous cacophony of explosions, happening virtually all the time. Since the formation of our own solar system, there have been on the order of 12 million gamma-ray bursts. Because of the size of the known universe, which is around 93 billion light-years across, this means that at any given time, there are millions of waves of gamma radiation, travelling through space at the speed of light. Having shot out from a pair of colliding neutron stars, and racing across the galaxy, they will end up crisscrossing each other's paths and intersecting in what we call Gamma-Ray Hot Spots.'

'So, these would be areas of unusually high levels of radiation?' asked Fiona.

'In a sense yes,' replied Lazenby. 'They aren't exactly *areas* as such, since the waves of radiation are travelling at the speed of light, but where the waves do intersect, the gamma-ray intensity could be extreme. Think of the waves in a pond if you drop two stones in it. Where the waves meet, they will tend to rise up more. The same principle applies to so-called *rogue waves*, which are regularly observed by shipping in the open ocean. Even on relatively calm days, suddenly a giant wave is observed travelling across the surface of the ocean. Those waves are simply multiple smaller waves with different frequencies that just happen to have converged on the same small spot in the ocean, creating an abnormally high wave.'

'So those gamma-ray hot spots are analogous to rogue ocean waves?' asked Andrew.

'Yes,' nodded Lazenby. 'And they can probably be quite intense. Especially considering that, due to the long initial duration of the neutron star collision, some of these waves can take several hours to pass through a volume of space. So, if you imagine a metallic meteoroid passing through one or more of those hot spots, it is clear that it could end up becoming exceptionally radioactive. It is even possible that entirely new radioactive isotopes might be created, which may turn out to have very long half-lives.'

'That is quite a fascinating idea,' said Fiona, clearly taken with the magnitude of what Professor Lazenby had explained. 'I shudder to think what would happen if a planet like ours found itself in one of those hot spots. I guess it would be all over for organic life there.'

'Probably,' said Lazenby. 'Although planets like ours have molten iron interiors, which give them a strong magnetic field, which in turn provides some protection from cosmic radiation. However, an interplanetary meteoroid would not have such protection, and so would end up absorbing the entire blast of gamma rays.'

Fiona shifted forward slightly on the sofa as if to get closer to the professor. 'You mentioned the idea of gamma-ray bursts creating entirely new radioactive isotopes in interstellar meteoroids. Is that likely to be possible?'

'I certainly wouldn't rule it out,' said Lazenby. 'As I said earlier, the creation of heavy elements requires such immense amounts of energy, in the form of temperature or pressure or both, that they can only be formed inside exploding stars.'

'Except,' said Fiona, and raised her hand cautiously. 'There is a Russian nuclear research lab that has succeeded in creating entirely new elements inside particle accelerators.'

Professor Lazenby hesitated for a brief moment, and then he produced an approving smile. 'The Flerov Laboratory. You certainly have done your homework, Miss Keane.'

Fiona sat up slightly and beamed.

'And you are right,' continued the professor. 'However, as I am sure you know, those new elements have proven highly unstable and short-lived. But who knows what multiple blasts of the most energetic radiation in the known universe might do to an asteroid. I believe new elements are perfectly possible in that scenario, and by implication, this could mean completely new types of radioactive isotopes.'

Fiona nodded and sat pensively for a few moments. 'I think that covers all the questions I had for you, Professor,' she said and looked up at the screen with a smile. 'Do you have anything else, Andy?'

Andrew shook his head. 'No, I think we have a lot to work with here. It seems like we have been moving in the right direction. Thank you very much for your time, Professor.'

'Harold, please,' smiled Lazenby benignly. 'It was my pleasure.'

'Have a lovely day,' said Fiona, and then she ended the video call.

They both sat silently for a few moments, reflecting on the conversation. Then Andrew leaned back in the sofa and exhaled heavily. 'That was pretty intense. There's a lot of information there to try to get your head around.'

'I agree,' smiled Fiona. 'As I said, physics was never really my strong suit.'

'You did really well,' said Andrew and looked at her. 'If it had just been me, I would probably never have been able to ask the questions you did.'

'Thank you,' she said and returned his smile. 'I guess I am used to absorbing large amounts of information. Anyway, it seems to me that everything Omran speculated might be true, actually turns out to be perfectly possible. I think we have now established that a meteoroid, such as the one described in the ancient Egyptian legends, is not necessarily a fictional object. It could really have happened.'

'I agree,' said Andrew. 'I suppose the next step is to try to find out if it is possible that such an object could have ended up in the Ark of the Covenant, and then brought with the Israelites out of Egypt.'

'I guess we will have to wait until we get to Jerusalem,' said Fiona. 'But I think we both need a bit of time to try to relax and think about all these different pieces of information. I am starting to see why Omran took such extensive notes.'

'Yes. Me too,' said Andrew.

'I keep coming back to what might have happened to Doctor Mansour,' said Fiona, looking concerned.

'I know,' said Andrew. 'There's only one way to try to work that out, and that is to keep pushing ahead and keep trying to solve Omran's mystery.'

Thirteen

Andrew and Fiona had just finished breakfast and were standing in an elevator taking them to the 10th floor of their hotel.

'Since our flight is not until late this afternoon,' said Fiona, 'I thought we might take the opportunity to go and see the city.'

Andrew looked sceptically at Fiona. 'Are you sure you want to go gallivanting around Cairo after what happened in Luxor?'

'Sure,' she replied and shrugged. 'We can't stay here the whole time. Isn't that what you people say about terrorism all the time? If we start behaving as if they have terrorised us, then they will have won.'

'I suppose,' grumbled Andrew. He did not relish the idea of Fiona subjecting herself to unnecessary risks. He felt confident that he would be able to handle himself, but looking after someone else who did not have combat training if something was to happen, was a whole different matter.

'Besides,' she said. 'I've got you to look after us. Just look like you're carrying a weapon, but don't look like you're about to murder someone, ok? I am sure you chaps have a way of doing that.'

Andrew shook his head with a wry smile. Fiona had a way of getting what she wanted.

'Alright,' conceded Andrew. 'I guess you're right. Where do you want to go? I am sure you have a long list of places you would like to see.'

'I do,' replied Fiona, 'But you just can't go to Cairo and not see the Egyptian Museum. It is like the National Museum in London, but bigger and with much older stuff.'

'Older stuff?' asked Andrew teasingly. 'Sounds very science-like.'

'Shut up,' she laughed. 'You know what I mean.'

'Alright then,' said Andrew as the elevator door opened on their floor. 'Egyptian Museum it is. Where in the city is it?'

'It is just a couple of kilometres south of here along the Nile. Shall we walk?

Andrew hesitated. His instincts told him this was not a good idea.

'Let's get a taxi,' he said. 'I don't want to be walking in the middle of the day. I will be soaking with sweat by the time we get there.'

'Ok. Fine,' Fiona replied, heading into the bathroom. 'Let's get a taxi then. I will phone the reception to make sure one is waiting for us in 10 minutes. Chop chop!'

Right on time, a white taxi with a thin strip of black and white chequered patterns running along its sides pulled into the hotel's drive. The concierge showed them out and told the driver where they needed to go. The driver nodded and gesticulated impatiently that he had understood the instructions.

'Ok?' he shouted, turning his head towards the two new passengers now sitting in the back of his taxi. His English was clearly just enough for basic communication with tourists.

'Ok,' said Andrew and shot him a smile and a thumbs up.

'Ok,' confirmed the driver, and took off as if he would be paid more to get there fast.

'I guess not everyone here speaks English as well as Khalil and Doctor Zaki,' smiled Andrew.

'No,' said Fiona. 'I read in a guide book about Cairo that most people here speak some English, but in Egypt as a whole, English proficiency is rated as "very low" by international standards, apparently. Can't really blame them after Suez. I know that was a long time ago, but still. There has got to be some animosity still there.'

'Probably,' said Andrew, looking out the window at the Nile sweeping past immediately to their right. 'It's not like we've let the Germans off the hook yet after World War Two.'

He briefly glanced back out through the rear window of the taxi. Traffic was picking up at this time of day, and he noticed that there were a few black limousines with diplomatic plates driving around central Cairo. One such vehicle, a large Range Rover with heavily tinted windows, was fifty meters behind them.

Fiona looked pensive for a moment as she looked out at the river. 'Did you know,' she said, 'that Egypt's official name is *Junhuriyah Misr al-Arabiyah*?'

'That's quite a mouthful,' replied Andrew. 'Something about Arabia?'

'It is obviously Arabic, and means the Arab Republic of Egypt,' replied Fiona. 'And the word *Misr* is the Egyptian Arabic name for Egypt. This is actually the original ancient name for this country. It is derived from the Aramaic name *Mizraim* who was the second son of Ham, who in turn was the son of Noah. You know, Noah from the Bible?'

'Oh him. Yes. The geezer with the boat,' said Andrew and shot her an irreverent look.

Fiona shook her head with a smile and sighed. 'Yes. The *geezer* with the boat,' she replied, sounding weary. 'Anyway, Egypt is actually described in The Book of Genesis as the Land of Ham, since he settled here with his second son Mizraim and his people. As for the English word *Egypt*, it was initially coined by the Greeks who ruled over the land in the roughly 300 years leading up to the year 0 BCE, under Alexander the Great. It is derived from the Greek word *Aegyptos*, which is a contraction of the term *Hi-Gi-Ptos*, which itself is a transliteration of the ancient Egyptian term *Het-Ka-Ptah*, which meant "Temple of the Soul of Ptah". Ptah being a tribal god in the city of Memphis in ancient Egypt.'

'How you manage to remember things like this is beyond me,' smiled Andrew.

'Anyway,' said Fiona. 'The Greek word *Aegyptos* clearly caught on with English speakers, and the rest is history, quite literally.'

'Your memory is frighteningly good,' said Andrew, looking impressed. 'How do you do it?'

'I don't know,' said Fiona and smiled coyly. 'If something is worth remembering, then I just remember it. You know, like your birthday.'

'Cute,' said Andrew and took her hand. 'Very cute. Right. It seems we're here.'

The taxi drove off the main southbound road on the east side of the Nile and entered the pick-up and drop-off bays at the Egyptian Museum.

The driver tapped the meter and turned to Andrew. 'Ok?'

Andrew nodded and fished out some cash from his inside jacket pocket. 'Ok!'

They got out of the taxi and headed towards the main building. A three-storey building, painted in a distinctive salmon pink colour, the Egyptian Museum was designed by the French architect Marcel Dourgnon and was completed in 1902.

'Quite the colour,' smirked Andrew at Fiona.

'Yes,' she laughed. 'It certainly stands out.'

'So, what's in there?' asked Andrew and gestured towards the building.

'In a nutshell, about 120,000 items mainly from ancient times.'

'That sounds like a lot,' said Andrew. 'I don't think we will have time for all that.'

'Don't worry,' replied Fiona. 'They only have a fraction of them out on display at any given time.'

'Phew,' laughed Andrew. 'I was worried I was going to have to man-handle you out of there at closing time. I have a feeling you could spend days in there.'

Fiona laughed, then took his hand and gave him a coy smile. 'Well, aside from being man-handled, I think I would probably object loudly to being removed from the premises.'

Fiona got two tickets for the museum from the ticket machine by the taxi drop-off. As they walked towards the front of the museum's main building, a guard who saw them approach got up slowly from his chair and walked lazily towards the turnstiles that they would have to pass through. Like all the guards at the museum, he was wearing a badly fitted black uniform and a beret, but he seemed to be unarmed, except for a baton attached to his belt. Seeming distinctly disinterested, and without making eye contact, he gave their tickets a cursory glance and waved them through.

'Top-notch security around here,' whispered Andrew with a sarcastic smile as they proceeded towards the entrance, 'That guy seemed like he was half asleep.'

'You think someone would try to steal the artefacts from here?' asked Fiona sceptically.

'I guess you can't rule it out,' replied Andrew. 'But I was referring to the fact that I have a firearm strapped to my side under my jacket, and he didn't even notice. I was also thinking about this place as a potential terrorist target. It is full of foreign tourists all day, and it is extremely easily accessible from the streets surrounding it. Tahrir Square is just behind it.'

'Alright, you,' said Fiona, and took his hand. 'Let's try to relax and just enjoy the experience. Snap out of work mode for a few minutes, will you?'

'Sorry,' smiled Andrew. 'Old dogs, new tricks and all that.'

They walked up the eight steps to the main entrance and entered the foyer. Inside it, were another couple of guards who were manning a metal detector.

'Let me just have a quick word with them.' said Andrew. 'I'm guessing this guy is the most senior chap here.'

Fiona waited just inside the building, while Andrew walked over to the guard who appeared to be the oldest, and who had the most impressive moustache. The two of them had a quick exchange, as Andrew handed him his firearms permit. After a couple of minutes and a phone call, the senior guard nodded and motioned for them both to proceed towards the metal detector.

One of the guards took Andrew's gun and placed it in a plastic tray on a shelf next to the metal detector. Then they were both waved through, and found themselves at a T-junction of three wide corridors, one straight ahead and the other two going left and right respectively. The ceilings were at least five meters above them, and the many columns and arches gave the impression of it being a temple of some sort.

'Let's go upstairs first,' said Fiona and pointed to the stairs leading up to the first floor. 'That's where they keep all the artefacts from Tutankhamun's tomb. That is definitely worth seeing.'

'Alright,' said Andrew, and found himself subconsciously moving his right hand to the left side of his chest where the empty gun holster was.

'I have already seen some of these things a few years ago,' said Fiona. 'The contents of his tomb were sent on a world tour, and exhibited in lots of different capitals around the world.'

'Sounds like a risky thing to do,' said Andrew. 'I hope they didn't break anything along the way.'

'I know,' smiled Fiona as they made their way up the stairs. 'Some of the items are big, like this one.'

As they had reached the landing at the top of the stairs, Fiona was already moving towards a large glass display box, roughly five by three metres.

'Tutankhamun's sarcophagus was found inside his tomb in the Valley of Kings in Thebes. It consisted of three coffins placed inside each other. This is the outer-most coffin.'

'A bit like Russian nesting dolls?' asked Andrew.

'Yes,' replied Fiona. 'Exactly like that, except the coffins were themselves placed inside four huge gilded wooden boxes. An extremely elaborate burial, especially considering that he died at the tender age of eighteen'.

'Wow,' said Andrew. 'Not many eighteen-year-olds today would get a burial like that.'

'The inner coffin was actually made of solid gold. It weighs more than one hundred and ten kilos.'

'Over one hundred kilos of gold just sitting in that tomb for more than three thousand years,' mused Andrew as he was inspecting the coffin. 'I wonder what that would be worth if it was melted down.'

'Melted down?' exclaimed Fiona. 'You absolute savage.'

'I was just wondering,' laughed Andrew and held up his hands defensively.

Fiona shook her head. 'Well. I am not exactly sure, but I am guessing in the region of five million dollars, give or take.'

'They really do need more guards here,' said Andrew.

Fiona moved along to another set of even larger display cases. 'These four gilded boxes, also called shrines, housed the three coffins,' she said. 'Yet more gold. And have a look at the sides.'

Andrew came over and stood next to her. 'What am I looking for?' he asked.

Fiona pointed to the gleaming gilded motif on the side of the wooden shrine. 'What do you see here?'

It took a moment for Andrew to realise what it was. There was an image of two winged creatures standing at either end of one side of the shrine, facing each other with their wings held up and out in front of them.

'Cherubim?' exclaimed Andrew. 'Like on the Ark of the Covenant.'

'Or something very similar,' replied Fiona. 'Just like we found at Medinet Habu in Thebes.'

'Amazing,' said Andrew. 'I feel like we are actually connecting some dots here.'

'Perhaps,' smiled Fiona, sounding, on the one hand, sceptical, and on the other like she wanted to believe him. 'There are definitely themes that seem to repeat across time and space in this whole affair.'

'I wonder what else is in here,' said Andrew, looking around the corridor. 'Was all of this stuff taken from tombs?'

'Yes, almost all of it. When you think about it,' said Fiona, looking pensive, 'this whole floor of the museum could be said to represent a type of desecration of King Tutankhamun's grave.'

'That is a bit harsh, isn't it?' asked Andrew. 'How do you mean?'

'Just look around you,' she replied and gestured to all the display cases, containing gold jewellery and other items. 'Everything you see here was placed in a tomb, with the intention of never seeing the light of day again. All these items had some significance to the dead king, and many were specifically intended to aid him in his transition to the next stage of existence. From the perspective of ancient Egyptians, removing those items and placing them here in this building for thousands of people to gawk at, would seem like a desecration and a humiliation of this highly revered king.'

'You are obviously right about that,' said Andrew. 'But without these sorts of displays, someone like you may never have become an archaeologist.'

'I understand that,' said Fiona reluctantly. 'But I still feel a sense of sacrilege watching his tomb having been disassembled and spread out like this. It somehow seems undignified. Some of the artefacts are even in other countries. On the plus side though, it is easy to make the case that an understanding of the past facilitates an understanding of the present and the future, so it does serve a larger purpose than just curiosity and spectacle.'

'Absolutely,' said Andrew. 'Without that Rosetta Stone, we would still be in the dark about what all the hieroglyphic writings mean.'

'More importantly,' said Fiona. 'I think the study of the rise and fall of empires and dynasties provide important lessons in how corruption, greed and mismanagement can doom an otherwise thriving civilisation. There is no reason to believe that those sorts of things won't happen many more times in the future. The only question is, which empire will fall next?'

'Interesting perspective,' said Andrew. 'I guess most people don't think along those lines. They just assume that everything will stay the way it is indefinitely.'

'That's right,' said Fiona. 'And yet every single person that has ever lived, would be shocked and confused if they were brought back to life, by the way the world looks now, compared with when they were alive. I guess, the problem is that we humans live for a very short amount of time, so we mostly fail to see how dynamic the world actually is, and how much it is capable of changing over just a few centuries.'

'That's a good point,' said Andrew, and proceeded another few steps along the wide corridor to another display case. 'Look at this. This must be Tutankhamun's funerary mask.'

The funerary mask had been made to fit the head of the Pharaoh, and was made of solid gold, and decorated with semi-precious stones. It includes blue stripes to depict the *nemes* headdress, worn by pharaohs in ancient Egypt, and it portrays the young pharaoh as a strong and decisive leader.

'Such craftsmanship,' said Fiona. 'This is probably one of the best-known pieces of art from ancient Egypt.'

'It is very impressive,' said Andrew and leaned closer to inspect it. 'How did he end up dying that young?'

'There have been various theories, but he seemed to be in generally poor health from birth. He had scoliosis and so his spine was unnaturally curved, his left foot was flat and his right foot was clubbed, and genetic testing has revealed traces of two different strains of the malaria parasite. This may ultimately have been the cause of death, but he was by all accounts a very frail boy.'

Andrew stared at the coffin for a few seconds. 'That somehow makes the whole thing feel a lot more real, all of a sudden. This was an actual human being. His parents no doubt grieving after his death.'

'Yes,' nodded Fiona. 'It was a very short life, and probably not an easy one. Even though he was supposedly the omnipotent Pharaoh, he might have dreamed of being a normal healthy boy, without the responsibility of being king. Who knows?'

'Right,' said Andrew and tugged gently at Fiona's sleeve to nudge her out of her reverie. 'Let's have a look in here,' he said and gestured towards a room off to the side. 'It says *Jewellery*,' he said in as enticing a voice as he could muster.

'You sound like a shifty real estate agent,' scoffed Fiona.

'Are there any other kinds?' asked Andrew and raised his eyebrows.

'Good point,' chuckled Fiona. 'Let's have a look at the jewellery then.'

In the side room, there were several long display cases arranged, one next to the other along all four walls. All of them were full of gold jewellery in the form of bracelets, necklaces and rings.

'They really did have access to a lot of gold,' said Andrew. 'Is it fair to say that mankind's fascination with gold started in ancient Egypt?'

'Quite possibly,' replied Fiona. 'Either here, or further south in Upper Egypt or Sudan where much of it was mined.'

'I can't believe how much is in just this room,' said Andrew. 'I might have to revise my opinion about the likelihood of someone trying to rob the place.'

'Oh, that reminds me,' said Fiona. 'You remember Professor Lazenby from the Kavli Institute for Cosmology.'

'Of course,' replied Andrew. 'What about him?'

'Well,' said Fiona. 'Remember when he said that gold was one of the heavy metals that can only be produced inside supernovae, and that heavy elements like that are distributed fairly evenly but in tiny amounts across the universe, including on this planet?'

'Sure,' said Andrew and leaned down to inspect an intricately ornamented bracelet.

'Well, that begs the question; How does gold end up being so concentrated in certain places here on Earth, that we can literally find huge nuggets of it in the gold veins?'

'Let me guess,' smiled Andrew. 'You've already worked it out?'

'Not exactly,' replied Fiona and laughed. 'But I have Googled it.'

'Alright,' said Andrew. 'How does it work then?'

'Well,' said Fiona. 'Like most things, it is simple when you break it down. The key is in the fact that gold is found in gold veins. These are long fractures in the bedrock, deep inside the earth. A team of researchers that I read about, examined gold deposits from British Columbia where the average gold vein is around 10 centimetres across, or roughly the thickness of a drinks coaster.'

'Wow,' said Andrew. 'That is incredible.'

'Yes. Especially considering what they found next. It turns out that in its original state, following a supernova, gold exists in tiny spheres just one to five nanometres across. That's just a few billionths of a meter. The spheres clump together or *flocculate*. These clumps then become suspended in water from what are called hydrothermal fluids, which is essentially just hot water inside the earth's crust, mixed with lots of different minerals and metals. These fluids then deposit the tiny gold specks inside the fractures in the rock, and over time, it results in a solid vein of gold. This process obviously takes millions of years, but eventually, you end up with extremely high concentrations of gold. Through tectonic processes, some of the rock eventually makes it up to the surface of the planet to make mountains, and that is when the gold veins become accessible to us.'

'Fascinating,' said Andrew. 'I almost feel like taking up gold prospecting in my spare time.'

As they exited the side room and emerged back out into the corridor, Fiona spotted something inside a long thin display case that was sitting in the middle of the corridor.

'Oh wow!' she said excitedly and hurried over to it. 'Look at this.'

Andrew joined her and looked inside the display case, where an ornately decorated gilded shrine with sloped sides sat, measuring roughly one and a half meters in length, and half a meter in width. On top of the shrine was what looked like a jet-black jackal, lying on its belly with its paws out in front of it, and its head held high. Its collar, eyes and ears were covered in a beautiful golden veneer.

'This is the portable simulacrum of Anubis, the jackal god of embalming and the dead,' said Fiona. 'Isn't it gorgeous?'

'Yes, but look down there,' said Andrew and pointed to the bottom of the sides of the shrine. 'Two staves for carrying it. It looks an awful lot like the Ark of the Covenant, don't you think?'

'Absolutely,' nodded Fiona, and peered at the intricate details of the gilded shrine. 'What was it you said a few days ago about seeing patterns? I am starting to understand exactly what you mean.'

'This place is amazing. Come on,' said Andrew, as he started walking slowly along the corridor. 'Let's see what is downstairs.'

'Am I mistaken,' said Fiona inquisitively, 'or are you starting to become really interested in this?'

'What do you mean?' said Andrew, walking backwards with his arms held out to the sides. 'I am always interested in interesting things. Just look at you. You're interesting.'

The two of them headed downstairs. Coming back down and out of the stairwell, they proceeded into the large central room, that housed various stone sarcophagi from the earliest Egyptian dynasties. At one end of the hall was placed a small black pyramid with a base of roughly one by one meter. Its sides were decorated with hieroglyphs, which had been with chiselled into its sloped sides.

'This is the *pyramidion* of the Pyramid of Amenemhat III,' said Fiona. 'It was recovered from Dahshur, about forty kilometres south of Cairo along the Nile. That location contains some of the oldest pyramids in Egypt.'

'What is a pyramidion?' asked Andrew and walked closer to inspect it.

'It is the capstone at the very top of a pyramid. They were typically covered in gold to reflect the sun's rays. You can imagine how spectacular that would have looked during sunrise and sunset.'

'Pyramids have a very appealing shape, don't they?' said Andrew, and studied the capstone while tilting his head to one side. 'It just seems like a perfect shape.'

'I agree,' smiled Fiona. 'Do you remember from your school days what Pi is?'

Andrew looked at her suspiciously. 'Where is this going?'

'Relax,' laughed Fiona. 'This is not a test. And I won't give you homework.'

'Alright, I'll bite,' replied Andrew and sighed. 'It's something to do with a circle. I can't say it has ever made a difference to me at any point in my life.'

'You might think so, but I am sure it has. Anyway, Pi is simply the length of the circumference of a circle with a diameter of 1.'

'I am sure you're going somewhere with this,' said Andrew.

'This means that if you divide the circumference of a circle with its radius, you obviously get two times Pi.'

'So?' said Andrew, looking perplexed.

'So,' continued Fiona. 'If you divide the circumference of the Great Pyramid of Khufu by its height, you get a number very close to two times Pi. Isn't that amazing?'

'Yes,' replied Andrew. 'I guess what it tells us is that ancient civilisations were more advanced than most people realise.'

Fiona suddenly started walking briskly towards what looked like a tall headstone on a plinth, with imagery at the top, and small inscriptions covering its entire front.

'This is the famous Merneptah Stele,' she said, looking over her shoulder towards Andrew. 'It was discovered in Karnak near Thebes in 1896, and it is over three meters tall, and believed to be from around 1208 BCE. We know this because it recounts the exploits of Pharaoh Merneptah, who was Ramesses II's predecessor.'

'What's so special about it?' asked Andrew and started to walk around it whilst studying it.

'It is also called the Israel Stele, because it contains here at the bottom the earliest reference to Israel ever found.' Fiona pointed to the last line of text on the stele.

'In 1208 BCE? What does it say?' asked Andrew, and joined her to inspect the bottom of the tall granite monolith.

'It talks about how several cities in both the north and the south of Canaan have been plundered and subjugated. These are listed by name, and refer to places we know existed at the time in what is today Gaza and Syria. And then it goes on to say on the second to last line: *Israel is laid waste and his seed is not.* It uses the determinative for 'people' instead of 'cities' when referring to Israel, so this essentially means that the Israelites were wiped from the face of the Earth.'

'Not to be flippant about this,' said Andrew. 'But I think the Israelis today would disagree with that statement.'

'Well, ancient Egyptian pharaohs were notorious for exaggerating when describing and recording their own military exploits. Much, if not all of it, was probably for domestic political consumption.'

'So, not much different from how things work in the modern world then?' said Andrew and sighed.

'That's right,' replied Fiona ruefully. 'But what it demonstrates is that there was a known entity in Canaan at the time, referred to as Israel.'

'Oh, I think I understand now,' said Andrew and looked at Fiona.

'Exactly,' she nodded affirmatively. 'If the people of Israel were a known quantity in 1208 BCE, then it is at least conceivable that their presence in Canaan was the result of an Exodus from Egypt, around say half a century earlier around 1250 BCE. It is fascinating to think that Egypt's ancient history spans so many millennia, that when looked at in its entirety, this country has only been Muslim for about twenty percent of its history, depending on when you start counting. The vast majority of its history was spent in the ancient Egyptian era.'

'I have to admit,' said Andrew, 'I feel like I have a new appreciation for your line of work.'

'Really?' smiled Fiona suspiciously, expecting some clever joke or sarcastic put-down.

'Yes,' said Andrew emphatically. 'It really is amazing what is kept in this building. I am still trying to get my head around just how old some of these things are.'

'I am glad you can get a little bit excited about archaeology,' replied Fiona. 'Most people think it is as boring as anything.'

'If I spent another six hours in here, I might start to feel a bit like them,' smiled Andrew. 'But in small doses, I can appreciate it. Anyway, shall we leave? I think we have seen what there is to see.'

'Sure,' replied Fiona. 'Let's go.'

They headed towards the exit, where the senior security guard made Andrew sign a form, after which he handed him back his gun. Andrew slotted it back into its holster under his jacket and instantly felt more complete. As if he had been walking around inside the museum, missing an item of clothing.

As they exited the building, he now felt fully dressed again.

Fourteen

The man had been sitting in the black Range Rover for over an hour and was beginning to become concerned that the two Europeans might have slipped out of a back entrance. But why would they do that, unless they had discovered that they were being followed?

He was sure that he had not been spotted at their hotel. He had been parked around a bend in the road, about fifty meters from the hotel entrance, and he had only started following them after the bell boy had sent him a text message to say that they had just got into a taxi.

At that point, he had slipped in behind them at a reasonable distance, and driven south along the Nile in as inconspicuous a manner as he had been able to. He had kept a distance of around one hundred meters for most of the journey, and he had even made sure to continue on past the Egyptian Museum and round Tahrir Square a couple of times, before finally parking off to one side behind some trees in the museum car park.

They had discussed whether he should follow them inside, but after the incident at Medinet Habu in Luxor, his boss had told him to stay well back and not draw any unnecessary attention to himself. Judging from their body language when they had entered the museum, they both seemed relaxed, and he felt confident that they did not suspect that they were being followed. The SAS soldier clearly seemed to be distracted by the woman he was travelling with, and the man in the car was sure that this could be used to his advantage at some point.

Now, he was just waiting for them to show up, so he could determine where they were going next, and if that might provide him with a clue as to the status of their investigation.

*   *   *

Darkness. Distant muffled voices. He was floating in a sea of drowsiness, detached from the world.

In the far distance, he heard a voice. 'Mansour.'

The darkness was still all around. Then the voices suddenly became clearer, as if he had surfaced from under the water in a swimming pool, to now be able to hear what people around him were saying.

'Mansour!?'

His eyes snapped open.

It was not a nightmare. He was still here strapped to the chair, and the man in the pin-striped suit was back. He looked down at his mutilated hands and instantly began to sweat profusely. What was coming next?

The man in the suit leaned in over the table and grabbed Mansour's jaw. The grip was surprisingly strong and made Mansour wince in pain.

'What did the notebook say about Medinet Habu?' hissed the man.

'I can't remember,' whimpered Mansour.

'What did the notebook say about the Egyptian Museum?'

'I don't know,' said Mansour, feeling the panic taking hold. 'Nothing. I swear, I can't remember now. I only looked at it for a few minutes. I told you.'

'Ok then,' said the old man and sighed. He let go of Mansour's jaw and leaned back slowly in his chair. 'Eight to go.'

Doctor Mansour's head jerked up, and he stared at the man with terrified eyes.

'Doctor,' said the suited man. 'Would you say that you are particularly attached to your right ring finger?'

Mansour whimpered and closed his eyes, trying to find some way to hide from reality inside his own mind. Trying to escape what he knew was about to happen.

* * *

Exiting the museum into the hot sun and hearing the noise from the traffic, felt like a return to the loud chaotic modern world. Their visit had given both of them food for thought, and some pieces of the puzzle seemed like they might be beginning to fall into place.

'Shall we grab some lunch somewhere?' asked Fiona and gestured to the surrounding area. 'There must be lots of interesting local cuisine here if we just start walking down one of these side streets.'

Against his instinct, Andrew agreed. Walking around Cairo like a couple of tourists, somehow felt like unnecessary exposure.

'Sure,' he said. 'I guess we can do that. What did you have in mind?'

'Well,' said Fiona excitedly, as they started walking towards a pedestrian crossing to get across the main road that ran next to the museum, connecting to Tahrir Square on the other side of the building. 'My Egyptian friend from university would never shut up about these things called *Hawashi*. They are almost like a fajita, apparently. Pita bread stuffed with minced meat, onion, peppers and some spices. It is supposed to be really delicious. And I also just love the name. Hawashi.'

As they walked along, with Fiona talking about lunch options, Andrew suddenly started tuning out, not hearing her anymore. For some reason, his attention was drawn towards the museum's car park. Without really realising it, he found himself scanning the area until suddenly he ended up staring at a car. He gradually slowed down, and eventually came to a stop, eyes now fixed on the black Range Rover in the car park.

'Hello?' said Fiona, and turned around to where he was standing. 'Are you listening?' She then joined him, looking in the same direction. 'Andy, what's going on?'

'Wait here,' he replied, and then started walking towards the car without taking his eyes off it.

'Andy?' exclaimed Fiona, sounding annoyed.

Andrew did not answer but walked briskly and in a straight line towards the black Range Rover. He could have sworn it was the same one he had seen driving behind them on the way to the museum earlier in the day. It looked exactly the same. It even had the same orange parking permit stuck in the same place on the left side of the windscreen.

I should have taken note of the bloody number plate, thought Andrew, annoyed with himself for not having done so earlier. If he had been by himself, he was sure he would have memorised the plate.

As he came within fifty meters of the car, he thought he saw it sway ever so slightly, as if someone inside the car was moving. His instincts were now screaming at him that there was something very wrong with this picture.

Guided almost entirely by impulses and threat assessment training, he started into a slow jog towards as the car, while his right hand moved up and inside his jacket to grip the handle of his gun, while at the same time unfastening the leather strap holding it in place inside its holster.

At that moment, the headlights of the car switched on, and a fraction of a second later its engine sprang to life with a growl. He could hear the driver rev the engine, and somewhere behind him he just barely registered the voice of Fiona calling his name.

Andrew was now sprinting towards the car with his gun out, and a couple of seconds later the car suddenly roared loudly and leapt forward. The huge

Range Rover was coming straight at him, and Andrew realised that whoever was driving it was trying to run him over. He now only had a few seconds to act.

At that moment his training took over, and he whipped out his gun and fired three shots in quick succession into the windscreen of the car. The bullets found their mark right where the driver would be, and they slammed into the windscreen, leaving three small white impacts where the glass had fractured. However, they did not penetrate.

Fuck. Bulletproof glass.

As the car roared the final few meters towards him, he threw himself to the side, narrowly avoiding being struck. As he hit the ground, he rolled once to regain control, trained his gun at the left rear tire as the car barrelled past him. He could feel the vacuum of the slipstream left by the car as he aimed and fired two more shots. Both of them missed.

A couple of seconds later when the Range Rover had made it around twenty meters away from him, it performed a violent handbrake turn. With its wheels screeching loudly, the back of the car swung out to one side, and the car rotated one-hundred and eighty degrees to leave it stationary with its front pointing in Andrew's direction.

Even though he could not see him, Andrew sensed that the driver inside the car was evaluating the situation for a moment. Then the car leapt forward again, bearing down on Andrew who was still lying on the ground.

He aimed and fired another two shots through the front grille and into the engine compartment, but to no apparent effect. In the distance, Fiona was now screaming at him to get up.

Andrew jumped to his feet and started running straight at the car. He knew he had only a few seconds to close the distance. Without thinking, and now operating purely on survival instincts, he leapt into the air and slammed his foot down on the hood of the car as it reached him. Using the hood as a ramp, and applying as much force as he could through his leg, he was sent up into the air just high enough for the car to pass under him.

The driver, realising what was happening slammed on the breaks, and the Range Rover screeched to a halt just a couple of meters away.

Andrew landed on his feet and spun around facing the back of the car. In that instant, he saw the white reverse lights come alive, and a split second later the Ranger Rover was roaring backwards towards him. He only just managed to throw himself clear of the two tonnes of metal hurtling at him, rolling twice before jumping to his feet again less than five meters from the side of the driver's door.

The Range Rover was now stationary, its engine growling with power, and there was a brief standoff between the two. Then, in one smooth and continuous movement, Andrew took half a step forward, raised his gun and fired two more shots into the driver's side window. Once again, the bullets slammed into the glass but did not penetrate.

At that point, the driver must have decided he had had enough. He revved the engine, and then the car shot forward and swerved round in a curve towards the car park exit.

Andrew was already moving, sprinting towards where he knew the car would be in a couple of seconds. Sweat was pouring off his face and into his eyes, and as he shoved his gun back into its holster, he had to blink a few times to see where he was going.

He and the car converged on the same spot just where Andrew had predicted, and as he leapt up into the air, he grabbed one of the two roof rack mounting rails running along either side of the roof of the car.

He had slightly misjudged just how tall the main body of the car was, so one of his legs slammed into the passenger door, but the rest of his body was high enough and carried enough momentum for him to end up on top of the car.

Using both hands, he managed to get a firm grip on both of the mounting rails, but the momentum of the car almost made him lose it. He grimaced as his fingers strained to maintain their grip, and pain shot up through his hands and arms.

The Range Rover barrelled out into traffic on the busy road towards Tahrir Square and started to pick up speed. Andrew was hanging on for dear life, realising that he did not actually have a plan for what to do next. Everything that had happened from the point where he had noticed the parked Range Rover, had been more or less automatic, as if he was simply following a program. Now, he needed to improvise, and fast.

The driver swerved the Range Rover violently from side to side, trying to throw him off whilst overtaking other cars, and Andrew only just managed to hang on. As they raced towards the on-ramp for the 6th of

October Bridge leading west across the Nile, the driver was forced to drive in a straight line whilst trying to overtake an enormous eighteen-wheeled car transport, that had somehow made it into the city centre.

Andrew knew that this was his only chance. Letting go of the mounting rail with his right hand, he swiftly reached inside his jacket and yanked out his gun. Pointing it downwards and slightly to the right, he pulled the trigger three times. The gun fired twice, and the clicked. It was out of bullets.

However, his suspicion had been correct. The roof of the Range Rover was not armoured, and so the bullets had gone straight through the metal. For a few seconds, he wondered if he had managed to hit the driver, but then he got his answer. The Range Rover accelerated even more quickly and was now barrelling past the eighteen-wheeler. Directly in from of them were two more cars, one in the process of overtaking the other.

The Range Rover did not slow down but instead continued to accelerate, and then slammed into the back of the open back truck that was in its lane. The Range Rover decelerated instantly because of the impact, and Andrew immediately lost his grip on the mounting rails, as his body continued forward at the same speed.

He was airborne for what seemed like an eternity, and then he landed inside the open back of the truck, which had been badly damaged from the collision. The truck swerved wildly and ended up sliding sideways along the road with its tyres screeching loudly. Andrew was flung out of the truck's open cargo space and went flying once more.

He hit the tarmac, and rolled over several times, banging his elbows into the road whilst trying to protect his head from impact. He heard the sound of his gun clattering along on the road.

Eventually, he came to a stop, as a loud cacophony of screaming tyres arose from the eighteen-wheeler that was braking frantically to avoid running him over. He could also hear the distinct sound of the Range Rover's engine as it sped off towards the bridge.

As he lay there panting for a few seconds, a taxi in the typical white livery with the chequered pattern down its side screeched to a halt next to him, and he heard one of its doors open.

'Get in!' shouted Fiona.

Andrew raised his head and whipped around to see Fiona sitting at the wheel of the taxi, with the passenger door open.

Without hesitation, he jumped to his feet, but then winced as pain shot through the left side of his rib cage. He threw himself into the passenger seat, and before the door had slammed shut, the taxi had taken off in pursuit of the black Range Rover.

Fiona could just see it ahead of them, and she floored the accelerator. It was the tallest vehicle on the road, and she could see its black roof gleaming in the sun as it swerved from side to side. The driver was overtaking and racing past the other cars on the dual carriageway leading west away from Tahrir Square, and over the bridge towards Zamalek.

'Are you alright?' shouted Fiona, briefly glancing at him while weaving the car through the traffic.

'Sure,' winced Andrew. 'I have been a lot worse.'

Fiona was not sure what to make if that, but she had to assume that he would have told her if he was severely injured and needed medical attention.

'Strap in,' she commanded in a no-nonsense tone of voice. 'This could get rough.'

Andrew glanced at her for a moment, wondering where this side of her had suddenly come from. This situation was far from what he would have called amusing, but he still found himself with a half-grin on his face, as Fiona man-handled the wheel of the taxi in pursuit of the Range Rover.

What a girl, he thought to himself.

As they raced after the Range Rover, weaving through the traffic ahead of them, Andrew shifted in his seat holding the left side of his chest.

'Are you injured?' asked Fiona.

'Just a bruise,' said Andrew. 'Don't let him get away. I want that bastard.'

'Just hold on and let me drive,' replied Fiona, throwing the car from left to right, as she weaved her way through traffic trying to catch up with the Range Rover.

They had reached the middle of the bridge, and up ahead she could see the Range Rover peeling off to the left to take the off-ramp for Zamalek. Fiona got in the left lane and overtook a slow-moving car on the inside, just in time to make the exit herself. The Range Rover drove down the off-ramp, where it made a hard right to go under the bridge and head north.

Fiona followed, the wheels of the taxi squealing as she took the corner.

By driving recklessly during the pursuit across the bridge, she had managed to gain some ground on the Range Rover. But the taxi's engine was nowhere near as powerful as that of the Range Rover, so it could not accelerate as fast. As the Range Rover turned down one street after the next, the distance between it and the pursuing taxi began to grow again as the Range Rover leapt ahead after each turn.

Doing a hard left turn whilst coming round a corner outside a fruit and vegetable shop, the taxi drove over what must have been a small amount of engine oil in the road. The back wheels of the taxi immediately stepped out to the right, and before they knew what had happened, the taxi had spun around. Fiona attempted to correct it, but it was too late. The taxi slammed backwards into a row of parked mopeds and came to a halt. She tried to get the car moving again, but the transmission had gone. They were not going anywhere now.

They both got out of the car, looking in the direction the Range Rover had disappeared in. There was no sign of it anymore. Then Fiona walked back towards the taxi.

'You piece of JUNK!' she screamed and kicked the driver side door.

'Alright,' said Andrew. 'Calm down. It's over now.'

Fiona turned to face Andrew, and then walked up to him and slapped hard him across the face.

'You utter moron!' she shouted. 'What the hell is wrong with you? You could have been killed. Again!'

Andrew placed his hands on his hips, and just stood there with his head down, without responding. He knew it was better to let Fiona decompress and get her feelings off her chest. He could not exactly blame her for being upset. When he had chased after the car, he had behaved as if she was not even there, and he had effectively left her by herself. That was not good teamwork, and he knew it.

'You can't just go running after people like that. And shooting up cars in a parking lot? That's crazy!'

'Look,' said Andrew calmly, spreading out his hands and wincing from the pain in his chest. 'The guy was trying to kill me. I had to do something.'

'Alright,' said Fiona reluctantly. 'But did you have to jump onto his bloody car when he tried to get away?'

'Perhaps not,' admitted Andrew. 'Honestly, I wasn't really thinking. There was no time to think it through. I just did what I felt I needed to do. I couldn't let him get away.'

'I understand,' sighed Fiona, now calming down a bit. 'I was bloody terrified.'

Andrew walked over to her and placed a hand gently on her shoulder. 'I am sorry,' he said. 'I should have thought it through first.'

Fiona stepped in front of him, put her arms around his waist and pulled herself in close to him.

He placed a hand on her head and wrapped his other arm around her. 'Ouch,' he smiled and winced. 'My ribs are killing me.'

'She looked up at him and returned his smile 'And if you ever do that again, then *I* am going to kill you.'

'Win-win then,' smiled Andrew.

'You muppet,' she replied and tucked herself into his embrace.

In the distance, they could now hear the sound of sirens from several police cars that were converging on their location. A few minutes later they were surrounded by three police cars and five officers from the Cairo Police Department.

Andrew had placed his gun on the ground, and they both held their hands up into the air. Neither of them knew if the Cairo Police had a reputation for being trigger happy.

Eventually, they were taken into custody and driven to the nearest police station, where they were placed in a holding cell. After about an hour, they were escorted into an interrogation room, where they sat opposite a pompous and self-important looking senior officer, who began asking them questions about who they were and what had happened. In front of him, he had a small stack of papers, which Andrew guessed was meant to give them the impression that he already had information about them.

Andrew attempted to deflect the questions, but it was not an easy job, considering the damage they had caused. The fact that he was carrying a gun, even if he did have a permit for it, did not make that task any easier.

Suddenly, there was a knock on the door, and a junior officer entered. Without looking at Andrew or Fiona, he walked over to the senior officer and leaned down to whisper something in his ear. The look on the senior officer's face instantly went from pompous to confused, and then to worried. He began collecting his papers, but before he was done, the door to the room opened again.

As soon as Major Elsayed from Egyptian Military Intelligence entered the room, the mood changed in an instant. The major had an assistant with him, also in military uniform. The previous self-important attitude of the senior police officer evaporated like morning dew in the Egyptian sun, and he picked up his papers and shuffled out of the room without saying a word, or even looking at Andrew and Fiona again.

Major Elsayed appeared to be so used to this sort of thing, that he did not even seem to notice everyone scurrying out of his way. He sat down slowly across from them, folded his hands in front of himself, and placed them on the table. Then he looked up at Andrew, shifted his gaze to Fiona, and then returned it to Andrew.

'Quite a show you two put on,' he said matter-of-factly.

Andrew and Fiona glanced briefly at each other. They both felt like naughty school children having broken a window playing ball in the schoolyard.

'Major Elsayed,' began Andrew. 'I can explain.'

'You don't have to,' said Elsayed wearily. 'I have seen the CCTV footage from the cameras at the museum, and we already have witness statements from motorists on the bridge and the witnesses at the grocery store. All I need to know is this. Do you have any idea at all who might have been following you two? And did you see anyone at all that appeared suspicious inside the museum?"

'I am pretty sure no one followed us into the museum,' said Andrew, and looked at Fiona who shook her head to confirm that she agreed.

'But I am also quite sure that the Range Rover was following us from the hotel,' continued Andrew. 'That's why I thought I recognised it.'

'I see,' said Major Elsayed. 'We will make sure we obtain the CCTV from the hotel then.' He glanced to his side and snapped his fingers, and his assistant immediately rose and left the room.

'Do you have CCTV of where the Range Rover went?' asked Andrew.

Major Elsayed shook his head and produced a bitter expression. 'We don't have the same level of traffic surveillance that you do in London,' he replied. 'It is about the money, they tell me.'

'So, we don't know where the Range Rover went after we lost him?'

'I am afraid not,' said the major. 'We will try to obtain CCTV footage from private businesses in the area, but I wouldn't get my hopes up if I were you. Most of them are internal cameras, and many of them don't work.'

'I see,' said Andrew. 'Please let us know if your people dig up anything. If we can identify the vehicle, we have a real shot at figuring out where Doctor Mansour might be kept.'

'I will keep you updated,' nodded the major.

'One final thing before I let you go, Mr Sterling,' said Major Elsayed gravely. 'Having a permit to carry a firearm, does not mean that you can freely discharge that firearm whenever you please. Luckily, no

Egyptian citizens were injured. If they had been, this would have been a different matter altogether.'

'I understand,' said Andrew, keen to convey that he had not done so flippantly.

'In this instance,' continued Elsayed, 'I have been able to protect you from criminal prosecution under Egyptian law, but if this happens again, I will not be able to prevent you from being placed in front of a judge. Is that clear?'

Out of the corner of his eye, Andrew could sense Fiona eager to interrupt and say something, but he quickly glanced at her and lifted his hand off the table whilst shaking his head slowly. Now was not the time for an argument.

'Yes, sir,' said Andrew. 'Completely clear.'

Major Elsayed looked at them both for a few seconds and then nodded. 'Ok. We are done here. I will have the police escort you out.'

A couple of minutes later, they were standing outside in front of the police station. Andrew had had his gun returned to him, and after a brief examination by the medical officer at the police station, he had been told that none of his ribs were broken.

'What a day,' said Fiona.

'I have had better,' smiled Andrew. 'But I have also had a lot worse.'

Fiona shook her head and smiled. 'I don't even want to know. Let's get back to the hotel. We need to get ready for the trip to Jerusalem tomorrow.'

'No rest for the weary,' said Andrew. 'Let's try not to break things when we get there.'

'Great idea,' replied Fiona sarcastically. 'Taxi?'

'Absolutely,' said Andrew. 'I don't feel like walking anywhere for the rest of today.'

Fifteen

The Royal Airforce BAe 146-200 came in to land at Jerusalem International Airport, known locally as Atarot Airport, just after 1 pm. The airport is located roughly 8 kilometres due north of the city centre, connected to it by highway 60. Andrew and Fiona had both managed to sleep for around an hour on the flight from Cairo and were looking out at the scenery passing underneath as they approached the runway. Located on a plateau in the Judean Mountains in central Israel, it is a sprawling city of fewer than one million people, yet it covers a large area of 125 square kilometres.

It was a clear day, and Andrew noticed how, despite the large footprint of the city, it seemed to have very few high-rise buildings. Where the city met the mountains in the east, and the plains in the west, the terrain looked dry and rocky.

They had arranged to meet Professor Finkelstein in central Jerusalem, despite the fact that the Hebrew

University of Jerusalem, was more or less on their way from the airport to the city centre. The professor had insisted on meeting in a café within walking distance of the Western Wall, and it took them less than an hour from when the aircraft's wheels had made contact with the runway until they were walking down one of the narrow, cobbled streets in Jerusalem's Old Town.

The café was tucked away in a side street, and was set in what appeared to be an old converted storage cellar partly below street level. As they descended the five steps down into the café, a cosy space with original limestone walls and a plethora of candles revealed itself.

'Lovely,' smiled Fiona. 'It looks so inviting. I like it here.'

'Very nice,' nodded Andrew, subconsciously scanning the room for a table that would allow him to sit with his back to the wall, facing the entrance.

The café was around half full, and people were sitting around small round tables drinking tea and coffee and having animated discussions in Hebrew.

'I literally don't understand a word anyone here is saying,' smiled Andrew. 'I guess we English get lazy when it comes to languages.'

'Yes, you do,' replied Fiona. 'Although, in your defence, Hebrew is a very difficult language to learn by any standards. It is nice to be in a completely foreign environment sometimes, though, isn't it?' beamed Fiona.

'Sure,' lied Andrew. The notion that 'foreign' was equal to 'threat', had become so hard-wired into this brain, that he had to make an effort to relax and be open-minded. *I really need to work on that,* he thought to himself.

A waiter swung past, wearing an apron and a welcoming smile. He showed them to a table at the far corner, where they sat down on one side of the table so that they could both see the entrance where they were expecting Professor Finkelstein to emerge any moment now.

'Do you know what he looks like?' asked Andrew.

'I had a quick peek at the university website,' replied Fiona. 'He has a beard.'

'Great,' said Andrew teasingly. 'He will be very easy to spot in this city then.'

Fiona elbowed him gently in the arm and smiled. 'I am sure he'll be able to spot us. You stand out like a sore thumb around here.'

'What do you mean by...' began Andrew.

'That's got to be him,' interrupted Fiona and nodded in the direction of the entrance, where a man had just entered.

He was short and slightly rotund, had a big grey beard and messy hair, and he was wearing a wrinkled white shirt with no tie and brown suspenders. The shirt was struggling to contain his belly, which bulged out in front of him. Under his arm, he was carrying a worn dark brown leather bag and an umbrella, even though there was no hint that it might rain.

He had a quick exchange with the waiter, who pointed in the direction of Andrew and Fiona, at which point Fiona raised a hand and waved discreetly at the professor. The man's face lit up in a smile, and then he shuffled towards them, bumping into a man who was seated at another table. He apologised profusely, which seemed to be enough to placate the offended party.

The professor eventually slumped down across from Fiona, placed his bag and umbrella on the seat next to him and wiped his forehead with a handkerchief. Then he turned to them both and, looking exhausted, produced a broad friendly smile.

'Hello,' he said, apologetically, with a heavy Jewish accent. 'Sorry about being late. I hope I did not keep you waiting. I am Professor Ari Finkelstein.'

Fiona looked at her wristwatch, and smiled. 'You're actually slightly early.'

'I am?' chuckled the professor. 'Oh. I am usually late, so I just assume that I need to apologise.'

'My name is Fiona Keane, and this is Andrew Sterling.'

Finkelstein nodded and smiled in Andrew's direction. 'Hello, sir. Nice to meet you.'

'Hello professor,' smiled Andrew. 'Thank you for seeing us.'

'Ah, it's no problem,' said Finkelstein with a benign smile, and waved his hands dismissively. 'If you can't be hospitable, what sort of person are you, right?'

At that point, the waiter came over and took their orders. After he had left, the professor leaned forward slightly with a conspiratorial look on his face. 'You know, I took my wife here on our first date.'

'That's lovely,' exclaimed Fiona. 'How did it go?'

'Well,' said Finkelstein. 'We've been married for thirty-seven years, so I guess you can say it went ok. Mind you, I was more handsome in those days. If I had shown up for that date looking the way I do now, I am sure she would probably have said 'Oy Gevalt!'

and left me there.' Then he erupted in infectious laughter, which made his belly jump up and down. He was an easy man to like.

'It is very characterful down here,' said Andrew. 'And cool.'

'Oh yes,' replied the professor. 'This used to be an underground storeroom for goat cheese. It is always nice and cool here, even when it is hot like the Negev desert outside.'

Finkelstein sipped at his coffee and then smiled at them both. 'So, what can I do for you today? You have come a long way.'

Andrew and Fiona exchanged a quick look, at which point Andrew nodded for Fiona to go ahead.

'This is your show,' smiled Andrew.

'We've actually just flown in from Cairo,' said Fiona.

'I see,' said the Finkelstein and raised his eyebrows. 'Lovely city. Especially the old parts.'

'Yes, it is an amazing place,' replied Fiona. 'Anyway, the reason we've asked to meet with you is because we are investigating the disappearance of an archaeologist there, as well as a possible security threat. We can't really go into much detail because most of it is classified at this point. But what we can say, is that there is a group of people who seem to be prepared to do whatever it takes to get their hands on a radioactive source.'

Finkelstein's eyebrow slowly moved up, and he nodded sagely. 'I see. That is serious business.'

'It is,' nodded Fiona. 'And as odd as this may sound to you, we believe that there may be a connection between what has happened in Cairo in recent weeks, and the story of Exodus.'

Finkelstein hesitated for a moment. 'Well, he said and produced a weary smile and shrugged. 'I guess you can say that most things in this part of the world are connected to Exodus.'

Fiona smiled. 'I guess you're right. But in this case, we're dealing with a tangible link between the story of Exodus and the later arrival of the Israelites here in Jerusalem, and an event that happened in ancient Egypt several thousand years ago.'

'I see,' said Finkelstein. 'That does sound very intriguing. 'How can I help?'

'To be blunt,' said Fiona, 'We would be very grateful if you could help us understand, from a scientific point of view, what Exodus was and what might actually have happened. And then we would like to try to understand what the Ark of the Covenant really was and whether it is likely to have been a real physical object at that time.'

Finkelstein smiled. 'Sure,' he said ironically. 'That should only take a few minutes.'

Fiona held up her hands apologetically. 'I know,' she said with a smile. 'It is an extremely complicated story, but what we're trying to understand is what the best and most accurate current scientific consensus is, regarding whether Exodus did indeed actually happen.'

The professor leaned back in his chair and put his hands on his belly. He looked up at the ceiling for a few seconds, tilting his head to one side, as if trying to decide the best approach. Finally, he leaned forward again and placed his hands on the white table cloth.

'Ok,' he said. 'I think what I should do is start by telling you about the story of Exodus from a biblical perspective. And then after that, I can tell you what the scientific evidence is saying and also what my own thoughts are. Does that sound ok?'

Andrew and Fiona both nodded. 'That would be great,' said Fiona. 'Any way you prefer.'

'Ok,' said Finkelstein, and lifted his hands from the table cloth. 'Let me just go back a little bit further and start at the very beginning, as far as the biblical text is concerned. And when I say biblical text, I am talking about the Old Testament, or the Jewish Torah, as we call it. As you may know, in the text, Abraham is the common patriarch of all the so-called Abrahamic religions. Christianity, Islam, and Judaism, all trace themselves back to him. There is no scientific basis for his existence as a real person, but the Tanahk, the Hebrew Bible, says he lived around 2150 BCE.'

Finkelstein sipped at his coffee and then continued. 'Abraham and his wife Rachel had a son called Isaac. Isaac and his wife Rebecca had Jacob, who in turn had one daughter and twelve sons with four different women, two of whom were his wives. Those twelve sons then became the patriarchs of the twelve tribes of Israel, which you may have heard of.'

Andrew was vaguely familiar with the story, but as he sat there listening to the professor, he began to feel grateful that Fiona was there with her notepad.

'The story goes that Jacob, who by then had also acquired the name Israel, and his wife Rachel favoured the two sons Joseph and Benjamin, and so the other ten brothers conspired to kill Joseph, but ended up selling him into slavery instead.'

'Friendly bunch,' said Andrew, and raised his eyebrows.

The professor shook his head and smiled disarmingly. 'There are plenty of hair-raising stories like that in the texts. You can say a lot about the scriptures, but they are never dull.'

'Anyway,' continued the professor. 'After a great famine in Canaan, which is what we today call the southern Levant, the ten sons of Jacob went to Egypt to buy grain, with Benjamin staying behind to look after their father Jacob. When they arrived in Egypt, they found Joseph, who had become the grand vizier of the Pharaoh's court, which was effectively like being the chief bureaucrat, answering only to the king.'

'How do you go from slave to vizier?' asked Fiona.

'Simple,' smiled Finkelstein mischievously. 'You become head of the household of your master, which in this case was the captain of the pharaoh's guard. You then interpret a dream the pharaoh has had, of seven lean cows devouring seven fat cows, as a coming famine. And when that famine actually arrives, and Egypt has plenty of stores of grain, the Pharaoh makes you his most trusted confidant.'

'Sounds simple enough,' smiled Fiona. 'I believe the term vizier is similar to the word viceroy in English. Like a chief advisor or deputy?'

'I think you are correct,' said Finkelstein and continued. 'Anyway, Joseph then helps Jacob move his entire clan to Egypt, to escape the famine in Canaan. There they meet the Pharaoh, and are given land because of Joseph's position in the Pharaoh's court.'

'Quite a story,' said Andrew.

'Oh yes,' exclaimed Finkelstein and chuckled. 'The emphasis here is on the word *story*, but I will get back to that.'

'Do go on,' said Fiona.

'Right,' said Finkelstein and shifted in his seat. 'This is where the story of Exodus starts to take shape. Joseph was given the wife Asenath, who was the daughter of an Egyptian priest. Together they have two sons, Manasseh and Ephraim, who later form the basis of the House of Joseph. They supposedly lived in Egypt for 400 years, give or take. During that time, one of Jacob's sons, named Levi, has a son called Koath, who has a son called Amram, who in turn has three children called Moses, Aaron and Miriam.'

'Ok,' said Fiona. 'And this is the point where Moses is raised by the Pharaoh's daughter, kills an Egyptian soldier, flees to Midian where he sees the burning bush, and then returns to Egypt to take the Israelites back to Canaan.'

'Nicely summed up,' smiled Finkelstein and nodded approvingly. 'You've done your homework.'

'Well, someone has to,' she said and shot Andrew a caustic smile.

Andrew smiled wryly. 'Do we have any idea when this might have been, and if it ever actually happened?'

'If it ever did happen,' repeated Finkelstein and held up an index finger, 'we think it may have been around 1270 BCE. The chronology is extremely uncertain, but I will come back to that in a bit. For now, let's assume the texts are correct. And also, this might help you,' he said and reached into his bag, producing a book which he opened on a page that had a map of the Levant. It also showed a dotted line from the Nile Delta into the Sinai Peninsula, down to its southern tip and Mount Horeb, then back up all the way to Mount Nebo in present-day Jordan and then over into Jericho and Jerusalem in what is today the state of Israel.

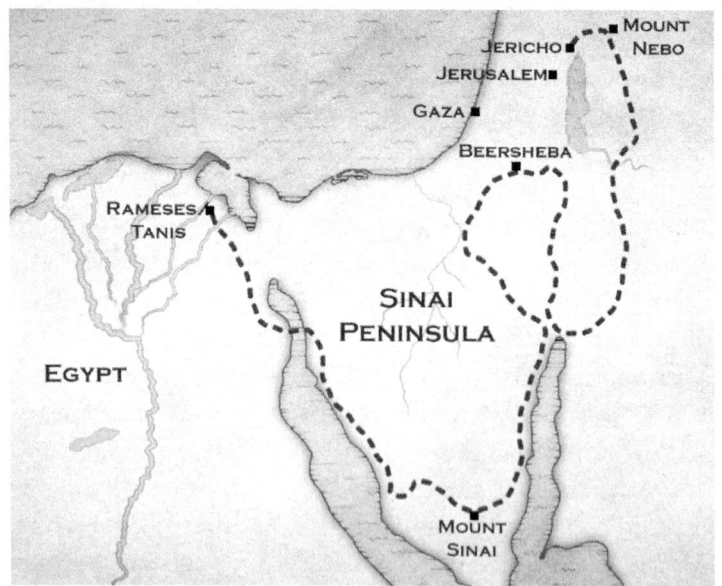

'No one really knows how accurate this is,' he said, 'but it more or less depicts what is laid out in the Bible.'

'By the way,' he continued. 'The term Exodus or Ex-*odus* literally means "the way out", which is an interesting term to think about both literally and figuratively in this particular context. The Israelites needed a way out of Egypt, and also a way out of slavery under the Pharaoh. So, they leave Egypt, and make their way to the Sinai Peninsula to Mount Sinai, and this is where Moses receives the Ten Commandments, which constitute the covenant between Yahweh and his chosen people, the Israelites. They then spend forty years wandering in the desert, not because it took even remotely that long to reach Canaan, but because Moses was trying to teach them a lesson about being subservient to Yahweh.'

'Tough boss,' said Andrew.

'Yes,' shrugged Finkelstein. 'It's fair to say there was a lot of bickering going on, so Moses apparently felt he needed to teach them a lesson. But eventually, they make it to Canaan via the southern route from the Sinai Peninsula, and up into what is present-day Jordan. The return to Canaan can be divided into five phases. First, the Israelites crossed from present-day Jordan at Gilgal near Mount Nebo, into the region of Judah. Second, they conquer Jericho, Ai, Jerusalem and several other cities. Third, a southern campaign takes several more cities. Fourth, a northern campaign takes the city of Hazor. Finally, they go back down south to Shechem and Mount Ebal, where the Covenant is renewed.'

Fiona tilted her head to one side, hesitated for a moment, and then asked. 'How did the Israelites manage to enter into the old kingdoms of Judah and then north, and win several battles on the way?'

'Well,' said Finkelstein and spread out his hands. 'This is where much debate has been taking place over the centuries. As you know, the Ark of the Covenant was supposed to have supernatural powers.

In fact, it is the only item in all the scriptures that supposedly possessed such powers. In Exodus 13:18, it clearly states that "The people of Israel went up armed out of the land of Egypt", so they were supposedly carrying some weapon with them.'

'And do you believe they carried such a weapon?' asked Fiona, now quite literally on the edge of her seat.

Finkelstein pressed his lips together and hesitated. 'I am not in the business of believing this, that or the other. I am in the business of trying to establish facts. And as far as that is concerned, there is no evidence to support any supernatural tales from the scripture. Archaeologically speaking, there is no evidence of the destruction of Jericho or Ai, anywhere near the time put forward by the Bible. In fact, there is no evidence of 'a destruction' of Jericho at all. There is some evidence of a destruction at Ai, but this has been dated to around 2500 BCE, which is around 1,200 years earlier than the supposed destruction by the Israelites.'

Fiona's forehead creased up. She was clearly ambivalent about what the professor was saying.

'The clue to this,' continued Finkelstein, 'is the fact that Ai literally means 'The destroyed place'. So, whoever wrote the Book of Joshua where these events are mentioned, probably around the 7th century BCE, was clearly looking around the area at the time of writing. He probably saw this "destroyed place", and he then concluded that this must have been done by the Israelites. So, this is a good example of how the historicity of the Bible should not be trusted. At least not with regards to specific events and times. It is more likely that the Bible paints a much broader picture of the general societal evolution of the time. And of course, the divine aspects are added for dramatic effect, or for religious and political purposes, which at that time was effectively the same thing. You simply could not make an even remotely legitimate claim to power, without somehow demonstrating or at least claiming that God was on your side.'

'So, what you're saying,' interjected Fiona, 'is that there is no archaeological evidence of the conquest of Canaan by the Israelites, the way it is described in the Bible?'

Finkelstein shook his head. 'Of the 31 locations in Canaan that are supposed to have been destroyed by the returning Israelites, only two show any archaeological evidence of having been destroyed at the time of the supposed Exodus. And the destruction uncovered at those sites is believed to be the result of clashes between local warring tribes.'

'Is there any evidence at all of the Israelites in Canaan at that time,' asked Fiona, now looking slightly dejected.

Well,' said Finkelstein. 'Let's take a place like Shiloh, which plays a prominent role in the Bible, not least because the Ark rested there for many years. We know exactly where the site is, and it has been extensively excavated by archaeologists. What was found was a settlement dating to around 1600 BCE, but basically nothing was found from around 1200 BCE, which is when the texts describe these events as having happened.'

'That sounds pretty conclusive,' said Fiona.

'Yes,' replied Finkelstein. 'There really isn't a single modern mainstream historian or archaeologist today, who even attempts to uphold the notion that the story of conquest presented in the Book of Joshua is in any way reflective of historical fact.'

'What about the Exodus itself?' pressed Fiona. 'Is there any archaeological evidence to support that narrative?'

'Let me put it like this,' said Finkelstein. 'There is ample evidence of people from the southern Levant, including Canaan, living in ancient Egypt, along with many other ethnic groups from the wider Middle-East at that time. But there is no evidence of a large group of Hebrews having been enslaved in Egypt, and then having left in a large Exodus back to Canaan.'

'I see,' said Fiona pensively. 'So, what is the consensus right now among historians and archaeologists regarding the Exodus?'

'The current consensus,' said Finkelstein, 'in terms of whether it really happened, and if so who left Egypt and when they might have done so, can probably be summed up like this. There is no serious Egyptologist or historian who actually thinks that Exodus, as described in the Bible, really happened. There is simply no evidential basis for believing that. There is, however, good reason to believe that there are historical kernels to be found in the biblical Exodus narrative. But those kernels have been picked from many different time periods and contexts, and then combined into a cohesive and compelling, although not actually historically accurate, narrative. This most likely happened for political purposes, to bind a group of tribes together, and create a common identity.'

Finkelstein sipped his coffee again and then continued.

'There are elements in the Exodus narrative that reflect things that may have happened in ancient Egypt. So, there were possibly people that would have been like the Israelites, linguistically, culturally and religiously, and who after coming under pressure from the rest of that society at that time, decided to leave for their former homeland in the Levant. There may well have been periods of slavery for some of Israel's ancestors in Egypt. We know from pictorial representations and texts found in ancient Egypt, that people from the Levant had long been present in the Nile delta, and sometimes enslaved there from time to time from at least the early 2nd millennium BCE. There are images of slaves making mudbricks, and even of Ramesses II himself beating foreign slaves. The Egyptians were fairly prolific in documenting their history, especially their successes and military victories. So, it seems strange that there should be no record at all of the subjugation and enslavement of a whole ethnic group. There are plenty of examples to be found at the mortuary temples in Thebes, of images of Pharaohs smiting Hittites or Babylonians or people from the southern Levant. But there is no explicit mention of such a group of Hebrews or Israelites living in Egypt and being subjugated or expelled. The first mention of the name *Israel* that has been found, is from the Merneptah Stele from around 1210 BCE. But again, it does not mention Israelites in

Egypt, but only mentions Israel as a location in the southern Levant, that was subjugated by the pharaoh.'

'Yes,' said Fiona. 'We saw the stele ourselves yesterday in the Egyptian Museum in Cairo.'

'Good,' exclaimed the professor. 'I have been there myself. Fascinating place.'

'So anyway, are you saying that the entire Exodus tale was constructed to serve a political purpose?'

'I think that is most likely,' said Finkelstein. 'The story itself could relate to a couple of major events in the history of the Canaanites through the centuries. The first is the historically verifiable story of the Hyksos, who were an ethnic group most likely from the Levant, who invaded and ruled as pharaohs in the Nile delta for about one hundred years around the 16th century BCE. This was the Fifteenth Dynasty of ancient Egypt, and it co-existed for a time alongside the Sixteenth and Seventeenth Dynasties in Thebes in southern Egypt. But they were ultimately seen as foreign usurpers of the indigenous Egyptians, and when they were eventually overthrown by Pharaoh Ahmose I around 1540 BCE, they are believed to have fled back to Canaan. It is very possible that the story of Exodus began as an oral memory of the Hyksos expulsion.'

'Fascinating,' said Fiona. 'I have read about the Hyksos, but I have never thought of that connection to Exodus. That sounds very plausible.'

'I think so too,' nodded Finkelstein. 'The second story that could have formed the basis for the Exodus narrative, is the story of the Israelites returning to Canaan after having been dispersed, following invasions of Canaan by foreign powers. This could have been after the expulsion from the Kingdom of Israel by Tiglath-Pileser III of Assyria in 733 BCE. Or it could have been during Babylonian captivity when some of the population was deported in 597 BCE, or in 587 BCE after the sacking of Jerusalem by the Neo-Babylonian Empire under Nebuchadnezzar II. These historical events could very well have served as a blueprint for the Exodus story, specifically with regards to the idea of being victimised, expelled and then eventually returning to their original homeland. In all of these cases, the Israelites or Canaanites would have needed some sort of origin story to help them survive as a diaspora after their expulsion, and then to resettle in the old country as a cohesive unit, after having been scattered for centuries.'

'That makes a lot of sense,' nodded Fiona sagely. 'Especially in this part of the world, which has pretty much always been contested.'

'Yes,' smiled Finkelstein and gesticulated. 'The one thing you must understand about this land that we sit on, and that we Jews now call our home, is that it is in the wrong place!' His infectious laughter quickly had both Andrew and Fiona chuckling.

'Present-day Israel,' continued Finkelstein, 'but also Palestine, Gaza, Lebanon. They all sit on a narrow land bridge between the deserts of what is today Jordan and Iraq on one side, and the Mediterranean on the other. And along this land bridge, several empires have spent millennia fighting each other. The North Africans, in the form of the Egyptians and the Libyans, and then the Mesopotamians in the form of Assyrians and Babylonians, have fought over control of this land and its trade routes since time immemorial. And of course, most recently, the meddling of the British did not improve things.'

Andrew shifted uncomfortably. 'I feel like I should apologise,' he said.

'Ah,' laughed Finkelstein. 'Don't be silly. Nothing to do with you. We can't change history, so let's not bicker about it.'

Fiona smiled sombrely 'If only more people thought like that, the world would be a much better place.'

'I feel like there are strong parallels in what you just explained to the modern Middle-East,' said Andrew.

'That's right,' exclaimed Finkelstein and gestured towards Andrew, as if to emphasise his point. 'Now as well as then, victimhood is a powerful way of creating a shared identity for a people. The modern Israelis rightly feel victimised by historical events such as the holocaust and the Six Day War. The Arabs, on the other hand, rightly feel victimised by the way the West carved up the region after WW II, and to some extent also by the Israeli treatment of the Palestinians. That sense of victimhood has become a defining character trait of both of those peoples. I think it is reasonable to believe that a similar dynamic was at play when this group of people, who were originally from the Levant, returned to Canaan after however many centuries, to try to re-establish themselves. A strong narrative about their common identity and origin would have been beneficial to their ability to function as a cohesive unit, in the face of the very real obstacles that would have faced them on their return to Canaan. There is no better way to pull people together than the notion of some external threat.'

'In other words,' said Andrew. 'The narrative was a way to give people a common focal point, and to try to make sure that whatever unity was there at the time, didn't fracture.'

'Exactly,' said Finkelstein. 'Another good example of this is the fact that the three Hebrew patriarchs Abraham, Joseph and Isaac, have strong connections with the region of Hebron in the south, the desert fringe of Judah, and the northern hill-country respectively. This is an obvious attempt to portray shared heritage and to evoke a sense of common ancestry for all the different tribes of the region. These three men were most likely originally separate regional ancestors, but in the texts, they were brought together in a single genealogy, in an effort to create a unified history. Similarly, characters like Joseph may represent memories from Levantines who did well for themselves in Egypt. Moses may represent memories from Levantines who were perhaps taken as slaves during Pharaonic military campaigns in the Levant, of which there were many. All of these different memories were then stitched together and the whole thing was mythologised into an Iron Age narrative, that could carry the weight of having to be the origin story of an entire people.'

Andrew and Fiona both looked slightly bamboozled by the amount of information the professor had laid out in front of them.

'I know,' laughed Finkelstein in a good-natured manner. 'It is a lot to think about. The biblical texts, we have to understand, have their own program, so to speak. They are theological documents, presented as revelation, but they are obviously a compendium with lots of different sources, which have always had a political and a religious purpose.'

Well,' said Fiona. 'Thankfully, we're not here to try to settle the question of whether the Exodus actually happened precisely in the way it is described in the Bible, or which group of people might have left Egypt or even exactly when. What we need to understand is whether an event similar to Exodus could conceivably have happened and whether they really carried with them something like the Ark of the Covenant. If Exodus never happened, what about the Ark? Was the Ark never real? Do you think the Ark is a mythological artefact, or could it actually have been a real physical object that was brought out of Egypt at some point?'

'I am not sure about that, to be honest,' replied Finkelstein. 'As you probably know, there was a religious practice at that time in ancient Egypt of transporting religious artefacts in arks carried by priests using staves. You might have seen the Anubis Chest from the Tomb of Tutankhamun in the museum in Cairo.'

Fiona nodded. 'We did.'

'So,' continued Finkelstein, 'It is quite possible that if the Israelites, or whoever may have left Egypt as a group, would have carried some type of reliquary with them. Of course, the Ark was supposed to have been made at the foot of Mount Sinai, but I guess that is a minor detail. Things like that can easily get lost as the story is told and retold through the ages.'

'We saw an example of such an Ark depicted in the mortuary temple of Ramesses II in Thebes,' said Andrew. 'That was quite an experience.'

Fiona glanced at him and smiled. 'Yes, it had quite an impact on Andrew.'

'I am glad,' said Finkelstein. 'It is a remarkable place. And there are several other places, where objects similar to the Ark can be seen in ancient Egyptian art. I am quite sure that if such an object was carried out of Egypt at some point, it would have borne the hallmarks of the local religious tradition of that time, especially if the group carrying it had spent centuries in that country.'

'Would you mind running us through the journey of the Ark,' asked Fiona, 'And perhaps if you could have a stab at where it might have gone. As I understand it, it has been missing for centuries now.'

Finkelstein laughed. 'I get all the easy questions today.'

'Sorry,' said Fiona, with a pained look on her face. 'I know we are asking a lot of you.'

'It's quite alright,' said Finkelstein, holding up his hands. 'I don't mind. These are all interesting topics to discuss.'

He then sat up in his chair and rubbed his chin. 'Let us for a moment pretend that the Bible is an accurate historical account. According to the texts, the Ark came into Canaan with the Israelites. This is supposed to have happened around 1200 BCE, but this is obviously hotly debated. It was then used as a weapon to lay waste to all of those different towns I mentioned earlier. It also supposedly inflicted terrible sickness on the foes of the Israelites.'

'Yes, I have been reading up on that,' said Fiona. 'Quite a gruesome tale.'

'It would have been, if it were true,' said Finkelstein.

'I suppose I don't have to ask you about the purported supernatural powers of the Ark,' smiled Fiona. 'I think I can guess the answer.'

Finkelstein placed his hands flat on the table cloth. 'Look, this is obviously an emotive issue, not least for my people. But let's be honest. There is no credible reason to believe that such supernatural powers exist. And I can't think of a single natural phenomenon that could have explained the powers that the Ark supposedly had, as described in the Bible.'

Fiona glanced briefly at Andrew, who shook his head almost imperceptibly. He was not keen on involving more people in this than absolutely necessary, if nothing else then simply for their own safety. Even if it turned out that they were on a wild goose chase, and that the Ark of the Covenant was entirely fictional, and that Jabari Omran's theory was entirely without merit, what really mattered was that there were some people who really believed it. And those people had already demonstrated that they would stop at nothing to uncover the supposed location of the radioactive meteorite.

The professor did not seem to notice their silent exchange and pressed on. 'As I said, the Ark went to Shiloh, where it rested for several centuries. Again, the exact timing is highly disputed, but the next major event was when the Ark was captured by the Philistines at the battle of Eben-Ezer around 1040

BCE. After having inflicted tumours and burns on the Philistines, it is then returned to the Israelites.'

The waiter swung past their table and asked if he could get them anything else. Professor Finkelstein asked for a glass of water, but Andrew and Fiona declined.

'Now,' said Finkelstein. 'We're approaching a time period where we can begin to use other known sources to hold up against the accounts in the Bible, to see if the dates and events match. At this point, the twelve tribes of Israel have settled in Canaan in twelve separate regions. The tribes eventually decide to have just one ruler, and the United Monarchy is formed. Its first king was Saul, who supposedly reigned for about 27 years from 1037 BCE. He is followed by David, famous from the story of David and Goliath, where he ends up becoming a hero of the people. Saul fears David's newfound influence, and David is forced to flee. He escapes to Philistia of all places, and when Saul is killed in battle against the Philistines, David returns, conquers Jerusalem and defeats Saul's only son Ish-Bosheth in the north around 1010 BCE. David reigns for forty years and is succeeded by his son Solomon, who becomes known for his wealth and wisdom, but also for his extravagant lifestyle. This is circa 970 BCE to 931 BCE, and during his reign, the famous Temple of Solomon is completed here in Jerusalem in 957 BCE, and the Ark of the Covenant is placed inside, where it supposedly remains for almost four hundred years.'

'And is this a historical fact?' asked Andrew.

'The Temple of Solomon was certainly real. It stood where the Al-Aqsa Mosque now sits on the

Temple Mount, just a stone's throw from where we are sitting.'

'Presumably, they would not have built that temple, if there had not been an Ark to place inside it,' said Fiona.

'I agree,' said Finkelstein. 'I think we can take it as fact that the Temple of Solomon did house some type of artefact or reliquary, which is likely to have been what we now know as the Ark of the Covenant.'

'So, I guess that is the first definitive tangible piece of evidence we have of the Ark's existence,' said Andrew.

'I am not sure I would call it *tangible*,' said Finkelstein. 'But the inference that the Ark existed and was kept inside the Temple is a reasonable one.'

Fiona scribbled furiously in her notebook.

'Anyway, following Solomon's death,' continued Finkelstein. 'The ten northern tribes rebelled, establishing the city of Samaria as their capital, with a new king by the name of Jeroboam. The land of Judah in the south, which had Jerusalem as its capital, remained loyal to Solomon's son Rehoboam. This land was occupied by the two remaining tribes of Judah and Benjamin.'

'Jeroboam?' said Fiona. 'I feel like I have come across that name when I was reading about ancient Egypt.'

'You probably have,' said Finkelstein. 'During Solomon's reign, Jeroboam, who was from the tribe Ephraim of the House of Joseph, was a superintendent of his tribesmen in the building of the fortress of Millo in Jerusalem. Here he became aware of the widespread discontent with the extravagant reign of Solomon, so he began to conspire against Solomon. But the conspiracy was discovered and Jeroboam fled to Egypt around 927 BCE, where he came under the protection of the Pharaoh Shoshenq I. There is no mention of Shoshenq I in the biblical texts, but there is a mention of a *Shishak*, who invaded Canaan with one of the largest armies in history. I feel quite certain that Shishak and Shoshenq I are one and the same.'

'Jeroboam fled to Egypt?' said Fiona. 'That seems a strange place to run off to. The twelve tribes had virtually just escaped that place.'

'It might seem odd,' nodded Finkelstein, 'But the Pharaohs were not above trying to meddle in the affairs of their neighbours, and this could have been a way of stoking division amongst the people of Canaan.'

'I guess so,' said Fiona. 'So how does Jeroboam end up back in the north as king of the Kingdom of Israel?'

'Well, first he returns from Egypt and joins a delegation attempting to get King Solomon to reduce taxes. This fails, and as a result, the ten northern tribes rebel, and this is where the Kingdom of Israel is formed in the north. Then, in the fifth year of Rehoboam's reign over Judah in the south, Pharaoh Shoshenq I invades and conquers Judah, making it a vassal state of Egypt. However, he does not attack the Kingdom of Israel, where Jeroboam is now king.'

'Really?' said Fiona, raising an eyebrow. 'So, there is a failed attempt to get Solomon to lower taxes, which results in the revolt by the ten northern tribes, and then Shoshenq I just happens to arrive in Canaan with one of the largest armies ever seen?'

'Correct' smiled Finkelstein.

'And Shoshenq then takes over the Kingdom of Judah, but he leaves the Kingdom of Israel alone? That seems highly suspicious.'

'It certainly does,' chuckled Finkelstein. 'You could be forgiven for thinking that Jeroboam and Shoshenq I had made a deal, during Jeroboam's time in Egypt. I believe Jeroboam assisted Shoshenq I in conquering Judah, in return for becoming king of the ten tribes in the Kingdom of Israel in the north.'

'That is some proper Machiavellian manoeuvring,' said Fiona.

'Very much so,' said Finkelstein. 'But I feel confident that this is what happened.'

'Ok,' said Fiona, looking intently at her notes. 'And during all of this, the Ark of the Covenant is in the Temple of Solomon, here in Jerusalem?'

'Yes. As far as we know,' replied Finkelstein. 'Of course, only the Levites were ever allowed to see it, including after it was brought to Jerusalem, but the generally accepted history states that the Ark remained inside the Temple of Solomon, until its destruction in 587 BCE by the Babylonian King Nebuchadnezzar II.'

'So, did Nebuchadnezzar II take the Ark back with him to Babylon?' asked Andrew.

'Not as far as anyone can tell,' replied Finkelstein. 'This is the essence of the enduring mystery about what happened to the Ark. It is recorded in the texts that Nebuchadnezzar II took all the treasures of the

Temple of Solomon, but there is no mention of the Ark.'

'Once again, that seems very strange to me,' said Fiona. 'There's just something here that doesn't add up.'

'Welcome to my world,' laughed Finkelstein and spread out his hands, whilst looking around the room. 'This mystery is at the heart of the conflict over Jerusalem to this very day.'

'I suppose so,' said Fiona. 'Is there any possibility that the Ark could have been transported out of Jerusalem somehow? I am starting to wonder if it was even here in 587 BCE when Nebuchadnezzar II arrived.'

'That's a very good question,' replied Finkelstein. 'There is one theory, which has yet to be proven right or wrong, but which seems to have become unverifiable.'

'That sounds intriguing,' said Fiona and leaned forward. 'What is it?'

'It relates to the brief mention in the biblical texts of an unnamed queen, who travelled to Jerusalem to meet King Solomon. She had heard of his wealth and wisdom, and she wanted to see him. She went to Jerusalem, and they exchanged gifts, and she was apparently very impressed. This is where the story ends in the biblical texts. However, in the *Kebra Nagast*, which is a foundational document to the Orthodox Ethiopian Church, the story is presented in much more detail. According to the Kebra Nagast, that queen is Makeda, the Queen of Sheba.'

'Do you mean *the* Queen of Sheba?' said Andrew.

'Yes. Most people have heard the name,' nodded Finkelstein. 'According to this narrative, the Queen of Sheba returns to the land of Sheba pregnant, and in due course gives birth to a son called Menelik. When he is twenty-two years of age, Menelik travels to Jerusalem to see his father King Solomon, who by then is an old man. King Solomon is so impressed with Menelik, that he tries to convince him to stay in Jerusalem and succeed him as King of the United Monarchy. Menelik declines and chooses to return to the land of Sheba, but he supposedly takes with him the Ark of the Covenant.'

'Really?' said Fiona sceptically. 'Solomon just hands over the Ark, leaving the Temple in Jerusalem empty? That seems unlikely.'

'I agree,' said Finkelstein, 'But the fact remains that the Ethiopian Orthodox Church to this day claims to hold the Ark inside the Chapel of the Tablet, next to the Church of Maryam Tsion in the city of Axum in Ethiopia.'

'That's quite the story,' mused Fiona. 'Has anyone ever been able to verify this?'

'No,' chuckled Finkelstein. 'If someone had, we would all know about it by now. In the same way that only the Levites were allowed to handle and lay eyes on the Ark, so too the Orthodox Church of Ethiopia appoints just one person, whose responsibility it is to look after the artefact. Needless to say, this is a job for life, and only this one person is allowed to see it.'

'Well, that's not very helpful,' said Fiona. 'It almost seems cruel to present this claim, and then deny anyone access to it.'

'Well,' smiled Finkelstein and shrugged. 'If the Ark really is there, and if it really has the terrifying powers that it is supposed to have, then perhaps that is a good thing.'

'I suppose,' said Fiona. 'It makes you wonder what would happen if one day the Orthodox Church of Ethiopia came out and said, "We have it. Here it is.".'

'Probably nothing good,' chuckled Finkelstein. 'These sorts of things never seem to make things better for anyone.'

'Perhaps,' said Fiona. 'Common understanding and tolerance between humans have always been a bit of a Sisyphean task.'

'A what?' asked Andrew, starting to feel like a third wheel.

'Oh,' said Fiona. 'Sorry. In Greek mythology, Sisyphus was a king who cheated death twice and was then punished by having to roll a boulder up a hill for eternity. Every time he got it near the top, it would roll back down again.'

'Sounds sadistic,' said Andrew.

'Oh. Speaking of mountains,' said Finkelstein, having seemingly just remembered something. 'There is another theory about the Ark that you might find interesting. The Hebrew Bible states, that the prophet Jeremiah was warned by God of the impending Babylonian invasion in 587 BCE, and that he therefore took the Ark out of the Temple in Jerusalem and placed it somewhere near Mount Nebo.'

'That is the mountain from which the Israelites first saw the Promised Land after their exodus from Egypt, right?' said Fiona.

'That is correct,' said Finkelstein. 'Bear in mind that this was written, not by Jeremiah himself, but by an unidentified author circa 150 BCE, so around half a Millennium after the event supposedly took place. So, I do not put much stock in this particular story either. But it is interesting nonetheless.'

Fiona hesitated as if choosing her words carefully. 'Professor, would you say that you personally give any credence to any of what we have just discussed, from a purely historical and archaeological perspective?'

'To put it bluntly, as far as the biblical texts are concerned, the only thing you can really rely on is that the Old Testament can't be relied on. Regarding the historicity of the Bible in general, I think it is fair to say that it is severely lacking. Some things are possibly true. Other things are certainly not true. Similarly, some events have an archaeological and scientific basis, but most things do not. As for the divine or supernatural elements of the Bible, there is obviously no evidence at all that any of that ever happened. But given the imperative at the time for any would-be rulers to somehow demonstrate that they had a deity on their side, it stands to reason that all of the legends from that time would include some type of divine or supernatural element. And as time passes, those elements do not tend to become smaller. They only ever get bigger. You know, when people tell stories about fishing trips, their fish never get smaller. They only ever get bigger.'

'True,' nodded Fiona.

'Look,' smiled Finkelstein benignly, and folded his hands on the table cloth in front of him. 'As I have said, this is a highly emotive issue. There are people who, despite the lack of evidence, think that the Bible, including its narrative about the Exodus and the Ark, is an actual historical record. Then there are people who believe that the Bible is essentially just a very long but well-crafted myth, designed for political purposes. And if it can't be backed up with archaeological evidence, then it should be disregarded. I probably lean towards the latter, but perhaps the truth is somewhere in between. Ultimately, everyone has to make up their own minds. By that I mean, that we all have to think about it properly, and then decide for ourselves, as opposed to someone telling us what to think and what to believe. That is the most important part.'

'I couldn't have said it better myself,' said Andrew and stretched his back. They had been sitting in the café for more than two hours, and his head was beginning to swim with the barrage of facts and conjecture that Finkelstein had presented them with.

Finkelstein looked at his wristwatch. 'And now I must get back to my wife,' he said. 'She is expecting me soon, and I don't want her to worry.'

'Well, thank you very much for your time Professor,' said Fiona. 'We are extremely grateful for this. I am sure it will help us put things into perspective. If nothing else it might give us a starting point for where to go next.'

'It has been my pleasure,' said Finkelstein and placed his hands on his round belly. 'I hope you will have time to see a little bit of the city while you are here. It is a magnificent place. You can practically feel the history oozing out of the stone in the walls and the streets.'

'We will hopefully find time to do that,' said Fiona.

And with that, they bid the Professor farewell and watched him shuffle out of the café, back to the wife he met in this very place thirty-seven years ago.

Sixteen

As they were walking away from the meeting with Professor Finkelstein towards the Al-Aqsa Mosque on the Temple Mount, Andrew noticed that Fiona appeared subdued.

'You seem a bit dejected,' he said. 'What's wrong?'

Fiona shrugged and smiled. 'I don't know. I almost feel disappointed that the Exodus story was mostly, if not entirely, fictitious.'

'Why?' said Andrew looking perplexed.

Fiona shrugged her shoulders. 'I suppose there is a certain romanticism to the whole thing that is just inherently attractive, so I almost find myself wanting to believe it. But I guess that was exactly the point of the whole thing.'

'How do you mean?'

''Like Finkelstein said. The whole thing is expertly crafted to achieve what is ultimately the political goal. The idea was to shape the mindset of a whole host of different tribes and peoples, and make them buy into the notion of shared trauma, common ancestry, and thereby a sense of belonging.'

'I see what you mean,' nodded Andrew. 'But what does this mean for the idea of the Ark of the Covenant actually being a real object?'

'Well,' she replied. 'Regardless of who the supposed Levites or Hebrews or Israelites really were, and whether they were ethnically originally Canaanites from the southern Levant, or whether they were Egyptians, it doesn't really matter for the basic structure of the Exodus story. At some point in history, it is conceivable, even probable, that a group of people left Egypt, possibly under duress, possibly not. And they took with them an artefact, which they carried in an ark since that is what all-important reliquaries were transported in during ancient times. What we need to do now is chase down that lead, and see where it takes us.'

'What about Jabari Omran's notebook,' said Andrew. 'Does it say anything about the idea that Menelik transported the Ark to Axum in Ethiopia?'

'Only briefly, and he placed a big question mark next to it. I assume he was not particularly convinced that this actually ever happened. I think it sounds a bit tenuous myself too.'

They were now walking along the cobbled streets of Jerusalem's old town, next to the walls of the Temple Mount.

'So, this is where the Temple of Solomon was first built?' asked Andrew and gestured to the walls.

'That's right,' replied Fiona. '957 BCE. Almost three thousand years ago.'

'But why is there a mosque here?'

'Simple,' said Fiona. 'Because the city was conquered by Muslim armies in 638 CE, so they immediately began building a mosque to rival the city's existing churches.'

'And what exactly is the gilded dome that is also in there?' asked Andrew.

'That's a separate building called the Dome of the Rock, which was completed about fifty years later. It is built over the rock on which all the Abrahamic religions believe God created the world and the first humans, Adam and Eve.'

'Right in there?' asked Andrew with a smile on his face and sounding sceptical. 'What about the dinosaurs? Were they also created in there?'

Fiona glared and him the way a teacher would look at a petulant student. 'Don't be facetious. A lot of people take this stuff very seriously.'

'I know,' said Andrew in a placating tone of voice. 'Relax. Just because they do, doesn't mean I have to. No one should tell anyone else what to believe.'

Fiona nodded. 'On that, we can agree. Anyway, just think about it. This is a Muslim monument built over a rock that is sacred to all three major religions, in a city under the control of the Jews, in a country that many Muslims don't recognise. It is no wonder there has been so much conflict here. It is part of the reason why this whole region is so contested, aside of course from the monumentally ignorant way in which the Brits and French carved up the whole of the Middle-East in 1916, with the secret Sykes-Picot Agreement.'

'Let's not go over that again,' smiled Andrew, sensing that Fiona was about to go on a roll.

'Ok,' said Fiona, 'I am just saying that this place has such a complicated history, and it has changed hands so many times, that it is simply not possible to unequivocally establish the answer to the simple question of, who was here first?'

'I guess Finkelstein was right when he said that the geographical bottleneck of this region, is largely the reason for why it is this way.'

'What is most ironic to me,' said Fiona, 'is that if we were to go all the way back to the beginning, whenever that was and whatever that really means, the two sides that are now fighting over it, were probably more or less the same group. They were all indigenous to this area. Different tribes, but still more or less one people. At least if you go back far enough.'

'Taking that logic to its extreme,' said Andrew, 'you could argue that if we go all the way back to the very beginning in Africa, then we are all undeniably the same people because we have the same ancestors. We are quite literally all part of the same family, genetically speaking.'

Fiona glanced at Andrew with a wry smile. 'I never knew you had a tree-hugging pacifist hippie inside you,' she said, teasingly.

Andrew shrugged and smiled. 'It has nothing to do with trees or hippies. I don't care where people are from or who their ancestors were. I care about what they do, and how they behave towards others.'

'Very wise, Mr SAS man,' smiled Fiona.

★   ★   ★

Fiona had suggested that they spend the night in Jerusalem to ponder their next move, and Andrew had agreed. After all, they did not exactly have a firm plan for where to go next or what to do.

When he woke up in the hotel room and drowsily opened his eyes, he was momentarily unable to remember where he was. It was pitch black outside, and there was no noise from the streets.

He lifted his head to find Fiona sitting on the sofa with her laptop in front of her.

'What on earth are you doing?' said Andrew, rubbing his eyes. 'What time is it?'

'Don't know,' replied Fiona without looking up.

She was staring intently at the screen of her laptop.

Andrew glanced at the clock next to their bed. It read 2:37 am.

'Are you alright?' he asked.

'Yes, I'm fine,' replied Fiona, without moving a muscle.

Andrew waited for a few seconds, expecting her to elaborate, but she just kept looking at her screen.

'Fiona,' he said firmly. 'Snap out of it. What are doing over there in the middle of the night? You need sleep just as much as anyone else.'

She finally lifted her gaze and shifted it towards him.

'Sorry,' she said, blinking a couple of times. 'Sorry, I just suddenly had a thought.'

'Oh those,' said Andrew wearily. 'Yes, those can be dangerous. What about?'

'Finkelstein mentioned Mount Nebo, and it has been bugging me ever since.'

'Why?'

'At first, I couldn't put my finger on it. But I was lying in bed, and I suddenly remembered a sketch in Omran's notebook. He hasn't written any notes on that page, except for the word *Jeremiah*, and a cryptic name in the bottom right corner of the sketch. But it is literally just a drawing of what looks like a hilltop. It is definitely not the peak that was depicted on the metal casket that he and Doctor Mansour were working on, because that looked like the two humps on a camel. This one is a smooth, rounded thing. But it has what appears to be an overhang with what could be a cavemouth. It is obvious that the drawing has been made from a very specific spot, because there are landmarks there, such as towns, other peaks as well as a river included in the sketch.'

'Where is this going?' asked Andrew impatiently. His body was trying to convince him to lie back down and go back to sleep.

'Get this,' she replied and quickly leafed through her Bible. 'In the Second Book of Maccabees, it says the following. "*It was also in the same document that the prophet, having received an oracle, ordered that the tent and the Ark should follow with him, and that he went out to the mountain where Moses had gone up and had seen the inheritance of God. Jeremiah came and found a cave-dwelling, and he brought there the tent and the Ark and the altar of incense; then he sealed up the entrance. Some of those who followed him came up intending to mark the way, but could not find it. When Jeremiah learned of it, he rebuked them and declared: "The place shall remain unknown until God gathers his people together again and shows his mercy. Then the Lord will disclose these things, and the glory of the Lord and the cloud will appear, as they were shown in the case of Moses, and as Solomon asked that the place should be specially consecrated.".'*

'Fiona,' sighed Andrew, sounding irritated. 'It is two-thirty in the bloody morning. What are you trying to say?'

'I am saying,' replied Fiona. 'The Book of Maccabees states that just before Nebuchadnezzar II conquered Jerusalem, the Ark was taken by the prophet Jeremiah, to a cave inside the mountain from which Moses saw the promised land. That mountain is Mount Nebo in Jordan.'

'I think I know where this is going,' smiled Andrew.

Fiona ignored him and continued. 'Jabari Omran has provided us with a sketch, so all we have to do is find the spot.'

'But we don't even know if this is anything other than speculation. What is the source? How did he create this sketch?'

Fiona looked at him with a drained expression. 'We don't know anything for a fact, obviously. I can't tell precisely what the source is, except that in the bottom right corner it seems to say, *Oil Painting: Zacchaeus Collection.*'

'What does that mean?' asked Andrew now sitting up in the bed, massaging his right shoulder. 'Who is Zacchaeus?'

'No idea,' said Fiona. 'Never heard of him, or her. It might be from someone's private collection, and the fact that it is an oil painting doesn't really help us much either. If I remember correctly, the first oil paintings in Europe were made in the 12th century, so it could technically have been made anywhere within a time span of 800 years. For all we know, the painting might also have been a copy of something else. There's no way of knowing.'

'It all sounds extremely tenuous,' said Andrew. 'I am pretty sure that Finkelstein didn't mention this because he thinks the Ark is inside Mount Nebo somewhere.'

'It doesn't matter what he thinks,' said Fiona. 'What matters is that this is a tangible clue and that Omran may have believed that this could be where the Ark is.'

'So, what do you suggest,' asked Andrew now sounding more awake.

'I think we need to go to Mount Nebo,' replied Fiona.

'How did I know you would say that?' he smirked.

Fiona smiled sheepishly. 'You never know. We might find something there.'

'But where?' said Andrew sceptically. 'It's an entire mountain.'

'Yes,' replied Fiona. 'But the sketch seems very specific in terms of where it was made from.'

Andrew hesitated and was about to try to talk her out of it, but he decided to fold. There was just no way he was going to dissuade her, and at least in theory, she was right. They just might find something.

★ ★ ★

Six hours and a couple of hours' sleep later, they were on the road towards the Israeli border with Jordan. The hotel had swiftly arranged for a rental car, and the trip itself was going to be quick. As the crow flies, the border is only around 15 kilometres due east from the outskirts of Jerusalem, although the winding roads down towards Jericho and the River Jordan, added many kilometres to the trip.

The wide plain where the River Jordan flows is called the Jordan Rift Valley, and is a divergent boundary between the African tectonic plate and its Arabian counterpart. It was formed over a period of tens of millions of years, beginning as early as twenty-three million years ago, when the Arabian plate began moving north-east and away from the African plate.

'Geologically speaking,' said Fiona, 'this area is almost twenty-five million years old. It sort of puts all the squabbling between us humans over the past few thousand years into perspective.'

'Sorry,' smiled Andrew, and glanced over at her. 'I am too tired for deep philosophical conversations right now. Someone woke me up in the middle of the night with a hair-brained plan to go to a mountain in a different country and look for the Ark of the Covenant.'

Fiona burst out laughing. 'When you put it like that,' she laughed. 'I guess it does sound pretty crazy.'

'Never a dull moment,' said Andrew, feigning long-suffering weariness. 'Anyway, we're coming up on the Jordanian border in a few minutes. Got the passports ready?'

'Right here,' said Fiona, and held them up in front of her.

'Alright,' said Andrew, thinking about the fact that his gun was in a small safe on their aircraft, which was still parked at Jerusalem International Airport. 'Hey, look at that sign,' he said and pointed ahead towards a big sign.

'*Allenby Bridge*,' read Fiona. 'Sounds like one of you lot again,' she smirked and looked at Andrew.

'Us lot?' said Andrew. 'What do you mean?'

'You Brits,' replied Fiona. 'Like this Bridge over the River Kwai. This is just the Bridge over the River Jordan, no doubt named modestly after the man who built it.'

'Quite possibly,' said Andrew, and shrugged. 'At least we won't have to swim.'

The border crossing was busy. Long queues of tour buses were parked and undergoing inspection, most of them on the way from Israel into Jordan, and probably about to embark on the 130-kilometre journey south to Petra.

Andrew drove their car through the designated crossing point for foreigners and presented the visas that had been expedited through the British Consulate in Jerusalem and delivered to their hotel early that morning. Fifteen minutes later they were headed south towards the town of Al Rama on the Jordanian side of the river. Just a couple of kilometres away they could see quite clearly the mountains rising up ahead of them. To call them mountains was perhaps a bit grandiose, since the highest peak at Mount Nebo is only around 700 metres above sea level. But because the approach from Israel happens over a wide flat stretch of land quite close to sea level, the mountain has the appearance of towering above anyone coming towards it from the northwest.

'How do you want to do this?' asked Andrew. 'We can't just drive up there and hope for the best, can we?'

'I was thinking we just drive up past the peak, and then down the other side of the mountain. I had a look at a simple 3D map of the area this morning, and I think I have a rough idea of the layout of the mountain. For now, though, let's just make our way towards the top so we can get a proper feel for this place.'

It was now a hot clear day, but at this altitude the air was pleasant. Mount Nebo is more akin to a very large hill, in that it has only a few sections that are steep. The rest consist of a series of hills that overlap to reach several hundred meters into the air. The hills themselves are a dusty pale-yellow colour, and mainly have a rounded shape to them, with only a few jagged peaks. Here and there, bits of vegetation in the form of low grass and bushes stick up from the rocks.

'Oh,' said Andrew. 'I forgot to tell you. I got this.'

He pulled out a plastic device that looked a lot like a handheld GPS tracker. Roughly the size of a small mobile phone, it was black with yellow trim around the edges. It had a display at the top and a range of large buttons with different colours on its front.

'Boys and toys,' smiled Fiona. 'What's that?'

'It a radiation detector, or Geiger counter,' replied Andrew. 'I was able to requisition one via MI6's station chief in the British Embassy in Jerusalem.'

'Really?' asked Fiona incredulously. 'MI6 has people working in the British Embassy in Israel?'

'Officially, the answer is no,' smiled Andrew.

'I don't even want to know about this,' sighed Fiona and shook her head.

'Good,' said Andrew. 'Because officially I don't know this, and even if I did, I would not be at liberty to tell anyone.'

'Spycraft, eh?' said Fiona, with a dubious look on her face.

'Something like that,' replied Andrew. 'Anyway, I figured this might come in handy since we're quite literally looking for something radioactive. We don't want to inadvertently walk into a torrent of gamma rays without realising it.'

'Good point,' said Fiona. 'I didn't think of that.'

'See?' grinned Andrew. 'Not just a pretty face.'

Andrew continued to drive the rental car along the winding road towards the summit. They were gaining altitude only very slowly, and the road was winding left and right with only a gentle incline.

'I guess this road has been here forever,' said Andrew. 'It seems to have been laid so that it is relatively easy to get to the top, even if someone is walking or pulling a cart.'

'It could easily have been here for centuries,' said Fiona 'Once a path to somewhere is picked, it eventually turns into a road, and once that happens, it never changes again. Just look at central London. Almost all the tiny little narrow roads are exactly where they were hundreds of years ago when the city really started growing. Some of them might even be in the same location as when the Romans put them down almost two thousand years ago.'

'It is fascinating to think about what has unfolded on this road through the ages,' said Andrew. 'This must have been a place of pilgrimage for several thousand years now.'

'It still is,' said Fiona. 'There is even a church near the peak called the Memorial Church of Moses. We should be coming up on it in a couple of minutes.'

Sure enough, after another few tight bends and another one hundred meters of altitude or so, they came round a wide bend to find a sign for the visitor's car park of the church. The car park was closed off, so they continued on for a few hundred meters along the road which now ran on top of a ridge and continued south-east through the mountains, and further into Jordan towards the major city of Madaba. On their left to the north-east, was a view towards what appeared to be a much more fertile plain than they had seen on the western side of the mountain.

'I don't think this is going to help us,' said Fiona. 'If Jeremiah came up on this mountain with a group of people carrying the Ark, they are unlikely to have gone to the peak of the mountain, and then proceeded down the other side. Also, wouldn't they have hidden the Ark somewhere that overlooks the Jordan Valley and Israel?'

'I suppose so,' replied Andrew and let the car come to a gradual stop. 'The whole point here is that this is the mountain where Moses first saw the Promised Land, so it makes sense to think that they must have hidden the Ark near the summit on the western side.'

'I saw a few interesting features when I was looking at the 3D map,' said Fiona. 'We should go back down the way we came, and then keep an eye out for those. I'll tell you when to stop.'

They drove back up to the Memorial Church of Moses, and then proceeded down the way they had first come up, now driving west along the winding road down towards the Jordan River Valley.

'Pull over here,' said Fiona just after they passed the church. 'I want to hop out and see the view from here.'

There was a warm dry breeze blowing gently over the mountain as they got out of their rental car, stepped over the guard rails and out to a slightly elevated spot from where there was a clear view of the entire Jordan Rift Valley. The Jordan River was below them, no more than 10 kilometres away, and its flood plains extended north for as far as the eye could see. The Dead Sea was stretching south from a point due west of them, where the flood plains end and the river meets the salty inland sea.

'Amazing view,' said Fiona, and stopped at the edge. She placed her hands on her hips and turned slowly from left to right as she surveyed the entire vista in front of them.

'Down there is Bethlehem,' she said and pointed towards the southwest. 'Over there, due west is Jerusalem, and the town of Jericho is just there,' she said and pointed towards the north-west, where the ancient city could be seen clearly on the western side of the River Jordan.

'Quite spectacular,' said Andrew and took a swig from his water bottle.

'Archaeologists have found evidence of as many as twenty distinct settlements on the site where Jericho now sits. The oldest ones go back eleven thousand years to around 9000 BCE.'

'That amount of time is difficult to wrap your head around, isn't it?' said Andrew. 'Most people think that something that happened a hundred years ago is in the distant past, but this is on a whole different magnitude.'

'It is,' nodded Fiona and tucked a lock of hair behind her ear. 'It is amazing to think that those three places are exactly where they were when Moses supposedly stood on this mountain top and looked at the Promised Land for the first time. Anyone standing here would find it very easy to work out exactly where they are, just based on the relative positions of those settlements.'

'They would also find it easy to come up here, hide something, mark a location, and then go down again whilst knowing exactly where that position was. You don't need GPS for that in this valley. There are so many landmarks, natural and man-made.'

'You're thinking of Jeremiah, aren't you?' asked Fiona.

'Yes,' replied Andrew. 'If the story in Maccabees is true, he would have come from roughly that direction over there, right?' said Andrew, and pointed towards Jerusalem due west some 30 kilometres away, as the crow flies. 'If they came in a more or less straight line, they would have skirted the very northern edge of the Dead Sea, which means they would have come from that direction.' He pointed west along a ridge that ran up towards the mountain peak.

'There is no way to access that point by road,' said Fiona. 'There simply aren't any.'

'I think we should drive back down towards the valley and have a look. There might be a dirt road.'

'Ok,' said Fiona. 'What we need to do is somehow get to a point where the view corresponds exactly to Omran's sketch. That is the only chance we have of finding the location of the cave he has marked.'

'Alright,' said Andrew, hesitating for a moment to savour the view. 'Even if we find nothing up here, it will have been worth it.'

'Definitely,' smiled Fiona.

They stepped back over the guard rail and returned to the car. A few minutes later, they came to several tight hairpin bends in quick succession on what was the steepest bit of road they had found. On their right, the terrain fell away towards the rocky and somewhat jagged foothills of the mountain's western side. On their left, the mountain towered up over them, and there was a particularly steep section with a sheer cliff, facing the valley.

Fiona stepped out and away from the car until she was standing on the very edge of the drop.

'Don't fall down,' said Andrew. 'I don't feel like climbing down after you in this heat.'

'Don't worry,' said Fiona and pulled out Omran's notebook from her shoulder bag. 'I won't, but you might have to do something similar.'

'Excuse me?' said Andrew.

'Looking at Omran's sketch,' said Fiona, 'this could be the right area. The River Jordan is down there, just as it is in the sketch, Jericho is over there on the left. The sketch also has a church spire in the far distance, which I am going to assume represents Jerusalem, which is that direction. And above us, there's a sheer cliff face not too far from the peak, just like in the sketch, and that is also where Omran has indicated a cavemouth.'

As she spoke, she marked out the different landmarks with her outstretched arm, while holding the notebook up in front of her with her other hand.

'This area also sits almost perfectly on the shortest route from Jerusalem to the peak of the mountain, so if Jeremiah and his men ever came here, they would almost certainly have come past this point.'

'Makes sense, I guess,' said Andrew.

'It's all here,' continued Fiona, 'but the perspective is wrong.'

'So, what do we do then?' asked Andrew, looking around the difficult terrain, whilst suspecting what was about to happen.

'I have an idea,' said Fiona. 'I take the car further down the road and peel off the small dirt road that is marked here on Google Maps.'

She showed him her phone, which displayed a satellite view of a map of the area, and a blue dot as their current location. Further down the road towards the valley, there seemed to be a small dirt road leading almost directly south and away from the mountain.

'I am sure the perspective from down there will match the sketch much better, which means that must be where the painting or sketch was originally made. Once I have that location, I can then direct you from this spot right here, and up the mountain.'

'Up the mountain,' repeated Andrew sceptically.

'Well, one of us has to,' said Fiona. 'You are much more fit than I am. And you're so strong and handsome,' she purred sarcastically.

'Don't try that with me, Miss,' he laughed. 'Where exactly do you want me to go?'

Fiona pointed to the cliff face above them. 'It must be close to that sheer face up there. But once I am in a position, I can guide you in with my phone. I have brought binoculars, so I will be able to see you easily. Wait, we do have phone coverage here, do we?'

They looked at each other for a brief moment and then checked their phones.

'I have three bars,' said Fiona.

'Me too,' said Andrew. 'Alright, fine. Let's do this. Let me have your water bottle. Mine is empty.'

Fiona took a quick sip and handed her bottle to Andrew. He was going to need it a lot more than she was. Then she got into the car in the driver's seat and rolled the window down.

'Give me five minutes, and then I will call you,' she said. 'I should be able to find the spot pretty easily, as long as the dirt road passes just roughly through it.'

'Take your time,' said Andrew. 'Dirt roads can be tricky, and we have all afternoon to do this.'

'Don't worry,' beamed Fiona, as she put on her seatbelt. 'I am a big girl, remember?'

Andrew had a sudden flashback to the first night they had met in London when he had offered to walk her home, and she had responded with the same phrase. That suddenly seemed a very long time ago.

'Ok,' he said. 'Call me when you want me to head out.'

'Ok. Talk to you in a bit,' said Fiona, and then she was off down the mountain at significant speed.

Never bloody listens, thought Andrew and smiled to himself.

He took another swig from the water bottle and turned to look up at the mountainside above him. It was in full sun and would continue to be so for several hours until the sun would set to the west over Jerusalem in the far distance. From this angle and looking up, he was only able to vaguely make out the cliff face that Fiona had pointed out to him, and he began to create a rough idea in his mind about the route he might need to take, and what it would require. He was in good shape, but it was hot, and they had not brought nearly enough water for a climbing adventure like this.

He could now spot their rental car making its way along the dirt road far below him. Dust clouds whirled up behind it as it made its way further south and away from Mount Nebo. After a few minutes, it stopped. It was too far for him to be able to see clearly, but he thought he could just make out Fiona stepping out of the car. A moment later, his phone rang.

'Hello handsome,' he heard Fiona say. 'What is a good-looking chap like you doing on a mountain like this?'

'Very funny,' smirked Andrew. He would never admit it, but he loved her compliments. 'How does it look?'

'Really good actually. I've got the whole mountain right ahead of me, the river seems to be in the right place, and Jericho sits exactly where it is on the sketch, relative to the valley and the mountain. The cavemouth on the sketch seems to be around the area where the cliff face is, so this is definitely the right place.'

'Alright,' said Andrew as he hopped over the guard rail and crossed the road to begin his ascent. 'I am going to start heading up there now. Call me if you can see that I need to adjust course.'

'Ok,' said Fiona. 'Good luck.'

Seventeen

As he began his climb, Andrew deliberately paced himself. Speed was not a priority, but energy conservation was. His approach to physical exertion like this was to start out slow, push until his heart rate was at a steady 120 beats per minute, and then keep it there by adjusting his speed. If the terrain got significantly steeper or more physically demanding, he would simply move slower to keep his exertion level and heart rate more or less stable during the ascent.

This strategy had proven extremely useful over the years, especially when he had been dropped with his SAS platoon in mountainous terrain in Afghanistan. Carrying a heavy backpack and weapons, moving fast was a guaranteed way of tiring themselves out much more quickly, and a highly variable heart rate would make it difficult for them to use their weapons effectively. In addition, it would be much easier to spot the platoon if they were scrambling over rocks and boulders in an effort to cover a lot of distance in a short amount of time. Their ability to recon the immediate area would also be severely compromised by excessive speed. None of this was conscious behaviour anymore. It was simply instinct and muscle memory. His body would take care of the 'how'. All he had to do was use his brain to decide the 'where'.

After about ten minutes, his phone chirped. He stopped and sat down on a rock, looking down towards where Fiona and the car was. At first, he could not see her because of the change in perspective as a result of him ascending, but then he spotted the car.

'How are you doing?' asked Fiona. 'You're making really good progress already.'

'I am alright,' said Andrew, breathing heavily. 'Where do you want me to go?'

'You're pretty much on the right path, but you might want to bear left a bit if you can.'

Andrew looked up and ahead of him, trying to scout a route that would take him slightly more to the left as he ascended.

'Ok,' he said and winced. The left side of his chest had not completely recovered from the incident in Cairo. 'How far do you reckon it is? I can't see the cliff face any more from where I am standing.'

'Perhaps another fifteen minutes, if you keep this pace,' replied Fiona.

'Alright,' said Andrew. 'Talk later.'

He took a couple of deep breaths and swallowed a big mouthful of water, and then he continued onwards. The terrain was gradually becoming steeper, and after a few minutes, he could see the cliff face towering over him up ahead. In order to get to it, he would have to approach an overhang and somehow find a way up and over it. That turned out to be easier than he had expected, since several large boulders had come down the mountainside and landed in a messy pile next to the overhang. They allowed him to climb onto them, and then jump up and grab the ledge above him.

Hauling himself up and over the small overhang, he stood up to discover what appeared to be a wide ledge with vegetation growing near where the rockface extended upwards almost vertically towards the peak of the mountain.

Right on cue, his phone rang again. 'Hey,' he said, sounding very out of breath. 'Is this it?'

'I think so,' said Fiona. 'It looks like the exact spot marked on Omran's sketch. What can you see? Is there a cave?'

Andrew grimaced from the effort of traversing the overhang and turned to look around him. 'It's just a wide ledge. Probably around ten meters wide. I don't see anything unusual here.'

'It should be right there,' urged Fiona. 'Are you sure there's nothing there?'

Andrew shook his head. 'There's nothing here, except for some boulders and some bushes.'

He took a few steps further along the ledge and focused on the vegetation. 'Hang on,' he said. 'There's a big bush over here by the rockface.'

Fiona hesitated for a moment. 'Andrew, if the next words out of your mouth are "There is a burning bush here", I swear, I will get in the car and drive back to Jerusalem without you.'

'Fair enough,' laughed Andrew. 'I promise, I won't tell you when it catches fire.'

He took another few steps towards a group of bushes that lined the back of the ledge in front of the sheer cliff face. 'You have got to be kidding me,' he said.

'What?' said Fiona curiously. 'What do you see?'

'I think there's something behind these bushes,' he said and walked closer.

The bushes looked like small olive trees about a meter tall, and several of them were growing in a tight group by a boulder right next to the cliff face. As he came over next to it, Andrew could see that on the other side of the bushes was what appeared to be a narrow opening into the rockface. He pushed aside the bushes, to reveal a small uneven crevice about twenty centimetres wide and a meter tall.

'There's an opening here,' he said.

'What's inside,' asked Fiona, struggling to contain her excitement.

'I can't see,' said Andrew. 'It is much too small to fit through. Hold on a second.'

He put the phone down on a rock next to him and stepped in between the bushes obscuring the crevice.

Peering inside, he was unable to make out how big it was or how deep into the rockface it might go. Then he noticed that one side of the crevice seemed to be part of the surrounding rockface, while the other had a slightly lighter colour and a smoother texture, almost as if it was a separate piece of rock. As if it had been placed there by someone.

He stuck both hands inside the crevice, grabbed the lighter piece of rock, and started pulling. The rock did not budge at all. He readjusted his stance, placing one boot on the rockface next to the crevice, and then pulled again. This time the rock moved ever so slightly. It was definitely not part of the rockface. Sweating profusely, and with his heart rate now well into running territory, he grimaced and put all his strength into trying to move the rock. Every sinew in his arms and back were straining under the power of his muscles, and ever so slowly the rock started to move out and away from the surrounding rockface.

Groaning loudly, Andrew put his final bit of strength into it, and then the rock came loose and fell towards him. He fell backwards, and just managed to move his legs out of the way as it toppled over onto the ledge with a loud thump.

'Andrew?' Fiona's voice said from his phone.

Andrew got up, dusted himself down and looked at the opening. It was now about one by one meters in size, and the inside of it was almost completely black.

'Andrew?' repeated Fiona.

He went over and picked up the phone. 'I am here,' he panted.

'Andrew, I am dying here,' breathed Fiona. 'What is going on?'

'I found a cave,' he said, trying to catch his breath. 'Just had to remove a rock that was blocking the entrance.'

'What's inside?' asked Fiona, almost shouting with excitement.

'Hold on,' replied Andrew. 'Give me a minute here.'

'Sorry,' said Fiona. 'I wish I could be up there with you.'

'You wouldn't enjoy the climb,' grimaced Andrew. 'Anyway, let's see what is inside this thing.'

He walked back over to the opening and knelt down. The bushes were partly blocking the sunlight coming through the opening, so only a small amount of light made it into the cave's interior.

'Let me just get my torch,' he said and reached into the side pocket of his trousers.

He switched on the torch and shone its light through the opening.

'That's better,' he said and crouched down to look into the cave.

'How big is it?' asked Fiona.

'Not sure,' said Andrew. 'Looks pretty big. About the size of an average living room, perhaps a bit smaller. I am going to have a quick look around, ok?'

There was no reply.

'Hello?' he said. 'Fiona?'

Still no reply. He checked the phone and noticed he now had zero bars. The connection to the mobile phone network had died as soon as he had started entering the cave opening.

Andrew slipped his phone into this pocket and proceeded through the opening and into a short tunnel. It had been cut neatly into the rock, and the sides and the ceiling were almost flat and meeting at right angles on either side above him. He had to remain crouched as he proceeded through the tunnel, but after less than two metres, he emerged into a large open square space. The floor was flat and covered in a thick layer of dust, which appeared deeper the further into the cave he looked. The walls extended up above him in a vaulted circular fashion, which made him feel like he was standing inside a very large igloo made of stone. The vaulted walls and ceiling were chiselled very neatly, in what must have been a time-consuming process. The space gave no hint as to how old it might be. It could have been made ten years ago or three thousand years ago. There was no way to tell, just by looking at it.

At the back of the cave, he spotted a raised platform with what at first appeared to be some sort of altar. On closer inspection, Andrew realised that it was a type of box made of several separate pieces of neatly hewn rock, that did not resemble the surrounding rockface into which the cave had been made.

There were no identifying marks on any of the sides or on the top of the box, or anything else providing a hint as to what its purpose might be, but it was immediately clear to Andrew that the lid was made so that it could be removed.

He walked slowly around the box while inspecting it, and then stood next to it with his feet placed apart, gripping the lid on two of its sides. He began to pull, and immediately the lid lifted from the box without much effort. It probably weighed around twenty kilos, so Andrew easily removed it and placed it carefully next to the box on the raised platform.

Not sure what he was going to find, he carefully leaned in over the box and shone the light from his torch into it.

'What have we here?' he whispered to himself.

Inside the box was what appeared to be a metal cylinder with patterns on it. It was covered in a thin layer of dust, so after a few moments, Andrew took a deep breath, leaned down and then blew hard. A cloud of dust blew up into his face, and he pulled his head away, whilst coughing and rubbing his eyes.

Leaning back in over the box, he could now see that the patterns appeared to be some form of writing, but he had never seen anything like it before. He reached in and placed his hands carefully under the cylinder, and lifted it up and out of the box. It was heavier than he had expected, and as he placed it gently next to the lid of the box, he realised that it was not a cylinder, but a rolled-up piece of metal.

He sat down next to it and moved his torch around it so as to see the writing more clearly.

The surface of the metal was a dusty pale green, but he could see a rich ochre colour where the metal cylinder had grazed the side of the stone box.

The patterns on the metal were completely indecipherable to Andrew, but it was obvious to him that it bore no relation to the Greek alphabet or to the primitive Cuneiform, which he had seen examples of in various museums. It was clearly also not pictorial in nature, in the way that hieroglyphs are.

He suddenly realised that it must have been at least fifteen minutes since he had lost the phone connection to Fiona, so he got up, dusted himself down and headed back out through the narrow tunnel and into the daylight. He had to squint as the warm afternoon sun shone right into his face as he came out.

He called her number, and she immediately picked up the phone. 'Andy? Are you alright?' She sounded agitated.

'Yes, I am fine,' replied Andrew. 'Sorry. I guess the phone signal can't make it into that cave.'

'I was worried sick,' said Fiona, in an almost accusatory voice, but then her tone softened and became excited and impatient. 'What did you find in there? Tell me!'

'Long story short,' said Andrew. 'I found a cave with some sort of box or shrine made of stone, and inside it were some metal scrolls with writing on them.'

There was no reply, but Andrew could hear her breathing.

'Are you there?' he asked.

'Yes, I am here,' replied Fiona, almost sounding distracted. 'Did you say writing? Are you sure?'

'I don't know what else it could be. It is not like anything I have ever seen before, but it definitely looks like writing to me.'

'Andrew,' said Fiona. 'If what you say is correct, then you may just have made a really important archaeological find.'

'What do you mean?'

'What you are describing sounds exactly like a copper scroll found as part of the so-called Dead Sea Scrolls at a site called Qumran in Israel. These are scrolls with ancient Jewish and Hebrew religious texts written on parchment and papyrus in the period between 300 BCE and 100 CE. This was a major sensation when they were first found in 1945. Archaeologists went on to find many more in the following decade or so. But they also found a copper scroll, describing a long list of sites where treasure was supposed to have been buried.'

'Are you pulling my leg?' asked Andrew sceptically. 'Treasure?'

'I know,' said Fiona. 'It sounds far-fetched, but I am not making this up.'

'Ok, listen,' said Andrew. 'I think you need to come up here and have a look for yourself.'

'Erh,' said Fiona, and paused. 'Yes. I guess you are right. If I don't, I will be kicking myself for the rest of my life.'

'You watched me climb up,' said Andrew, 'So you should be able to follow the same path. I'll help you get up and over the overhang and onto the ledge once you get here.'

'Ok,' said Fiona. 'I will be there as soon as I can. When does the sun set?'

'In about two and a half hours,' replied Andrew. 'We've got time.'

'Alright,' said Fiona. 'See you there.'

Andrew put the phone back in his pocket but then decided to take it out again. Whatever happened, he was going to take a bunch of pictures of the find. They might have to alert the Jordanian authorities, and he did not feel completely convinced, that whoever they ended up contacting, would treat this as the archaeological find that it clearly was.

After having taken pictures of the cave, the stone box and the scroll, he made his way back outside and sat down with his back against the rocks, and closed his eyes. The sun felt warm on his skin, and the gentle breeze kept him at a perfect temperature. Within a couple of minutes, he was asleep.

When he woke up, it was because his phone was vibrating in his trouser pocket.

'Hello,' he mumbled drowsily.

'Where were you?' asked Fiona. 'I've been trying to reach you for a couple of minutes now.'

'Oh,' said Andrew and got up. 'I just fell asleep. I guess lack of sleep is beginning to catch up with me.'

'Well,' said Fiona. 'I am at the ledge. Get your butt over here and pull me up.'

A couple of minutes later they were both standing over the scroll inside the cave, shining their torches down onto it. Fiona knelt down and peered at it closely.

'This is an amazing find,' she said. 'This is definitely very similar to the copper scroll found at Qumran.'

'You said that one of them was like a treasure map?'

'Well,' said Fiona and hesitated. 'It wasn't exactly a treasure map. I mean, there was no map as such. But it contained a list of sixty locations in Israel, and for each location, there was a detailed list of what had been buried there. Gold and silver mainly.'

'Sounds like a plot for a Hollywood movie. Has anyone been able to work out who made the copper scroll?'

'No,' said Fiona. 'There were no signs as to who made it. The text was hammered into the copper plate with a hammer and chisel, and there has been some speculation that it might have been a copy of an original because there are signs that whoever made it might have been illiterate.'

'So, you are saying you think this scroll here is similar to the Qumran copper scroll?'

'I think it might well be,' replied Fiona. 'I can't tell just from looking at it. It was written in an unusual dialect of Hebrew, but the style of writing is more akin to Greek. It even includes Greek letters, which no other Hebrew writings from that time do.'

'So perhaps they are fakes?' asked Andrew.

'It's unlikely, but we can't rule it out. All efforts to date them have come to the same conclusion about their age.'

'Well,' said Andrew and pointed at the scroll in front of them. 'This thing here is very real.'

'It certainly is,' replied Fiona, admiring the ancient relic in front of them.

'So, what are we going to do about it?' asked Andrew. 'We can't take it with us. That would probably be a crime.'

'Absolutely,' replied Fiona. 'This is the property of Jordan. Taking it would be theft. We have to leave it here, and then contact the proper authorities in the capital Amman. I will ask a colleague back in London to find out whom to reach out to. We don't want this to fall into the hands of robbers.'

Andrew was rubbing his chin. 'I hate to say this, but as exciting as this is, it probably has nothing to do with the Ark of the Covenant.'

'I think you're right,' said Fiona, pressing her lips together and looking around the cave. 'This place was clearly created to hide this scroll, and if it is anything like the Qumran copper scroll, then it has nothing to do with the Ark, or anything else related to religion. It is just about money.'

'Just?' smirked Andrew. 'We could be talking about a lot of money here.'

'I know,' smiled Fiona. 'I have seen estimates of the value of the treasures mentioned in the Qumran copper scroll as high as a trillion dollars.'

Andrew's jaw fell open. 'A trillion? What is that? One thousand billion dollars?'

'Yes,' nodded Fiona. 'Or one million million dollars. Just about enough to retire on.'

'I should have become a treasure hunter,' said Andrew sarcastically.

Fiona shot him a scolding glare. 'You really are a savage,' she said.

'Anyway, how was Omran able to make this sketch, if it has nothing to do with the Ark?' asked Andrew.

'I don't know,' replied Fiona. 'For all we know, it could be a sketch of a sketch. But somehow, he got his hands on some sort of original sketch or painting, and he clearly thought it was related to the Ark of the Covenant.'

'But it was actually a depiction of the secret location of a scroll similar to the Dead Sea copper scroll? That sounds very odd.'

'I know,' said Fiona. 'It seems confusing.'

'Anyway,' said Andrew. 'We should get out of here. We don't want to be descending a mountain in the dark.'

'Ok,' said Fiona hesitantly. 'I think we should put the scroll back in the stone box. It somehow seems wrong to leave it here on the floor.'

'Alright,' said Andrew. 'Let's do it.'

They carefully lifted the scroll up and put it back inside the stone box, and then placed the lid back the way Andrew had found it.

As they exited the cave, the sun was moving rapidly towards the horizon due west of them, and they could just make out Jerusalem in the far distance immediately below the orange orb in the sky.

'Gorgeous,' smiled Fiona pensively. 'I wonder if I will ever come back to this place.'

'I guess that depends on what the Jordanians end up concluding about that scroll,' said Andrew, with a conspiratorial tone. 'If it is another treasure map, I know I will be back here with a shovel at some point.'

'Incorrigible,' smiled Fiona and shook her head.

Half an hour later they were back by the car. They shared the rest of the water they had brought, and then set off for the Israeli border.

'I feel as if I have left something behind,' said Fiona, looking out at the Jordan Rift Valley as they traversed it in the direction of Jericho and towards the Israeli border. 'It is almost as if I am missing something.'

Andrew smiled and glanced at her. 'You did not like leaving that scroll behind, did you?'

'No,' she said and shook her head with a resigned smile. 'It just goes against my instincts to walk away from something that special. I am also terrified that someone else will find it and rob it.'

'I wouldn't worry if I were you,' said Andrew, reaching out to gently squeeze her hand. 'We will get a message to Jordanian authorities as soon as we can. That scroll has been in there for many centuries. The odds are virtually nil that someone else will stumble upon it again over the next few days.'

'Unless someone was following us,' said Fiona, and shot Andrew a concerned look.

Andrew sucked his teeth and winced, and then involuntarily checked the rear-view mirror. They seemed to be the only people on that road. He could see no other cars in front or behind them.

'I don't think that is likely,' he finally said. 'Whoever those bastards back in Egypt are, I am pretty sure they would not have been able to get themselves visas to Jordan overnight the way we did.'

'I hope you're right,' replied Fiona. 'Who the hell are those people anyway? What is their game?'

'If I had to guess, they are your standard lot of religious zealots. In a way it is simple. If they are terrorists, then they are obviously trying to get their hands on the most terrifying thing they possibly can. And an extremely highly radioactive meteorite would fit that bill very nicely.'

'Can you imagine a world where people no longer fight and try to kill each other?' asked Fiona dreamily as she gazed out at the flood plains stretching along the eastern bank of the River Jordan.

'Honestly?' said Andrew. 'No, I can't. I just don't see that as being realistic. I feel that conflict is part of our nature. It is a defining characteristic of human beings. It might even be possible that we have been able to develop our civilisation, precisely because we are that way.'

'You mean, conflict drives innovation?' asked Fiona.

'Something like that,' replied Andrew. 'It is a fact that a huge amount of our technological progress through the millennia came directly from weapons development and research.'

'It is a depressing irony, isn't it?' asked Fiona, now sounding glum. 'Humans progress and evolve the fastest when they are pursuing destruction and death on an industrial scale. It's like we're trapped by our own basic nature.'

Andrew smiled and looked at her. 'Come now. It's not all bad. Most people are good people that want to do good things for themselves and for others. We all just need to talk to each other.'

Fiona laughed and smiled at him. 'Mr SAS man. You really are a hippie.'

Eighteen

The next morning, they checked out of the hotel and went straight to the airport. Their aircraft was fuelled and ready to take them on the 2000 km journey to Axum in Ethiopia. The town is relatively small with less than seventy thousand inhabitants, and it lies in the far north of the country, less than 30 kilometres from the border with Eritrea.

Their pilot had warned them that the landing might become slightly 'entertaining', as he had put it. The town only had a small regional airport next to it, and it would only just be long enough to accommodate their aircraft.

'What are you reading?' asked Andrew.

'I am just going over my notes about the Exodus,' said Fiona. 'Listen to this. This is what a researcher called Ronald Hendel wrote about Exodus. He describes it as "a conflation of history and memory. A mixture of historical truth and fiction, composed of authentic historical details, folklore motifs, ethnic self-fashioning, ideological claims and narrative imagination.".'

Fiona looked up at Andrew and smiled. 'I don't think I could have said it better myself.'

'But where does that leave us?' he said.

'Well,' said Fiona pensively. 'We know that the Temple of Solomon was real and that it housed a reliquary that was almost certainly the Ark of the Covenant. Even if the story of how the Israelites, and therefore the Ark came to be in Jerusalem, is still highly uncertain, there is no reason to doubt that something like the Ark was present in the Temple for a long time after it was built.'

'What do you make of the story about the Queen of Sheba having a child with King Solomon, and the child carrying the Ark out of Jerusalem as a grown man?'

'I think it is perfectly possible,' replied Fiona. 'Although I am slightly perplexed as to why we would even know about it.'

'What do you mean?' asked Andrew.

'If the son of Solomon and the Queen of Sheba, Menelik I, took the Ark out of Jerusalem around 950 BCE, then why would it not have been kept a secret? Why is it apparently common knowledge that this happened? The Orthodox Ethiopian Church is clearly very open about it.'

'Good question,' said Andrew. 'You would have thought that the motivation for taking the Ark away from the Temple in Jerusalem would have had to have been a pretty serious one.'

'Exactly,' said Fiona and paused for a few moments. 'Maybe it was seen as a way to keep it safe.

As Finkelstein said, the Levant has virtually always been a battlefield, with armies from all the major empires sweeping through it time after time through the ages. Perhaps Solomon really was as wise as they say he was. Perhaps he understood that if the Ark stayed in Jerusalem, then it would be a question of time before it was captured or destroyed.'

'Which is what supposedly happened when Nebuchadnezzar II sacked Jerusalem in 587 BCE,' interjected Andrew.

'Very good,' smiled Fiona, looking impressed. 'So, you *did* pay attention.'

'And,' continued Andrew. 'It is fair to say that Ethiopia is well out of the way of the Levant. And it has never been a particularly juicy target for would-be empires. A quiet backwater, you might call it.'

'But,' said Fiona, as if a thought had just occurred to her. 'What if there is a reason that the story of Menelik and the Ark is so well known? What if that was part of the plan all along?'

'I don't understand,' said Andrew, creasing his forehead.

'Ok,' said Fiona and shifted in her seat to better face Andrew. 'What if a replica of the Ark was made, and then after that Menelik took an ark to Axum. And then, later on, Solomon let it be known that this had happened, but that the ark taken to Axum was actually a replica.'

'Why would he do that?' asked Andrew, looking perplexed.

'Just to sow confusion,' said Fiona. 'Not only has the real Ark been taken to safety, but an ark is still present in Jerusalem, and on top of that, Solomon leaks the story about Menelik and the Ark, which makes it ambiguous which of the two is actually the real Ark.'

'But what would that achieve?' asked Fiona.

Fiona held out both of her hands in front of her and made fists of them. 'Imagine that I have £10 in one of my hands, and you don't know which one it is. What is then the value of what I am holding in my right hand?'

'I don't follow,' said Andrew. 'I don't know what is in your right hand.'

'Exactly,' said Fiona. 'The value of what I am holding in my right hand is £5 because there is a fifty percent chance that it is a £10 note.'

'Oh,' said Andrew and smiled. 'I think I get it. You're saying that the ambiguity about the location of the Ark, makes it a less juicy target for would-be invaders of Jerusalem.'

'Precisely,' smiled Fiona.

'It doesn't make it any simpler for us though. If anything, it actually makes it more complicated.'

'Perhaps,' said Fiona and sat back in her seat. 'But we have to go where ever the evidence takes us. Or in this case, where ever the most credible speculation takes us.'

'I have got to be honest though,' said Andrew. 'I find it difficult to believe that King Solomon would have parted with the Ark and allowed it to be taken out of Jerusalem and down to Axum in Ethiopia.'

'Me too,' said Fiona. 'But that may have been exactly why he did it. No one would have believed that the real Ark was no longer in Jerusalem, which meant that it would have been safe in Axum.'

'I suppose that makes sense,' said Andrew.

'Alternatively,' said Fiona. 'It is also possible that the entire story about Menelik and the Ark was invented by Ethiopian rulers, and tagged onto the short mention in the Bible about the Queen of Sheba, in order to lend credibility to their claim to power.'

'Also perfectly possible,' nodded Andrew. 'So many different permutations. This is getting complicated.'

'Welcome to my world,' smiled Fiona. 'For all the focus on hard physical evidence, archaeologists invariably end up with lots of conjecture, simply because we never have the full picture.'

'Well,' said Andrew. 'Hopefully, something more tangible turns up at some point. I don't think I need to remind you that people have been searching for the Ark of the Covenant for more than two millennia, ever since it somehow disappeared from Solomon's Temple. It was never going to be easy.'

'That's another thing that I don't really understand,' said Fiona.

'What is?'

'When Jerusalem was sacked by Nebuchadnezzar II in 587 BCE, there is no mention of the Ark being taken or destroyed. The only record we have is from the Second Book of Kings in the Bible. Listen to this. Here's what it says.'

Fiona flicked through her notebook and found the correct page. '*And he carried out thence all the treasures of the house of the Lord, and the treasures of the king's house, and cut in pieces all the vessels of gold which Solomon king of Israel had made in the temple of the Lord.*'

Andrew looked at her sceptically. 'You do understand that this is not a historical record of events, right?'

'Of course,' said Fiona. 'But still, if the Ark had been in the temple when Nebuchadnezzar II looted it, don't you think we would know about it? I mean, the Babylonians travel hundreds of kilometres from the area around the river Tigris in present-day Iraq, lay siege to Jerusalem, which they obviously know is where the Israelites are. They also know that there is a huge Temple there, erected specifically to keep safe the very thing by which the Israelites define themselves, namely the Ark of the Covenant. This religious artefact is the physical manifestation of, and in some sense also contains, the covenant between Yahweh and the Israelites, in which he makes them God's chosen people. The idea that Nebuchadnezzar II either doesn't know this and lets the Ark be destroyed with the Temple, or that he knows it and takes the Ark but never brags about it, as had been the custom in every civilisation for thousands of years, is just not credible.'

'I can't really argue with that,' said Andrew.

'Imagine the opportunity this would have represented,' continued Fiona. 'Not only did he destroy Jerusalem. He had the chance to destroy the very thing that defines the Israelite or Hebrew identity and their special covenant with God. But there is no mention of it at all. I am just not buying it. I mean, just imagine it for a moment. When Nebuchadnezzar II sacked Jerusalem, he would have gone straight for the Temple. Either the Ark was not there, or what he found was an obvious replica. Either way, this is the only thing that explains why there is exactly no mention of the Ark at all, after 587 BCE. The very fact that he does *not* brag about it, and that there are no references to it in subsequent Babylonian writings, should tell you that if they found anything inside the Temple at all, it was not the real Ark. Nebuchadnezzar II kept meticulous records of all the things that were looted and taken from the places he conquered and plundered, and the Ark just simply isn't mentioned anywhere.'

'So does that mean that you think Menelik really did take the Ark to Axum?'

Fiona spread out her hands and shrugged. 'I don't know. All I know is that I don't believe the Ark was in Jerusalem in 587 BCE.'

'Your line of thinking does sound credible,' said Andrew. 'But ultimately, this is all just speculation on our part. What we really need is hard evidence, one way or another.'

'I agree,' sighed Fiona. 'We just have to press on and see what we find.'

★   ★   ★

After three and a half hours, the aircraft descended through a thin wispy layer of cloud and began its approach to the runway. They were coming in to land on the airport's only runway, which ran almost perfectly north to south.

As they looked out of the windows, they could see farmland as well as tiny villages dotting the landscape. It was clear that this was a perennially hot and dry country, and they could make out small irrigation canals that had been dug, connecting the fields with the local river. The town of Axum was ahead of them on their right, and from the air, it appeared particularly small.

'It seems almost surreal that something as monumental as the Ark of the Covenant should be located in this place,' said Fiona.

'I know,' said Andrew looking down at the terrain that seemed to be moving steadily up towards them. 'But as you said, that might have been part of the whole idea. Three thousand years ago, no one would have come looking for it here, and even if they wanted to, it would have been an awfully long walk from Jerusalem.'

'Right. Anyway,' said Fiona. 'I am really hungry. Fancy trying out the local cuisine?'

'Sure,' said Andrew hesitantly. 'Do you think they have burgers?'

'I said *local*, you oaf,' laughed Fiona. 'Let's see what a typical lunch menu looks like around here.'

They strapped in, and a couple of minutes later the aircraft touched down at the very northern end of the runway, and immediately began breaking hard. The runway was somewhat uneven, and the aircraft felt like it was bouncing up and down slightly as it decelerated. There seemed to be no serious crosswind, so the aircraft went straight down the middle of the runway, without swerving.

The pilot had judged the speed of the aircraft and the length of the runway perfectly, and at the end of it he made a neat right turn onto the taxiway which took them to the tiny terminal building.

Having spent more than three hours in a temperature-controlled environment, stepping out onto the tarmac was like running into a wall of hot humid air. They both instantly reached for their water bottles.

'Wow,' said Fiona. 'This is quite something.'

'I like it,' said Andrew. 'Better this than freezing cold. Let's get inside and get ourselves some transport. There is supposed to be a motel by the airport, so I think we should grab a room there. We need a base of operations.'

'This is not a military exercise, you know?' said Fiona.

'Yes, I know,' smiled Andrew. 'Old habits.'

They checked into the hotel and dumped their luggage in their room while the taxi waited outside. The room was basic but comfortable, and its air-conditioning was working like a dream. After quickly freshening up, they left and got into the waiting taxi.

The town of Axum was only 3 kilometres away from the small airport, so within half an hour they had hired a taxi and made it into the town centre. It was a small but very neat town, considering that it was in many respects in the middle of nowhere in the Ethiopian bush. The driver took them to a small arcade of shops lining the road near the Axum Tsion St. Mary Church, where the Ethiopian Orthodox Church maintains the Ark of the Covenant is located.

They got themselves some *Injera*, which is flatbread made from sourdough, wrapped around spiced lamb. Fiona was appalled to find a huge selection of fizzy drinks like Coca-Cola and Pepsi, and ended up opting for another water bottle.

The two of them sat down on a bench under a huge tree, facing the church on the other side of the square. The sun was beating down on the town, but the tree provided them with shade, and the light breeze made for a pleasant temperature.

'So, this is it then,' said Andrew and nodded towards the church.

'Well, not exactly,' replied Fiona.

Andrew turned and looked at her, perplexed. 'What do you mean? Is this the wrong church?'

'No,' smiled Fiona. 'This is definitely the right one, but apparently, the Ark is no longer in here. It's over there,' she said and pointed at a small chapel, in what appeared to be a somewhat overgrown plot behind a metal fence, next to the church.

'What's that?' asked Andrew.

'That is the so-called Chapel of the Tablet,' replied Fiona. 'Supposedly, the Ark was moved from the church to that chapel, because a "*divine heat*" emanating from the Ark was damaging the stonework of the church.'

Andrew looked at her sceptically. 'Really?'

'Yep,' replied Fiona. 'That's what they said, so now it is in there.'

'If it is here at all,' added Andrew.

'Of course,' nodded Fiona, taking a swig from her water bottle and looking at the chapel for a few moments. 'But if it really is in there,' she continued. 'It does seem odd that we can sit here and look at that building, and inside it may well be the most important reliquary in the history of mankind.'

'You sound almost disappointed,' said Andrew and looked at her.

'Maybe I am,' said Fiona. 'It all just seems so... unremarkable.'

'What did you expect?' smiled Andrew with a mischievous grin. 'God rays, singing and angels playing harps?'

'Of course not, you oaf,' she replied and punched him playfully on the arm. 'I guess these things always seem more magical in our minds than they are in real life.'

'Sorry,' smiled Andrew. 'Anyway, when was the Ark supposed to have arrived here?'

Well,' said Fiona. 'This church obviously wasn't here back then. The original church was built around 400 AD by King Ezana, who was the first Christian ruler of the Kingdom of Axum.'

'It was a kingdom?' asked Andrew and tucked into his Injera. 'Mmm. Delicious.'

'Yes,' replied Fiona. 'In its heyday, the Kingdom of Axum covered northern Ethiopia, Eritrea and much of Sudan and Yemen. It was a pretty big deal.'

'So presumably the Ark was placed inside when the original church was built?'

'You would think so,' replied Fiona. 'But its precise location prior to that is not known with any degree of certainty. And remember, the period from when Menelik supposedly carried the Ark out of Jerusalem, until it was placed inside this church, spans in the region of a thousand years.'

'That is a very long time,' said Andrew, dubiously. 'And there is no record of where it might have been kept during that period?'

'Well, presumably somewhere in this area,' said Fiona. 'But there is no information available on precisely where it might have been, or who would have looked after it.'

'I have to be honest,' said Andrew, shaking his head slowly. 'The whole thing seems pretty far-fetched to me.'

'I know it does,' smiled Fiona. 'But if I had told you last week that this week you would end up making a significant archaeological find inside a cave on Mount Nebo in Jordan, then that would have seemed equally far-fetched. But look at what happened.'

Andrew nodded pensively. 'I guess you're right. But do you know what I think is really odd?' he asked.

'What?' said Fiona.

'I think it is almost beyond belief that something as significant as the Ark could have sat here in a church in this tiny backwater for centuries, and at no point has anyone ever tried to force themselves inside to verify that it is actually here.'

Fiona looked at him suspiciously. 'You're not thinking what I think you're thinking, are you?'

Andrew smiled and shrugged. 'I'm just saying. What if it was never there?' he said. 'Or what if it really is there right now?'

'I understand your frustration,' said Fiona. 'But we are talking about probably the most significant religious artefact of all time. You can't just break in and have a look. That would cause an outrage, and you would probably end up either locked up in prison or dead.'

'I agree that it would be a bit of a sticky situation,' said Andrew. 'And it would probably ruffle a few feathers. But think about it this way. If the terrorists somehow work out that the Ark carried a section of the meteorite, and that it ended up here, you can bet anything that they will come looking for it. And I am pretty sure they won't ask nicely before entering.'

'It sounds a bit like you're equating this to breaking down the front door of a house, in order to get inside and stop a gas leak.'

'That's not a bad analogy,' said Andrew. 'If we don't do it, someone else will. And if there really is a highly radioactive piece of a meteorite in there, it will eventually become known. And then there is no knowing who will get their hands on it, and what they will do with it. But I think it stands to reason that anyone sufficiently interested in acquiring it, will want to use it to harm others.'

'Yes,' said Fiona. 'I can't really argue with that logic. But I also can't bring myself to take part in something like this. It feels like desecration or sacrilege or something.'

'Well,' said Andrew cheerfully. 'Luckily, I don't suffer from hang-ups like those. I am just interested in making sure a bunch of crazies don't get hold of a weapon of mass destruction.'

'So, what are you going to do?' asked Fiona incredulously. 'Go over there with a sledgehammer and smash in the door?'

'Please,' said Andrew overbearingly. 'Have a bit more faith in me than that. I am sure I can think of something a lot more elegant than that.'

Fiona looked at him suspiciously. 'You're starting to sound like a cat-burglar planning a heist. Whatever you do, I can't take part in it. I would also quite like to not spend the rest of my life in a prison cell in

Ethiopia. I read some reviews on Tripadvisor, and they really aren't that great.'

'Ok,' said Andrew. 'You just stay in the motel room at the airport. If things go south, we board the plane and get out of here right quick.'

Fiona shook her head. 'I can't believe you're talking me into this.'

'Relax,' said Andrew and spread out his hands. 'You're not actually in it. I am.'

Fiona looked up at him with an admonishing look on her face. 'Just remember, I am not coming to visit you in jail.'

'Fair enough,' said Andrew and stood up. 'Let's get back to the motel.'

Several hours later they were back at the motel, resting on the bed. It was late afternoon and the TV was on, but there were no channels in English. Andrew was flicking absentmindedly between them, finding nothing he understood or that looked interesting. The only things that were vaguely familiar were the commercials. Happy people. Happy babies. Happy products. And a number to call. Happiness delivered straight to your door.

'Are you sure you don't want to come along?' said Andrew teasingly, as he swung his legs off the bed and started gathering his things.

'Yes, I am,' replied Fiona. 'I am completely sure. I understand why you are doing it, but I just can't bring myself to participate.'

'Alright,' said Andrew, checking his pockets and making sure he had everything he needed. 'I almost certainly won't find anything there, so in that sense, you probably don't have to worry. The whole Menelik legend just doesn't seem credible to me. But I could be wrong.'

'Just be careful,' said Fiona as he opened the door to leave.

'I will,' said Andrew and winked. 'Don't wait up.'

Then he closed the door and walked to the taxi that had been arranged for him. It turned out to be the same taxi with the same driver.

Maybe there is just this one taxi in the whole town, he thought to himself.

Nineteen

The sun seemed to be balancing on the horizon, and Andrew noticed that there was a thick cloud cover closing in from the north. This would probably be useful later, as it would block out any moonlight and make the night even darker.

He asked the driver to stop at the end of the street with the arcade of shops. Most of them were closing up for the day, and the vendors were busy wrapping up their goods and placing them behind metal shutters inside their shops. He walked along the road, carrying a book and looking like just another tourist, and when he came to a small alley that peeled away from the main street, he walked down to the end of it and stopped for a few moments.

There was no one else around, and he was now only a couple of hundred meters from the Chapel. He jumped onto an abandoned oil barrel and leapt over a fence and into what looked like a private garden. Calling it a garden was perhaps a bit imprecise, since it was quite overgrown by tall grass, and it had what appeared to be self-seeded trees and bushes dotted all over it.

He made his way through the garden and onto a large plot that appeared to belong to a building contractor. It had stacks of timber and stone-lined up in neat rows, as well as piles of gravel and sand. He quickly made his way to the far side of it, where the fence to the chapel grounds was. The fence was made of wood and was clearly not designed to actually keep anyone out. He was easily able to rip two boards off and crawl through the opening.

On the other side, he found himself sitting behind a row of dense bushes, that obscured the view of the chapel. It also meant that anyone on the chapel grounds would be unable to see him.

There was no sign of anyone there. In fact, there were no lights either around or inside the chapel, and it was now becoming dark enough that anyone inside a building would need to turn on the lights.

He had already decided not to attempt the front door, and so made his way up to the chapel wall and around the corner to the back of the building. Here he located a window and broke the glass as quietly as he could. There were clearly no alarms installed, so he reached inside and unfastened the latch. The window popped open easily, and as he pulled himself up and over the windowsill, he couldn't quite believe how easy it had been up to this point. It made him feel as if he was breaking into an empty building that no one had bothered to protect, possibly because there really was nothing to protect in there.

He dropped down onto the floor in a crouched position and found himself in a dimly lit corridor that seemed to wrap around the entire building, with a large central chamber in the middle. He reached into a pocket and took out a small LED headlamp with a strap, and placed it on his head. He dialled the light intensity down to where it was just enough for him to see clearly ahead of himself. This was a far cry from night vision goggles, but it would have to do.

As he moved silently along the corridor, he was listening out for noises that might betray the presence of anyone else in the building, but he could hear nothing.

Following the corridor along the exterior wall, he came to the corner of the building, where the corridor turned ninety degrees towards where the front door of the chapel was. He peeked around the corner but saw nothing except for the inside of the tall sturdy wooden door.

Approaching it carefully, he noticed that opposite the front door was another doorway, which did not have a wooden door. Instead, there was a tall curtain made of what looked like heavy velvet in a dark red colour.

Andrew hesitated for a moment, but then pulled the curtain aside and peeked inside. As he had suspected, the entire interior was one big room, and at its centre was an area sealed off by tall heavily ornamented wooden panels with carvings of various motifs and patterns. Together they seemed to make a type of shrine, and through the wide gaps he could see that inside it was what appeared to be a large square box, covered by an intricately woven cloth.

The central chamber had no natural light coming into it, and the scene was dimly illuminated by what appeared to be small oil lamps affixed to the walls at regular intervals. Clearly, someone would be coming in here on a regular basis to refill the oil lamps.

He was about to take another step towards it, but then stopped dead in his tracks. He looked down, reached into the side pocket of his trousers, and pulled out the Geiger counter. Momentarily unsure of where to point it, he looked up and around the room, and then decided to simply switch it on and see what happened.

The device sprang to life with a robotic-sounding chirp, and the small LCD screen lit up. After a couple of seconds, a sparse series of muffled clicks could be heard from its tiny speaker. The number on the screen fluctuated but settled after a few seconds to read 0.14, which indicated that the device was currently picking up radiation levels consistent with an hourly exposure of 0.14 microSieverts.

Andrew kept looking at the screen, observing the reading settling firmly on that same value. What the device was telling him was that it was picking up only the normal levels of background radiation that can be expected anywhere on the Earth, with only small variations from location to location. Background radiation comes mainly from the radioactive gas radon, which seeps from the ground in the form of various isotopes, and makes up around half of the annual radiation dose that humans are subjected to naturally.

Andrew held the device still for around ten seconds, and then started slowly moving it from side to side, pointing it in different directions inside the chamber. The reading momentarily jumped to 0.15, but then went back down to 0.14. Clearly, there was nothing radioactive in this room other than the normal background radiation.

He slipped the Geiger counter back into his pocket, took a couple of steps towards the shrine, and peered in through the gaps to look at the cloth. It seemed to have gathered a lot of dust and appeared not to have been moved for a long time.

Carefully, he grabbed the edge of one of the large ornate wood panels and shifted it outwards just enough for him to squeeze through and enter the interior of the shrine. It scraped against the dusty stone floor, but it hardly made a noise and would be barely audible outside the chapel.

Andrew stood inside the shrine for a few moments, looking around at various sections of the cloth, and trying to decide which part to grab hold of. Eventually, he simply grabbed the nearest corner with both hands, and in one slow move pulled the entire thing off and onto the floor.

He was met with the sight of a small wooden shrine, very similar to the large surrounding shrine, sitting on a low plinth. It was similarly ornate and had wooden sides with intricate carvings of various motifs that appeared to relate to Christianity. It was evidently very old since it had long thin fracture lines running along its sides, but apart from that it did not appear damaged. The fractures were simply a product of the wooden relic being subjected to thousands of cycles of warm dry days and cold humid nights, possibly for hundreds of years.

What was clear though, was that it was definitely not the Ark of the Covenant. The dimensions were all wrong, it was not gilded, and it had no cherubim or staves. But most importantly, the Christian motifs meant that it was clearly a much later relic, created at some point well into the first millennium CE.

Andrew got out his phone, turned the flash on and took several pictures whilst walking slowly and gingerly around the artefact. When he came round the back of it, he noticed that a slab in the floor next to the plinth that the shrine was resting on, was significantly darker than the ones surrounding it. He knelt down and tapped on the slab with his knuckles. He then tapped on the three slabs immediately next to it. The latter three made a short muffled sound, but the darker slab produced a much more drawn-out higher pitch hum. The darker slab clearly had a void underneath it.

Feeling around with his fingers, he managed to get his fingertips into the grooves between the slabs. After a couple of attempts, he was able to get enough purchase to begin to pull the slab out. It was surprisingly light, and with some effort, it eventually came free of the floor. It turned out to be only a few centimetres thick, and Andrew placed it carefully on the floor with a clonk.

It revealed a pitch-black hole in the floor, but when Andrew shone his light into it, he could see a square stone shaft leading down roughly two meters to what appeared to be an underground passage leading away from the centre of the chapel and towards the back of the plot of land it was sitting on.

He moved his head slightly from one side to the other to try to gauge how big the passage was, but all he could make out was that it was probably big enough for him to move through.

He sat down on the edge of the shaft with his legs dangling into it and placed his hands on either side.

Well, here goes nothing, he thought to himself and dropped down through the shaft and into the passage.

As his boots hit the ground, a small cloud of fine dry dust exploded up from the floor of the passage, and he had to cough a few times to clear his throat. As he was rubbing the dust out of his eyes, Andrew heard a dry rustling sound just behind him, and he immediately scrambled to turn around inside the narrow passage.

Right in front of him were two snakes with their heads raised and their fangs exposed. Cobras. He froze, trying not to move a muscle and thereby invite a strike. His mind was racing and his eyes were darting around the cramped space looking for something to defend himself with.

With the two snakes swaying their heads from side to side and gauging the distance to their foe, Andrew slowly moved his right hand towards the knife in his belt. He silently released the small leather strap and gripped the knife. Then his left hand moved gingerly down on the floor of the passage, which was covered in a layer of sand and dust. He watched the two snakes both following the movement of his left hand with their eyes. Slowly he closed his hand around a handful of sand, then in a flash, he threw the sand towards the two snakes, instantly creating a cloud of dust between him and them.

One of the snakes took the opportunity to go for his extended left hand, but Andrew pulled it back again immediately after letting go of the sand, and the snake missed. However, the momentum of its strike caused it to lurch forward onto the floor right in front of him. He instantly slammed his knife down onto its head, skewering it through its brain. The tip of the knife went clean through the snake's head, penetrated the soft sand, but then hit the hard rock below, sending a jolt of pain through Andrew's wrist.

The pain caused him to involuntarily let go of the knife, and as it slipped out of his hand the other snake launched itself at him. He instinctively pulled his head down whilst also lurching backwards and away from the snake's strike. The result was that the snake came straight at his head with its mouth open and its fangs pointing forward, and when it reached his head, its mouth snapped closed around the headtorch.

Momentarily confused by what had happened, Andrew then reached up with his left hand and grabbed the head of the snake. He then yanked it forcefully off the headtorch. His right hand was scrambling around on the floor next to him until it found a rock the size of a fist. Still holding the snake, he put his left hand onto the floor and then raised his right hand holding the rock above his head. He then brought the rock down onto the head of the snake with all his power and kept pounding it again and again, until he could feel its head disintegrating in his hand.

Blood from the snake had squirted onto his left forearm, but it was the sensation from his forehead that suddenly got his immediate attention. He could feel a bead of liquid running down his forehead, and he quickly brought up his hand, wiped it and then held his hand out in front of his eyes. The headtorch revealed, not red blood from his head, but a small amount of clear liquid. At first, he thought it was sweat, but then he brought it up to his nose, and the distinct smell of rotten eggs filled his nostrils. This was the smell of the snake's musk.

Andrew slumped down and breathed a sigh of relief. For a terrifying moment, he thought it was the neurotoxin from the cobra's fangs. Contact with the skin could lead to severe tissue damage and even necrosis.

He looked up and down the length of the underground passage but mercifully could not see any other snake or creatures anywhere. He then dialled the intensity of the LED headtorch up to maximum and started to make his way along the passage towards what appeared to be where it opened up into a cavity of some sort.

As he reached the end of the passage, he exited it by sliding his feet through the opening and down onto a floor about a meter below where the opening was. He found himself standing stooped in a perfectly square room, with a ceiling roughly 1.5 meters above the floor. The floor was covered in a thick layer of dust and was made of the same slabs as the one he had prised loose in the chapel above him. The walls and the ceiling were made from large rough slabs of rock, and the ceiling was held up by four pillars arranged around a low platform in the middle of the room.

Slightly crouched over, he took a few steps towards the platform, which rose roughly 30 centimetres from the floor. It had the same amount of dust on it as the floor, and it was empty except for a small stack of what appeared to be square slabs at its centre.

Andrew walked closer and peered at the slabs. He then knelt down and swiped his hand over the top one. It was not a stone slab. It was some sort of dull grey metal.

Andrew whipped out his Geiger counter and pointed it at the metal slabs. The device instantly came to life and the muffled clicks were now coming in very rapid succession. The LCD screen read 236 microSieverts, still not anywhere near dangerous, but several orders of magnitude above background radiation. He took a step back and looked at the stack of slabs, then down at the screen, and then up at the slabs again. He was not sure what he was expecting to find here, but it certainly was not this.

After a few moments, he took out his knife and knelt down next to the slabs. Holding a corner of the top slab, and hoping to shear off a small flake, he placed his knife on top of it and began performing a sawing motion. The metal was surprisingly soft and malleable, and within a few seconds, he had cut off a tiny piece the size of a pea.

He stood back up and slipped the piece into the front left pocket of his shirt. Turning around, he let the light from the headtorch sweep over the rest of the room, just to make sure he had not missed anything. There was nothing else there, so he got out his phone and took a number of photos of everything in the room, including close-ups of the stack of metal slabs. He checked his wristwatch. It was just before midnight, and he decided he had seen enough.

He made his way through the passage, past the dead snakes and back to the shaft, where he stood up, grabbed the ledge above him, and pulled himself up and out of the hole and into the chapel. Here, he slid the slab back into place. He picked the cloth up off the floor and draped it over the shrine. He knew that anyone looking closely would be able to see that the cloth had been pulled off, but he was hoping no one would notice through the narrow openings in the larger wooden shrine surrounding it. Having dragged the large ornate wood panel back to where he had found it, he made his way out of the room and back to the window where he had entered.

It was completely dark and very quiet outside. As he exited the chapel and made his way back to the alley, he noticed that there were only a very small number of electric lights on in the town at night. Whatever power plant supplied this small town was probably many tens of kilometres away, and the cost of electricity was most likely prohibitive for the inhabitants to allow their lights to burn through the night.

Andrew walked casually towards the east to the edge of town, where he decided to jog back to the airport. It was only a few kilometres away, and the air was now nice and cool.

When he arrived back at the motel, Fiona was lying on the bed reading a book. She jumped up and onto the floor as Andrew entered.

'It's only me,' he grinned.

'Crikey,' exclaimed Fiona with a smile. 'Could you knock?'

'What?' smiled Andrew. 'Are you naked?'

'You wish,' smirked Fiona and shook her head.

He proceeded to tell her what he had found in the chamber below the chapel but left out the part about the snakes. He did not want to worry her, and he also did not want to be shouted at again for being reckless.

'That is amazing,' said Fiona. 'What do we do with that piece of metal?'

'We need to get it looked at,' said Andrew. 'I am sure Doctor Zaki can help us out. Radiation levels were nowhere near what you could call hazardous, but they were certainly way above background levels, so there's something strange going on here.'

'Surely it can't be a coincidence that we find radioactive metal in the exact spot where we are looking for the Ark?' said Fiona emphatically. 'There's clearly a connection here. There has to be.'

'I agree,' said Andrew. 'Is there nothing in Omran's notebook that could throw any light on this?'

'No,' replied Fiona. 'I don't think he put any stock in the Menelik story at all. It seems that he only mentioned it because he was trying to cover all the bases.'

'Right,' said Andrew, and threw himself onto the bed, exhausted. 'So, what now? I guess we head back to Cairo, right?'

'Or we head to Aswan,' said Fiona.

'Aswan, on the Nile?'

'That's right' replied Fiona. 'It is 150 kilometres further south from Luxor and Thebes. It used to be the southernmost edge of the ancient Egyptian empires, and was the primary source of most of the stone used to construct statues, obelisks and other monuments throughout ancient Egypt.'

'Why do you want to go there?' asked Andrew.

'There are quarries there that have a particular type of granite rock called Syenite, which is rose coloured and an ideal material for shaping and carving.'

'But what does it have to do with the Ark?'

Well,' said Fiona. 'I have been studying Omran's notebook in some more detail, and I think I came up with something that might provide a clue.'

'Really?' asked Andrew and turned to look at her. 'What is it?'

'Omran was looking into a place called Elephantine Island,' said Fiona. 'It is an island in the Nile just across from where the ancient city of Aswan lies. His notes are incomplete, but there are entries about a Jewish or Hebrew community there some time in the 6th century, and it seems to somehow be related to the Ark of the Covenant. There is also a mention of the destruction of Jerusalem in 587 BCE.'

'Sounds intriguing,' said Andrew. 'What do you make of it?'

'I will have to do some more research,' replied Fiona. 'But it is definitely worth visiting. There are more sketches in Omran's notebook, but I don't think any of them will make sense until we actually get there.'

'Alright.' said Andrew. 'I have never been to Aswan. It is supposed to be a very interesting place.'

'It is,' smiled Fiona. 'Especially for people like me. Oh, and by the way. Dress appropriately. Aswan is one of the hottest and driest places on earth. I believe they get about 1 millimetre of rain per year on average.'

'So, basically no rain then,' said Andrew. 'Lovely. Listen, I think we should get out of here. If anyone discovers that an intruder has been inside the chapel, it won't be too hard for them to guess who it might have been.'

'Andy,' said Fiona, and looked admonishingly at him. 'Even if we leave right now, they will work out exactly who we are. The aircraft alone will give us away.'

'I know,' said Andrew and held up his hands. 'But I am sure the Foreign Office and MI6 will find a way to iron that out. I would just rather not be here when that happens.'

'The mindset of a criminal,' said Fiona and tutted.

'The mindset of a pragmatist,' countered Andrew in a reasonable voice and smiled at her. 'Anyway, we should pack up and head for the plane. There's nothing more for us to do here.'

'I agree,' said Fiona. 'I don't feel like we are any closer to solving the mystery of the Ark, or even to pass judgement on the Menelik legend, but at least we discovered that the Ark is not here. I guess we will have to wait and see what Doctor Zaki says about our little souvenir.'

'Come on,' said Andrew and grabbed his bag. 'Let's go.'

Twenty

Night had fallen in Zamalek, and the lone guard on the ground floor of the townhouse was standing by the window in the kitchen, looking out onto the empty street outside. Only occasionally did a car drive past, and there were no pedestrians at this time of night. All the lights in the house were off, and as he stood there in almost complete darkness, he reached inside his suit jacket and took out a packet of cigarettes. Putting one in his mouth and lighting it, he could now see his reflection in the kitchen window, as his face was lit up by the small bright flame of the lighter.

He looked at himself as the glow from the cigarette's ember pulsed along with him inhaling the smoke. This was a far cry from the rough deprived streets where he had grown up. When he was a small boy, he could not in his wildest dreams have imagined living in a city like this, and being paid to do a job like this. But his childhood had prepared him for it, in the sense that he was capable of things most people would not be able to do.

It was a long time since he had stopped thinking about what his various employers through the years were doing. He had decided that he was going to remain loyal to his paymasters, and then deal with whatever consequences would arrive later on. This assignment was no different. He was simply doing a job, and he did not lose any sleep over it.

He finished his cigarette, stubbed it into an ashtray, and walked to the fridge. Here he grabbed a small water bottle and a sandwich wrapped in greased paper. Then he turned to walk towards the concealed stairwell down into the basement. At the bottom of the stairwell, one of the twins was standing guard. They never seemed to say a word to anyone, not even each other, and they always made him nervous when they were in the same room as him. Somehow, they seemed less like human beings, and more like animals. Being near one of them was like being in a cage with a hungry jackal. They made him jumpy, and he never had his back turned to them.

The twin looked at him with no discernible sign of emotion, and then unlocked the door and let him through.

On the other side of the door, inside the windowless underground apartment, was the other twin, creepily dressed exactly like his brother. He was standing by the door, keeping an eye on Doctor Mansour who was still strapped to the same chair. He had been there for days, without being allowed to move, and he had now lost a part of three of his fingers. The severed parts had been placed in a jar of alcohol in front of him on the table because the boss had complained that the smell was becoming unpleasant.

Mansour was hunched over with his chin on his chest. He seemed to be sleeping, or perhaps he had passed out again. He was dribbling onto what used to be a white shirt, but which was now mottled with dirt and sweat.

The guard placed the water bottle and the sandwich on the table in front of him but did not wake him or untie him. He simply turned and walked over to the wall where he sat down on a chair.

A few minutes later, the door opened again, and the boss entered.

As if sensing what was happening, Mansour stirred, yanked at his restraints, and then woke up. Once again, the horror of his situation hit him like a hammer blow to the heart, and he seemed to shrink into an even more defeated and diminutive man than he had been just a few minutes before.

The man in the pinstriped suit sat down across from Mansour without saying a word.

Mansour looked up at him. 'I can't help you,' he begged. 'Don't you understand? I don't remember all the details. There were so many pages, and they were all handwritten.'

'I am starting to think you may be telling the truth,' sighed the man.

'Why do you want it?' sobbed Mansour. 'What is it you want it for? To destroy it?'

The man in the suit sneered and scoffed at the question. 'Our plans are not your concern. You should simply assume that we will stop at nothing to find it.'

Then he looked down at Mansour's stumps and then back up at his eyes. 'I thought you would have understood this by now.'

'Please,' breathed Mansour. 'I am begging you.' His voice was trembling, and he was panting, partly from the pain, and partly from the crushing realisation that his life would be over shortly unless he somehow found a way to give his captors what they wanted.

'I can't do anything without the notebook. Omran's notebook. I must have it to give you what you want.'

The old man stared at him with his penetrating eyes for what seemed like an eternity. Then he turned to one of the twins.

'Make it happen,' he said and then turned back to look at Mansour. 'You had better be telling the truth.'

★ ★ ★

It was pitch black as the Royal Airforce BAe 146-200 shot across the runway, raised its nose and lifted off in a northerly direction, from the small regional airport just outside Axum. The green and red strobe lights on its wingtips flashed brightly, and the forward-facing landing lights were illuminating the runway as it lifted off. It banked slightly to the left, setting course for Aswan in Egypt, and then began its climb towards its cruising altitude of thirty thousand feet. Within ten minutes it crossed over the border into Eritrea and made another course adjustment, which would take it the 1,300 kilometres to Aswan International Airport within a couple of hours.

Andrew and Fiona were slumped in their seats with cold drinks, both feeling relieved that they had been able to leave Axum without incident. If Andrew's intrusion into the chapel had been discovered, the news had not yet reached the border officials at the airport.

'I can't believe how easy it was to get inside that chapel,' said Andrew. 'You would have thought that there would be a whole army of people protecting something as important as the Ark of the Covenant. It is honestly a mystery to me why this has not happened before.'

'Well,' said Fiona, and looked at him with her disapproving school teacher gaze. 'Perhaps it is simply because no one else has ever had the irreverence and utter disrespect for religious sensibilities that you have.'

Andrew shrugged. 'Or perhaps it was because they all knew that there was nothing there? At least, no Ark.'

'The underground chamber is intriguing though,' said Fiona. 'It definitely seems like there might have been something important stored in there. Whatever it was, it must have been placed there as the chapel was being built, and then the access passage you came through was made later. From how you described it, it would have been much too narrow to bring something the size of the Ark through.'

'I agree,' said Andrew. 'It was obvious that the platform with the metal slabs was intended for something very specific, and the size of it would seem to correspond to the size of the Ark.'

'But that doesn't mean that the Ark was ever there,' said Fiona. 'It is all very mysterious. I guess there is a reason why no one has ever found it.'

'Well,' said Andrew, 'Technically, we are not actually looking for the Ark of the Covenant, just in case you have forgotten. We're looking for the meteorite or a piece of it that may or may not have been carried inside something like the Ark.'

Fiona shrugged and looked slightly annoyed. 'Well,' she said. 'You look for the meteorite, and I will look for the Ark. The latter is much more significant to me.'

'Deal,' smiled Andrew and took her hand. 'I will look for a radioactive glow, and you keep your eye out for a burning bush.'

Fiona shook he head and smiled. 'I am so glad you're not a comedian.'

* * *

A little under three hours later, at half-past four in the morning, they were leaving the arrivals terminal at Aswan International Airport and walking towards a taxi stand. The airport is a few kilometres to the south on the west side of the Nile, and anyone wanting to make it to Aswan city has to travel by road across the Aswan High Dam. The sun was just peeking over the hills to the east, as their taxi made its way out of the airport complex towards the highway.

A few minutes after joining Highway 75 going eastbound, they passed a huge monument on their right that looked like a very tall crown with five sharp spikes protruding up into the air high above them.

'I believe this is the Soviet-Egyptian Friendship Monument,' said Fiona. 'Seventy metres tall. It is supposed to resemble a lotus flower, and it was built in 1971 to commemorate Soviet support for Egypt over the preceding decades. Soviet engineers and contractors actually played a big part in the construction of the dam.'

'That's geopolitics for you,' said Andrew. 'The Soviets did what they could to curry favour with countries in the Middle-East after the Second World War.'

'As did the Americans, and the Brits, and anyone else with global ambitions,' said Fiona and raised her eyebrows.

'And those,' conceded Andrew.

A couple of minutes later the highway took them over the Aswan High Dam.

'Quite an impressive thing,' said Andrew and looked out the window at the four-thousand-meter wide dam as they drove over it. 'Must have cost a fortune.'

'Probably,' said Fiona. 'I think it took them ten years to build it, but it did put Egypt in a much stronger position in terms of independent energy production, which in turn translated into regional political clout. And of course, it benefitted the economy significantly.'

'What about out there?' said Andrew and pointed to their right across the huge water table of the now blocked Nile River. 'This thing must have caused huge flooding upstream.'

'Oh, it definitely did,' replied Fiona. 'Look at how high the water table is there, compared with on the other side. It must be at least one hundred meters higher. All that water on our right is called Lake Nasser, and it is only there because of the dam.'

'That must have flooded an enormous area,' said Andrew.

'It did,' said Fiona. 'I read that the lake is about 500 kilometres long, covers more than five thousand square kilometres, and holds over one hundred cubic kilometres of water. That is about a hundred billion tonnes of water.'

'Wow,' said Andrew. 'Let's hope the dam doesn't break tonight. Didn't it flood a whole bunch of towns and villages then?'

'Yes, eventually,' said Fiona. 'It took many years for Lake Nasser to reach its current size and for the water table to reach all the way up to the edge of the dam, but it obviously ended up flooding a large number of towns, and also some important archaeological sites up-stream.'

'I guess that's the price of progress,' said Andrew. 'I hope those displaced were offered new homes.'

'I think they ended up settling in Aswan,' said Fiona. 'That city is now home to around 1,6 million people, so it is quite big.'

They soon got a glimpse of just how many people live in the city, as Highway 75 cut straight north through the newest suburbs, where row after row of identikit apartment blocks had been built. There were hundreds of them, and not a single park or green space anywhere, which gave the impression of the buildings having been dropped from the sky onto a barren desert.

'They look like those Soviet housing complexes from the 1980s,' said Fiona.

'Yes,' said Andrew. 'Aesthetics seem to have taken a back seat since the time of the Pharaohs.'

Eventually, they peeled off the highway and headed through the city centre towards the Nile and Elephantine Island.

Fiona had booked a room for them at the Sofitel Legend Old Cataract Aswan Hotel, which was situated right on the edge of the Nile, directly opposite the Elephantine Island. As their taxi pulled into the drop-off area, a porter came running towards them to offer his assistance. When he saw that they were carrying only small hand luggage, he smiled apologetically and motioned towards the main building, which lay on the other side of a long promenade lined with palm trees wrapped in long chains of fairy lights. Down the centre of the promenade ran a long water basin with three fountains. The hotel had a calm and pleasant feel to it, and the two of them ambled towards the reception desk in the main building whilst enjoying the scenery.

Another ten minutes later, they had been shown to their room, tipped the bellboy, and had thrown themselves onto the bed.

'Andy,' said Fiona. 'Could I just see the pictures you took under the chapel in Axum again, please?'

'Of course,' said Andrew and handed her his phone. 'What's going on?'

'Something just occurred to me,' she replied. 'I just need to check whether it makes sense.'

'What's going on?' said Andrew.

Fiona flicked through a couple of pictures on Andrew's phone, before handing it back to him.

'Look at that,' she said. 'What do you see here?'

Andrew shook his head in confusion and looked at her. 'The metal slabs. I know what they look like. I was down there, remember?'

'But what do you think they were there for?' asked Fiona. 'And count them. Why do you think there were five of them?'

'No idea,' said Andrew, beginning to become frustrated. 'Just tell me what you are thinking please.'

'How many sides to a box?

'Uhm. Six,' replied Andrew. 'So?'

'And there are five slabs here, so if you were to make a box from those, one side would be open, right?'

'Yes?' said Andrew. 'Enough with the riddles. Fiona for the love of all that matters in this world, will you just tell me what is going on?'

'I think those slabs are made of lead, and I think they are radioactive because together they make a five-sided box, that once contained a highly radioactive source.'

'But why five sides?' asked Andrew. 'If one side was missing, then the radiation would shoot out of that side.' He hesitated. 'Oh,' he finally said. 'I get it now. The five-sided box would be a way of directing the radiation coming from the source. And the lead would absorb all the other radiation and make it safe to carry the box.'

'Possibly,' said Fiona. 'It's just a theory, but it sort of makes sense, doesn't it? Lead absorbs gamma radiation, and the slabs were quite thick.'

'I guess so,' replied Andrew. 'Whoever was carrying the lead box, possibly inside an Ark or by some other means, could theoretically have directed the radiation towards their enemies, just by pointing the box in their direction.'

'Yes,' added Fiona, 'And at any point the lead box could just be rotated inside the Ark, to direct the radiation upwards into the sky where it would do no harm to anyone standing near it.'

'Simple but effective,' nodded Andrew. 'But are you now saying you think the Ark was actually in Axum after all?'

'I don't know,' replied Fiona. 'I guess I am just pointing out that the radioactive slabs could well have become radioactive because of proximity to a highly radioactive source, like the meteorite. And I find it suspicious that those slabs should be sitting under that particular chapel in Ethiopia when that is supposedly where Menelik brought the Ark?'

'But the Ark was not there,' said Andrew.

'I know,' nodded Fiona patiently, 'but is it possible that it could have been there in the past?'

'Alright,' said Andrew. 'But then why would the lead box have been disassembled and left there, if the Ark and the meteorite were taken away? That doesn't make any sense.'

'I know that too, Andrew,' said Fiona, sounding frustrated. 'I am just trying to throw things up in the air to see where they land. We might have missed something. Perhaps there's a connection here that we are just not seeing.'

'Ok. fine,' said Andrew. 'I guess it is also conceivable that those slabs were irradiated somewhere else, and then transported to Axum, even if the Ark never was?'

'It is starting to feel like a giant smokescreen,' sighed Fiona. 'I don't know how we are going to make progress here.'

'Well, I want to go back to the front desk later,' said Andrew. 'I will have them post the metal fragment overnight to Doctor Zaki in Cairo. He might be able to tell us what it is.'

'Ok,' said Fiona. 'Just as long as the package is safe.'

'I will get the most expensive service they have,' replied Andrew. 'There must be a secure international shipping firm that operates out of Aswan.'

'Alright,' said Fiona, and yawned.

'Aside from that, we have got to just keep on plugging away at what we have,' said Andrew. 'We can't do anything else.'

'Well, I could really do with a nap,' said Fiona.

'Me too,' said Andrew and closed his eyes. 'All this adventuring is draining.'

'Let's catch up on some sleep,' said Fiona and tucked herself in close to him. 'Then we can have brunch in the restaurant and then go explore the island.'

'Sounds good,' yawned Andrew.

A couple of minutes later they were both asleep.

Twenty-One

Fiona sat up in the bed and slowly swung her legs out over the edge to let them drop gently to the floor. It felt strangely cold underfoot, and not how she remembered it.

It was almost pitch black in the room, and in her drowsy state, she reached out for the lamp next to the bed, but could not find it. Outside the window, she could hear the sound of cicadas, and the muffled sound of voices in the distance, speaking a language she did not understand.

Rubbing her eyes, she stood up and started walking unsteadily towards the door. To her surprise, she was able to push it open. Had it not been locked?

Outside in the corridor, the air felt warm and humid, and as she made her way over the tiles, she noticed that the dim illumination was coming, not from electric lights but from small oil lamps mounted along the walls. She did not remember seeing those when they checked in to the hotel.

When she came to the end of the corridor, she pushed open the double doors and found herself in another much wider corridor made entirely of neatly chiselled blocks of sandstone. Both sides were richly decorated with ancient Egyptian cartouches of battle scenes. They had been painted expertly in red, blue, white and orange colours, and they depicted pharaohs engaged in battle against what she thought might have been Hittites, or perhaps the so-called *Sea People,* who wreaked havoc on coastal towns in the Nile delta during several ancient Egyptian dynasties.

At that point, Fiona looked down and realised she was wearing a long white flowing robe, with a small belt around her waist. On her feet were leather sandals, and she noticed a long lock of hair having been made into a corkscrew, dangling next to her face. Who had done this to her?

As she pushed through a second set of double doors at the end of the wide sandstone corridor, she entered into an enormous chamber, with huge stone columns supporting an ornate ceiling high above her. At the centre of the chamber, was a tall obelisk made from the syenite granite that had been dug out of the quarries in Aswan for millennia.

Still feeling strangely dazed and detached, she walked slowly up towards the obelisk that was towering above her. It was a couple of metres wide at the base and tapered ever so slightly towards its top, where a small pyramid sat. Its sides were covered in hieroglyphs, which she had some experience in reading, but for some reason, none of them made sense to her.

She then noticed a huge mural on the back wall of the chamber, behind the obelisk. It was perhaps five meters tall and at least as wide, and it depicted what appeared to be some sort of ceremony. There were Egyptian priests holding jugs of water, and they were pouring it over a central figure who was much taller and imposing-looking than anyone else in the scene.

He was standing tall with a confident look on his face, and holding the ancient Egyptian regalia, the crook and the flail. This was clearly the pharaoh. Around him, everyone else was kneeling in reverence, except for two women on the left side of the mural. One was obviously his queen, dressed in elegant clothing with elaborate woven patterns and jewellery.

The other woman seemed older and was dressed in plain white clothes that looked like a type of dress, but with several layers of fabric bulging out slightly to create three overlapping sections as it flowed from her waist to her feet. She looked familiar somehow. She was the only person in the mural to wear a thin headband, and on her feet, she wore leather sandals.

Fiona looked down at her own feet. They were the same. Her dress also looked like that of the woman in the mural.

As she raised her head and looked again at the pharaoh, his head seemed to turn towards her. She blinked a few times, but the movement in the mural continued in a strange flowing fashion, giving the impression of the mural coming alive. She took a step backwards, and as she did, the pharaoh's giant arms extended from the mural in slow motion and pointed straight at her. His face suddenly looked furious and he spoke angrily whilst baring his teeth, but there was no sound. Then he stepped out of the mural and onto the floor of the chamber, and took several huge steps towards Fiona whilst raising his crook above his head, ready to strike.

Fiona fell backwards onto the floor and tried to scream, but she was unable to make a sound. She turned over and started to crawl away frantically, but the pharaoh was bearing down on her with giant steps that shook the whole chamber, making dust fall from the ceiling and cracks appear in the columns.

Suddenly she sensed a big hand on her back, as if she was being held down against the dusty floor.

'Fiona,' said a deep booming voice.

She tried to wriggle free, but to no avail, and in a final desperate attempt she flailed her arms around and tried to roll out from under the giant hand. She managed to get the hand to relinquish its grip, but then she instantly felt herself in free fall, as if she had rolled off a tall ledge.

She hit the ground and woke up. She was lying on the floor of the hotel room, right next to the bed, looking up at the ceiling.

Andrew's face appeared over the edge of the bed.

'Are you alright?' he said, looking concerned, and sounding groggy, as if he had just woken up himself. 'I think you just had one hell of a nightmare.'

Fiona closed her eyes and exhaled in relief. She was sweating, her heart was pounding, and she took a few moments to try to calm down. Then she sat up and shook her head.

'Yes, I did,' she said. 'It was terrifying.'

'Come back up here,' he smiled. 'You can't sleep down there.'

She climbed back up into the bed and tucked herself in close to him.

'That was intense,' she said. 'I hope I am done dreaming for tonight.'

Andrew put his arm around her, and a couple of minutes later they were both soundly asleep again.

★   ★   ★

'Hello?' said a stern authoritative-sounding voice.

'Yes. Hello sir. It is me.'

'What did you find out?'

'Their plane has landed in Aswan. Looks like it came from Ethiopia.'

'Any idea what they did there?'

'No, sir.'

'And their trip to Israel? Any sign of them finding anything?'

'No, sir. We were unable to follow.'

Pause.

'Sir? What do you want us to do?'

'I want you to take two of your best men, and get down there immediately. I don't care how you get there, or how much it costs. Get there fast and get that notebook from the girl.'

'We're already prepped, sir.'

'Good. I knew I didn't make a mistake calling you up for this task.'

'Thank you, sir.'

'Any questions?'

'Yes, sir. Rules of engagement?'

'None. You just do whatever you have to do. No restrictions.'

'Ok, sir. Got it.'

'Keep me updated as soon as you have news.'

'Yes, sir. Thank you for putting your faith in me.'

'You have come through for us many times before. Don't mess this up.'

* * *

Andrew and Fiona woke up in the early afternoon, having had several hours of much-needed sleep. They went out to sit on the balcony of their 3rd-floor hotel room, which was facing due west, overlooking Elephantine Island less than 100 meters away. It had a dry dusty look to it, and the light brown rock and dirt made it look decidedly unwelcoming. There were a few trees and bushes further north, but on the southern tip, there was hardly any vegetation at all.

'So, what do you know about this place?' asked Andrew. 'What is its historical significance, and what is the connection to Menelik I?'

'Well,' said Fiona. 'We don't know for a fact if there ever was a connection to Menelik, but after what you found under the chapel in Axum, I would say chances of that connection actually being there are pretty good.'

She shifted in her seat to face Andrew. 'Ok. In 1906, a small series of papyri that were found on Elephantine Island was acquired by a Mr. Robert Mond and edited by Professor Sayce and Dr. Cowley, of Oxford. Another larger quantity was then unearthed in the course of excavations by the Berlin Imperial Museum in 1911, and edited by Professor Sachau of Berlin. The papyri were in Aramaic, and detailed the existence of a community of Jews living on Elephantine Island in the 6th century BCE. This was during a period when the area was under Persian control.'

'That means they are more than two-and-a-half thousand years old,' said Andrew. 'That is a very long time for papyrus to survive.'

'It is,' nodded Fiona. 'And the only reason they did survive is because of the exceptionally dry and stable climate there. If it is very hot all year round, and there is next to no humidity in the air, then organic materials take a very long time to decompose, if they ever do so.'

'Ok,' said Andrew. 'So, what did these papyri say?'

'Well,' said Fiona. 'They do not present a narrative or some sort of religious or political dogma. They include letters, legal contracts, divorce settlements, documents related to the freeing of slaves, and all sorts of other business. So, what they represent, when looked at together, is an incredibly detailed view of the daily lives of this group of Jewish settlers several thousand kilometres from the southern Levant where they would have come from.'

'How did they come to live here?' asked Andrew. 'It seems like an odd place to end up unless of course there was a very good reason for them to be here.'

'Exactly,' said Fiona emphatically. 'Why would a small community of Canaanites live this isolated life on an island opposite the city that was quite literally considered as the very edge of the ancient Egyptian empire? Remember, this was around the same time as the destruction of the Temple in Jerusalem, or possibly a number of years later.'

'Are you saying they might have been guarding the Ark?' asked Andrew.

'That is precisely what I am thinking,' said Fiona. 'Knowing what we know about the Ark, and maintaining our speculation that someone, possibly King Solomon, was trying to move the Ark out of Jerusalem to safety, it does seem like the obvious place. If the aim was to bring the Ark to a safe location, then the very edge of the ancient world would seem like a good candidate.'

'The Ark of the Covenant on Elephantine Island,' mused Andrew. 'I guess they could have brought it along the Nile from the delta in the north. Or it could have come via the land route from Axum.'

'Both are a possibility,' said Fiona. 'Whether this happened before or after the Ark went to Axum, if it ever did, is difficult to say. My sense would be that if the Menelik legend is true, then the Ark was eventually taken from Axum, and back to Egypt, where it was kept and protected inside the temple on Elephantine Island.'

'But is there any evidence at all that the Ark was on Elephantine Island?' asked Andrew.

'This is the really amazing thing,' said Fiona. 'Remember, the whole of Aswan served first and foremost as a quarry for the sought-after syenite stone used for ancient Egyptian monuments. So, the island has been occupied and inhabited for millennia. This, in turn, means that over the centuries, buildings have been torn down or destroyed, and then other buildings have been erected on top of the old ones.'

'Just like in so many other places around the world,' said Andrew. 'Same old principle. And sometimes using some of the same stones, right?'

'That's right,' said Fiona. 'When archaeologists started digging on the island in 1967, looking for remnants of pagan temples, they discovered the buried remains of a Jewish temple from the 5th or 6th century BCE. This was obviously a big deal, but it was only when they mapped it out precisely, that the true significance of the structure became obvious.'

'What was it?' asked Andrew, sounding intrigued.

'The footprint of the temple on Elephantine Island matched the Temple of Solomon in Jerusalem perfectly. In other words, it appears to have been an exact copy, right down to the dimensions of the holy of holies at its centre.'

'Wow,' said Andrew. 'That's bizarre.'

'Was it, though?' asked Fiona. 'What was kept in the holy of holies in the Temple of Solomon in Jerusalem?'

Andrew hesitated. 'The Ark of the Covenant!' he replied, clearly impressed.

'And it gets even better,' smiled Fiona. 'You may have heard of the Bible's Book of Deuteronomy. It formalises the special covenant between the Hebrews and their god Yahweh. It states that it is only permissible for the Hebrews to build one temple in which to worship Yahweh, and the Ark of the Covenant must therefore reside inside that temple. There clearly was a temple here on Elephantine Island, so it stands to reason that the Ark must have been here during that period.'

'So, what happened to the Jewish colony here?' asked Andrew.

'Unknown,' said Fiona. 'There is some evidence to suggest that the Jewish colony existed here because there were a large number of Jewish mercenaries working for the Persians. Their empire at the time stretched from present-day Iran to Greece and all the way down here to the southern border of ancient Egypt. When the Persians were ousted by the Egyptians around 400 BCE, the Jewish mercenaries would have been in a precarious situation, and might even have been accused of treason. But we don't know exactly what happened to them or where they might have gone.'

'That's quite a story,' said Andrew. 'But when did they first come here? That would be relevant when trying to work out if the Ark was really here.'

'It is not known exactly when they arrived, but the earliest record demonstrating their presence was from 525 BCE, which is around sixty years after the destruction of the Temple of Solomon by Nebuchadnezzar II.'

'It seems plausible that it could have been transported here,' said Andrew. 'But what do you suggest we do when we get over there. I bet the whole place is completely overrun by tourists.'

'Yes,' said Fiona. 'There are quite a few tourists on the northern half of the island. There are some large resorts there, but the southern part, where the temple is supposed to have been, is not particularly busy.'

'How big is Elephantine Island?' asked Andrew.

'Around 1200 metres long, and 300 metres wide at its widest point,' replied Fiona. 'So, there is quite a bit of real estate there to explore.'

'By the way,' said Andrew and looked at her. 'This hotel. Its name sounds familiar somehow.'

'It should be,' smiled Fiona. 'It is the same hotel that was in Agatha Christie's *Death on the Nile*.'

'Oh, that's where it is from,' chuckled Andrew.

'Yes,' said Fiona grimly. 'Let's hope it doesn't come to that for us.'

'Don't worry,' said Andrew. 'We can take care of ourselves.'

Fiona did not look convinced.

'What is that over there,' said Andrew and pointed at a two-storey building on the south-eastern edge of the island, facing Aswan and their hotel.

'That is the Aswan Museum,' replied Fiona. 'They apparently have several mummies in there, as well as exhibits of things found on Elephantine Island. Most of them were uncovered by various German expeditions, going as far back as the early 20th century.'

'Such as?' said Andrew, and sipped some orange juice.

'Mainly statues of various pharaohs if I remember correctly. But the most prominent thing on the island is probably the ruins of the Temple of Khnum.'

'Who?' asked Andrew.

'Khnum,' repeated Fiona. 'Elephantine was supposedly the dwelling place of this ram-headed god of the cataracts. He was worshipped as the guardian of the waters of the Nile. You can see the remains of it just over there,' she said and pointed to two tall pillars standing by themselves in a large square.

'Not much left,' said Andrew. 'What about the Jewish temple? Where was that located?'

'Only hints of it have been found, but it is believed to have been over there on the southwestern edge of the island.'

'We should take a look for ourselves,' said Andrew. 'But I have to say. Sitting up here and looking at it from a distance, most of it looks like piles of rubble.'

'Well,' said Fiona and scoffed. 'That is often how archaeological sites look, until someone who knows what they are talking about comes along, maps it out and makes sense of it all.'

'Someone like you,' said Andrew and winked at her.

'Yes,' said Fiona and smiled. 'Someone like me.'

'Well, let's get changed, get some food, and then get on our way,' said Andrew.

* * *

Doctor Zaki had asked to see his Malpannah again. He was sitting in his usual spot on the pavement in the ahwas in Mohandessin. The Teacher arrived on time as usual and sat down across from him with a gentle smile.

'How are you, my son?' he asked in a hushed voice.

'I have been contacted by the SAS soldier Andrew Sterling again,' replied Zaki. 'They sent me a small fragment of metal, and asked me to examine it.'

'Oh?' said the old man and raised his eyebrows slowly.

'They said it was radioactive, and that proved to be true. It is a small piece of lead, and it must have been exposed to a powerful radioactive source.'

'Where did they get it from?' asked the old man.

'They did not say,' replied Zaki, 'But I think they must have been to Axum, and entered the chapel there. I guess they found the underground chamber.'

The old man produced a resigned smile. 'That would seem a logical conclusion. Another step closer.'

'We can't sit idly by and let this happen, can we?' asked Doctor Zaki, looking concerned.

The old man hesitated. 'We may be approaching a turning point for the brotherhood,' said the old man pensively.

'You mean, give up?' asked Zaki, sounding appalled.

'No no,' replied the old man reassuringly. 'I mean, we might have to finally change the way in which we manage this burden of ours. Perhaps the time has come to end the old ways. The world has changed so much, and what has served us well for centuries may no longer be the right thing to do anymore.'

Doctor Zaki nodded sagely. 'Are you saying we should intervene?'

The old man nodded. 'We may have to now. They may need our help to prevent the Source from falling into the hands of truly evil people. If the choice is between the Source being employed for destruction, and our secret being revealed, then that choice is clear.'

Doctor Zaki nodded. 'What shall I do?'

The old man leaned forward and spoke softly into the scientist's ear.

Twenty-Two

Andrew checked his pockets one more time, to make sure he had everything he thought they might need. Then the two of them walked down to the small boats that were moored by the river's edge immediately below the hotel.

A hotel employee in a burgundy uniform and a black hat greeted them and arranged for a small rowing boat that could take them the fifty meters across to Elephantine Island. The river flowed marginally faster as it made its way around the island, but it was still a calm and pleasant trip.

Once they were moored on the other side, Andrew hopped onto the jetty and helped Fiona up and out of the boat. They then walked up several sets of steps, until they found themselves within a stone's throw of the Temple of Khnum, or what was left of it. The two pillars that rose up in the middle of the cobbled stone square cut a lonely figure, and Fiona closed her eyes for a few seconds to try to imagine what that temple might have looked like almost two and a half thousand years ago. There would have been many buildings surrounding it, and some of the ruins of those were only just visible as rows of neatly stacked chiselled stones from the quarries on the island.

'Come on,' said Fiona. 'Let's have a closer look.'

Andrew pulled out a small tourist map that he had picked up in the hotel's reception. It showed all the major points of interest on Elephantine Island, including where various temples and other structures were. They walked across the square and stood next to the pillars that were around four meters high, and looked slightly unsafe.

'This whole area used to be a courtyard leading into the interior of the temple over there.' Fiona gestured to the elongated space behind the pillars. 'They used to make animal sacrifices and other offerings to Khnum here. But interestingly, this temple existed alongside other temples for other deities, including the Jewish temple for quite a while, as far as we can tell.'

'All sounds very amicable and tolerant,' said Andrew.

'It was,' replied Fiona. 'For as long as it lasted. Once the Persian overlords were kicked out, the Jewish mercenaries here were squeezed out apparently.'

'Any idea how many people lived in this community?' asked Andrew.

'Several hundred,' replied Fiona. 'They were here for generations. They obviously had children here, and by all accounts, those entered into the mercenary trade like their parents. Another interesting note is that the women here had extraordinary powers over their own lives, at least compared with their contemporaries in the rest of Egypt and in most other places at that time. Some of the papyri recount verbatim statements by women, who in the context of legal wranglings over property, threatened to divorce their husbands.'

'Sounds like a ferocious bunch of ladies,' said Andrew. 'Were they also mercenaries?'

Fiona smiled. 'Not as far as we can tell, but they clearly took after their men in some respects. In Jewish culture, women have probably always been a force to be reckoned with. Just take something like the concept of matrilineal descent.'

'Which is what?' asked Andrew.

'It is the simple notion that Jewish descent goes through the maternal line. So, from that perspective, you are only a real Jew if your mother was Jewish. Apparently, orthodox Jews maintain that matrilineal descent dates at least to the time of the covenant at Mount Sinai.'

'That's topical,' said Andrew. 'I admit that I am no expert on the Bible, but given the existence of things like matrilineal descent, there is a serious absence of female characters in those stories. Everything seems to revolve around men.'

'You're finally getting it,' said Fiona, grinning. 'It's always the men that are the centre of attention.'

'Alright,' smiled Andrew and held up his hands. 'Let's not get into this right now. We have work to do.'

'Fair enough,' smiled Fiona. 'Come this way,' she said and motioned towards the ruins of a building just a few meters away. At the front of the building next to the doorway, was a pillar with a beautifully carved face of a woman with long hair and full lips.

'This is a bust of the goddess Hathor,' said Fiona. 'She was the goddess of love, beauty, music, dancing, fertility, and pleasure.'

'Quite the lady,' said Andrew.

'And, she was the protector of women,' continued Fiona, 'But men also worshipped her.'

'I can see why,' smirked Andrew and winked at her.

'Oaf,' smiled Fiona and shook her head. 'Anyway, what is really interesting about her are her facial features, which are clearly Nubian, and look at her neck. Those are neck rings, which you also see in many other African cultures.'

'I guess that makes sense,' said Andrew. 'After all, we are at the edge of ancient Egypt's border with Nubia. We can't be far off the halfway mark between the Nile delta in the north, and Khartoum in Sudan. This place must have been a melting pot of cultures and religions through the ages.'

'Exactly,' said Fiona. 'This probably also explains why so many different buildings and temples here ended up being built on top of each other, century after century.'

'Speaking of which,' said Andrew and looked towards the southwestern part of the island. 'Where was the Jewish temple supposed to have been?'

'Let me show you,' said Fiona, and started walking slowly in that direction. 'I had a look at a map created by a researcher by the name of Stephen Rosenburg, and he theorised that the Temple would have been aligned more or less in the same way as the Temple of

Solomon in Jerusalem, with the entrance to the main courtyard facing east.'

They were now well past the temple of Khnum, and around fifty meters from the edge of the island.

'This would have been the entrance,' said Fiona, and held out her arms wide to indicate where the exterior walls would have been.

'How big was it?' asked Andrew.

'If it really was a copy of the Temple of Solomon, right down to using the exact same dimensions, then according to the Book of Kings, it would have been around thirty meters long, ten meters wide, and fifteen meters tall.'

'And if it did contain the Ark, or a replica of the Ark, where would that have been located?'

Fiona turned and walked towards the edge of the small rocky plateau where the temple would have been, but stopped some ten meters short of the edge.

'Roughly around here,' she said. 'The holy of holies was around ten by ten metres, and would have been set back at the other end of the temple from where the entrance was.'

Andrew placed his hands on his hips. 'It seems small,' he said, and looked around on the ground as if expecting to spot some remnant of the temple.

'Yes,' she said. 'The Temple of Solomon was not very big at all.'

'But there is no trace of it now?'

'None,' said Fiona. 'At least not anything that has been uncovered yet.'

'Unless it is below all these other buildings and rocks,' said Andrew. 'You said this place is basically just buildings on top of the ruins of other buildings.'

'That's correct,' said Fiona. 'What often happened was that the remains of ruined buildings would be picked up and used to build other buildings decades or centuries later. So, it is possible that some of the stone blocks you see here in these other structures actually came from the Jewish Temple.'

'Fascinating,' said Andrew, and pulled out his Geiger counter.

'What are you doing?' asked Fiona perplexed.

'Just checking,' said Andrew. 'You never know.'

He turned on the device and waited a few seconds. Then followed a sparse series of intermittent clicks.

'Nothing,' he said. 'Just background radiation. If something like a radioactive source had been kept here, I might have been able to pick up a marginally higher level.'

'Really?' asked Fiona. 'Even after all this time?'

'Sure,' said Andrew. 'Remember, some of these isotopes have half-lives of tens of thousands of years, or even millions of years. But I am not picking up anything.'

'Well, I wanted to have a look at something else,' said Fiona, and started walking back towards the eastern side of the island. 'Remember how the Nile more or less dictated life in ancient Egypt, and how many of their gods had some relation to the river?'

'Sure,' he replied.

'Well,' she continued. 'The best way to keep track of what the Nile was doing and how it flowed during the seasons, was with nilometers. And Elephantine Island has two of them.'

'Don't you just need one?' asked Andrew.

'Yes,' replied Fiona. 'But for some reason, two were built here. One was a quite simple one, down in that direction by the edge of the river-facing our hotel on the other side.' She pointed southeast, towards the hotel. 'The other is up here near the Aswan Museum. Let's go have a look.'

They walked through the remains of the temple of Khnum again, and past several other temples built to worship other ancient Egyptian gods, to arrive at the largest nilometer, which was also the most recently constructed. It was accessed via a long corridor leading down ninety steps to the water's edge.

'Look at this,' said Fiona and gestured towards the entrance. 'This was built during the 17th Dynasty, so around 1550 BCE. Let's go down.'

They descended the first section of steps and entered into a tunnel that led further down into the bedrock. It was cool and damp in there, and at one point it turned at a right angle to reveal where it ended by the edge of the Nile. The brightness of the sunlight made them both squint as they exited the tunnel onto a small stone platform right by the water's edge.

'This is where they used to make their water measurements,' said Fiona and pointed to carvings in the side of the tunnel's stone blocks.

'So has the water level been more or less the same since then?' asked Andrew.

'Yes, as far as we can tell,' said Fiona. 'Let's go and have a look at the other one.' She started back up the steps towards the raised plateau of the island's southern part.

Andrew walked along behind her, looking up at the inside of the tunnel. His eyes were getting used to the darkness again, and just as he was turning the corner where it was darkest, he noticed a small carving into one of the blocks of granite that the tunnel was constructed from.

The carving was almost at head height, which is why he had not noticed it before. Walking through the damp gloomy tunnel, anyone walking past would be busy watching where they were putting their feet, especially by the ninety-degree turn. He had done the same, and so had not noticed the carving on the way down.

The carving itself was only about the size of a drinks coaster and seemed to depict a sun with rays shining out in all directions.

'Fiona?' he called. 'Take a look at this.'

She came back down to stand next to him, looking up at the carving. 'What is it?' she asked, but then immediately gasped. 'Oh my God,' she whispered. 'Do you see what that is?'

'What?' said Andrew. 'A sun?'

'No,' said Fiona shaking her head. 'That is no sun. That is the same sort of image as what was depicted on Omran's metal casket.'

Andrew squinted at it, and then pulled out a Zippo lighter from his pocket. He flicked the wheel, and the flame sprang to life in his hand. The orange light accentuated the contours in the carving, making the shadows appear dark, and the granite much lighter.

'See?' said Fiona. 'Remember how in ancient Egyptian imagery, the sun is always depicted as a circle with rays of light shining downwards only?

Well, this has the same outward radiating patterns as the front of the metal casket.'

'You're right,' he said. 'Wait. Are you saying this is a depiction of a meteorite?'

'What else could it be?' said Fiona excitedly.

'Has anyone else ever noticed this?' asked Andrew incredulously.

'Probably,' said Fiona. 'But if you don't know what it means or what it relates to, then you have no context to interpret it in any meaningful way. It's just an unusual image of the sun.'

'Take a picture of it,' said Andrew and stepped back for a better look, to make sure he would be able to find it again.

Fiona took several photos and then became quiet. She was pondering what this could mean. She also had a strange feeling that this was related to something she had seen before, but she could not put her finger on it.

'This is so frustrating,' she said. 'There is clearly a connection to the casket here, but I just don't understand what it is.'

'Let's go to the other nilometer,' said Andrew and took her hand. 'Perhaps that will help us figure this out.'

They ascended the steps and came back out into the warm bright sunlight. The dry dusty air was suddenly quite noticeable, and they both took a swig of their water bottle.

'It's just down this way,' said Fiona and pointed along the edge of the island towards the south.

Just off to their left on the other side of the river, was their hotel. For a brief moment, Andrew felt slightly silly going adventuring in a place like this that was so overrun with tourists, and that had been combed through by archaeologists for centuries. But as Fiona had said. If they did not know what to look for, then they would not be able to put the pieces together and find what might still be hidden here.

The second nilometer was a large open square, carved into the bedrock and built up on the sides with neatly chiselled blocks of granite. On one of its sides was a series of steps leading down to the bottom of it, where the water level could be measured. Similar to the first nilometers, there were a set of carvings in the granite blocks next to the steps, which would allow for accurate measurements of the water level. The nilometer was almost completely dry, and most of the underlying bedrock was exposed. Only at the very bottom of the steps did the river lap gently at the stone steps.

They descended the steps and started to examine the blocks of granite near them. There was nothing to be found. They were all smooth with no images or writing carved into them.

'I am going to have a look over here,' said Andrew, and stepped off the stone steps and onto one of the large boulders that protruded from the base of the nilometer. He walked along the boulder, looking intently at the granite blocks above him that made up the walls of the nilometer.

'Well, will you look at this,' he said. 'It's right here in plain sight.'

'What?' said Fiona, sounding incredulous. 'There's another one?'

'Yes,' replied Andrew and pointed at a block about a meter above his head. 'Right up there.'

'I don't believe it,' whispered Fiona. 'All this time these carvings have been sitting there, and no one seems to have had a clue what they were.'

'Well,' said Andrew. 'We might have an idea about what they depict, but we don't know what they mean. Why are they here?'

'True,' conceded Fiona, again having the feeling that she knew something about this that she was just unable to recall.

She took several more pictures, and then they walked back up the steps to the plateau with the temple of Khnum. Her face now looked anguished as she desperately tried to connect what they had just seen, to what she knew was filed away somewhere in her memory.

'Interesting that they decided to place two nilometers this close to each other,' said Andrew. 'There can't be more than a hundred meters between them.'

As they were walking along the path away from the second nilometer, Fiona suddenly slowed gradually to a halt and stood still without saying a word.

Andrew looked over his shoulder and then turned around to face her.

'Are you alright?' he asked.

Fiona did not reply, but her hands started grabbing at the latches on her shoulder bag.

'What's going on?' said Andrew, and walked back towards her.

'Give me your map,' she said, staring straight ahead of herself, without actually looking at anything.

'This map?' asked Andrew.

'Yes,' she replied impatiently. 'Your map. That map right there in your hand.'

He gave it to her and looked at her perplexed.

Fiona opened her shoulder bag and pulled out Omran's notebook.

'I've seen this before,' she said. 'I know I have.'

She flicked through the pages until she arrived at a very simple sketch. It showed two small circles on either side of the page, connected by two parallel lines. Halfway between the circles was another line perpendicular to the first two lines, stretching up to the middle of the page, where it met a rectangle.

Beneath the sketch was written a few words, in what she had concluded was Jabari Omran's handwriting. *At the temple where the river begins.*

'What do you mean?' asked Andrew. 'What have you seen?'

'Well,' said Fiona and shook her head, as if irritated with herself. 'I haven't seen this exact thing, but I have seen the pattern, and it is right here on this page.'

'I am sorry,' said Andrew. 'I don't follow.'

'Sorry,' smiled Fiona. 'Look at this map,' she said, and then knelt down and placed the tourist map of Elephantine Island on the ground.

'This is the southern part of the island, and this right here is where the two nilometers are.' She pointed to them both in succession.

'Ok?' said Andrew, still not understanding.

'And this is where the remains of the temple of Khnum are,' she continued and pointed to the large square where the two tall pillars stood. 'Khnum was the ancient Egyptian god of the first cataract of the Nile. But not only that. It was believed that the Nile started right here under Elephantine Island, guided by Khnum.'

'Well, that's obviously nonsense,' said Andrew. 'The Nile clearly flows north for hundreds of kilometres before it gets to Aswan.'

'I know,' said Fiona. 'But the point is, that is what the ancient Egyptians believed, and so when Omran wrote "At the temple where the river begins", that must mean that his sketch relates to this very place in Aswan.'

'So, what are those circles and lines then?' asked Andrew, no nearer to understanding where this was going.

'Simple,' said Fiona. 'If you overlay Omran's sketch on a map of the southern part of Elephantine Island so that the two circles are on top of the two nilometers, then the nilometers become connected by the first two lines.'

'So, what do you suppose that means?' asked Andrew.

'I think it might be a tunnel or a passage between the two,' said Fiona.

'And the other lines connected to the rectangle?' asked Andrew.

Fiona looked up at him with gleaming eyes. 'I think that might be another passage to a chamber underneath where the Jewish temple used to be. It fits perfectly with the location of the temple that archaeologists have guessed at.'

'So, are you saying that just because the original Jewish temple is long gone, it doesn't mean that there isn't still a chamber deep inside the bedrock of the island?'

'Exactly,' said Fiona. 'That is the only explanation for the images chiselled into the granite in both nilometers.'

'You could be right,' said Andrew and nodded. 'And if you are, then I bet the access to the underground tunnels are behind those blocks of granite with the image of the meteorite carved into them.'

'But then the question becomes this,' said Fiona, and held up her index finger. 'If the carving of the meteorite is on those granite blocks, does that mean that what is actually under the old temple site is the Ark, or the meteorite?'

Andrew looked at her for a moment, and then pulled out his Geiger counter. 'I don't know, but I am sure this thing will come in handy.'

'Well, we can't go looking for it now,' said Fiona. 'We should wait until after dark.'

'Yes,' said Andrew. 'I think we should come back between three and four in the morning when everyone else is sleeping. I also need to go shopping first.'

'Shopping?'

'I think we might need some tools for this,' he replied. 'Let's get back over to the hotel. If you want to go back up to the room, I will go and talk to the reception about where to find a hardware store.'

'Ok,' said Fiona. 'I could do with a bit of time to myself, just to try to think this through.'

'Alright,' said Andrew. 'Let's go.'

Twenty-Three

Fiona was sitting on the hotel room balcony overlooking Elephantine Island, when Andrew returned about an hour later. She had been going over the same pages in Jabari Omran's notebook over and over again, but nothing new had occurred to her. It was as if each insight from the notebook was contingent on a previous insight, so it was impossible to unravel the whole thing in one go. They simply had to proceed step by step and see where things would take them, and then try to connect the dots later.

'Did you get what you needed?' asked Fiona and turned to look inside the hotel room.

Andrew came outside and joined her on the balcony, holding a very large shopping bag from what looked like a builder's merchant. He sat down next to her and reached into the bag. Pulling out a crowbar, he beamed at her. 'Nice huh?'

Fiona just gave him a blank look.

Andrew shrugged, reached into the bag again, and pulled out a huge flathead screwdriver. He raised his eyebrows and gave her a cautious smile.

Fiona looked at him impassively.

Then he shook his head and reached into the bag for a third and final time, and produced a small pickaxe.

Fiona dropped her head and scowled at him from under her eyebrows. 'Are you kidding me?' she finally said.

'What do you mean?' asked Andrew.

'Are you planning to level the whole island? Why didn't you get some explosives as well?'

'Well,' grinned Andrew. 'They didn't have any.'

'Ok,' said Fiona. 'I am going to trust you on this, but let's just agree to not break anything unless we really need to. I am already feeling uncomfortable with this whole thing as it is.'

'Done,' nodded Andrew. 'No breaking things unless it's a good idea.'

Fiona pinned him down with a disapproving stare for a few seconds.

'Anyway,' she said. 'I think I have a theory about the metal casket that Omran was working on.'

'Really?' said Andrew intrigued. 'What is it?'

'It is a bit tenuous,' replied Fiona, 'But I think it makes some sense. Basically, when the first of the famous papyri of Elephantine Island were uncovered in 1906, they were obviously a bit of a sensation in archaeological circles. Researchers immediately launched themselves into trying to translate them and analyse their content. And for good reason. Finding this many ancient writings in such excellent condition was almost unheard of. But all that attention probably took away from other things they might have found.'

'Such as?' asked Andrew.

'The metal casket,' replied Fiona. 'Possibly.'

Andrew raised his eyebrows. 'Now, there's a thought,' he said, looking impressed.

'Any items found around the area of the Jewish temple, would not have been taken to the new Egyptian Museum in Cairo, which you might remember was completed in 1901. The reason is that they aren't related to ancient Egyptian religion, or even to Egypt's pre-dynastic belief systems. And they could not have gone into the Aswan Museum just over there on the island, because that did not open until 1912.'

'So, what do you think happened to them?' asked Andrew.

'I think items like those would have found their way to the Coptic Museum in Cairo. After all, Coptic Christians, along with all other Christians, are effectively a splinter group that broke away from Judaism in the 1st century. So, it would have made sense for those items to be kept there for later analysis and research. And it doesn't take too much imagination to think that perhaps some of the items were not properly catalogued, or that records of items might have gone missing.'

'And you think Omran stumbled upon one down in that basement in the Coptic Museum?' asked Andrew.

'I think it is plausible,' replied Fiona. 'It fits everything else we have discovered. And it would explain why Omran in some ways seems to be stumbling around in the dark. I am not even convinced that he realised that the casket was from Elephantine Island.'

'Either way,' said Andrew. 'It ties the casket and the meteorite more closely to this place, which means the odds of there actually being something here are pretty good. We just have to go find it.'

'There's something else that I just realised,' said Fiona.

'What?' asked Andrew, looking out over Elephantine Island.

'If we're going to go poking around in the dark on the island, tonight is not a bad night to do it.'

'What do you mean?' asked Andrew.

'It is New Year's Eve,' said Fiona and smiled.

'What?' said Andrew looking confused. 'But it's September. September 11th in fact.'

'Yes,' smiled Fiona. 'And Coptic Christians celebrate the start of their year today. It's called *Nayrouz*, and it is a commemoration of martyrs and confessors.'

'Charming,' said Andrew. 'This puts September 11th 2001 into a whole new perspective. Several of the hijackers on those planes were Egyptians.'

'I know,' said Fiona. 'Hardly a coincidence, if you ask me.'

'Anyway,' said Andrew. 'Let's not get distracted here. Nayrouz will help occupy the locals, and any tourists will probably be wining and dining in the local restaurants, taking in the local culture.'

'That was my thought as well,' said Fiona. 'It ought to be very quiet on Elephantine Island tonight.'

'Especially at 3:30 in the morning.'

'Let's get some early dinner,' said Fiona. 'And then we should get some sleep. We need to be well-rested if we're going to go adventuring in the middle of the night.'

'Agreed,' said Andrew, and put his newly acquired tools back into the shopping bag. He then carried them inside the hotel room and packed them neatly inside a backpack.

★ ★ ★

'Sir?'

'Yes, what's the situation?'

'We've just landed. It seems our local contact has delivered on his word, and the equipment is in a hotel room waiting for us.'

'And your targets?'

'Staying at the Sofitel Legend Hotel.'

'How fitting. What is your plan?'

'Our man is watching the hotel. When they leave, we'll be on them.'

'Good. You know what you need to do.'

'Yes, sir. We'll get it done.'

'Good luck.'

'Thank you, sir.'

★ ★ ★

Fiona woke up first, wondering for a moment where she was. She had set the alarm on her phone to two-thirty in the morning, and its vibrations had woken her without disturbing Andrew. It was dark and quiet in the hotel room, but in the distance, she could hear voices and music from the festivities that were still going on in the city.

She sat up on the edge of the bed, and then rose to walk over to the sliding doors to the balcony. The air was cooler now, but still pleasant. She could see Elephantine Island lying there on the other side of the river, bathed in the pale blue light from the full moon above the city. She could see the river-facing entrance to the southern-most nilometer from the balcony, and it felt surreal to her that they were about to go over there to attempt something no one had ever attempted before.

She walked back inside and woke up Andrew. They then got themselves ready, packed their equipment, and just before three o'clock they quietly left their room and made their way to the side of the hotel facing the Nile. On the way, they could see the reception down at the end of a corridor, and there seemed to be no one there except for the receptionist and another member of staff. They were talking, and oblivious to Andrew and Fiona making their way quietly to the back of the hotel.

The jetty was quiet with no one in sight, and Andrew quickly unmoored a small boat that was bobbing calmly in the river.

They climbed in without a word, and Andrew pushed off with an oar and quickly brought them across to Elephantine Island which was around fifty meters away. Here Fiona jumped out and tied the boat to another jetty. Andrew followed, and then they made their way up the steps to the plateau, and along the path towards the northernmost nilometer.

'We should go for the one in the tunnel,' said Andrew in a hushed voice. 'The one to the south is too exposed, and the granite block is too high up and difficult to get to. If we go to the one in the tunnel, we won't be overlooked.'

'Ok,' whispered Fiona.

The whole of the island seemed deserted. There were a few lights still on along a couple of the footpaths, but all of the temples lay in darkness. On the other side of the river, towards the city centre, they could hear a final few celebrations still going on, but most of the city had now quietened down, and very few people were awake. Their hotel, just on the other side of the river, was quiet and only a couple of rooms still had the light on inside them.

Andrew and Fiona quickly slipped out of view and down into the underground tunnel leading to the northernmost nilometer. After about ten meters, they switched on their torches and proceeded down to the ninety-degree right turn in the tunnel. Andrew quickly found the granite block with the carving of the meteorite, took off his backpack, and placed it on the ground.

'I am pretty sure no one saw us,' said Fiona. 'But we still need to hurry. Whatever we do here has to be done by sunrise which is about two hours away.'

'I know,' said Andrew, and pulled out the crowbar. 'I will try to make this quick. You just make sure no one comes down here.'

He stood up to examine the granite block that had the carving. Then he placed his feet slightly apart for a firm stance, held up the crowbar horizontally at shoulder level, and then rammed its end hard into the gap between the granite block with the carving and the one next to it. It produced a loud metallic clonk.

'Crikey,' said Fiona. 'That was loud.'

'I know,' winced Andrew. 'No way around it, I'm afraid. I have to get a really good purchase here.'

He wriggled the crowbar from side to side, breaking off small flakes of granite on both of the blocks in the process. Then he pulled the crowbar out, and then once more slammed it back into the gap, which was now a little bit bigger. He repeated the process several times on both sides of the granite block until he was able to insert the crowbar on the right side and get a good purchase on the block. He shifted his stance, and then he leaned into the crowbar, pushing it with all his strength, and the granite block shifted ever so slightly.

He flashed Fiona a grin. 'I think I've got this.'

'I am going to go topside and have a look around,' she said. 'I am worried about the noise we're making.'

'Alright,' said Andrew, now panting slightly from the effort.

Fiona turned and walked up the long series of steps to poke her head up and out over the edge of where the sides of the tunnel began. She could see no movement anywhere, and the only sounds she could hear was the sounds of Andrew's crowbar grinding against the granite inside the tunnel. Out here it did not sound nearly as loud as she had feared, so after a few minutes, she turned around and headed back down to him.

Andrew had now managed to nudge the block of granite several centimetres out from its position in the wall, and it was turned at a slight angle.

'Have a look at this,' said Andrew, his eyes keen and gleaming with excitement.

Fiona came over and stood next to him. 'What?' she said.

'Look,' he said. 'The block is not even remotely shaped like a cube. I can already see behind it. It is almost as if it is just a thin slab placed here to look like any of the other blocks. It can't be more than twenty centimetres thick.

'Are you saying it was meant to be removed?' asked Fiona.

'That is the only reason I can see for it being shaped like this. It isn't load-bearing, and it is clearly concealing a cavity behind it.'

Fiona looked at him with her mouth open. 'Really? Let me see.'

She pushed past Andrew and shone her torch through the small gap between the slab with the carving, and the solid block next to it. She adjusted the light slightly, and could now see what appeared to be a crawlspace about one meter wide and one meter high.

She looked at Andrew with wide eyes. 'Omran's map was correct,' she whispered excitedly. 'This is the tunnel between the two nilometers.'

Andrew nodded. 'It must be. Stand well back please.'

He waited for her to take a few steps backwards, and then slammed the crowbar into the gap between the slab and the block next to it, and pushed one final time. The slab groaned against the other three pieces of granite still holding it in place, but then it finally tipped out of the cavity and landed with a thud onto the granite steps below.

They looked at each other whilst listening out for noise, but they could hear none.

'Ok,' said Andrew in a hushed voice. 'Who wants to go first?'

Fiona looked at him, hesitating for a moment. She wanted to get in there to see for herself, but she also knew that Andrew was probably better equipped to handle this situation than she was.

'You should go first and have a look inside,' she said. 'I will follow you if it seems safe.'

Andrew nodded. 'Deal.'

'I'll pop up and have another look around,' said Fiona, and then she pointed at the granite slab lying on the ground. 'That was pretty loud.'

'Alright,' said Andrew. I will just have a quick look in there to see what I can see.'

He placed a foot on top of the slab lying on the ground. Shining his torch inside, he could see a neat and straight tunnel with no obvious end in sight. The air inside it was dry, but seemed slightly dusty, so the light from the torch was not able to reveal to him how far the tunnel went, or how it ended. It appeared to have a thin haze inside it, stretching away in the distance.

Fiona was back after less than a minute. 'Still no sign of anyone,' she said.

'Ok,' said Andrew, and switched on his head-mounted torch. 'I am going to crawl through here and see where it goes. If Omran's map is correct, then there should be another tunnel going off to the right, is that correct?'

'Yes,' said Fiona. 'But it could be as much as forty or fifty meters away. Around halfway to the southern nilometer. That's an awfully long way to crawl in there. Are you sure you're ok to do this? SAS or not, claustrophobia is a very real thing for a lot of people.'

'I will be fine,' said Andrew. 'We've trained for these sorts of things, but if it feels unsafe, I can come back out. The tunnel is wide enough to turn around in.'

'Alright,' said Fiona. 'Good luck.'

Andrew stepped up onto the slab and reached inside the passage with both hands. Then he put a knee on the edge of the passage and hauled himself up and into it. He was now lying on his side inside the passage, but there was enough space for him to turn his upper body and face Fiona. She was standing in the tunnel leading to the nilometer, with a concerned look on her face.

'I will try to make it halfway through the passage to start with, 'said Andrew. 'If Omran's sketch is correct, then there should be another passage going off to the right roughly at the midpoint.'

'Ok,' said Fiona, and watched as Andrew began crawling his way through the passage, holding his torch out in front of himself.

He made good progress and was around twenty meters in when Fiona decided to go up and check for anyone coming their way. She made her way up the steps again and poked her head up to look around. Everything still seemed quiet, although she thought for a moment that she could hear hushed voices in the direction of the hotel fifty meters away on the other side of the river, but when she looked she could see no one.

After about a minute, she decided to try to call Andrew. Her phone connected to the local network but was unable to get through to Andrew inside the passage.

'Damn it,' she mumbled. 'Not this again.'

After looking at the phone for a few seconds, she resolutely started walking back down the tunnel towards the newly exposed passage. When she turned the corner, she could neither see nor hear any sign of Andrew. Only when she went to stand on the slab on the ground, could she make out Andrew in the distance, still making his way along the passage. The light from his torch shifted slightly from side to side as he made his way forward through the passage. He was now at least thirty meters away, which suddenly felt like an enormous distance to Fiona. If the passage collapsed, Andrew would be trapped deep underground, and there would be nothing she could do to help him.

Suddenly he stopped moving for several seconds, but she could see him shining the light from his torch around his immediate vicinity. Then he directed the light back down the passage towards her.

'Fiona,' he said, in as loud a voice as he dared. 'Are you there?'

'Yes,' replied Fiona, conscious of the noise she was making.

Another loud whisper from Andrew. 'It's here. The second passage is here.'

For a moment, Fiona felt like hopping up and into the passage herself, but then she thought better of it.

'What can you see?' she asked, trying not to shout.

'More of the same,' replied Andrew. 'I am going to push on.'

Fiona watched him as he made his way to the right and into the second passage that ran in further underground, under the temple of Khnum and in the direction of where the Jewish temple was supposed to have been.

She watched his head and upper body disappear around the ninety-degree corner, then his legs, and then finally his feet. She could still see the light from his torch spilling back out behind him, but eventually, that disappeared too. The dry scraping sound of his clothes against the dusty passage interior had also faded to nothing. She suddenly felt very alone and exposed there in the tunnel by herself.

'Andy,' she called, but then instantly regretted it. The last thing he needed was to have to go back, and every time she spoke, she ran the risk of attracting attention to what they were doing.

She placed her hands on her hips and looked down at the ground. She hesitated for a few moments, but then looked up at the passage again.

'Shit,' she finally whispered to herself in a hushed voice. 'I am so going to regret this.'

Then she stepped up onto the slab, wriggled her way up and into the dark dusty passage, and began crawling forward towards where Andrew had disappeared a few moments earlier.

Twenty-Four

Andrew continued moving forward at a good pace, pulling himself through the second passage on his hands and knees. It was already clear to him that this passage was much longer than the first one, and as much as he tried to suppress it, he could feel a sense of claustrophobia beginning to creep in on him. No one had probably been through these passages for centuries, perhaps even millennia, and for all he knew the whole island could have settled and shifted during that time, in a way that made some of the massive blocks of granite above his head unstable and lose.

He pushed those thoughts out of his mind and continued forward. After another couple of minutes, and with no clear idea of how far he had come, he suddenly spotted something up ahead. A solid block of granite. The passage ahead of him was sealed.

He hesitated for a moment, turned to look behind him, and then directed his torch back towards the granite block. Taking a few breaths, and trying to peer ahead, he eventually decided that he had to push on, even if this seemed like a dead end. Going back was just not an option. He had come too far to give up now.

He made his way through the final stretch of the passage, crawling through thick veils of cobwebs, and eventually, he found himself next to the block of granite that was blocking his way. He examined it closely, shining the light from his headtorch around its edges, but there was nothing to indicate whether or not it was a thin slab similar to the one he had removed from the tunnel by the nilometer.

'Only one way to find out,' he said to himself and pulled out the crowbar from his backpack. He rammed it into the small gap between the granite block and the wall on the right, just as he had done half an hour earlier in the tunnel leading to the nilometer. He repeated this several times, trying to clear the rock around the block. He wriggled the crowbar from side to side, but the granite block did not budge.

After having opened up a gap all the way around the edge of the granite block, he pulled his legs up under himself, to then extend them in the opposite direction towards the block. Putting his fingers inside the gaps between blocks on either side of him, and making sure he had a good grip, he then placed both feet onto the middle of the granite block and pushed as hard as he could. The block did not move, and he suddenly became worried that he might be unable to make it any further.

He repositioned his hands slightly and tried again, this time groaning under the effort. He gave it everything he had, but the block did not move even a little bit.

As he relented, his pulse was racing, and he was breathing heavily. Lying back on the ground, panting loudly, he suddenly heard something back in the passage he had just come through. Out of the corner of his eye, he also saw the light from a torch.

In an instant, he had grabbed his knife from its sheath and spun around to face in the other direction.

'Fiona?' he exhaled, partly relieved that it was her, and partly unsettled that she had made her way in here by herself.

'I got really sick of waiting,' she said, trying to put a brave face on it, but it was obvious that she was scared and very much out of her comfort zone.

'Are you alright?' he asked, putting his knife away.

'Not really,' she smiled sheepishly. 'I am not good with tight spaces.'

'Well, you crashed the wrong party then,' he smiled sympathetically. 'Come over here. I could use your help.'

'With what?' she asked making her way towards him, and now sounding calmer.

'The passage is blocked,' he said.

'What?' exclaimed Fiona, instantly becoming agitated, and looking like she was about to panic. 'Can't we get out?'

'I am sure we can make it back, although it is a long way,' said Andrew, doing his best to sound in control. 'But the way ahead is blocked by this granite block. It might be another thin slab like the one in the tunnel, but it is wedged, and I can't move it.'

'Well, if you can't then I certainly can't,' she said, her voice trembling and sounding scared.

She had now reached him, and he placed his hands gently on either side of her head.

'Fiona,' he said calmly. 'Look at me.'

Her eyes were welling up and her lower lip was trembling as she looked into his eye, trying and failing to appear brave.

'It's ok,' he reassured her. 'We're going to be fine. We will get through this together. All we have to do is push this thing out of the way, alright?'

She nodded. 'Ok,' she said trying to pull herself together.

'Deep breath,' he said. 'Breathe with me.'

He took a long deep breath, inhaling slowly, and she did the same. Together they exhaled calmly.

'Ok,' she smiled, trying to convince herself that it was true. 'I'm ok. What can I do?'

'If you just come up here next to me and grab onto the gab in the wall,' he said. Then place your feet on the block like this.'

The two of them were now right next to each other in the cramped space. He placed his own feet onto the block and grabbed the gaps on his side of the passage.

'Ready?' he asked.

'Ready,' she replied

'Ok,' he nodded. 'One, two, three, go!'

They both pressed as hard as they could, and they immediately felt the block shift a couple of millimetres.

Fiona's head whipped up to look at Andrew. She was smiling, and suddenly again looking like the Fiona he knew.

'It's working!' she exclaimed.

'One more time,' he said. "One, two, three, go!'

They both kept the pressure up, and straining every sinew in their bodies, they managed to make the block begin to inch forward ever so slowly.

'Keep going,' groaned Andrew, his face now covered in sweat.

Fiona had her jaw clenched, and she was baring her teeth as she channelled all her energy into pushing her feet against the block.

Slowly the block moved forward a few centimetres, and then a few more, until it suddenly slid off the edge of the end of the passage, and fell with a loud crash onto the floor beyond.

They both exhaled violently and lay panting on their backs for a few seconds.

'Bloody hell,' said Andrew breathlessly. 'Well done. I knew we could do it together.'

Fiona turned her head and looked at him, a cautious smile on her face.

'Join Andy,' she said sarcastically. 'Go to Egypt. It will be fun.' Then she smiled.

They both lifted their heads and looked towards the square black hole they had just revealed. There was not enough light for them to see anything, so Andrew sat up and slid himself towards the opening. Peering through the hole, it seemed like there was a large chamber there, not dissimilar to the one he had found in Axum, but this one was bigger. It also had support columns almost identical to the ones he had found under the chapel, and at its centre, the chamber had a raised platform, very similar to that in Axum.

'This all seems eerily familiar,' he said in a hushed voice.

As he stepped out into the chamber, Andrew's head-mounted torch flickered.

'Wait,' he suddenly said. 'Stop here. Let me just check something.'

Then he pulled out his Geiger counter. He switched it on, and it immediately began clicking away in his hand.

'Definitely way above background radiation,' he said.

'Is it dangerous?' asked Fiona, moving forwards to sit next to him on the edge, where the passage met the chamber.

'No,' said Andrew and shook his head. 'Levels are not in dangerous territory, but there has clearly been something here that was very radioactive. What it was and how long ago, I can't say.'

'Let's see what's here then,' said Fiona.

They both proceeded carefully and slowly into the interior of the chamber, fanning their torches across the floor and the walls of the otherwise pitch-black chamber.

Circling around the raised platform towards the other side of the chamber, they could see that one of the walls and some of the ceiling there had partly collapsed in on itself.

'This makes me nervous,' said Fiona. 'The rock here is clearly not as stable as it once was.'

She took another few steps closer to the rubble and shone her light across it several times.

'Wait,' she said, and then tilted her torch up to the ceiling and then down along one side of the wall. 'This used to be an entrance. It looks like it would have been narrow, and very low, but it seems like it must have been a proper doorway. Which direction is this?' she asked, and held her arm out straight in the direction of the collapsed doorway.

Andrew lifted his left arm and looked at a small compass inset into the strap of his wristwatch.

'It is roughly southeast,' he said.

'Ok,' she replied. 'If we are under the site of the old Jewish temple now, then that doorway must once have led to an exit right on the river's edge somewhere in the sheer rockface facing towards the south.'

'But an entrance like that should be obvious on the outside,' said Andrew. 'Any boat sailing past from the south should be able to see it.'

'Yes, but I am pretty sure there is nothing to see from the outside now,' said Fiona.

'It was probably sealed off at some point,' said Andrew, and turned around to shine the light from his torch onto the empty platform. 'Perhaps the doorway and the access to this chamber was collapsed on purpose after whatever was here was removed.'

'What do you mean?' asked Fiona, and came over to stand next to him.

'Well,' said Andrew and knelt down next to the platform, holding the Geiger counter out in front of him, and listening to the lively clicking that was now happening in rapid succession. 'Something large and radioactive was clearly here on this platform, and it didn't just walk out of here by itself. So, at some point, whatever it was, must have been removed. The question is. What was it, and who removed it?

'And why did they remove it?' asked Fiona rhetorically.

'Could this have been where the meteorite was kept?' asked Andrew, and looked up at Fiona, who was standing next to him with her hands on her hips, and a pensive look on her face.

'It could very well be,' she replied. 'It is a very interesting thought. 'What if the temple above us actually held the Ark of the Covenant during that time? And what if this hidden chamber below it held the meteorite that the power of the Ark originated from?'

'That would make a lot of sense,' said Andrew.

'And,' said Fiona, now looking like a sequence of events was beginning to take shape inside her head. 'What if the chamber was here first, as a place used by the ancient Egyptian priests to keep and protect the meteorite? It is possible that the location of a dangerous object like the meteorite was kept a secret among such a small number of people that when they died, the secret was eventually lost.'

'But its location might have been rediscovered by the Israelites somehow,' interjected Andrew.

'Yes,' said Fiona, sounding excited. 'Remember, Aswan was first and foremost a quarry used for centuries to source granite for construction projects all throughout the ancient Egyptian empire. Also, remember that Joseph was the grand vizier of Egypt, the top administrator on behalf of the Pharaoh. He might somehow have learned of the existence of the meteorite and its secret location, and eventually passed that information on in a way so that it found its way to Moses.'

'Or,' said Andrew. 'If the Israelites really were enslaved here, Moses and his followers could have stumbled upon it during the work in the quarry. Either way, they could then have used it to mobilise the Israelites, and eventually lead them out of Egypt, possibly carrying a large chunk of the meteorite itself for protection.'

Fiona nodded. 'It obviously would have to have been encased in gold or lead, like the plates you found in Axum, but it is definitely a possibility.'

'It also fits neatly with why there was this strange but sizeable colony of Jewish mercenaries all the way down here on Elephantine Island on the very border of ancient Egypt. If they knew that the source of the power of the Ark of the Covenant stemmed from a meteorite hidden inside the bedrock on this island, what better way to protect it and its power, than to build a religious temple here, and use a large group of highly trained soldiers to guard it?'

"Very good point,' said Andrew, looking impressed.

'And also,' continued Fiona. 'If this place had remained hidden for centuries or perhaps even millennia, as a place for the ancient Egyptian priests to hide this powerful weapon, then it would have made sense for the Jewish colony to assume that protecting it here, would be better than trying to move it somewhere else.'

Andrew rubbed his jaw and raised his eyebrows. 'All of this is just conjecture, but it all does seem to fit together quite nicely with everything we have discovered so far.'

'I am trying to remain cautious,' nodded Fiona, 'But I have to admit that I find this idea extremely plausible.'

'Did Omran arrive at anything like this sort of conclusion?' asked Andrew.

'No,' she replied. 'Not as far as I can tell. There's nothing in his notebook about this. Elephantine Island only gets a small mention, in the form of the sketch on the two nilometers and the underground passages. There is also no indication as to where he might have got that sketch from.'

Andrew stood and looked at Fiona.

'I do agree that it is all very plausible,' he said and shone his light onto the empty platform. 'But it still doesn't explain why the meteorite disappeared. I mean, look at this platform. It is huge. If the meteorite was even remotely as big as this, then it would have weighed many tonnes. Not an easy task at all. And they must have felt that they had no other choice. Why else take on such a dangerous task?'

'I think it is fair to say that the logistical side of things would have been possible,' said Fiona. 'After all, this whole area of Aswan, revolved around moving large heavy objects hundreds of kilometres. It was literally the industry the entire city was built on. And as for the risks associated with moving it, I guess they must have thought that the risk of it falling into the wrong hands was the lesser evil, if they believed they were about to be overrun. Remember, they were ostensible mercenaries for the Persians, so when the Egyptians revolted and re-took power here, the Jewish mercenaries probably quite rightly assumed that it would be a question of time before they were overwhelmed by the locals and the forces of the new pharaoh.'

Andrew let the light from his torch move over the dusty surface of the platform. 'So, instead of leaving it here and hoping it would not be discovered, they decided to move it somewhere else?'

'I think that is likely,' said Fiona.

'So, where is it now?' asked Andrew.

Fiona smiled 'That is the question, isn't it? Along with the question of where the Ark of the Covenant has ended up.'

'Didn't you say that if we found the Ark, then we would also find the meteorite?' smiled Andrew.

'That could still happen,' said Fiona and spread out her hands. 'But honestly, I don't know what to make of this now. There is nothing in Omran's notebook that provides an obvious or tangible clue. The only things that are left are a few lines of text that I haven't been able to make sense of, another very simple sketch with no additional information, and a small poem about what I guess must be his wife.'

'Perhaps we should go and talk to her then,' said Andrew. 'She might know something.'

'Yes, but let's just focus on getting out of here in one piece,' said Fiona and turned to shine the light from her torch in the direction of the hole in the wall they had entered through. It suddenly looked small and cramped, and not like a place she wanted to go back into.

'You're right,' said Andrew. 'I am not sure there is anything more to find in here. And we're not getting out that way,' he said and pointed to the collapsed wall where the doorway had once been.

'I agree,' said Fiona. 'We need to get back out before sunrise.'

As they walked back towards the passage leading out of the chamber, Andrew spotted something to their left. The entire chamber was pitch black, and it was difficult to see much without shining a torch directly onto it, but somehow this stood out from the rocky walls and small rocks and stones that were lying scattered along the walls of the chamber.

'Hang on,' he said and tugged gently at Fiona's shirt. 'What's this?'

Pointing his torch at an object roughly the size of a shoebox, he walked towards it, and as he did so its shadow danced around on the wall behind it. It looked to be made of several strips of metal that were tied together with what appeared to be partly decayed leather straps. Although it now looked deformed, it was very obviously made by human hands, in the shape of a box.

As he knelt down next to it, he realised that it was a small cage, and inside it was the dry remains of what appeared to be a mouse. Its muscles had dried out and shrunk to almost nothing, and the fur and skin were shrivelled up and mottled. As the skin had dried, it had shrunk and was now peeled back from the mouse's limbs, exposing its skeleton. This had also happened to its head, which gave it the appearance of grinning maniacally as it lay there semi-decomposed and virtually mummified.

Andrew grabbed his crowbar, poked it through one of the gaps in the cage, and lifted it off the ground. Some of the partly decomposed parts of the mouse fell out of the cage onto the dusty floor.

'What on earth happened here?' asked Fiona, and knelt down next to Andrew to inspect the cage.

'No idea,' replied Andrew. 'Some sort of canary in the coal mine, brought in to detect radiation?'

'Possibly,' said Fiona. 'What reading does it give you?'

'Good question,' replied Andrew and got out his Geiger counter again.

As soon as he switched it on, the device issues a torrent of clicks, making Fiona stand up and back away a couple of steps.

'What the hell is going on here?' asked Andrew surprised, dropping the cage and standing up to step backwards towards Fiona. 'This thing is still red hot with radiation.'

'How is that possible?' asked Fiona. 'After all this time. Or is it recent?'

'No,' said Andrew. 'I am pretty sure this thing has been here for a long as this chamber has been sealed. But this cage is probably made of iron, and iron in those days was not very pure. So, it would have contained all sorts of other metals in its liquid form, when the local blacksmith made the metal strips. Some of those different metals could probably easily have been turned into various isotopes if this cage was exposed to a very high dose of gamma radiation. And because the half-lives of some of these isotopes are thousands of years, it is basically still almost as radioactive as the day this mouse died.'

'I think your hunch about this mouse being a canary in a coal mine was probably spot on,' said Fiona. 'Someone brought it down here to verify the presence of radiation, even if they would not have understood precisely what that really was, and the mouse ended up dead. That's awful.'

'Well,' said Andrew. 'It is literally ancient history by now. Let's get out of here. The sun is coming up soon.'

★ ★ ★

Halima Omran was in her small flat in Cairo's Abdeen district, sipping a cup of tea in their living room. Or rather, in *her* living room. She suspected she would never get used to Jabari no longer being there. The apartment had been tidied and the front door had been fixed and had several more locks fitted after the burglary. Dealing with this on her own without Jabari had made her feel very lonely and fragile. She had spent a lifetime with him, and she was able to remember as if it were yesterday, the way it had been when they were both young and they had first fallen in love.

Jabari had always been a hopeless romantic, and he had written her poetry, which he had always been too embarrassed to read out loud to her. It was never particularly good, but that did not matter to the young Halima. It had put a smile on her face and made her feel very special. He was bright and funny, and she was flattered to have someone as clever as him being interested in her.

She had grown up in an austere and traditional Egyptian home, with her father as the omnipotent patriarch. For the young Halima, this had been a difficult time, as she watched her society quickly evolve and transform into something much more open and westernised, with everything that brought with it for young women in particular.

Jabari was very different, and he seemed to truly respect her for who she was as a person. Looking back, she had often wondered whether her attraction to Jabari was partly a rebellion against her father, but in the end, it had not mattered. What they had together had been unique and special from the beginning, and not a day went by when she did not miss him profoundly. In many ways, she was happy and content in her new life with her friends and her various social activities, but deep down she still felt as if half of her soul had gone that morning when Jabari had drawn his last breath and passed away. The trip back from the El Rhoda Hospital later that day, just a few streets away from their apartment, had been a confusing daze. It had taken her many weeks to begin to live again.

Her gaze shifted absentmindedly from her teacup to the shelf opposite her armchair. Up there, next to several other books, was a small cigar case where she had kept safe the first poem he ever wrote to her. She had not touched it for years.

She looked at the cigar case for a moment, and then rose slowly and made her way over to the shelf. Reaching up, she picked the cigar case off the shelf and flipped the lid open. Inside the case, the poem, written on a piece of yellowed paper, lay folded neatly as it had done for many decades now. She picked it up gingerly with her hand and was suddenly struck by how old her hand looked compared with that day when he had first given it to her and had made her swear never to read it aloud to anyone else.

She put the cigar case down and carefully unfolded the piece of paper to look at the poem again. As she did so, a much smaller piece of paper fell out onto the floor. She bent down, picked it up, and looked at it curiously whilst turning it over. It was clearly not old like the poem, because the paper was a crisp white colour, and it was quite thick and showed no sign of wear or ageing.

It was only the size of a business card, and at the top it simply said. *'For those who seek, this is the key. You will know them.'*

Below it was a long series of pairs of letters, each pair separated by a semicolon.

Halima looked at it, utterly perplexed. Jabari loved riddles and brain teasers, but it had never been something she enjoyed.

'You will know them,' she mumbled, and sat down in her armchair again, holding the poem in her hands, along with the small piece of paper with the cryptic text on it.

These words might have been the last thing Jabari ever wrote, yet she had no idea what they meant. She closed her eyes, and a tear made its way slowly down her cheek.

Twenty-Five

After more than twenty minutes of crawling, Andrew and Fiona made it back to the tunnel by the Nilometer, and as Fiona looked back into the passage, she felt profoundly grateful that none of the granite blocks had chosen this day to finally collapse into the passage and seal them inside. A chill ran down her spine at the thought of being buried alive in there.

'Are you alright?' asked Andrew, dusting himself down.

'Yes,' said Fiona. 'I am fine. Let's get out of here. I have had quite enough of being underground for one day.'

They walked up the steps towards the top of the corridor that ended on the plateau, from where they would be able to see the temple of Khnum as well as their hotel on the other side of the river. Fiona was walking ahead of Andrew as they emerged and cautiously looked around to see if they could spot anyone. The coast appeared clear, so they continued on in the direction of the jetty where their small boat was moored.

As they walked along, they suddenly saw a man wearing black clothes, ambling slowly towards them. He appeared drunk and was walking unsteadily along the path towards the northern end of the island, where there was a large hotel. As they came nearer, the man stopped, held up a hand apologetically, and clumsily attempted to step aside to let them pass.

'Sorry,' he slurred and nearly tripped over his own feet trying to get off the path, pushing himself against a bush next to him.

Fiona kept walking but turned around to look sideways and back at Andrew, with a tired but sympathetic smile. She clearly thought he looked like he needed a hand.

'Oh dear,' she smirked. 'Someone's had a few too many....'

In that instant, her face changed from jovial and relaxed, to abject terror.

'Andrew!' she yelled, wide-eyed and instinctively reaching out towards him. 'Behind you!'

Andrew had focused only on the man in front of them, sensing that something was off about the whole situation, but he only had time to register a noise behind him that sounded like a few quick steps on the gravel path.

A split-second later, a hard blow struck the back of his head, and he only just had time to register his knees buckling under him. The images his eyes were sending to his brain contracted almost instantly into a small spot in the middle of his field of vision, after which everything faded to black. As he fell, he heard Fiona screaming in a terrified voice, but she sounded like she was far away. He never even felt himself hit the ground.

When he came to, it was as if no time had passed, but it could have been several minutes. The first thing he registered was the muffled voices of several men, interspersed with angry yelps and insults from Fiona. The voices quickly grew louder and clearer, as if he was surfacing from having been submerged underwater.

After a brief moment, his vision came back, then the sensation in his arms and legs returned, and then the pain hit him like a freight train. His head was pounding with deep searing pain, like the worst headache he had ever had, and he could feel a warm burning sensation on the right side of his forehead.

He was lying on the ground with his face in the dry dirt on the path. One arm was behind him, and the other was just in front of his face. Over the top of his hand, he could just make out a blurry melange of figures silhouetted against the moon, and he quickly recognised Fiona.

She was being held by two large men, while a third was rummaging through, first his backpack and then her shoulder bag.

'Let go, you bastards!' Fiona yelled. 'Help!'

As soon as she had called out for help, the man going through her bag slapped her hard across the face, and she produced a short whimper. The two burly men kept holding her up, while one of them produced a roll of duct tape. He deftly ripped off a piece and slapped it onto Fiona's mouth, her protestations now reduced to muffled noises. After a few more moments, the man going through their bags had found what he was looking for.

Andrew, still barely unconscious and reeling from the pain, heard the men exchange a few words in Arabic that he did not understand. His mind was racing to try to predict what they might do next, but his chances now were not looking good. However, all he thought about was what they might do to Fiona if he did not manage to intervene somehow.

The man holding her bag, who was clearly the leader of the group, issued a couple of quick commands, and from the tone of his voice, as well as from the way in which the two others reacted instantly and in unison, he was in no doubt that these people had military training. They might be active military personnel or possibly ex-military mercenaries.

The two burly men immediately began dragging Fiona along the footpath. They were about ten meters away, and as they dragged her swiftly along the footpath towards the jetty, the leader of the group walked calmly towards where Andrew was lying motionless on the ground. Andrew closed his eyes and stayed immobile, hoping that the man had not spotted him watching them.

He could hear the sound of heavy boots on gravel coming closer until they stopped right next to him. Andrew kept perfectly still with an impassive face, trying to look like he was still unconscious. For a few moments, it seemed as if the man standing over him was just watching him, perhaps deciding what to do with him.

Then he heard it. The unmistakable sound of a gun being pulled from its leather holster, and a second later, the sound of a metal silencer being screwed onto the barrel of the gun.

As soon as he heard the turning sound of metal grooves against metal, he spun around on the ground, using his arms as leverage. In a flash, he had repositioned himself and brought his right leg up to deliver a powerful kick to the man's right ankle. The man instantly lost his balance, taking a step backwards and flailing his arms, his pistol still in his hands. The silencer was now attached, and the man managed to hold on to the pistol as he tried to steady himself.

But Andrew was already on him. Having whipped out his hunting knife from his belt, he was already on his feet and charging towards the man. As Andrew closed the final distance between them, the man tried to bring his gun down in front of himself to aim at Andrew. He nearly managed to do it, but Andrew was already inside the reach of his arms, slamming into him.

He could have killed the man there and then, but for some reason, he had hesitated. The man was flying backwards through the air and landed on his back with a groan. Almost as soon as he was down, he brought up his gun and shot at Andrew, pulling the trigger twice in quick succession. The gun produced two quiet pops, and Andrew could feel a bullet tearing through the air next to his head. As soon as the man had fired at him, Andrew launched himself through the air with the knife raised. A second later he came down on top of him, slamming his knife into the man's chest just under his left collarbone.

The man's gun was pointing out and away from them both, but he must have panicked at the realisation of what had happened, because he pulled the trigger several times, even though there was no chance of the bullet hitting Andrew.

Without hesitation, Andrew yanked out the knife and then slammed it back into the man's heart. He froze instantly, looking wide-eyed up into the black night sky, as if he understood that this was the end. Then his gaze shifted slowly down to Andrew's face, and a couple of seconds later his arms went limp at his sides. The gun clattered onto the gravel path, and he exhaled for the last time.

Andrew kept his weight on the man for a few more seconds, making sure that he was dead. Then he pulled out the hunting knife from the man's chest and wiped the blood onto his black shirt. He quickly checked his own body to make sure that none of the bullets had grazed him. He seemed ok, but his attention was now on Fiona. He grabbed the man's gun, jumped to his feet, and started running cautiously in the direction the two burly men had taken her just a couple of minutes earlier. They must not have heard the scuffle and the silenced shots, otherwise, they would surely have come back to help their comrade.

Andrew was crouched over as he moved forward, trying to minimise how visible he was and how much noise he was making on the gravel path. Moving along the narrow winding path, around boulders and past bushes, he was constantly checking around bends to make sure he did not suddenly stumble into them.

When he was almost at the steps leading down to the jetty, he heard the voices of the two men. He could not hear Fiona. Slowing further and crouching down behind some boulders where the steps to the jetty began, he stopped and peeked around the boulder and down towards where he and Fiona had tied up their boat a few hours earlier.

He was just in time to see the two men push off from the jetty. The boat that he and Fiona had come over to Elephantine Island in, had been cut loose and was now floating sideways downstream some twenty meters away.

The two men started rowing their boat across the river towards the jetty on the other side. Andrew was momentarily confused by not being able to see Fiona, but then he spotted her lying motionless in the bottom of the boat.

He felt a chill run down his spine, and hesitated for a few moments, trying to decide what to do. The men had clearly been after Omran's notebook, and he was kicking himself for not being more cautious. If they had taken Fiona with them, then that meant that she was still alive. But what did they want her for? As a bargaining chip? Or were they planning to force her to help them find the meteorite?

The boat was making swift progress towards the jetty on the other side. The jetty on the Aswan side of the river was offset some twenty meters from the jetty on the island, so the men had to row their boat at an angle and slightly upstream, which slowed them down. Andrew looked straight across the river to the other side, which was a much shorter distance, and the river bank over there was dotted with large boulders that would provide good cover for anyone in the water.

He decided that it was his only chance, and leapt from his hiding spot and started running down the steps towards the wooden jetty. He quickly made it all the way down and proceeded at pace out onto the jetty where he picked up speed. His footsteps were now very loud, as his boots connected with the wooden boards.

His eyes were fixed on the end of the jetty, but in front of him and off to his right he could hear the agitated voices of the two men in the boat. They had clearly spotted him by now. Through the noise of his boots pounding on the creaky wooden jetty, and the air rushing past his ears as he sprinted the last few meters towards the end of the jetty, he was still able to hear the distinct sound of a weapon being cocked.

He used his very last step on the jetty to slam his foot down and launch himself up and forward into the air, and a couple of seconds later he dove into the river, letting his momentum carry him several meters underwater.

He was surprised at how much he could see. The river had seemed murky from the jetty, but the moonlight allowed him to see underwater plants and several rocks dotted around on the bottom.

He pulled himself forward under the water with powerful strokes and kept going for as long as he could. Eventually, he needed to surface for air, and only a couple of seconds later, he heard the sound of a bullet smacking into the water next to him. Then another.

Still swimming forward, he took a couple of deep breaths and dove down again. His blood oxygen levels were becoming depleted, so he was not able to swim as far underwater as before, but it was enough for him to make it to the first of the large boulders on the river bank. It suddenly flashed through his mind that the reason Elephantine Island had got its name, was because of these groups of boulders, which from a distance looked like herds of elephants.

These elephants were bulletproof, and as he surfaced next to one, two more bullets slammed into the boulder next to him and ricocheted off into the air with a high-pitched whine. He was now safely behind cover, and when he peeked out, the two men had reached the jetty and were bundling a limp Fiona out of the boat and onto the jetty.

He could only just see them past the boulders, but that also meant that they would probably be unable to spot him as he stood up and moved the last few meters through the water to the river bank. They were now also undoubtedly busy trying to get themselves and Fiona onto the jetty and away from there.

Andrew scrambled up over the last few small boulders, and up a steep grassy incline towards a small alley that ran next to the hotel grounds. The end of it connected to the main road, which was about one hundred meters away.

As far as he could remember, there was no other way of getting from the hotel jetty to the road than straight through the ground floor of the hotel, past the reception and out along the promenade leading to the hotel's outer gates. This was a brazen move by the two burly men, but at this point, they did not have any other options.

As Andrew started jogging towards the main road, he was listening out for noise inside the hotel grounds. The boundary between the alley and the hotel grounds was a barbed wire fence, only just visible through tall bushes that had been planted close together on both sides, along the length of the alley.

At first, all seemed quiet, and all he could hear was the sloshing sound of his wet clothes and boots as he ran. Then he heard a woman scream. It was not Fiona, but it had probably been a guest or a member of the staff. He imagined how the two men were in the process of dragging what would appear to be the lifeless body of a woman straight through one of the most iconic hotels in the country. Anyone seeing this would react with horror.

The two men had seemed very fit, so Andrew knew he had to hurry in order to get to the road before they did. He picked up the pace, and as he ran, he quickly popped out the gun's magazine to check how many bullets were left. It looked like at least four, but he could not see clearly as he ran along the dimly lit alley.

There were no more noises coming from the hotel grounds, which probably meant that everyone was taking cover. This would give the two men a clear run towards the outer gate. In all likelihood, the hotel's security guards were cowering somewhere. They almost certainly had no proper training, military or otherwise, and seeing two men with guns drawn moving in the swift and deliberate manner of trained soldiers, they had probably concluded that today was not the day to play heroes.

Andrew was now almost at the main road, and as he approached the corner where the tall bushes reached the pavement, he slowed to a jog and then a walk. He held the gun low and behind his back. The last thing he needed right now was to run into a police officer or even a hotel guest who would almost certainly give his position away if they spotted his gun. Luckily, there were only a couple of cars on the road, and there were no pedestrians in sight.

He peeked around the corner to the right, just as the two men appeared through the hotel's gate, dragging Fiona's limp body along with them. They were holding her under her arms, her head flopped down in front of her and her feet dragging along the ground behind her.

Andrew felt a hot burst of rage coursing through his body, as if he had just been given an intravenous shot of adrenaline straight into his bloodstream.

He barely had time to consider his next move, before a car came barrelling around a bend, racing towards the front of the hotel. Andrew instantly recognised the model. It looked identical to the one he had sparred with in Cairo about a week earlier. A black Range Rover with dark tinted windows. The growling engine noise was disconcertingly familiar.

The car came to a screeching halt by the side of the pavement, just as the two men dragged Fiona the last few meters towards the road.

Andrew looked around frantically for a way to intervene. It was at least thirty meters to the van, so if he tried to run straight at them, they would have plenty of time to aim and fire. He had already dodged two bullets today and did not feel like taking a chance on a third.

As the car came to a stop and its passenger door swung open, Andrew spotted a row of parked motorcycles off to his left. His head whipped back towards the car, where he just caught a glimpse of Fiona's feet disappearing inside it. Then he began sprinting towards the motorcycles. The two men were busy getting into the car themselves, one in the front passenger seat and the other next to Fiona in the back seat, and they had not spotted Andrew bolting from his concealed spot towards the motorcycle parking rack.

When he got to it, he slowed down but kept moving swiftly along the row of motorcycles, to see if any of them might still have a key in the ignition. None of them did, so he pulled out his knife, and ran over to the one that looked like it had the biggest engine. It was a bright yellow Kawasaki Z-series, and it looked sleek and fast. He rammed the knife into the plastic housing of the ignition keyhole.

The housing cracked, and as he twisted the knife, it popped open, with several plastic and metal components clattering to the ground beneath it. With one final forceful twist, the whole thing came apart, exposing three wires. He slotted the knife back into its sheath and glanced over his shoulder. The car doors had just slammed shut, and the Range Rover had started moving away in the opposite direction from where he was.

He looked down frantically at the mess of wires, then grabbed them all and ripped them loose. He then pushed one against the other, working his way through the limited number of combinations, until a connection was made that allowed the electric current to connect to the started motor. The engine sprang to life with an aggressive high-pitched noise, and he knew instantly that this motorcycle was a high-performance beast.

As he pulled it out from the parking rack and jumped on, the Range Rover disappeared down the street and around a corner. Revving the powerful engine a couple of times, Andrew flicked the gear lever with his foot and twisted the throttle firmly towards himself. The motorcycle leapt forward with a loud and enthusiastic high-pitched whine, and within a few seconds, he was racing after the car, the wind making his wet clothes flap violently against his body. The air was warm, and as he tore through it, it quickly began to dry out his wet hair.

When he spotted it again, the Range Rover was at least two hundred meters away, but he was gaining on it quickly. There was no other traffic in the streets, and he was able to focus on closing the distance as quickly as possible, without running the risk of an accident. The engine of the Kawasaki was screaming furiously as it propelled the motorcycle forward through the dimly lit streets, and after less than a minute Andrew was within fifty meters of the car.

The driver of the Range Rover must have spotted him at that point, because he seemed to be speeding up, and swapping lanes in an attempt to make their pursuer back off. The closer Andrew got, the more violently the driver swerved from side to side, trying to stop him from getting close or overtaking. Both he and the car were now racing through the nearly deserted streets of Aswan at over one hundred kilometres per hour.

Andrew swerved first to the right, then to the left, but each time the car mirrored his movements, and suddenly the front passenger window was rolled down, and one of the burly men from Elephantine Island leaned out facing Andrew. He was holding a gun.

As soon as he aimed, Andrew ducked down and swerved as much as he dared without risking falling off the motorcycle. His swerving caused the driver to swerve too, which in turn made it difficult for the gun-wielding man who was leaning out to hold his aim steady. Andrew accelerated whilst pressing himself down against the bike, until he was on the opposite side and immediately behind the car, making it impossible for the man to get a clear shot.

The man squeezed off several rounds, but they were nowhere near finding their mark. They were, however, enough for Andrew to decide that he had had enough of providing target practice on wheels for the man.

He reached behind him, and pulled out the gun he had taken from the dead attacker, and had kept in a side pocket of his trousers. Because he needed his right hand to keep twisting the throttle, he was forced to use his left hand to aim with. This felt about as awkward as trying to write his name with his left hand. His muscle memory had revolved through decades around the feel and the weight of a gun in his right hand, so he felt extremely clumsy and out of his comfort zone.

Luckily, his target was only a few meters away. He knew he had to be extremely careful to not shoot at the car itself, but aimed instead for the right rear tyre. The bumps in the road and the swerving of the Range Rover made it difficult to aim, but he allowed himself a few seconds to wait for the right moment, and then pulled the trigger once. The bullet missed and ricocheted off the wheel rim. He fired again, and this time the bullet tore through the rubber and punctured the tyre.

The effect was immediate. The tyre deflated within less than a second and started tearing itself apart because of the centrifugal forces at play at the speed they were now travelling. Strips of tyre flew off and slammed into the wheel hub and the chassis of the car. The driver immediately began to struggle for control, swerving all over the road, and for a few terrifying seconds, Andrew thought the car was going to fish-tail, tip over and start rolling along the road at speed. That would be extremely dangerous for anyone inside, especially if they were not strapped in with a seatbelt, which Fiona probably wasn't.

The driver regained control, but the Range Rover's speed was now dropping fast. Andrew let up slightly on the throttle to match its speed. The driver was braking and swerving wildly, trying to cause Andrew to crash into the car. Andrew managed to break just in time and let himself drop back around ten meters. Here he took aim again and squeezed off another two rounds, both of which found their target and punctured the left rear wheel.

The car was now effectively disabled, and it seemed like the driver realised this, because the brake light came on and stayed on, as the Range Rover slowed down rapidly until it came to a complete stop.

Andrew barely had time to react as the front passenger door and one of the rear doors opened simultaneously, and the two men from Elephantine Island threw themselves out and onto the road where they both rolled a few times, to come to a stop with their guns trained at Andrew.

Still moving forward at speed, Andrew twisted the throttle hard and leaned the bike left while shifting his own weight to the right. This caused the bike's rear wheel to fishtail out to the right, and the bike to end up lying down on road and sliding towards one of the men. Andrew had already let go of the bike and was rolling on his knees and elbows when the motorcycle barrelled into one of the men. It was only travelling at around thirty kilometres per hour at that point, but weighing in at more than half a tonne, it was as if the man weighed nothing when it made contact with him. It simply slammed into him and continued on, pushing him in front of it as if he was not even there.

Andrew could have sworn he heard the crunching sound of bones breaking during the impact, and the man's initial shout of pain was replaced by only the sound of the bike careening across the road. It came to a stop some thirty meters further along the road, it's engine still running.

Andrew was already up and running for cover behind a series of concrete blocks placed along the central reservation. He threw himself down onto the ground, out of sight of the other man who was getting to his feet unsteadily whilst looking briefly in the direction of his comrade who lay lifeless next to the motorcycle.

Andrew popped his head over the edge of the concrete block, and at that point the driver opened his door and stepped out with his gun raised, already firing in Andrew's direction. Andrew ducked down again and felt several bullets whiz over his head, and at least three others slam into the other side of the concrete block.

As soon as there was a break in the shooting, Andrew popped up and aimed at the driver, who was still moving forward but now in the process of changing magazines. He had let the magazine drop straight out of the gun, and as it clattered onto the road, he was already slotting the next magazine into the gun. This was clearly something he had done hundreds of times before, and Andrew saw enough of it to recognise the characteristic slightly crouched, slow-paced but deliberate walk towards a target that he himself had performed an endless number of times at the training grounds at Hereford. The whole thing took the driver less than a couple of seconds, but it was more than enough for Andrew.

He took a fraction of a second to make sure he aimed properly, and then he fired two bullets in quick succession. They both found their mark in the man's centre mass, and he reacted as if someone had punched him hard in the chest. His forward momentum stopped, and his arm came out to his sides, while his knees buckled. He fell to his knees with the gun clattering onto the road. Here he sat for a moment with a stunned look on his face, and then he tipped backwards onto his back, with his head making an unpleasantly loud noise as it made contact with the road.

Andrew ducked back down again to check his gun. He only had one bullet left in the magazine, plus the one sitting in the chamber. He quickly poked his head up again, but could not spot the second of the two men that had hauled Fiona off on Elephantine Island.

Emerging from his cover with his gun up in front of him, he moved towards the car which still had three of its doors open. The passenger door facing him was the only one still closed, and Fiona would be behind it. He suddenly felt sick at the thought of the thugs having killed her before engaging him, but then that would have gone against whatever the reason had been for bringing her along in the car. They clearly wanted her alive, along with Omran's notebook.

As he advanced towards the Range Rover, he could hear the engine still growling softly. He walked swiftly but cautiously behind it and swung his gun around the back left corner to check on the far side of the car, but there was no one there. Then he looked inside the car.

Fiona was lying on the back seat, her wrists tied together with duct tape behind her back, and her mouth still taped over. He could see her chest moving, so she was still alive. At that moment, she groaned and attempted to move, and after quickly scanning his surroundings again, Andrew stepped right next to the passenger door, leaned in and adeptly cut the duct tape behind her back. He then reached in and ripped the tape from her mouth.

'Andy?' she moaned. She sounded like she had been drugged. 'What's happening?'

'I'm here,' he replied.

She was trying to sit up but was struggling, so he reached in again, grabbed her shirt and pulled her upright.

Just as he did so, he heard the familiar sound of the Kawasaki engine being revved. He stepped back away from the car and moved swiftly towards its front, pointing his gun towards where the motorcycle had come to a stop a couple of minutes earlier.

The last of the two men who had taken Fiona from Elephantine Island had mounted the motorbike. He was revving the engine and struggling with the gear change, and as he looked over his shoulder in Andrew's direction, Andrew could see that he had Fiona's bag slung over his shoulder.

The motorbike suddenly leapt forward, surprising both Andrew and the man, and as he swerved forward, Andrew struggled to keep his aim steady. Quickly, the man regained control over the bike, and he took off down the road at speed.

Andrew held his breath, aimed, and then fired twice. The first shot missed, but the second shot connected with the man's right shoulder. His torso jerked forward on the right side from the impact, and he almost lost control of the bike, but after a few seconds, he managed to steady it and accelerate away.

Andrew lowered his gun and exited his firing stance.

'Fuck,' he spat.

He had no more bullets, and the distance was too great now anyway. He looked back at the Range Rover's rear tyres. Both flat and one of them ripped to shreds. It was over.

He dropped the gun on the road and ran back to the car to check on Fiona. She was sitting up in the back seat, her head down and her eyes closed, breathing heavily.

'Are you alright?' he asked, placing his hand gently on her shoulder.

'They have the notebook,' croaked Fiona.

'I know,' replied Andrew, now sounding more agitated. 'Fiona, are you alright?'

She nodded, still keeping her eyes closed. 'I think so. They drugged me somehow. Put a cloth to my mouth. I don't remember leaving the island.'

'I do,' said Andrew. 'I will tell you about it later. Right now, we have to leave. We won't be able to talk our way out of this one.'

In the distance, they could now both hear the sound of sirens blaring and getting louder each second.

'Fiona, we have to leave right now,' he repeated firmly.

'Ok,' she panted. 'Help me out please.'

She steadied herself on him as she exited the car, and the two of them started making their way towards the nearest alley, her left arm slung around his neck, and his right arm around her waist. The streets were empty, but above them, several lights had come on in the apartments facing the road, so they hurried down the alley and made their way to another street that ran parallel to the one where the gun battle had taken place.

Here they flagged down a lone taxi, pretending to be just another pair of tourists that had consumed too much alcohol. They piled into the back of the taxi and repeated the name of their hotel several times to make sure the driver understood where to go. Then they leaned back in their seat and tried to relax.

'Are you ok?' Fiona asked, suddenly realising that she had no idea if he was injured. 'I heard shots.'

'I am fine,' said Andrew dismissively. 'A few bruises on my elbows from jumping off the bike, but that is all.'

'Jumping off the bike?' she asked, sounding incredulous. 'What happened? I was out the whole time.'

'I will tell you later,' said Andrew and glanced up at the rear-view mirror. The driver was watching them, although that was hardly a surprise, given the state they were in.

Another ten minutes later they were back at their hotel. Outside the gate several police cars were parked, clearly having been called here by the hotel staff after the two men had dragged an unconscious Fiona through the hotel grounds. Andrew asked the driver to continue past the hotel, and then pull over in a parking space close to where he had stolen the motorcycle.

'This might get tricky,' said Andrew.

'Yes. We can't just walk in there,' said Fiona. 'They are bound to be looking for me, and before long they will be looking for you too.'

Andrew nodded. 'Alright, listen,' he said. 'I am going to go in there, slip past the police and hope the staff don't recognise me and put two and two together. I'll get our stuff from the room, and sneak out the back. Whoever those people are who now have Omran's notebook, they are suddenly much closer to uncovering the location of the meteorite.'

'Or the Ark,' said Fiona, and raised her eyebrows.

'Or the Ark,' repeated Andrew and nodded. 'We need to get out of here, and try to work out what to do now.'

'I think I already know,' said Fiona.

'Really?' asked Andrew. 'What?'

'We let Khalil make copies of all the pages in Omran's notebook, remember?' asked Fiona. 'We need to get to him, and get those copies back.'

'Oh yes,' replied Andrew. 'I had almost forgotten about that. It is probably our only chance now, and I think we need to move fast. I have a bad feeling that whoever took the notebook are the same people holding Doctor Mansour, and with the notebook, he might be able to help them find what they are looking for.'

'Are you saying he is working with them?' asked Fiona sceptically.

'No, of course not,' replied Andrew. 'But he is almost certainly assisting them under duress.'

'So much more reason for us to get a move on, and get to the bottom of this whole thing,' said Fiona resolutely.

Andrew glanced back up at the rear-view mirror. The taxi driver was no longer watching them, but was busy on his phone, seemingly texting someone.

'Stay here,' said Andrew and placed a hand on her leg. 'I will be back in a few minutes with our things. While in the room, I am going to make a quick call to our pilots in the airport hotel. They are on standby, and can have the aircraft ready in less than an hour.'

'Ok,' said Fiona. 'I'll be right here waiting for you.'

'Hold on to this,' said Andrew, and slid his hunting knife across the seat to her. 'Don't hesitate to use it if someone tries anything.'

Fiona looked at the large knife aghast. 'Are you kidding me?' she asked in a hushed but tense voice. 'I don't know how to use that on a person. And I don't want to!'

'It's all we have right now,' he replied calmly. 'Just do me a favour and keep it here, ok? I will be back as soon as I can.'

Fiona nodded, seemingly accepting his request. 'Ok,' she replied. 'Just hurry, please.'

'Back in a flash,' he said and stepped out of the taxi, and as he made his way through the gates of the hotel, Fiona explained to the taxi driver that he would be paid for waiting, and asked him to stay where they were for a few more minutes.

Less than ten minutes later, Andrew was back with both sets of hand luggage. He opened the boot of the taxi and dropped them inside. Then he opened the passenger door and slumped down next to Fiona.

'Ok,' he breathed, sounding relieved. 'Let's go.'

Twenty-Six

The trip back to Aswan International Airport on the other side of the Nile went swiftly and without incident. A couple of minutes past seven in the morning, their aircraft was racing down the runway and taking off towards Cairo International Airport, a two-hour flight north of Aswan.

They were both relaxing in their comfortable leather seats, trying to get a bit of rest after their nocturnal adventure. Andrew was just about to nod off, when Fiona suddenly sat up in her chair, with a short gasp.

'Are you ok?' asked Andrew.

Fiona just sat there, gripping the armrests with both hands, and staring blankly in front of her. Then she finally turned and looked at him.

'My dream,' she said, turning to look in Andrew's direction, but appearing to see right through him.

'What?' he asked. 'What dream?'

Fiona hesitated for a moment, and then leaned forward and looked him in the eyes.

'I had that dream where I was in a large temple. I think it could have been the Temple of Solomon, or perhaps somewhere in Egypt. One of the walls had a huge mural with ancient Egyptian depictions of a pharaoh during his coronation.'

'Oh, that dream,' said Andrew.

'As you might remember, it turned into a bit of a nightmare in the end, to be honest,' continued Fiona. 'But before it did, I saw two women in the mural. One of them was clearly the pharaoh's queen, but the other looked so much more ordinary, and she was wearing clothes that I have never seen before in an Egyptian mural. And her hair was arranged in a completely different style from what we normally see in depictions of ancient Egyptian women. She just seemed very out of place in that scene.'

'But it was just a dream,' interjected Andrew. 'It was all created by your subconscious.'

'I know that,' said Fiona, slightly irritated. 'That's not the point. The point is, all of those things I saw did not come from anything. They came out of what I have seen and experienced, and I suddenly realise where I might have seen something almost identical to that mural.'

'Where?' asked Andrew, his brow furrowing.

'I can't say for certain,' replied Fiona. 'But I am almost convinced that I once saw it in a sketch made by a German archaeologist, who did extensive excavations in and around Thebes. I think it might have been related to the so-called Ramesseum, which is the mortuary temple for Ramesses II.'

'Can you find that source somewhere on the internet?' asked Andrew.

'Probably,' replied Fiona. 'But I have a better idea.'

'So, what do you propose?'

'We need to go there instead,' said Fiona. 'I need to go back to Thebes and search the murals in the Ramesseum. I have a rough idea where to look, but it might take a while, so I am going to need your help.'

'Of course,' said Andrew, looking confused. 'But we have virtually just taken off to fly to Cairo. We need to get to Khalil and get his copy of Omran's notebook. And we need to talk to Doctor Zaki about the metal I got from the chamber in Axum.'

'Well, just tell the pilot to ask for landing permission at Luxor International Airport,' said Fiona impatiently. 'It is practically on the way there. How hard can that be? With a bit of luck, this should not take more than half a day.'

Andrew hesitated for a moment, but then nodded, stood up and headed forward towards the plane's cockpit.

★ ★ ★

Once again Doctor Mansour was awoken by the sound of the door to the room being unlocked and opening. He was sitting in the chair by the table, arms and legs tied to the chair, and the leather straps cutting into his skin. His hands were gently resting on the edge of the table, and he tried not to move them since the straps were hard and thin with sharp edges.

He kept his eyes closed, breathing steadily, and waiting for the inevitable. More questions. More despair. More pain.

He had stopped wondering how this would end, and had started hoping against hope that it would. And if that required him to leave this life, then so be it. He was broken, and he was tired. So very tired.

Suddenly, there was the sound of something hitting the table in front of him, and he could feel the weight of it through his mutilated hands. He opened his eyes slowly and blinked several times to get used to the light again.

In front of him on the table, lay Omran's notebook.

His eyes opened wide, and he looked up at the man in the pin-striped suit.

'How did you…?' he began, but then decided not to ask. No answers were ever forthcoming anyway, and he did not want to upset his captors.

'I will have your arms untied,' said the man. 'And I will let you look inside this notebook. And I would advise you to make sure you produce clues to the location of the Ark or the meteorite. I don't need to tell you how important this is to us, and to you.'

Doctor Mansour closed his eyes and nodded.

'I will do whatever I can. I just need time.'

* * *

Slightly less than three hours later, Andrew and Fiona got out of the taxi that had taken them from Luxor International Airport to the mortuary temple of Ramesses II, also called the Ramesseum. It lies a few hundred meters northeast of Medinet Habu, the temple of Ramesses III, which they had visited just a week earlier.

Andrew paid the driver and walked over next to Fiona, who was trying to look things up on her phone.

'The connection here is terrible for some reason,' she said, sounding frustrated. 'I wish I had my notes.'

'If I were to guess,' said Andrew. 'They are currently in the process of being read by whoever is behind this whole thing.'

'Let's make sure we don't get jumped again,' said Fiona. 'I really quite like not being drugged and unconscious.'

Andrew pulled up one side of his shirt slightly, to reveal the concealed gun that was sitting in its holster on his belt. 'Not going to happen this time,' he said. 'Let's go.'

They walked through the gates of the Ramesseum complex and headed towards the main structure.

'This looks a lot less impressive than Medinet Habu,' said Andrew. 'Is this much older?'

'Only about a century,' replied Fiona. 'Both complexes are more than three thousand years old, so there is hardly any difference in age in the grand scheme of things. The fact that the Ramesseum is in a relatively poor condition is mostly due to the fact that it is located on the very edge of the Nile floodplain. This has meant that annual floods gradually undermined its foundations and made many of its structures topple over. Apparently, it was also used as a church during the early Christian era of Egypt, long after the last pharaonic dynasties had died.'

'I'm guessing it was also a quarry for building materials in the local area,' said Andrew.

'Almost certainly,' said Fiona.

'It still looks impressive though,' commented Andrew as he looked towards the tall main structure in the middle of the complex. 'That over there looks familiar,' he said and pointed to a row of columns.

'It should,' said Fiona. 'This used to be the first courtyard of the temple, almost identical to the courtyard in Medinet Habu. In fact, Medinet Habu was largely modelled on this complex, except it was on an even grander scale.'

'That would make sense,' said Andrew.

'Yes,' smiled Fiona sarcastically. 'Men always have to try to outdo each other, even after they are dead.'

Andrew raised his eyebrows and smirked. He decided not to take the bait and just kept walking.

'So, what are we looking for?' he asked as they walked between the tall columns and through to the remains of the second courtyard that once connected to the temple and its inner sanctum.

'I am trying to find a mural similar to the one in my dream,' said Fiona. 'I know it sounds like a long shot, but I am sure I have seen a sketch from that German archaeologist that showed a mural from this mortuary.'

'Who was he anyway?' asked Andrew. 'The German guy.'

'His name was Uvo Hölscher, and he was an architect and Egyptologist in the nineteen-thirties, who drew a huge number of incredibly skilled and detailed sketches of the mortuaries here in Thebes.

He made hundreds of them, and they still serve as an accurate record of the ancient art in these temples.'

Andrew glanced at her askance. 'Nothing to do with the Nazis I hope?'

'Not as far as I know,' said Fiona. 'I have never seen his name come up anywhere in the context of the *SS Ahnenerbe*, or even the Nazi party. He seemed mostly to be an enthusiast, who also happened to be a very gifted illustrator. Anyway, I think it might be over this way.'

Fiona walked briskly through where the second courtyard had been, and into the remains of the temple itself. Most of the columns still stood where they had been placed more than three thousand years ago, and on top of them were placed several giant slabs of stone to make a flat roof.

Inside the structure on their left, were several relatively intact walls, some of them with large motifs carved into the sandstone.

'Here it is,' said Fiona. 'This mural is special because it is believed to have been made centuries after the death of Ramesses II and the completion of the mortuary. The elements have taken their toll on the carvings through the millennia, and the colours are almost completely faded, but you can still make out what is happening here.'

Andrew walked over next to her and looked up at the mural to study it in detail. It depicted some sort of ceremony, involving what appeared to be a pharaoh at the centre of the scene, surrounded by what could have been priests, as well as several other people.

'Is this what you saw in your dream?' asked Andrew, sounding intrigued.

Fiona nodded and smiled. 'Pretty much,' she replied. 'It was extremely vivid, and the basic scene was this one. And look over here to the left.'

She walked over to the wall and pointed to two women depicted standing next to each other. One of them was clearly a queen, dressed in elegant clothes and jewellery, with the characteristic royal crown of Ancient Egypt. The other was much more plain-looking.

'Look at this woman here,' said Fiona. 'She is dressed in a simple long-sleeved white dress or gown, with several overlapping layers of fabric. You can probably barely make it out, but the dress is edged in red and blue, and her hair is held up by a simple ribbon tied around her head.'

'Yes? So?' asked Andrew.

'None of what you see here has anything to do with ancient Egyptian culture. This woman is dressed in what is called a *Galabeya*, or a long Syrian robe, which is what women in the Levant wore at that time.'

'So, she is from the Levant?' asked Andrew. 'From Canaan?'

Fiona shot him a conspiratorial smile.

'But if she is not Egyptian,' continued Andrew. 'And if she is from the Levant, then what on earth is she doing in a mural of the coronation of an Egyptian pharaoh?'

'Exactly,' said Fiona emphatically and pointed at Andrew. 'Why would a simple Levantine woman be here in this scene depicting nothing less than the coronation of a pharaoh? The only other Levantines that have been found to have been depicted in ancient

Egyptian art, are either wretched slaves being beaten, grovelling emissaries offering tribute, or foes being killed on the battlefield.'

'Well, what do *you* think is the reason?' asked Andrew, sounding impatient. 'What does all this mean? And what does it have to do with the Ark of the Covenant, or the meteorite for that matter?'

Fiona took a moment to gather her thoughts, and then turned to Andrew, holding out her hands in front of herself, as if to present her case to him.

'It all has to do with something Professor Finkelstein told us when we went to see him in Jerusalem,' she said.

'Alright,' said Andrew, looking at her expectantly.

'I have been reading up on all of this,' said Fiona. 'And I think I have a theory.'

'Ok,' said Andrew. 'Fire away.'

'Well,' said Fiona. 'Remember how he told us about the Egyptian pharaoh Shoshenq I, and how he supposedly gave refuge to Jeroboam, who had tried to overthrow King Solomon in Jerusalem?'

'Yes,' said Andrew. 'He gave shelter to Jeroboam to sow unrest in Canaan, right?'

'Just hang on a second,' smiled Fiona. 'Do you also recall that Solomon supposedly held the Ark of the Covenant inside the Temple in Jerusalem?'

'Yes, that too,' replied Andrew.

'So, after Solomon's death,' continued Fiona, 'Shoshenq suddenly invaded Canaan, subjugated the whole thing, but left Jeroboam to rule over the Kingdom of Israel in the north.'

'Yes, that did seem highly suspect,' nodded Andrew.

'And the reason why he did so, is that the real purpose of Shoshenq's invasion was not simply subjugation and plunder.'

'What was it then?' asked Andrew.

Fiona smiled. 'It was to acquire the Ark of the Covenant, and bring it back to Egypt.'

Andrew looked at her. 'Are you serious?' he asked.

'Yes,' said Fiona. 'Remember, when Solomon died, Jeroboam returned to Canaan from Egypt, and took part in a delegation to try to request that Solomon's son Rehoboam, who was now the new king, lower the taxes in the United Monarchy. But I think that all of this was just a ruse, carefully planned by Shoshenq and Jeroboam during Jeroboam's stay with the pharaoh. They knew that Rehoboam would reject the request and that many of the tribes of Israel would then rebel because of it. When this actually happened, Jeroboam became king of ten break-away tribes who formed the Kingdom of Israel in the north of Canaan. This then, in turn, gave Shoshenq the perfect pretext to overrun Solomon's southern Kingdom of Judah to get his hands on the Ark of the Covenant, and as part of the deal, Shoshenq left the Kingdom of Israel and Jeroboam alone when he invaded.'

'Am I remembering correctly that Shoshenq didn't actually sack Jerusalem?' said Andrew. 'Even though he had clearly brought overwhelming force, and could easily have done so.'

'That's right,' said Fiona. 'And you have to wonder why, right?'

'And you think it was because he was only ever interested in the Ark of the Covenant?' asked Andrew.

Fiona nodded and pulled out a book from her backpack. 'Listen to this,' she said. 'The first-century Jewish historian Flavius Josephus wrote in his twenty-volume history work *Antiquities of the Jews*, that *Shishak*, a.k.a. Shoshenq, brought a contingent of 400,000 infantrymen into Canaan. And his army met with no resistance throughout the campaign, taking Rehoboam's most fortified cities *"without fighting."* Finally, Shoshenq conquered Jerusalem without resistance. Shoshenq did not destroy the city of Jerusalem, but forced King Rehoboam to strip the Temple of its gold and movable treasures, because *"Rehoboam was afraid".'*

'So Shoshenq basically extorted Rehoboam to hand over the Ark of the Covenant, or else?' asked Andrew. 'In other words, Rehoboam handed the Ark of the Covenant over to Shoshenq, in return for Jerusalem being spared.'

'Yes,' said Fiona. 'Something along those lines.'

'And this was written when?' asked Andrew.

'Around the year 93 BC,' replied Fiona.

'But why on earth would Shoshenq even want to take the Ark back to Egypt?' asked Andrew, looking perplexed. 'What good was it to him?'

'Well,' she said. 'It all comes back to this mural right here.'

'How so?' asked Andrew, looking confused.

'I think what we are seeing here in this mural,' replied Fiona and pointed to the Levantine woman. 'is none other, than pharaoh Shoshenq's mother.'

Andrew blinked a couple of times as he took a moment to process what Fiona had just said.

'You think Shoshenq's mother was Jewish?' he asked, sounding astonished. 'That would make pharaoh Shoshenq a Jew, according to matrilineal descent.'

'Yes, it would,' replied Fiona. 'And that is the real reason why Shoshenq invaded Canaan. His goal in harbouring Jeroboam, who was obviously also Jewish, was to try to engineer a scenario that would allow him to invade Jerusalem and then take back the Ark of the Covenant. He must have thought it belonged in Egypt.'

Andrew shook his head, trying to keep up. 'On the one hand it makes sense,' he said. 'But on the other hand, it seems really far-fetched.'

'I know,' smiled Fiona. 'But that doesn't mean it isn't true. There is actually a reference in the Hebrew Bible to the fact that Shoshenq I and Jeroboam were related.'

'Really?' asked Andrew incredulously.

'Yes,' replied Fiona. 'It describes how Shoshenq gave the eldest sister of his wife, a woman called Ano, to Jeroboam to be his wife.'

'That is an amazing detail,' said Andrew. 'And that is actually in the Bible?'

'Yes,' nodded Fiona. 'It is in the Greek Old Testament, if I remember correctly.'

Andrew exhaled, blowing his cheeks out as if the last few minutes had been physically exhausting.

'I feel slightly bamboozled,' he said. 'I am not sure what to think, or how to make sense of it, or even what it means for our search for the Ark and the meteorite.'

'Me neither,' said Fiona. 'All I know is that I am now convinced that the Ark of the Covenant is definitely back here in Egypt somewhere and that it hasn't been in Israel since 926 BCE when Shoshenq's army swept through Canaan. The same is almost certainly true for the meteorite. Remember, Jeroboam stopped at the gates of Jerusalem and did not destroy or plunder it. At least, there is no record of that happening during this campaign, which was otherwise documented in great detail in murals and steles.'

'So, what about the legend of Menelik and the Ark being transported to Axum in Ethiopia?' asked Andrew. 'We did find something there that seemed to indicate a connection to Jerusalem and the Ark, and the time frame fits nicely.'

'I know,' said Fiona. 'But I am becoming convinced that the whole story about Menelik and the Ark was invented as an elaborate smokescreen, to hide the fact that the Ark had already been taken by Shoshenq centuries earlier. Menelik might have taken an ark to Axum, but I think it was a replica. This also explains why the real Ark was no longer in Jerusalem when the Babylonian armies of Nebuchadnezzar II sacked Jerusalem in 587 BCE.'

'You mean, the Temple in Jerusalem had not had the Ark within it for around four hundred years when Nebuchadnezzar II arrived?' asked Andrew.

'That is the only logical conclusion to what we have discovered,' said Fiona. 'It all fits perfectly.'

'I guess so,' said Andrew, looking like he needed to lie down. 'But why were the metal slabs in the chamber in Axum radioactive then?' asked Andrew.

'I am not sure about that,' replied Fiona. 'They might have been used temporarily in Jerusalem when the replica was made. There's no way of knowing. Anyway, there is one final thing that I wanted to show you here in the Ramesseum. It is this way.'

She led them into the ruins of a second area inside the remains of the temple. On one of the walls was another large mural, with a battle scene and dozens of soldiers. In the middle of it was depicted a pharaoh smiting a Levantine soldier. The pharaoh was holding the soldier by the hair with one hand, and had his other hand, holding a weapon, raised above his head, ready to strike the soldier.

'This is a mural of the sacking by Egyptian soldiers of a place called *Shalem*,' said Fiona. 'The hieroglyphs right here state that quite unambiguously. There is no way to verify the idea, but it has been speculated that Shalem, is the same as Jerusalem.'

'But Ramesses II never invaded Jerusalem, did he?' asked Andrew.

'No, he did not,' replied Fiona, 'But perhaps this mural was also created long after Ramesses II's death, and perhaps it pays homage to Shoshenq's conquest.'

'There's something I don't understand about this,' said Andrew. 'Why were Shoshenq and Jeroboam so determined to bring the Ark back to Egypt? If they were both Jewish, then surely they would want the Ark to remain with the Israelites in Canaan?'

'I am not sure what the answer to that question is,' said Fiona. 'But there might be a clue to be found in the fact that the Israelites in Canaan were beginning to split at this point. The tribes of Judah and Benjamin were in the Kingdom of Judah in the south, and thereby in control of Jerusalem and the Ark. This might have bred resentment amongst the other ten tribes, and Jeroboam and Shoshenq might have exploited that split. There is probably a lot more to it than that, but I can't work out what it might be yet.'

Andrew nodded. 'Ok,' he said. 'There will be plenty of time for you to ponder this on the flight to Cairo. Have you seen what you wanted to see here?'

'Yes,' said Fiona and looked around, sounding like she wanted to stay for longer. 'I guess so. Let's get back to the plane.'

They walked briskly back to their cab and got in, and an hour later they were boarding the aircraft at Luxor International Airport, for the two-hour flight back to Cairo.

Once they had reached cruising altitude, they sat back in their seats and relaxed with a drink. Fiona was reading a book, and Andrew was writing an email to Colonel Strickland in London, updating him on their progress. Strickland had already offered increased support several times over the past week. Andrew had declined, on the grounds that their movements were very unpredictable, and also that coordinating active support and providing logistics around it in a foreign country, would cause a lot of noise that would not help them make progress in their investigation.

At one point, Andrew looked over at Fiona with a smile on his face. It took her a few seconds to realise that he was looking at her.

'What?' she said self-consciously. 'Have I got something on my face?'

Andrew laughed and shook his head. 'No,' he said. 'I just can't believe you dreamt your way to figuring out the link between the Ark of the Covenant and Shoshenq I.'

Fiona lowered her book and smiled. 'The subconscious is a very powerful thing, you know. Every day, your brain takes in multiples more information than you consciously register. Where do you think all that information goes? It doesn't just disappear. It all settles somewhere in your brain, like silt on the bottom of the ocean. Just because you don't see it anymore, doesn't mean it is not there. And sometimes, during your sleep, the subconscious trawls through that ocean when it needs to process something that requires a solution. And then it brings back up all the things you thought you had forgotten, and all the things you never realised you knew. And that's what happened with me, that's all.'

Andrew just kept looking at her with a smile on his face. 'You're amazing,' he finally said.

Fiona shrugged and lifted her book back up to continue reading. 'I know,' she said chirpily. 'And modest too.'

Twenty-Seven

After they had made it back to the hotel in Cairo, Andrew and Fiona decided to go back up to the roof terrace to have lunch. Andrew had tried to contact Doctor Zaki by email, but he had not responded. He then got in touch with Colonel Strickland in London, to see if they could reach him. Strickland returned to him an hour later, to say that he had been in touch with the Nuclear Research Facility north-east of Cairo, and had been told that Doctor Zaki was off work due to illness.

'What do we do now?' asked Fiona. 'We need someone to analyse the metal shard from Axum, don't we?'

Andrew sipped his tea. 'We do, but perhaps it isn't actually that important now. We already know it is radioactive, and I feel pretty confident that it is simply a piece of lead, so the only thing Zaki might be able to tell us, would be an estimate of its age.'

'And that would be very useful,' said Fiona.

'It would,' replied Andrew. 'But it actually wouldn't change much for us. Even if we discovered that the metal slabs were made around the time of Menelik I, then that would simply suggest that he did indeed bring something radioactive out of Jerusalem. But it would not tell us whether it was the Ark of the Covenant or the radioactive meteorite piece that was inside it, or perhaps even just part of the meteorite piece. It would be interesting to find out, but it would not help us locate the Ark or the meteorite.'

'Still,' said Fiona. 'Can we find out where Zaki lives and perhaps go to see him?'.

'Not a chance,' said Andrew and put down his teacup. 'Zaki is one of the top researchers at the Egyptian government's primary nuclear research facility. There is no way they are just going to hand out his home address.'

'Do you think we can trust him?' asked Fiona.

'I would like to think so,' said Andrew. 'But you just never know. There was something not quite right about the way he reacted when we told him about what we were searching for.'

'I agree,' said Fiona. 'Perhaps we should get in touch with Khalil instead. He might have been able to come up with something.'

'Good idea,' said Andrew. 'I will try to get hold of him. In fact, let me do that right now.'

Andrew got out his phone, and quickly composed an email to Khalil, asking if he would be able to meet them.

Only a couple of minutes later, his phone pinged with a reply from Khalil.

'That was quick,' said Andrew and looked at Fiona. 'He is asking if we can meet him later this afternoon in the botanical gardens just opposite Cairo University.'

'Sounds great,' said Fiona. 'Is he saying what he wants to talk about?'

'No,' replied Andrew. 'Probably sensible not to discuss anything by email at this point. You never know who might be listening.'

'You think our emails are being monitored?' asked Fiona, looking disturbed.

'I wouldn't rule anything out at this point,' replied Andrew. 'We've made quite a lot of noise since we arrived in this country, and frankly, I am not sure who to trust anymore.'

'Except for Khalil,' said Fiona.

'Yes,' nodded Andrew. 'Except for him.'

★ ★ ★

A few hours later, Andrew and Fiona stepped out of the taxi that had taken them from the east side of the Nile, across the small island of Zamalek, and down Charles De Gaulle Street to the botanical gardens, opposite the Cairo University campus.

They walked towards the north entrance and entered the gardens. As soon as they entered, the noise from the busy traffic outside died down. It was like standing in a busy shopping centre and putting in earplugs. The gardens covered a large area, some three hundred by one hundred meters, but it was densely packed with flower beds, neatly trimmed bushes, and a plethora of displays of ornately arranged flowers. Throughout the gardens, there were several hundred very tall palm trees planted at regular intervals, giving the whole place a distinctly tropical feel.

'Where did he ask to meet?' asked Fiona.

'On the other side, near the university,' replied Andrew. 'We can walk there in five minutes or so.'

'Good,' said Fiona. 'This is a lovely place. If I lived near here, I would probably be in here on a regular basis. It feels like such a nice break from the busy streets outside.'

'It also feels a lot cooler, have you noticed?' asked Andrew. 'It must be the shade from the trees and bushes, and I guess they must water the grounds every day in here to keep the plants alive.'

'It is certainly not like Aswan,' smiled Fiona. 'That place was a furnace.'

After another few minutes of walking, they approached the southwestern exit, nearest the University of Cairo.

'Ah, there he is,' said Andrew. 'Let go and say hello.'

At that point, Khalil spotted them and his face lit up in a friendly smile. He started walking towards them with his hand stretched out to greet them.

'Khalil,' said Andrew. 'Very good to see you again.'

'Mr Sterling,' replied Khalil. 'Miss Keane.'

'Please,' smiled Fiona. 'Call us Andrew and Fiona. We're all friends here.'

'Alright,' nodded Khalil. 'Andrew and Fiona. If you would like to follow me, there is a small café just on the other side of these trees. I would like to buy you a cup of traditional Egyptian coffee.'

'Sounds good,' smiled Fiona.

'Excellent,' said Andrew. 'Please lead the way.'

They walked together along a footpath that wound its way around a group of trees, to a small café with tables and chairs out in front of it. Here they sat down, and a waiter was quick to come and take their orders. Khalil ordered *kanakas* with coffee for each of them. Small, tall saucepans with long handles, each only large enough for one cup of coffee, they are the traditional way of brewing coffee in Egypt and much of the rest of the middle-east. Finely ground coffee beans are poured into the kanaka, along with hot water and a generous amount of sugar. Instead of filtering the coffee, it is left to settle for a few minutes, after which it is poured into a cup.

'Feel free to add lots of sugar,' smiled Khalil. It has to be lovely and sweet. Bitter coffee is only for funerals.'

Fiona smiled questioningly at him.

'It's true,' said Khalil. 'That is the only occasion where coffee is served with no sugar.'

Fiona nodded. 'That seems fitting somehow,' she said and took a sip. 'Oh, this is lovely.'

'I am glad you like it,' said Khalil. 'How are you both?'

'We've been busy,' smiled Fiona.

'Have you made any progress finding Bahir?' asked Khalil, sounding concerned. He was clearly impatient for news about his missing friend.

Andrew and Fiona glanced at each other.

'Well,' said Andrew. 'The short answer is no, unfortunately. But as Fiona just said, quite a lot has happened, so perhaps we should tell you what we have come up with so far, and then we can take it from there.'

Khalil nodded his acceptance. 'Ok. I am just very worried,' he said.

'We understand,' said Fiona sympathetically.

Andrew then went on to lay out their findings, including what had happened outside the Egyptian Museum in Cairo, their meeting with professor Finkelstein in Jerusalem, the trip to Mount Nebo in Jordan, what they found in Ethiopia, and what happened during their investigation in Aswan. Fiona laid out their theory that Shoshenq was Jewish, and that he worked with Jeroboam to take the Ark of the Covenant from Jerusalem and back to Egypt. Andrew then took over and relayed to Khalil their confrontations with the likely kidnappers of Doctor Mansour. He decided to downplay the most dramatic episodes that had unfolded over the past week or so, but he made it clear to Khalil that the threat from whoever was holding Doctor Mansour was very real.

'Do you have a firearm?' asked Andrew.

'I have one in a safe at home,' replied Khalil. 'I was in the army for six years, and I experienced things and met people there that made me want to be able to defend myself. Unfortunately, civil unrest is never far away in this country. Certain sections of the armed forces are not necessarily aligned with democratic values, the way most modern Egyptians are.'

'I understand,' said Andrew. 'I assume you have a permit for it?'

'Yes, I do,' said Khalil. 'Do you think I should have it on me?'

'I think that might be wise,' replied Andrew. 'You never know what Mansour's captors might do next. If they knew you have a copy of Omran's notebook, I am sure they would have paid you a visit already.'

'Ok,' said Khalil. 'I will make sure to carry it on me from now on.'

'I assume you have had some time to go through Omran's notebook?' asked Fiona. 'What have you learned so far?'

'I have,' said Khalil, extracting a small stack of papers from his bag, and placing it on the table. 'If you remember, during our trip to Luxor and the temple of Ramesses III, we saw a clear link between ancient Egyptian and Hebrew religious practises and culture.'

Fiona nodded.

'Well,' continued Khalil. 'I have been looking into this a lot more, using Omran's notes as a guide for which direction to go in. It is difficult to put all the pieces together because the sources for what really happened either don't exist or they were delivered orally for centuries until they were eventually written down for obvious political purposes.'

'That is, unfortunately, the curse of archaeology,' smiled Fiona.

'Indeed,' said Khalil. 'Anyway, something has always struck me as peculiar about the way the Israelites were presented in the story of Exodus. I have spent a fair amount of time researching this over the past several days, and it is clear that the Israelites are mostly talked about as one entity, when they were in fact many different tribes, from different parts of the southern Levant. You see this in how they behaved more or less as one people during captivity, but as soon as they were free from the yoke of the pharaoh, they started squabbling amongst themselves. This was the reason Moses forced them to spend forty years in the desert, rather than go straight to Canaan after their escape. It was a type of punishment.'

'Yes, I have come across that notion myself,' said Fiona.

'And if we just focus on Moses in that context,' continued Khalil, 'then something interesting emerges. Moses was a direct descendant of Levi, one of Jacob's 12 sons. We also know that the Levites were the carriers of the Ark, so this means that all the carriers of the Ark of the Covenant were all directly related to Moses. It is therefore reasonable to say that the Levites were effectively the Hebrew equivalent to the Egyptian priesthood, and they would have existed in that role in Egypt for generations before the Exodus. In my opinion, the clear amalgamation of ancient Egyptian religious traditions and practices with Hebrew religious practices is strong evidence of this. As we have already discussed, this is probably best exemplified by the design and function of the Ark of the Covenant itself, which in many ways is similar to the barques that the ancient Egyptian priests used for their religious artefacts during processions.'

'I completely agree,' nodded Fiona.

'Now, in the Bible,' said Khalil, 'there are several mentions of the Levites which seem to indicate that somehow they were treated differently from the other Israelites by the pharaoh. For example, they were allowed to come and go as they pleased, and as far as I can tell, they could even meet with the pharaoh himself. They were also the only tribe not to be enslaved. In effect, the Levites were a religious cult or priesthood within the Israelite people, and they presumably intermingled with the ancient Egyptian priesthood. This might have allowed them to obtain certain knowledge from the Egyptians.'

'Interesting point,' said Andrew. 'But what is the implication of this?'

'Well,' said Khalil. 'If we now also look at the House of Joseph, there is a good chance that they were also enmeshed into the ancient Egyptian priesthood, because Joseph was such a powerful figure, being the grand vizier, the chief administrator. Since power in the ancient kingdoms ultimately flowed from the gods through the pharaoh and on to the grand vizier, Joseph would have been closely involved with the priesthood. Anecdotally, Joseph's wife was the daughter of an Egyptian high priest, and together they had two sons, Ephraim and Manasseh. Those two sons, who formed the House of Joseph, were half Hebrew and half Egyptian, and they were born into a priestly family with enormous political influence. So, there is a definite connection between The House of Joseph and the Egyptian priesthood.'

'So, what is the bottom line here?' asked Andrew.

'The bottom line is this,' said Khalil. 'I think that between them, the House of Joseph and the tribe of Levi, would have had enough access and intermingling with the Egyptian priesthood through many generations, to potentially learn the secret of the meteorite and possibly even its location in Aswan.

It is even probable that Joseph himself would have had direct access to this knowledge through the Egyptian priesthood.'

'Or they might have uncovered records of it somehow,' said Fiona. 'As you know, the ancient Egyptians were very keen on record keeping in general, so it seems highly likely that the Egyptian priesthood would have kept written records of something as important as the meteorite, which in those days would have represented almost divine power.'

'Precisely,' said Khalil. 'If the story of Exodus and the arrival of the Israelites in Canaan are anything to go by, then those powers clearly made a difference when the Israelites left Egypt and eventually conquered Canaan. And interestingly, when Moses arrived in Canaan on Mount Nebo where he later died, he was supposedly instructed by Yahweh to hand over power to Joshua, who was also of the Ephraim tribe, and thus part of the House of Joseph. In other words, the religious and political power of the Israelites remained firmly in the hands of a small circle of people throughout the story of Exodus.'

'That is fascinating,' said Fiona. 'In that context, I have also discovered something else that is really interesting. Jeroboam was of the tribe of Ephraim. In other words, he was a direct descendant of Joseph. Therefore, if the House of Joseph had acquired the knowledge of the meteorite and its secret location at some point, then Jeroboam would almost certainly have known about it.'

'That ties in very nicely with what I have found too,' nodded Khalil sagely. 'If Shoshenq's mother was not only Jewish, but actually from the house of Joseph, then it all fits neatly together. But that must remain speculation on our part. There is just no way for us to verify that. As far as I have been able to ascertain, there is no record of anything like that. The only thing we have is the mural in the Ramesseum, and that provides no exact detail, other than the fact that she was indeed Jewish.'

'Hang on,' said Fiona pensively. 'It suddenly occurs to me that this theory explains something else that I have been wondering about.'

'Yes?' said Khalil.

'It is simply this,' replied Fiona. 'If the original covenant was between Yahweh and Abraham, and the Covenant at Mt Sinai was between Moses of the Levi tribe, which meant that only the Levites could carry the Ark, then why would the ten tribes in the north accept letting the tribes of Judah and Benjamin have possession of the Ark for centuries, between the time of Jeroboam's reign and the destruction of the Temple in Jerusalem in 587 BCE? And the answer is of course, that the ten tribes, led by the tribes of Joseph and Levi, knew all along that the real Ark of the Covenant was no longer in Canaan.'

'That is a good observation,' said Khalil and raised his eyebrows. 'I did not think of that myself.'

'On top of that,' smiled Fiona. 'I have been wondering if somehow the House of Joseph and the Levites saw themselves as special amongst the Israelites. Perhaps they felt that the covenant was between Yahweh and them only. Perhaps they believed that somehow those two tribes were the chosen people. It also helps explain why Shoshenq never laid a hand on the ten northern tribes. If Shoshenq's mother was from the House of Joseph, then both Jeroboam and Shoshenq were descendants of Joseph.'

'It is possible,' nodded Khalil. 'Almost impossible to prove, but definitely possible.'

'Well,' said Fiona. 'It feels like a very compelling theory to me, and it explains a lot of things, right from the discovery of the meteorite, to before Exodus happened, through Exodus itself and right up to the point where Shoshenq plots with Jeroboam to take the Ark back to Egypt. Of course, we still don't really understand why they would want to do this. And we also still don't have any clue as to the current location of the Ark or the meteorite. But as I have said to Andrew already, I feel convinced that both of them are here in Egypt somewhere.'

'I agree,' said Khalil and sipped his coffee. 'But anyway, that was only one strand of what I have discovered. There is another fascinating aspect of the Exodus story that I have been looking into.'

'Alright,' said Fiona and smiled. She was clearly in her element now. 'Let's hear it.'

'It has to do with the origin of the Ten Commandments,' said Khalil.

Fiona raised her eyebrows. 'Really?' she asked.

'As you know,' continued Khalil. 'These were supposedly handed to Moses at Mount Sinai after the Exodus from Egypt.'

'We're not going to go chasing after them too, are we?' asked Andrew sceptically, half-joking and half-serious.

'No,' laughed Khalil. 'That would have to be a different adventure. But I have been looking into them from the perspective of the ancient Egyptian legal system.'

'Interesting,' said Fiona. 'What did you find out?'

'Well,' said Khalil. 'Ultimately, the pharaohs were omnipotent, because they were the representative of the gods in ancient Egypt. But since not every single issue can be put in front of the pharaoh, or even his vizier, there had to be a more formalised legal system put in place. During the Old kingdom, roughly between the 26th and the 21st century BCE, the local courts, known as the *Kenbet*, would hear disputes between individuals, and then the priests would decide. There were no lawyers to represent individuals. Judgement, especially in the context of moral questions, was decided by the priesthood. Later on, in the Middle Kingdom and the New Kingdom, the legal system was increasingly codified and rational, using concepts such as legal precedent, but it was still the priests who functioned as judges.'

'So, the priests were not just religious leaders?' asked Fiona. 'But they were also lawgivers, or I suppose the main interpreters of the laws?'

'Very much so,' replied Khalil. 'And if this structure was carried over to the way the Israelites conducted their legal affairs, then that just emphasises what a unique and powerful position the priestly Levites would have held.'

'But what is the connection to the Ten Commandments?' Asked Fiona.

'It is fairly straightforward,' said Khalil. "In the same way that the Hebrews or Israelites adopted many religious and cultural elements of ancient Egypt, so they also borrowed heavily from the ancient Egyptian legal system.'

'How so?' asked Fiona.

'Well,' said Khalil. 'Even as the ancient Egyptian legal system became more formalised and codified through the centuries, one thing never changed and that was the fact that all power was ultimately derived from the gods. Specifically, the goddess *Maat*, who represented balance, truth, morality and justice.'

'I think I remember her,' said Fiona. 'Is she the goddess always depicted wearing a feather on her head?'

'Yes. That is the one,' said Khalil. 'She was in charge of weighing the heart of a deceased person and deciding if that person was to be allowed to progress to the afterlife, or whether they would be devoured by the crocodile-headed god *Ammit*. If the heart was lighter than Maat's feather, they would be allowed to move to the afterlife, but if it was found to be heavier than the feather, the person would be consumed by Ammit.'

'A bit like Saint Peter at the gates of Heaven?' said Andrew.

'Very much like that,' nodded Khalil. 'And who knows. That particular idea might also have been borrowed and adopted by later religions such as Christianity and Islam.'

'That is very interesting,' said Andrew. 'I never knew these concepts existed thousands of years before those other religions were created.'

'There is more to this,' continued Khalil, and held up an index finger. 'And this is where things become really interesting. The weighing of a person's heart did not happen in some arbitrary fashion. It was done by forty-two principles or laws, by which an individual was expected to live their life in ancient Egypt. These principles were so-called negative confessions, that a person would ultimately end up making in front of Maat. They included things like, "I have not stolen", "I have not slain men and women", I have not committed adultery", "I have not told lies", and so on. Forty-two of these in total.'

'Sound awfully familiar,' smiled Fiona.

'The Forty-two Commandments?' said Andrew.

'Exactly,' said Khalil.

'So, the Israelites got the skinny version?' smiled Andrew.

'Something along those lines,' laughed Khalil. 'The key point here is that when looked at in the context of the principles or laws of ancient Egypt, the Ten Commandments are clearly a smaller derivative of those forty-two principles.'

'So basically, what you are suggesting, is that even if one were to completely disregard the entire biblical Exodus tale as fiction,' said Fiona. 'You are saying that there is still an actual historical connection from the ancient Egyptian legal system, to the later Israelite legal system, the inception of which was the mythology of the Ten Commandments.'

'That's right,' replied Khalil.

'And if a character from the tribe of Levi such as Moses really existed,' continued Fiona. 'Then it would make sense for him to have been both a priest and a lawgiver. This fits neatly with the idea that Moses produced the Ten Commandments as a new legal and spiritual focal point for the many different Hebrew tribes, as they left Egypt together and headed towards Canaan. As a people, they would have needed some sort of new legal structure in order to remain coherent, especially with a view to eventually arriving in Canaan, and then trying to re-settle themselves after centuries in foreign lands.'

'Exactly,' said Khalil. 'And irrespective of divine elements in the stories of a group of Hebrews from Egypt to Canaan, this just adds yet more weight to the idea that at some point in history, something very much like the Exodus actually happened, and that it happened in circumstances more or less similar to what is described in the Old Testament, or the Hebrew Bible.'

'Just another thread in the fabric of the story,' mused Fiona.

'Exactly,' nodded Khalil.

'It doesn't really help us pin down the location of the Ark or the meteorite,' said Andrew. 'But I guess it does make the existence of the Ark as a real historical artefact more credible. And, at least theoretically, this means that the likelihood of actually finding it, should be above zero.'

Khalil smiled. 'I wish I had been able to contribute something more tangible,' he said. 'But people have searched for this artefact for almost three thousand years, so I was never under the illusion that this would be easy.'

'We are all very much on the same page here, smiled Fiona. 'I suppose at this point, we might have a much better chance of finding the meteorite than the Ark.'

'Which, I should probably remind you, is also what we initially set out to do,' said Andrew. 'The meteorite has a huge destructive potential, and finding it will probably also give us a chance of finding Doctor Mansour.'

'That is certainly why I am here,' said Khalil and nodded sombrely. Then he hesitated for a moment and looked at Andrew. 'I almost forgot to tell you something. I made contact with Jabari Omran's widow. She lives in Al Manial on Rhoda Island here in Cairo, and I wanted to make sure she was ok. Her apartment was broken into a little over a week ago.'

'Really? That is no coincidence,' said Andrew. 'Is she alright?'

'She is ok,' nodded Khalil. 'When I spoke to her, she seemed mystified as to why anyone would break in and ransack her apartment, but it is quite obvious that they were looking for Omran's notebook. I did not tell her I have a copy of it. I thought that it would be safer for her not to know.'

'Good thinking,' said Andrew.

'Anyway,' said Khalil. 'When I mentioned that the disappearance of Doctor Mansour is being investigated by the two of you, she asked me if she might be able to meet you.'

Andrew and Fiona looked at each other.

'Really? Us?' asked Fiona. 'What for?'

'She wouldn't say,' replied Khalil. 'She only said she was trying to do something for Jabari.'

'Well,' said Andrew, looking slightly unsure. 'I suppose there is no harm in meeting her. She might have some information about Omran that we are not aware of, and perhaps that can point us in a direction that could help us find Doctor Mansour.'

'Are you able to arrange a meeting?' asked Fiona.

'Certainly,' nodded Khalil. 'I will get in touch with her this evening.'

The three of them finished their coffees, agreed that Khalil would let them know as soon as a meeting with Halima had been set up, and then they said their goodbyes. Khalil walked back to Cairo University, and Andrew and Fiona returned to their hotel to await his call.

Twenty-Eight

Khalil held up his hand in front of Halima Omran's door and turned slightly to look at Andrew and Fiona. They both nodded, and then he knocked three times in quick succession. He then took a step back, and let his arms drop down along his sides.

After a few moments, there was the sound of shuffling feet on the other side of the door, and a couple of seconds later, the sound of locks turning and a chain coming off its clasp. Then the door opened slowly, to reveal an old woman, slightly stooped and wearing a dark blue dress and a light grey cardigan. Her face was wrinkled, but her brown eyes were bright and keen, and as she greeted Khalil, the warm smile of a calm and sensitive person slowly spread across her face.

'Mrs. Omran,' said Khalil and bowed his head slightly. 'Thank you for seeing us.'

The old woman nodded silently, perhaps feeling out of her comfort zone with two foreign visitors on her doorstep. Fiona sensed her unease and stepped forwards with her hand outstretched.

'Mrs. Omran,' said Fiona with a gentle smile. 'My name is Fiona Keane, and this is my colleague Andrew Sterling. We're very grateful that you would spend time with us.'

Halima smiled, took Fiona's hand in hers, and held it there for a moment whilst looking into her eyes. Then she shifted her gaze to Andrew who nodded respectfully. Khalil had told him that when greeting, men only take the hand of a woman if she offers it to him.

'Mrs. Omran,' he smiled. 'It is a pleasure to meet you.'

Halima studied his face for a moment, and then smiled gently and beckoned them inside.

'Please come inside,' she said, her voice soft and friendly.

They all followed her inside the apartment, after which she showed them to the living room and gestured for them to sit on the sofa opposite her armchair.

'Thank you for coming,' smiled Halima, and looked at Fiona and Andrew in turn.

Khalil had prepared himself for the role of interpreter, however, Halima spoke a heavily accented but self-assured English, whilst looking intently at her two foreign visitors.

'I asked Khalil to request that you come to visit me,' she said. 'I understand that you are here to help search for Omran's colleague, Doctor Mansour.'

'That is correct,' said Andrew.

'And are you also looking for something else?' she asked and looked at Fiona with eyes that seemed to study every detail of her face.

Fiona hesitated and glanced sideways at Andrew.

'Perhaps Miss Keane and I could speak, just the two of us for a moment?' asked Halima and looked first at Andrew and then at Khalil. There was a natural authority behind her gentle exterior, which made them both nod their agreement and stand up.

'Let's go out on the balcony and enjoy the view of the city,' said Khalil.

Andrew bowed his head slightly and followed Khalil outside.

Then Halima held out her hand towards Fiona.

'May I see your hand?' she asked.

Fiona was momentarily uncertain how to react but then agreed. 'Of course,' she said and move closer to offer her hands to the old woman.

Halima held Fiona's hands gently in hers, looking Fiona in the eyes. Her hands were soft and warm, and as she held them there, Fiona felt as if the old woman was looking deep inside her. It was not unpleasant, but there was a sense that Halima was somehow able to look deep inside her soul.

'Why are you here?' asked Halima gently.

Fiona shifted slightly but did not look away.

'To help find Doctor Mansour,' she said.

Halima nodded and smiled. 'And I hope you succeed. He is a nice man and a gentle soul.'

'We're doing everything we can,' said Fiona. 'But it is complicated. There are a lot of things going on right now.'

'Are you also looking for an artefact?' asked Halima, still keeping her gaze on Fiona's eyes.

Somehow, the old woman made Fiona feel safe, and she knew that she could trust the old woman sitting there holding her hands.

'Yes,' replied Fiona. 'We are looking for one of the oldest and most mysterious artefacts in history, and we think it might be connected to an event that happened several thousand years ago.'

'The power of the heavens,' said Halima. 'A meteorite.'

'Yes,' whispered Fiona surprised. 'How did you…?

Then she stopped. 'You worked with Jabari on this, didn't you?

'We discussed it,' smiled Halima. 'I was always his sounding board. I helped tame some of his wildest ideas.'

'His ideas might have seemed wild, but as far as we can tell, he was right about this one.'

'And if you find it?' asked Halima. 'What will you do then?'

'We will make sure it stays out of the hands of people who would abuse its power,' replied Fiona.

Halima did not reply but sat with an impassive face and her eyes locked onto Fiona's. Fiona did not dare look away, and she felt like an open book. After a couple of seconds, Halima smiled again and nodded.

'Very good,' she said and let go of Fiona's hands. 'I would like to give you something I found a few days ago. I do not know what it is or what it means, but I think it might be useful to you. Jabari never did anything for no good reason, so I am sure he left this for me to find and pass along to someone like you following in his footsteps. I am giving it to you so that it might help you in your quest.'

She handed Fiona the small piece of paper that had fallen out of the poem a few days earlier. Fiona studied it briefly, and then looked up at Halima, who suddenly looked like a frail old woman again.

'Thank you,' said Fiona. 'We will do our best to make sense of it.'

Halima nodded and smiled. Then she rose and walked slowly over to the balcony, where Khalil and Andrew had been chatting quietly. After exchanging a few words in Arabic, Khalil thanked Halima and motioned towards the front door.

'We should leave,' he said. 'Mrs. Omran is tired and would like some rest.'

Andrew glanced at Fiona who nodded at him as if to say that it was alright. He decided to trust her judgement and followed her out to the front door. Here, here turned around and looked at Halima.

'My condolences about your husband,' he said.

'Thank you,' said Halima and bowed her head slightly. 'He was very ill, but I know he is in a better place now. He was called home to God.'

'Thank you again for seeing us,' said Fiona.

Khalil took the old woman's hand and bowed. Then the three of them made their way back down the stairs and out onto the pavement in front of the apartment block. Here they hailed a taxi and got in to drive back to Andrew and Fiona's hotel.

'Well, that was interesting,' said Andrew and looked at Fiona. 'What did you two talk about?'

Fiona relayed her conversation with Mrs. Omran, as they wound their way back through the streets of

Cairo. Then she showed Andrew and Khalil the small piece of paper she had been given.

'What does this mean?' asked Khalil.

'I am not sure,' said Fiona. 'And neither was Mrs Omran. I am going to have to do some thinking on my own. I feel like the answer is inside my head somewhere, but I just can't see it right now.'

'Let's just get back to the hotel,' said Andrew. 'I am sure it will come to you.'

* * *

An hour later the three of them were back in Andrew and Fiona's hotel room, lounging on the sofas with cold drinks. They discussed their respective findings, and Andrew provided Khalil with more detail on the dramatic events that had unfolded on Elephantine Island.

'Who are those people,' asked Khalil, looking concerned. 'You said you think they might be military?'

'Yes,' replied Andrew. 'Either that or they are ex-military mercenaries. We were both lucky to get away unharmed, if I am honest.'

'So, the people holding Bahir are highly trained and heavily armed,' said Khalil. 'Don't you think we need help if we are going to solve this?'

'Probably,' replied Andrew. 'The problem is that we can't know for sure who to trust. Somehow, they, whoever they are, have been able to track and monitor us, at least part of the time we have been here. So, I am extremely hesitant to reach out to anyone, except for my own unit back in the UK. But they won't be able to respond with actual assistance here on the ground, unless there is something very tangible to respond to.'

As the two of them were talking, Fiona was lying back in a soft armchair, looking at the wall opposite her. It had a painting, a lamp and a clock. She was watching the hands on the clock as the seconds were ticking by. The numbers on the clock were Roman numerals, which she had always liked the aesthetic of. When she had first learnt to read them as a child, it had seemed like a confusing system, but there was something about the way the letters were combined in a rigid structure to denote time that had always attracted her.

Then her brow furrowed, and her head came up and tilted to one side. She lay there for several seconds, then sat up and grabbed the little piece of paper that Halima had handed her. She looked at it intently for a moment and then started paging through Khalil's copies of Omran's notebook. Eventually, she found the page she was looking for.

'Bloody hell,' she breathed.

Andrew and Khalil both turned their heads to look at her.

'What's going on?' asked Andrew.

Fiona turned to look at him. 'It's a cypher,' she said. 'It is a simple Caesar cypher.'

'The letters on the piece of paper Mrs Omran gave you?' asked Khalil.

'Yes,' replied Fiona.

'What is a Caesar cypher?' asked Andrew, looking perplexed.

'It is a super simple encryption technique,' replied Fiona. 'It just replaces letters with other letters, but unless you know which ones are replaced with what, it can be surprisingly difficult to crack. Imagine you have a text, and you replace all instances of the letter "a" with the letter "k", and you do something similar with the letters "n" and "r". Already your text is going to look quite different. Now imagine that you swap every single letter in the text for some other letter. The text will then become completely illegible.'

'Unless you know which letters were replaced with what,' said Andrew.

'Exactly,' said Fiona. 'And that is precisely what this piece of paper tells us. It contains pair of letters, separated by a semi-colon, and each pair has a number below them. They are the key to deciphering a text.'

'What are the numbers for?' asked Andrew.

'They almost certainly indicate the word to be deciphered in a text. In other words, the number 7, indicates the seventh word in the text.'

'But which text?' asked Andrew.

'This one,' said Fiona and placed her right index finger on a paragraph of text from Omran's notebook.

Khalil and Andrew rose and came over to look.

'But that text isn't encrypted,' said Andrew.

'I know,' said Fiona. 'It doesn't have to be. The pairs of letters and numbers can be used to encode a message into any text, just as long as the words of the original text are chosen carefully.'

'So, what does it say?' asked Khalil.

'The text is unremarkable,' said Fiona. 'When I first saw it, I was surprised that it was in this notebook because it is just a simple poem about two young people falling in love whilst walking by the Nile here in Cairo.'

'Jabari and Halima,' said Khalil.

'I think you are probably right,' nodded Fiona.

'And the deciphered text?' asked Andrew. 'What does it say?'

Fiona grabbed a pen and paper, and the Caesar cypher. She then quickly wrote down the deciphered text, using the sequence of pairs of letters, and their corresponding numbers indicating which letters in the poem to extract.'

'Glowing mountain home,' she said, looking perplexed.

'Glowing mountain home,' repeated Andrew slowly. 'What on earth does that mean?'

Khalil shook his head. 'I don't think I have ever heard that phrase.'

Fiona leaned back in the sofa, staring into empty space in front of her.

'Is this about Mount Nebo?' asked Andrew. 'Because if it is, this is almost certainly a dead end. We followed Omran's trail to that place, and it turned out to be something completely different.'

'Glowing,' said Fiona quietly, as if hoping that repeating the word would somehow jolt her into understanding what it meant.

Then she suddenly sat bolt upright. She blinked a couple of times, and then grabbed her pen and started scribbling furiously on another piece of paper.

'What?' said Andrew. 'Do you know where it is?'

Fiona's eyes were now narrow slits, and her forehead was creased as she scribbled away, attempting to combine a number of disparate thoughts and memories into something coherent.

'Halima,' she said. 'Omran's wife. She said something to me just as we were saying goodbye.'

'What was it?' asked Andrew, sitting down next to her.

'She said Omran had *gone home to God*,' said Fiona.

'Well. Who knows?' said Andrew. 'That might be true. No one can really say, can they?'

Fiona shook her head slightly. 'You're missing the point,' she said. 'This is about the word *home*.'

'I don't understand,' said Andrew, looking confused.

'What is the Ark's home?' asked Fiona.

'The Temple in Jerusalem?' asked Andrew.

'No,' said Fiona. 'The home of the Ark of the Covenant, is the place it came from. The place where it was made three thousand years ago.'

'Which is where?' asked Andrew.

'Mount Sinai,' said Fiona and looked at him, her eyes sparkling with excitement. 'Or rather, Mount Horeb. The glowing mountain.'

'Mount Horeb?' said Andrew. 'Where is that?'

Khalil sat down in the armchair next to them.

'It is the same as Mount Sinai, isn't it?' he asked.

'Most likely, yes,' replied Fiona. 'The name Horeb means *glowing* or *heat*.'

'Seems appropriate somehow,' said Andrew.

'What is your line of thinking here?' asked Khalil. 'Why do you think Omran concluded that the Ark has gone to Mount Horeb.'

'Ok,' said Fiona, and placed a hand flat on the piece of paper she had just scribbled her thoughts onto. 'During the reign of King Ahab of Israel in the 9th century BCE, there was a prophet called Elijah. King Ahab and his wife Jezebel were worshippers of the horned demon god Baal. According to the Book of Kings, Chapter 19, believing he was carrying out Yahweh's wishes, Elijah slew the prophets of Baal with his sword, but Jezebel then threatened to do the same to him. Elijah fled south into the desert to the town of Beersheba, and there he despaired at what he had done.'

Fiona quickly flicked through her Bible and held it up to read a passage.

'Chapter 19, verse 4,' she said. '*But he himself went a day's journey into the wilderness, and came and sat down under a broom-tree, and he requested for himself that he might die, and said: "It is enough now, O Lord, take away my life, for I am not better than my fathers."*.'

Andrew and Khalil sat impassively, allowing Fiona to lay out her theory.

'An angel then appears,' said Fiona. 'And the angel tells Elijah to eat and drink ahead of a long journey.'

'Then it continues,' said Fiona. 'Verse 8. *And he arose, and did eat and drink, and went in the strength of that meal forty days and forty nights unto Horeb the mount of God.*'

Andrew raised his eyebrows. 'Mount Horeb, where the Ten Commandments were handed down to Moses.'

Fiona continued. 'Verse 9. *And he came thither unto a cave, and lodged there.*'

She lowered the Bible and placed it back on the table.

'So, the mountain of God is Mount Horeb, the mountain of glowing heat. And there is a cave there that Elijah visited, which is large enough to lodge in. And if Omran was correct, then the Ark was taken back there to the place where it was made. Its true home.'

They all sat in silence for a few moments.

'Forty days and forty nights,' said Khalil pensively. 'As the crow flies, there is probably around four hundred kilometres from Beersheba in Israel to Mount Sinai in Egypt. So, assuming the distance by foot is around twice that, it would certainly be possible to walk that distance in forty days.'

'I am sorry,' said Andrew. 'Can I just point out that none of this is in any way likely to be historically accurate. We are talking about myths here.'

'I know,' said Khalil, holding up his hands placatingly. 'I am just saying that regardless of how accurate the Bible is, it is possible that someone might have made such a journey over roughly that time frame, and it is perfectly possible that there was a cave somewhere on Mount Horeb that could have been used.'

'But Mount Sinai has two peaks close to each other,' said Fiona. 'What if one of them is Sinai, and the other is Horeb? If I remember correctly, Sinai is the southern peak, and Horeb is the northern peak.'

'You might actually be on to something there,' said Khalil. 'As you mentioned, the name Horeb refers to glowing heat, which could be a reference to the Sun. Sinai, on the other hand, may come from Sin, the

Sumerian deity of the Moon. So Horeb and Sinai could be the mountains of the Moon and Sun, respectively.'

'And with two peaks, that would make perfect sense,' said Fiona. 'So, if Elijah found a cave to stay in, it would almost certainly have been inside Mount Horeb, since that is the northern peak, which would have been the direction he was coming from, setting out from Beersheba.'

'Okay,' said Andrew. 'Let me get this straight. You're saying that after pharaoh Shoshenq took the Ark from Jerusalem, under the threat of destroying the city, he then brought it back to Mount Horeb.'

'That is correct,' nodded Fiona.

'And why would Shoshenq and Jeroboam conspire to do that?' asked Andrew.

'Simple,' said Fiona. 'For the same reason that King Solomon might have allowed Menelik I to take the Ark out of Jerusalem, and down to Axum in Ethiopia. Both Jeroboam's and Shoshenq's ancestors were Levites, and they wanted to protect the Ark. To keep it out of the way. As we have already discussed, Canaan in general and Jerusalem in particular, sit in a bottleneck between huge empires to the north and to the south. With invasions sweeping through that land from both directions on a regular basis, it is logical to arrive at the conclusion that eventually the Ark would be destroyed along with the city of Jerusalem. And as it turned out, this did indeed happen when Nebuchadnezzar II's armies conquered the city in 587 BCE.'

'And by that time, the Ark had been safe inside Mount Horeb for centuries,' said Khalil.

'Precisely,' said Fiona.

'I think I know what is about to happen,' smiled Andrew.

Fiona looked at him, with a determined look on her face.

'We have to go,' she said imploringly. 'It is our best lead so far.'

Andrew held up his hand and nodded. 'I know,' he said. 'And I agree. We should try to find this cave. I just don't have the first clue where to start.'

'I am going to get in touch with a friend in London,' said Fiona. 'He produced the 3D topology map of Mount Nebo, and I am sure he would be able to do something similar for Mount Horeb.'

'There are likely to be many caves there,' said Khalil sceptically. 'I have spent some time hiking in the southern Sinai, and the mountains there are beautiful, but they are tall and steep. There is a fair amount of geological activity there, so it is not unusual to have the bedrock crack open to reveal caves and crevices.'

'We still have to give it a shot,' said Fiona.

'I think we should also keep in mind that whoever is holding Doctor Mansour, now has access to Omran's notebook. They may be piecing things together just the way we are. Or they might even be ahead of us. This is not going to be without risk.'

'If what you say is true,' said Khalil. 'That just means that there is no time to waste.'

'We should get going without delay then,' said Andrew. 'I will call ahead and make sure the plane is ready when we get to the airport.'

The three of them agreed to meet at the Almaza Airforce Base two hours later for the flight south-east to the southern tip of the Sinai Peninsula.

Twenty-Nine

'Saint Catherine International Airport,' said Andrew as they stepped off the plane. 'Never heard of it before today.'

Khalil smiled. 'It is not exactly a major hub. It is mainly a domestic airport, but it does have a few arrivals from Israel and a couple of other countries, so technically it qualifies for the term *International*.'

'How large is the town of Saint Catherine?' asked Fiona as they walked across the tarmac towards a waiting rental car.

'Small,' replied Khalil. 'Less than ten thousand permanent residents. But the area is well visited by tourists.'

The three of them got into the car, with Khalil in the driver's seat. It was a beige Toyota Land Cruiser with wide tyres, and an elevated chassis that would allow it to comfortably go off-road, even in very uneven terrain with large rocks. The sun was heading down towards the horizon as they set out from the airport, and the dry mountain air was fresh and invigorating. Behind them rose a cloud of fine sandy dust as the car made its way out of the airport complex and southwest towards the town of Saint Catherine.

'I have arranged for us to stay at a small guest house in Saint Catherine Town,' said Khalil. 'It is basic, but it is cosy. And the local food is delicious.'

'Sounds good,' said Andrew.

'I would have liked to go up the mountain without delay,' said Fiona. 'But I do understand. We can't go running around on a mountain trail as the sun is setting.'

'Yes, it's not safe.' said Khalil. 'It also gets very cold here at night. This entire area is essentially high desert and mountains, and even though it gets hot during the day, the heat radiates away from the rock very quickly at night. Add to that the fact that there is rarely any cloud cover to retain that heat, and also the fact that we are a couple of kilometres above sea level, and the result is that temperatures can drop by quite a lot during the night. Up here is one of the few places in Egypt that gets snow on a fairly regular basis during the winter.'

After less than fifteen minutes, they pulled into the drive of a small characterful lodging by the side of the road in the western part of the town. It had a cobbled courtyard, where the stones were worn smooth by feet having shuffled across it for decades. The rooms were small but comfortable, and there was a small restaurant serving local dishes, mainly made from lamb and chicken.

'This is very charming,' said Fiona as they sat down. 'Does this area get a lot of tourists all year?'

'Mainly during spring and autumn,' replied Khalil. 'Summer is usually too hot down here in the valley, and winter is too cold in the mountains for most people's liking.'

'What are the main attractions here?' asked Andrew.

'There are quite a few things to visit,' said Khalil. 'Aside from mount Sinai, which is about three kilometres south-east of here, there is also the Saint Catherine Mountain, which is the highest mountain in Egypt at over two thousand six hundred metres. That is further to the south.'

'I read that there are several monasteries here too,' said Fiona.

'That is correct,' said Khalil. 'There is a very large one in the valley just north of Mount Sinai. The mountain itself is actually called *Jabal Musa* in Arabic, which means Mount Moses. It is just under two thousand three hundred meters tall.'

'I am guessing there are footpaths up to the peak?' asked Andrew.

'Yes, there are,' said Khalil. 'They mainly approach the peak from the south-east, because the ascent is much easier from that direction. There is a small Greek Orthodox Chapel at the peak, but we're not going to be going up that way.'

'Where did you have in mind then?' asked Fiona.

Khalil brought out a map of the southern Sinai Peninsula and unfolded it on their table.

'This is the town of Saint Catherine, and this is Saint Catherine's Monastery down here,' he said and pointed to a small collection of buildings in a valley southeast of the town. 'Its official name is Sacred Monastery of the God-Trodden Mount Sinai.'

'Sounds promising,' said Andrew.

'As you can see here,' continued Khalil. 'There is a walking trail that starts at the monastery and goes south-east along the mountain and then curves west to wind its way up to the peak. Apparently, there are 3750 steps from the monastery to the top, if anyone wants to test that.'

'No thanks,' smiled Fiona. 'That does not sound like my kind of fun.'

'Good,' said Khalil. 'Because we're not going that way either.'

'Where are we going then?' asked Andrew.

Khalil slid his finger from the monastery southwest towards the mountain.

'There is a ravine here that leads to a place called *Farsh Elijah*,' he said and drew a circle around a small area with a pen.

'Interesting name,' said Fiona. 'What does Farsh mean?'

'In the local Bedouin dialect,' replied Khalil, 'a Farsh is a *wadi*, or a stretch of land at high elevation in the middle of a mountain range. I guess the best English word would be *basin*.'

'So, is that where you think the cave that Elijah took shelter in might be?' asked Fiona.

'Possibly,' replied Khalil. 'It is easy to dismiss place-names like that as being too obvious, but a place like Farsh Elijah was named for a reason. And once it had been named eons ago, there is really no good reason why that name would ever have been changed to something else, especially when both Christianity, Judaism and Islam all recognise Elijah as a real person that may have come to this mountain from Beersheba in Israel. I think there is a good chance that if Elijah was actually a real person, then this is the place he would have ascended the mountain.'

Khalil tapped the small circle on the map and then leaned back in his chair.

'But this is a huge area,' said Fiona. 'It might have lots of ravines and crevices and caves. How on earth are we going to be able to know where to look? And also, there have been people crawling over this mountain for centuries. Surely they would have found whatever there was to find here.'

Andrew smiled. 'Yes. You would think so, wouldn't you? But if they didn't have the proper eyes to see, then they would have found nothing.'

'Andrew,' said Fiona, looking at him sceptically. 'You're beginning to sound vaguely religious. Are you alright?'

Andrew laughed. 'Nothing like that,' he said, dug into his trouser pocket for his Geiger counter, and placed it on the table. 'What I meant was, if you can't pick up the trail left by the Ark, then you will probably never know where to look.'

'That is genius,' smiled Fiona. 'That might actually work.'

'Well,' said Andrew. 'Let's just hold our horses on this. In order for this thing to pick up anything, there would have to be a radioactive source strong enough to leave a trail. And that is not at all a given.'

'I think we should make our way up towards Farsh Elijah, and start our search there,' said Khalil. 'It is a steep climb, so hardly anyone ever goes up that way. It is our best lead.'

'Speaking of leads,' said Fiona. 'I have been looking at the copy of Omran's notebook again. There are several pages that I can't make sense of, including one that has a sketch of what appears to be a floorplan for a large building or complex. There's nothing to indicate what it might be, or where it might be located, but there is one thing about it that I found intriguing. I am wondering if Khalil has been able to make sense of it."

'Can you show us?' asked Khalil.

'Of course,' replied Fiona, and pulled out a sheet of paper.

The sheet showed a complicated schematic of what appeared to be a multi-room complex, with only one point of entry. The rooms were more or less square, but of varying sizes, and they all connected to a large central room leading to and from the entrance. Inside the larger room were what appeared to be pillars or some other type of support structure. At the other end from the entrance, was a circular shape, offset from the rest of the complex On the right-hand side of the schematic was a hand-drawn compass rose, showing that the complex did not appear to be aligned with the north or south, but seemed to have its orientation defined by what appeared to be the outside, possibly a cliff face.

'Does this look familiar to you?' asked Fiona and looked at Khalil.

'I am not sure,' said Khalil, and pressed his lips together. 'I did have a look at that back in Cairo, and I think it might be some sort of burial chamber. I have seen many of these from the archaeological digs in the Valley of Kings near Luxor, and even though this is very similar, I don't think I have seen this particular one before. And this circular room back here seems very unusual. I have never seen anything like it before.'

'Do you think it could be an undiscovered tomb in the Valley of Kings?' asked Andrew.

'It is possible,' replied Khalil. 'It has more or less the same layout as that of Thutmosis III or Seti I. They seem very similar to me.'

'What about an underground complex here at Mount Horeb?' asked Fiona.

'Very unlikely,' replied Khalil. 'Even though this area was part of the ancient Egyptian kingdoms, no pharaonic tombs have been discovered here.'

'Okay,' said Fiona. 'We might have to try to come back to this one. It can't be in the notebook for no reason. Omran must have thought it important somehow. If only he had made more notes on his sketches.'

'I don't think he ever imagined that anyone else would ever be reading his notebook,' said Khalil.

'You're probably right,' sighed Fiona.

'I can't actually believe we're about to do this,' said Andrew. 'Looking for the Ark of the Covenant. It seems quite surreal. And a bit naïve, to be honest.'

'I agree,' said Fiona. 'But that type of thinking is probably precisely why hardly anyone has tried seriously to find it here. And even if it seems naïve, that doesn't mean that there isn't anything here to be found. Especially if, as you say, people have not been using the right eyes to look with,' she said, and pointed at the Geiger counter.

'Well,' said Andrew. 'There is only one thing to do now. Let's get some dinner and some sleep, and then we meet here again tomorrow morning at first light.'

★   ★   ★

When they got up the next morning, it was only a few degrees above freezing, and they were all wrapped up warm as they got into the Toyota Land Cruiser for the short drive south-east to Saint Catherine's Monastery.

The approach ran through a valley that became increasingly narrow as they approached their destination. The ground was dry and dusty, and as Fiona looked out of the window, she could not spot a single plant growing anywhere in the light brown terrain.

'It looks so arid here,' she said.

'This place gets virtually no rain,' said Khalil. 'The only reason the monastery is able to exist here in this valley is because it sits at the lowest point between two mountains, and it has a deep well that is just about able to access the groundwater table.'

The monastery still lay in the shadow of the mountain range to the east, but Mount Sinai, which was towering above them to the west, was lit up by the Sun's rays, bathing it in a warm orange glow.

'Horeb. The glowing mountain,' said Fiona as they stepped out of the car.

'Fitting name,' said Andrew and joined her, gazing up towards the peak high above them.

The mountainside was steep, and the entire area at the foot of the mountain and around the monastery looked extremely dry. Everywhere they looked, there were rocks and boulders that had come down from the mountain over eons, and looking up at it, there was no obvious way to approach it.

'It seems like a very steep approach,' said Fiona and turned towards Khalil. 'I can't see anywhere where it looks possible to ascend.'

'I know,' said Khalil. 'It looks impossible from this side, which is why the trail goes past the monastery and down to the south for the easy climb from the west.'

He pointed south along the narrow road to where the monastery lay a few hundred meters away, with its high walls and a church spire poking up above them. Built around 565 CE, it is the size of a football field, and the encircling walls are upwards of fifteen meters tall. Inside it are multiple buildings, including the oldest continually operating library in the world. As it lay there in the shadow of the mountain to the east, it looked the way it has probably looked every morning for centuries, and a visitor from the 10th century would feel quite at home there.

'The trail goes along that exterior wall there, and then winds its way around the base of the mountain to the right, and up that side, you can just see beyond the monastery. But we're going up over there,' he said and pointed at a narrow ravine that stretched several hundred meters up the mountain slope, and then seemed to stop at what appeared from their vantage point to be a sheer wall of rock.

'Well,' said Andrew, and adjusted his backpack. 'No time like the present. Let's go.'

The three of them set off across the valley floor towards the ravine some two hundred meters from where they had parked the car. The ground was rocky and covered in small boulders that had tumbled down from the mountains above over many centuries.

There was no one else around, and the valley was quiet except for the occasional screech of an eagle circling high up above them on the thermals from the mountain range. A thin wispy column of smoke was rising serenely from a chimney on one of the buildings inside the monastery walls, and since the cool morning air was almost completely still, the smoke drifted calmly up above the building where it seemed to dissolve.

'We need to get over to that ravine,' said Khalil and pointed ahead of them. 'It leads further up this side of the mountain, and should provide us with a way to get to the plateau where Farsh Elijah is.'

They continued across the increasingly uneven ground and eventually reached the lower part of the ravine. It was wide and relatively easy to navigate, but as they proceeded further into it, it became narrower and steeper, and they soon had to place their feet carefully to avoid sliding or tripping. There was no proper path, although it was evident that people had made the journey up this side of the mountain before. Whenever they reached small chokepoints where there was only one route further up the ravine, they could see a semblance of a path and a few flat rocks that looked like they had been worn smoother than the surrounding rocks.

After another fifteen minutes, Fiona turned around to look behind them. As she looked down towards the monastery below them, it became clear how their ascent had become increasingly steep as they went, and they were now several hundred meters above the valley floor. From this vantage point, she was able to look down and into the monastery, where a number of buildings with very different designs, possibly from very different time periods, were placed in what appeared to be a disorderly way. This was clearly a building complex that had grown organically over the centuries, with no clear plan from the outset. On the other side of the monastery complex, beyond the high walls, was a patch of green, with bushes and what looked like vegetable patches. A solitary figure was on its knees there, seemingly tending to the plants.

'The steepest bit is up ahead,' said Khalil. 'We might have to help each other over the boulders to get to the plateau.'

Khalil turned out to be right. The final thirty meters of the ravine were a sheer rockface with a few huge boulders laying in front of it. They seemed to have come down the mountain, dropped down here and come to rest on their way down the mountain.

'Let's hope no more of these things come tumbling down in the next few minutes,' said Andrew as he adeptly climbed on top of one of them.

'Give me your hand,' he said to Fiona.

Gripping on tightly to Fiona's hand, he pulled her up the side of the boulder and then helped Khalil come up the same way. This allowed Khalil to give Andrew a leg up, which in turn let him grip the ledge above them that led to the plateau. Lying on the ledge above, Andrew then reached down with both arms, and helped first Khalil and then Fiona to scale the final few meters.

They all stood up and dusted themselves down. The sun was now peeking over the mountain to the east, and its rays were bathing the Farsh Elijah plateau in warm sunlight. The air was crisp and cool, but they could clearly sense that it would become much hotter in a few hours.

Fiona walked a few meters out onto the plateau.

'I can't believe this is actually it,' she said, placing her hands on her hips and gazing up towards the summit of Mount Horeb several hundred meters above them.

'What do you mean?' asked Andrew.

'Look up there,' said replied and pointed. 'Just beyond it is Mount Sinai. The actual place where Moses received the Ten Commandments.'

'Well. Possibly,' said Andrew. 'There is no way of knowing. But if the Hebrews really did flee ancient Egypt, then this would have been a spectacular place to assemble and lay down new laws for themselves.'

'It certainly does inspire a certain amount of spirituality,' said Khalil.

'That I can agree with,' said Andrew. 'Mountains have always made me feel small, and that can be a healthy thing from time to time.'

The Farsh Elijah plateau was small and quite flat. It was nestled between several lower peaks on one side, and Mount Horeb on the other. At this time of day, the Sun managed to bathe it in its warm light, but it would be in shadow as soon as the sun began to pass its zenith and make its way towards the horizon around mid-afternoon. The plateau looked decidedly barren and windswept, and at one end near where they had come up, it had a single shelter made from mudbrick, and next to it was a well. It was impossible to determine their age just by looking at them. They were clearly constructed from materials found on the plateau, but they could have been built ten years ago or five hundred years ago.

At the far end of the plateau where it sloped up slightly, they could see a narrow footpath begin to wind its way up the steep incline towards the summit, but it looked precarious and not like something one might want to undertake in bad weather.

'I am not surprised this side of the mountain barely has any visitors,' said Fiona. 'That climb looks treacherous.'

'So, this is where Elijah spent the night and was visited by an angel?' said Andrew and looked at the shelter. 'Somehow I expected more.'

'I am pretty sure this is just a shelter,' smiled Fiona. 'It was probably built by local Bedouins, in case they got caught out by weather and had to spend the night up here. According to the scripture, Elijah stayed in a cave, so that is what we should be looking for.'

'I don't see anything like that,' said Andrew and turned slowly to scan the surrounding area. 'We might have to make excursions around the edge of the plateau. I will use the Geiger counter to see if I can pick up any residual radiation. It will be faint, but if something radioactive like the meteorite was brought through here, there still ought to be faint traces of it. Small variations in background radiation should give it away.'

They spent the next hour or so walking around the perimeters of the plateau, investigating crevices and smaller ravines that led away from it. The rock formations leading up and away from the plateau were a mix of light yellow and dark brown, often with large angular shapes.

Andrew used his Geiger counter to scan for radioactive traces, slowly sweeping it from side to side and trying to create a mental map of the variations in radiation that the device was picking up. The variations that it did detect were very small, and none of the readings were significantly above the levels that could be expected from simple background radiation.

'I don't see anything remotely like a cave here,' said Fiona almost an hour later, after they had searched the entire circumference of the plateau.

Andrew shook his head. 'Me neither,' he said. 'It feels like we're chasing a myth. There's nothing here.'

'Let's make sure we're hydrated,' said Khalil and dug into his backpack for bottles of water. 'It will get very hot here in a few hours, and we should not wait until we're thirsty to drink.'

They all slumped down, leaning their backs against the well next to the small shelter.

'Could it be much higher up?' said Andrew and looked towards the narrow path at the other end of the plateau.

'It's possible,' said Khalil and took a big gulp from his water bottle. 'Although caves tend to be nearer the base of mountains. I don't think there will be anything up there, but it is worth a try.'

'Wait a minute,' said Fiona suddenly.

She rose and took a few steps away from the well, turned around and looked at it, whilst tilting her head to one side and furrowing her brow.

'What?' asked Andrew. He and Khalil looked at each other perplexed.

'Why is there a well here?' asked Fiona.

'Why would there be a well anywhere?' asked Andrew rhetorically. 'To provide water to drink, of course. If you get caught out by the weather, you will need a source of drinking water.'

'But there is virtually no precipitation up here,' said Khalil. 'This place gets less than one millimetre of rain per month on average, so there is no water for the well to catch.'

'Exactly,' said Fiona. 'And we are also much too high up for a well to be able to reach the groundwater table. That must be hundreds of meters below where we are now.'

Andrew and Khalil both got to their feet and stood back from the well, looking at it. Then Fiona walked to its side and leaned in over it. The circular sides of the well were made from rocks that had been chiselled into the shape of small squares blocks. The hole was roughly two meters across and reached down at least ten meters.

'There's no water in here,' said Fiona. 'In fact, it looks like there hasn't been any water in here for a long time. The bottom is covered in dry sand and rocks. Not a single plant.'

The two men joined her and looked down into the well.

'You're right,' said Khalil. 'This does look strange.'

'Are you thinking what I am thinking?' asked Andrew and turned to Fiona.

'You packed a rope, didn't you?' she replied.

'Yep,' said Andrew and swung his backpack off his shoulder and reached into it, pulling out a thick rope made of hemp.

'There is nothing to tie it to,' said Fiona. 'But if Khalil and I hold on to the end of it, you should be able to use it to climb down.'

'Alright,' said Andrew, and looked at Khalil. 'Are you up for this?'

'Of course,' smiled the big man. 'We can do this easily.'

They unfurled the rope, and Khalil grabbed it with his large hands and wrapped it around his right lower arm. He then gripped the rope with both hands, and Fiona then placed herself in front of him, also holding on to the rope.

Andrew dropped the rest of the rope into the well and turned to his two companions.

'Ready?' he asked.

Fiona and Khalil both nodded, and then he sat on the wall surrounding the well and swung his legs over the edge. He then gripped the rope with both hands, adroitly turned himself to face the inside of the well, and started his descent towards the bottom of the well. Placing the tips of his boots inside the gaps between individual rocks in the wall of the well, he was able to quickly make his way down towards the bottom of the well. He pushed himself off the wall and let go of the rope to let himself drop the last meter to the sandy bottom.

'Down!' he shouted and looked up towards the small circular patch of blue sky above him.

After a few seconds, the heads of Fiona and Khalil peeked over the side.

'Are you alright?' called Fiona. 'Any sign of water?'

'I am ok,' replied Andrew. 'Not a drop of water here. I don't think this well has ever held any water. I am going to have a quick look around.'

He fished out his Geiger counter from the side pocket of his trousers and waited for it to start up. After a couple of seconds, the display lit up, and the familiar clicking sound began. They were few and far between at first, but as he started turning around slowly, holding the device out in front of him, the readings began to fluctuate beyond what he had seen up on the plateau. He stopped turning at the spot where the reading showed a spike and knelt down. The Geiger counter started producing more regular and frequent clicks.

'Hello,' said Andrew to no one in particular.

'What's that?' called Fiona.

'I've got something,' Andrew called back.

His eyes were still getting used to the relative darkness at the bottom of the well, but he was soon able to make out that the last meter of the inside of the well, was constructed with much larger stones than the walls above.

And that is when he spotted it. It was small, covered in dirt and dust, and placed at the centre of one of the larger stones making up the inside of the wall just above the well's sandy bottom. It was the same mark that he and Fiona had seen inside the tunnel leading to the Nilometer on Elephantine Island, and it was carved into a stone that looked to be roughly half a meter by one meter in size.

'What the…,' he whispered slowly.

He let his fingertips move gently across it, and as the dust was wiped from the small groves in the stone, it was clear that this was the exact same motive.

'Hey Fiona,' he said and looked up. 'I think you should come down and have a look.'

'Really?' she replied sounding apprehensive.

'Yes, really.' replied Andrew. 'I need you to confirm that I am looking at what I think I am looking at.'

'Fine,' said Fiona, and started climbing onto the wall of the well. 'You've got this, right?' she said and turned to look at Khalil.

'Absolutely,' he replied and repositioned his hands on the rope. 'You're safe to go down.'

Thirty

Fiona took a deep breath as if steeling herself for the descent, and then resolutely lowered herself down along the inside of the well. Less than a minute later she was kneeling next to Andrew, looking at the carving of the meteorite motif that was now so familiar to them.

'Bloody hell,' she breathed while inspecting the carving. Then she looked at Andrew. 'Could the meteorite be here at Mount Horeb?'

'It's possible,' replied Andrew. 'Have a look at this,' he continued and showed her the Geiger counter, which was now busily clicking away in his hand as he pointed it at the stone with the carving.

'There has got to be something here,' said Fiona.

'It gets even better,' smiled Andrew.

He had taken out his knife while she had been on her way down, and he now knocked the handle against the stone with the carving. It did not sound like solid rock. It almost rang, clearly indicating that the rock slab was thin and that there was a cavity on the other side of it.

'Stand back,' he said and got his small pickaxe out of his backpack. 'I am going to try to get through.'

'Just don't make the whole thing come down on us,' said Fiona and stood up.

'It will be fine,' said Andrew. 'This slab of stone is not carrying any weight. If it did, it would have crumbled ages ago.'

'You sound confident,' said Fiona. 'I hope you're right.'

Andrew shifted the pickaxe, feeling its weight in his hands, then gripped it tightly and held it out to the side and behind him. Then he swung it powerfully down and forward, connecting with the centre of the slap. He was expecting to perhaps be able to crack the slab, but the pickaxe split it into several pieces, and the pickaxe continued its forward momentum so that he had to hold onto it tightly to avoid it slipping out of his hands.

'Crikey,' he said. 'That was easy.'

Fiona knelt down again and shone her torch through the gap. There was clearly a cavity on the other side, and it seemed as if the sandy base of the well continued seamlessly into the cavity.

'Everything alright?' called Khalil.

'Yes. We're fine,' said Fiona and looked up towards the small patch of blue sky where Khalil was looking down towards them. He suddenly seemed far away to her. 'There seems to be a hidden compartment down here.'

Andrew put the pickaxe down and shone his own torch into the hole.

'It's a passage of some sort,' he said. 'I am going to crawl in there and have a look.'

'Be careful,' said Fiona.

'I'm always careful,' said Andrew and winked at her. 'This is my new full-time job. I know what I am doing.'

Then he removed the broken pieces of the stone slab and crawled through the hole into the cavity.

'Wow,' he said. 'It's bigger than I thought. I can almost stand up straight in here.'

'Is it a cave?' asked Fiona.

'No,' said Andrew. 'It is more like a tunnel. About one and a half meters to the ceiling, a bit less than a meter wide.'

'Where does it lead?' asked Fiona

'I can't tell,' said Andrew. 'I will have to make my way further in. There's a strange smell in here.'

'What does it smell of?' asked Fiona.

'I am not sure,' replied Andrew. 'But it is not pleasant.'

'I need to go with you,' said Fiona. 'It would be reckless of you to go in there by yourself.'

'I can handle myself,' said Andrew.

'You always say that,' replied Fiona, sounding irritated. 'But we're safer if we both go in.'

'Alright,' replied Andrew.

'Khalil,' called Fiona. 'There's a tunnel down here. We're going to go inside and have a look around, ok? Please just wait for us. We'll need your help to get out again.'

'Absolutely,' nodded Khalil. 'I won't be going anywhere.'

Fiona ducked down and crawled through the gab to join Andrew, who had just donned his LED headlamp. The inside of the tunnel was made of the same dark brown granite that they had seen above them on the plateau, and it stretched away in a straight line towards some as-yet invisible destination. When they shone their torches along it, all they could see was more of the same granite walls, and the tunnel appeared remarkably straight as it receded into the darkness ahead.

Fiona was already looking uncomfortable, but was trying to put a brave face on it.

'You really don't like confined spaces at all, do you?' asked Andrew and placed his hand gently on her shoulder.

'I'm ok,' said Fiona bravely. 'Let's see what's up ahead.'

The two of them started walking carefully and slightly hunched over along the tunnel. It began to curve ever so slightly downward as they progressed, and after around fifty meters it was descending noticeably. It kept going down at an angle for another thirty meters, and then it levelled out again and ended abruptly with an open doorway leading into a large cave. It was the shape of a square, roughly five by five meters in size, with statues of what appeared to be angels on either side. At the opposite end of the room from where they had entered, was a wide but narrowing stairway that led up beyond where they could see from their vantage point.

'Who on earth made this place?' said Fiona.

'People who wanted to hide something far out of both sight and reach of anyone else,' replied Andrew.

Fiona walked over to one of the statues and shone her light on it while looking at it closely.

'I might be imagining things,' said Fiona. 'But I would put money on this being the same red granite we saw in the quarries on Elephantine Island.'

'That's incredible,' said Andrew. 'It is hundreds of kilometres to Aswan from here. And how did they get them down here? They are much too big to pass through the tunnel.'

'I guess there's another way into this place,' said Fiona and touched one of the statues with her hand.

Andrew shone his torch on the stone floor. It was covered in a fine layer of dust. 'I don't think anyone has been through here for eons,' he said.

'Let's see what is up here,' said Fiona, and began moving towards the stairs.

They were cut neatly into the bedrock, and the stairway narrowed as it went up, until it was only as wide as the doorway that sat at its top a couple of meters above the square room's floor level.

Through the doorway was another corridor, similar to the first one they had already passed through, but this one was only around ten meters long and perhaps as much as three meters wide. It ended in a black void at the other end where their torches could not properly illuminate. Along its centre was a narrow path covered with stone slabs less than a meter wide, and on either side were what appeared to be trenches cut deep into the bedrock. Along the walls were wide pillars that appeared to be holding up a ceiling made of very wide slabs of stone. The pillars had been placed close together all the way along both sides of the corridor, and they each seemed to have a neat hole the size of a tennis ball cut into their base facing the trench in front of them.

'This place is making me nervous,' said Fiona as she shone her torch across the pillars, and along the wide trenches between the path in the centre of the corridor and the pillars. 'What are these trenches for?'

'I haven't got the faintest idea,' said Andrew and walked forward slowly. 'Let's be very careful now. I have a bad feeling this place was not made to be welcoming to strangers.'

They proceeded along the central path in the corridor towards the other end, stepping carefully and gently on the slabs. At one point Andrew leaned out to one side and shone his torch down into the trench next to him. The air seemed slightly misty down there, and he was unable to see the bottom.

'What the devil is this place?' he whispered.

Just then, he heard a dull metallic click from underneath the slab he had just placed his foot on. He also felt the slab give way ever so slightly beneath his foot.

'Shit,' he said.

'What happened?' asked Fiona.

'I am not sure,' said Andrew, raising his head and looking around.

At first, he thought he was imagining things, but after a few seconds, he knew that his senses were not deceiving him. He could hear the sound of a faint rumbling, followed by a strange hissing sound. Fiona heard it too.

'Andrew?' she called, her voice sounding anxious.

At that moment the first grains of sand began to trickle out of the holes at the base of the pillars. First, it was just a couple of them, but soon sand was coming out of the holes in all the pillars. The trickle then increased steadily, until after a few seconds it was pouring out of all of them and into the deep trenches cut into the bedrock between the path and the pillars.

'I think we may have just set off some sort of ancient burglar alarm,' said Andrew, looking concerned. 'We need to get out of here. Come on.'

The two of them started walking faster towards the end of the corridor, and when they reached it, they emerged into a huge natural cave with stalactites hanging down from the uneven and vaguely dome-shaped cave ceiling. The cave was perhaps twenty by thirty meters in size, and the ceiling was at least three meters above them. At the centre of the room was what appeared to be a large box-like sarcophagus, roughly three metres long, two metres wide and just over a meter high.

'What is this place?' asked Andrew looking up at the ceiling and around the circumference of the cave.

'I don't know,' said Fiona. 'But it definitely isn't that complex that is depicted on the sketch in Omran's notebook.'

Andrew started walking slowly and carefully towards the sarcophagus, while Fiona followed after him walking backwards and shining her torch back at the corridor. The sand was still pouring audibly out of the columns and into the trenches.

'Andrew,' said Fiona nervously. 'I am not sure what is happening here, but I don't think we have a lot of time.'

'I know,' said Andrew, sounding tense and shining his torch onto the sarcophagus-like box. Its sides were adorned with various symbols and ornamental patterns. He then brought out the Geiger counter, and it immediately started clicking away. The readings were not at dangerous levels, but they were significantly above background radiation levels.

'Fiona, could you take a look?' he asked. 'What do you make of this?'

Fiona turned around and looked at the box.

'Wow,' she said and knelt down next to it, shining her torch along its side. 'This is definitely Levantine. There is no writing, but the imagery and the symbols seem distinctly Hebrew.'

She looked up at Andrew who was now looking back towards the corridor again.

'This could be it, Andrew,' she said, her eyes gleaming. 'This really could be the Ark of the Covenant. We need to open this.'

'Whatever we do, we need to do it fast,' said Andrew. 'I have a really bad feeling about this whole thing now.'

He had barely finished his sentence before they both heard and felt a rumble throughout the cave. It was like a distant earthquake, that made the floor under their feet tremble and dust begin to fall from the ceiling.

'I am worried this whole place is about to come down on our heads,' said Andrew.

Fiona looked up at the ceiling as if it might tell her whether it was safe to be here or not. All she ended up with was the claustrophobic realisation that an entire mountain, weighing billions of tonnes, was bearing down on the cave.

They both stood up and were about to grab the lid of the sarcophagus when Andrew suddenly placed his hand on Fiona's arm.

'Wait,' he said. 'Let me check something.'

He quickly scanned the stone lid for radioactivity, and found the same levels as before, but with a very high reading coming from the centre of it.

'There is definitely something highly radioactive in here,' he said. 'For some reason, it has only made a small area in the middle of the lid radioactive.'

'I think I know why,' said Fiona, glancing nervously towards the corridor, just as another tremor rippled through the cave.

'There were five lead slabs in the chamber in Axum, right?' she asked.

Andrew nodded.

'So, if this is the Ark, and it has a radioactive source inside it, it would be shielded on five sides, except for the side pointing upwards.'

'And that's why the lid of the sarcophagus has been so irradiated,' said Andrew.

'Correct,' she nodded.

'Ok, so what you're saying is that it is safe to do this, as long as we don't put ourselves near the centre of the sarcophagus?' asked Andrew.

'Exactly,' said Fiona.

'Let's do it then,' he said and placed his hands on one corner of the lid.

Fiona moved to the other end of the sarcophagus where she placed her hands on the corner that was on the same side as Andrew's.

'Ready?' said Andrew. 'One. Two. Three. And push!'

They both pushed hard, and the slab seemed to move a fraction of a millimetre. As they did so, a powerful tremor made the cave shake, and in that instant, one of the wide stone slabs in the ceiling of the corridor collapsed and shattered onto the narrow path with an ear-splitting crash.

'Well,' said Andrew, now out of breath. 'We're not getting out that way. We need to hurry.'

More dust and tiny pebbles were now dropping from the ceiling of the cave, and Andrew glanced briefly up at the ceiling to make sure there were no stalactites hanging directly above them.

'Again,' he shouted.

They both re-adjusted their stance as well as their grip on the lid.

'One. Two. Three. Push!' said Andrew, and groaned as he focused every muscle in his body on pushing against the stone lid.

Finally, it seemed to come loose and began sliding across the top of the sarcophagus.

'Keep pushing,' Andrew shouted with gritted teeth as the lid continued moving towards the edge of the sarcophagus, where it eventually tipped over and landed with a crash on the floor of the cave.

They both stood back from the sarcophagus, panting heavily, as yet another of the immensely heavy ceiling slabs inside the corridor crashed down and broke into several pieces. Fiona was first to approach it and shine her torch inside it, and she stopped dead in her tracks as soon as she reached the edge of it.

Andrew took a couple of cautious steps towards the sarcophagus and then shone the lights from his torch and his headlamp into it.

The gleaming gold of the Acacia wood seemed as clean and shiny as it must have been the day Bezalel gilded the vessel. The wings of the cherubim stretched elegantly towards the middle of its lid, and every feather seemed to have been carved delicately into the wood from which they were made. The light from their torches reflected off the Ark of the Covenant, and it lit up the entire centre of the cave, shining up onto the ceiling with golden light.

Dumbfounded, Andrew and Fiona stood there for a few moments just gazing at this small wooden reliquary, which had been thought lost for more than two millennia.

Fiona's lower lip trembled, and her eyes started to well up with the emotion of being in the presence of this powerful artefact, that had in many ways been the foundation stone of all three of the world's most dominant religions for thousands of years.

Just then, a much more powerful tremor rippled through the cave, causing the entire corridor they had entered through to collapse in a barrage of loud dry crashing noises, as the remaining ceiling slabs buckled under the immense weight of the granite rock above them. A split second later, a large stalactite that hung overhead broke off the ceiling and crashed loudly onto the cave floor less than two meters from where Andrew was standing. It shattered in a cloud of dust, sending tiny pebbles of rock flying off in all directions.

'I hate to say this,' shouted Andrew, over the loud rumble of the mountain around them, and the noise from the falling rocks. 'We need to leave right now.'

'Shit,' whispered Fiona, stealing one last intent look at the Ark, as if trying to commit it to memory. The agony of having to leave the artefact now after all they had been through, was etched onto her face.

She quickly reached into her pocket and pulled out her phone, selected camera mode and pointed at the Ark. But then she hesitated. She closed her eyes, bowed her head and grimaced, consumed by some internal conflict.

'Damn it,' she whispered. 'I can't.'

'Let's go,' shouted Andrew as he ran past her, grabbing her hand and pulling her along towards the other side of the cave.

Fiona shoved her phone back in her pocket, and ran along next to Andrew, with an anguished look on her face.

'I think there is an opening over here,' shouted Andrew. 'It's our only shot.'

They ran across the cave floor towards what seemed to be another dark corridor leading out of the cave.

'Let's hope this is not a dead-end,' shouted Fiona.

As they raced into cover from the falling rocks and stalactites, they slowed down momentarily to try to see where this corridor led to. At that moment they realised that it seemed to be identical to the one they had entered the cave through, and which was now a pile of huge broken granite slabs.

'Oh, bloody hell!' exclaimed Fiona. 'I don't believe this!'

'I can't see where it leads,' said Andrew, fanning the light from his torch out ahead of them. 'We just have to press on and hope for the best.'

They sprinted along the corridor, and they had barely entered it before sand started spilling out through holes in the pillars that lined the sides of it. By the time they were at the other end, sand was gushing out through the holes and into the trenches. At the end of the corridor were steps leading up to another tunnel similar to the one they had entered from the well at Farsh Elijah. The tunnel had a slight incline to it, and Fiona felt her heart soaring at the sensation of running upwards towards the surface, wherever that might end up being.

Within less than ten seconds, the first of the stone slabs that made up the ceiling in the second corridor collapsed and crashed to the floor. They felt the rush of air and dust coming up behind them, even as they ran away from it.

'This tunnel had better take us to the surface,' panted Andrew. 'Otherwise, we're screwed.'

He had barely spoken those words before they arrived at a ninety-degree right turn, after which the tunnel levelled out again and continued on for another twenty meters before it stopped abruptly.

'Oh shit!' exclaimed Fiona. 'Dead end. What do we do now? We can't go back to the cave.'

Andrew walked swiftly towards the end of the tunnel. It looked exactly like the dark brown granite that made up the wall in the rest of the tunnel.

'We're trapped,' said Fiona, with panic creeping into her voice. 'We're trapped under a mountain.'

She bent over and placed her hands on her knees, gasping for air.

'Easy now,' said Andrew, trying to sound calm. He could hear that Fiona was beginning to hyperventilate. 'We'll figure this out.'

'Figure it out?' said Fiona and shook her head. 'There's nothing to figure out. We'll never get out of here.'

'Fiona,' said Andrew sternly. 'Look at me please.'

She stood back up and looked at him with a distraught and resigned look on her face.

'We need to stay calm now,' he said. 'If there is another way out, we won't find it unless we use our heads, ok?'

Fiona swallowed hard and nodded. 'Ok,' she said, sounding as if she was trying to convince herself that he was right.

Andrew got out his Geiger counter and scanned the tunnel's dead end, but there was no variation in the readings that might have provided them with a hint as to what to do.

Then he knelt down and pulled out his pickaxe from his backpack. He started tapping it against the rock blocking their way, but it had the distinct sound of solid granite, and barely a pebble came loose when he did so.

He tried again, this time slightly lower on the wall, and with much more force. The pickaxe bounced off the granite with a high-pitched clang, and Andrew almost lost his grip.

He glanced over at Fiona, who was now looking ashen-faced. Then he turned back to the wall and swung the pickaxe hard at the lower part of it. With a loud clang, the pickaxe struck the stone, but this time the metal tip penetrated and stuck into the wall.

Andrew changed his stance and gripped the handle, and then used his weight to lever the pickaxe free. It quickly popped out of the wall, ripping pieces of rock with it.

'I've got something,' he said and looked back at Fiona who was sitting on her knees watching him.

He swung the pickaxe again, with the same result. It stuck into the rock, which was clearly much more brittle than that higher up on the wall. Again, he used leverage through the handle of the pickaxe to break more pieces of rock away from the wall. He kept doing this until he could see a light-coloured stone behind the brittle section of rock.

'What is that?' said Fiona, her voice trembling with trepidation.

'I don't know,' said Andrew. 'But it looks like the slab I found inside the well at Farsh Elijah. This could be a way out.'

After a few more tries, the dark brittle rock was cleared away, and they could now see the light-coloured stone slab clearly. Andrew tapped on it with the pickaxe, and it had the distinct resonance of something thin.

'Here goes nothing,' he said and swung the pickaxe hard.

The tip of the pickaxe shattered the stone slab, and light poured into the tunnel.

Behind him, Andrew heard the sound of Fiona gasping in relief at seeing sunlight again. He turned around to glance at her.

'See?' he said with a smile. 'We're ok.'

Then he turned back to the wall and used the pickaxe to clear away the shattered stone slab along with the pile of brittle granite lying in front of what was now an opening to the outside. He hacked away at the remnants of the slab, until the gap was big enough to get through, and then he crawled on his belly to the other side.

'Oh,' Fiona heard him say from the other side. 'Déjà vu.'

'What do you see?' she asked.

'Another well,' he replied. 'Just like the first one. Only this time, we don't have a rope to climb up.'

Fiona crawled through the opening to join him. She stood up and dusted herself down 'And no Khalil to help us.'

She then reached into her pocket and brought out her phone.

'Damn it,' she said. 'There's no signal down here.'

They both looked up towards the blue disc of sky above them. It was only about ten meters away, but it might as well have been ten kilometres. Without a rope, there was no way of scaling the inside of the well.

Fiona sighed. 'Just when I thought we were ok.'

Andrew was struggling to think of something encouraging to say. Even he was beginning to feel a sense of doom creeping in on him.

'Let's just have a look around,' he said and began walking around the perimeter of the bottom of the well. 'We might be able to find a way.'

After a few seconds, Fiona spoke again.

'I don't think we'll have to,' she said.

Andrew looked at her and saw that she was looking up towards the top of the well. He followed her gaze upwards, to see the dark silhouette of three people looking down on them. They stood immovable by the side of the well, and they seemed to all be wearing hoods.

'Oh shit,' whispered Andrew.

'Do you need a hand?' asked a familiar voice.

'Khalil?' asked Andrew confused.

'No,' said the voice. 'This is Ibrahim Zaki.'

Thirty-One

'Watch out down there,' called Zaki, and a few seconds later a rope dropped down the well and unfurled itself to where Andrew and Fiona stood.

'Wait a minute. This is my rope,' exclaimed Andrew, and looked up towards the top of the well. 'Is Khalil with you?'

'In a manner of speaking,' said Zaki.

Andrew and Fiona looked at each other perplexed. Then Andrew shrugged and pointed at the rope.

'You first,' he said. 'I'll stay here in case you fall.'

'Thanks,' said Fiona, sounding relieved.

Then she grabbed the rope, put her right foot on the wall, and started working her way hand over hand up the rope whilst using her feet for support. As she reached the top, Zaki and one of the other hooded men reached down to grab her arms and help her up and out of the well. A minute later, Andrew had followed her up and made it safely over the edge of the side of the well. The well itself was almost identical to the one they had found on the Farsh Elijah plateau, but this one was located on the west side of the mountain at the bottom of a wide ravine.

Zaki and his two silent companions were wearing all black loose clothes, with hoods that completely covered their heads, except for a slit to allow them to see. They were all armed with rifles and wearing belts that seemed to have both small weapons and grenades attached.

The third hooded man was standing a few meters back, with his gun trained at Khalil, who was tied up and kneeling on the ground with a gag in his mouth.

'Set him free!' demanded Andrew angrily. 'He is with us. You can trust him.'

'Do you vouch for him?' asked Zaki.

'Absolutely,' replied Andrew. 'All he is trying to do is find his old friend Doctor Mansour.'

Zaki took a moment to study Andrew's face, and then he nodded, took a step to one side and looked at the hooded man.

'Release him,' he said, and immediately the man swung his rifle over his shoulder, untied the gag on Khalil's mouth, and produced a knife to cut the rope tying his hands together.

Khalil rose and rubbed his aching wrist, and then brought his hand up to his jaw, working it to open and shut his mouth a few times.

'Apologies,' said Zaki to Khalil. 'We couldn't take any chances.'

'Apology accepted,' said Khalil reluctantly. 'I am just glad you are not the same people holding my friend.'

'We are not,' said Zaki. 'In fact, we have been trying to locate him too. But without any luck, I am sad to say.'

'Who are you really?' asked Fiona sceptically and pointed at Zaki's clothes. 'And what's with the outfits?'

Zaki reached up and took off his hood, whilst bowing his head slightly. Then he took a deep breath, hesitated for a moment, and then looked up at them.

'We are the Brotherhood of Horeb,' he said, sounding as if he was reluctantly admitting to something he would rather not tell anyone.

'The Brotherhood of Horeb,' repeated Fiona, looking puzzled. 'I have never heard of it.'

Zaki smiled benignly. 'I am glad. We are not really in the habit of advertising our existence to anyone. The brotherhood was founded by a small group of Levite priests more than three thousand years ago, just before the exodus of the Israelites from Egypt. As I think you might have guessed by now, they had uncovered the secret location of a radioactive meteorite, which had been kept hidden by the ancient Egyptian priesthood for more than a thousand years by that time.'

Andrew and Fiona looked at him, dumbfounded.

'I guess you were right, Fiona' said Andrew finally.

'So, it's all real,' she said sounding incredulous.

Then she looked from Andrew to Doctor Zaki. 'Does that mean that a piece of that meteorite was brought out of Egypt to this mountain?' she said and gestured to the massif above them.

'That is correct,' replied Zaki. 'Bezalel was one of our founders, and he oversaw the construction of the

Ark of the Covenant to be a vessel for safely carrying a piece of the meteorite that the Israelites had retrieved from Elephantine Island. The goal was to transport it out of Egypt, in order to provide them with a weapon for protecting themselves on their journey back across the Sinai Peninsula to Canaan.'

'So, you are Jewish?' asked Andrew.

'Yes, we are,' replied Zaki and gestured to his two companions. 'Please excuse my companions for not speaking. Secrecy is paramount, and these two gentlemen both occupy important positions in the Egyptian military. We cannot afford for their identities to be revealed.'

'Are you saying you have infiltrated the Egyptian military, and that you have sleepers on the inside?' asked Andrew.

'I would not call them that,' replied Zaki, and winced at the use of that word. 'We are all descendants of those Levites who played a role in the retrieval of the meteorite all those years ago. And for generations, we have taken it upon ourselves to guard its secret, as well as that of the Ark after it was made here at the foot of Mount Horeb.'

'Does this mean that Moses himself was part of this effort?' asked Andrew.

'Yes,' nodded Zaki. 'According to our legends, he was the one whose tribesmen uncovered the secret of the meteorite. They discovered that Joseph, in his capacity as grand vizier of Egypt under Ramesses II, had managed to uncover its existence, and that it had been hidden by the ancient Egyptian priesthood almost five thousand years ago. He then instructed Bezalel and Aholiab to construct an Ark that could serve both as a vessel for transporting a large piece of the meteorite, and as a weapon against the enemies of the Israelites. Ever since then, we have been tasked with protecting the secret locations of the Ark and the meteorite.'

'Are all the brotherhood's members people of Levite lineage then?' asked Fiona.

'Yes,' replied Zaki. 'This was built into our code from the very beginning.'

'So, you are all descendants of Levite priests?' asked Andrew.

'Yes, we are,' said Zaki.

'How did you even know we were here?' asked Fiona.

'We have been tracking your aircraft's location ever since our first meeting,' replied Zaki. 'When we saw it had landed at Saint Catherine Airport, it wasn't too difficult to work out where you were going. I have to admit that I am impressed that you managed to find a way into the chamber.'

'Why didn't you try to stop us?' asked Fiona. 'We could have been killed down there.'

'You could,' replied Zaki. 'Our helicopter set down on Farsh Elijah a couple of hours ago, but by the time we got there, you two had already gone through,' he said and nodded in the direction of Andrew and Fiona.

'So, what happened?' asked Fiona and looked at Khalil.

Khalil shrugged. 'I was holding on to the rope, waiting for you two to get back when this sleek black corporate looking helicopter arrived over the mountain and landed on the plateau next to the well.

At first, I didn't know what to do, but I was about to reach for my gun when these three gentlemen jumped out pointing their guns at me. Good thing I decided not to resist.'

'Yes,' said Zaki. 'I am glad too. But unfortunately, we were unable to get here fast enough to prevent you from entering the cave. That would have been better.'

'We almost got ourselves killed down there,' said Fiona.

'I am afraid that was the intention of the builders of this place,' replied Zaki. 'It is not for the uninitiated.'

'What were those sand contraptions in the cave anyway,' asked Andrew. 'Was it a burglar alarm?'

'I suppose you could say that,' smiled Zaki. 'The chamber for the Ark was constructed so that only people from the brotherhood would be able to navigate it safely. Each slab was marked to indicate whether they were safe to step on, but you probably did not know that.'

'No, we didn't,' said Fiona. 'We didn't know what to look for, and we were too focused on getting to the cave.'

'Like I said. That is how it was designed,' said Zaki. 'So, in that sense, it worked as planned. Although the original intent was to trap any unwelcome visitor in the cave.'

'So are you saying you would have preferred it if we had been trapped down there,' asked Fiona, looking horrified.

'We have spent a good amount of time monitoring you,' replied Zaki. 'And we do believe that your intentions in this affair are honourable. So, the answer to your question is no. In addition, we also now believe that we need each other.'

'How so?' asked Andrew.

'As I am sure you have worked out,' replied Zaki. 'Whoever is holding Doctor Mansour, is now also on the trail of the Ark or the meteorite. And I am guessing they are more interested in the meteorite than in the Ark. We in the brotherhood are sworn to protect both, and you may be our only way to do so now. We will need to work together.'

'Whoever they are, they now have Jabari Omran's notebook,' said Fiona, looking concerned.

'And they have my friend,' interjected Khalil with a grim look on his face. 'With both him and the notebook in their possession, they might be on their way here right now.'

Doctor Zaki nodded sagely. 'Unlikely,' he said. 'But if they have Omran's notebook, then that is still very bad news indeed. They may not have been able to determine the location of the Ark, but they could conceivably have uncovered the location of the meteorite. We have to hurry.'

'What do you mean?' asked Andrew.

'I will explain later,' said Zaki. 'Right now, we need to get moving.'

He reached inside a pocket and got out his mobile phone, and had a brief conversation with someone on the other end.

'Come with me,' he said and started walking briskly down the ravine towards a large flat area nearer the valley floor below them.

A couple of minutes later the distinctive buffeting sound of helicopter rotor blades could be heard in the distance, and suddenly a black Sikorsky helicopter swooped over the mountain, pitched up to bleed off speed, and then descended rapidly towards them. The noise was deafening, and as the helicopter's wheels touched the ground, a cloud of light brown dust was whirled up into the air around it. They all had to kneel and close their eyes for a few seconds as the rotor blades spun down.

Sitting there with his eyes closed in the noise, the rush of wind and the sensation of sand against his skin, Andrew suddenly felt transported back to Afghanistan, where he and his comrades in arms had been exfiltrated after covert missions almost exactly like this. As the engine revved down and the dust storm abated, he found himself involuntarily reaching for his weapon as he stood up. His hand felt nothing but the shirt on his chest, and he had the uncomfortable feeling of being partly naked.

'Let's go,' shouted Zaki over the engine noise. 'We have to get back to the airport. And we will need your plane to get back to Egypt fast.'

'Ok,' shouted Andrew, and helped Fiona inside the passenger compartment behind the pilots. 'I will make sure it is on stand-by by the time we get there.'

Zaki and his two companions entered the helicopter last, and then it lifted off into the sky and headed over the ridge next to the mountain, and proceeded in a north-easterly direction towards Saint Catherine International Airport.

★ ★ ★

After a flight lasting less than fifteen minutes, the helicopter landed at Saint Catherine International Airport, only a short distance from the Royal Airforce BAe 146-200, which by then was refuelled and ready to depart.

'My men will take the helicopter back to Cairo, where they are needed tomorrow,' said Zaki. 'I will come with you, if you don't mind. I fear that I am only too correct in saying that this is now a race against time.'

'Of course,' said Andrew. 'Just tell us where we need to go.'

The group made their way swiftly aboard the aircraft, and a few minutes later it lifted off from the runway, retracted its landing gear, and headed southwest. Doctor Zaki had asked Andrew to instruct the pilot to take them to Abu Simbel in the far south of Egypt on the border with Sudan. Out of the windows on the left side of the aircraft, they could see the twin peaks of Mount Horeb and Mount Sinai below them. After less than ten minutes in the air, they crossed out over the Gulf of Suez towards southern Egypt.

The four of them we sitting in pairs across from each other, sipping cold drinks and snacking. The dramatic events under Mount Horeb had taken their toll on Andrew and Fiona.

'Ok, so please tell us. Why are we going to Abu Simbel?' asked Andrew.

'Abu Simbel is the final resting place of the meteorite,' replied Doctor Zaki.

'So, you have known where it was this whole time?' asked Fiona.

'Of course,' replied Doctor Zaki. 'It is the very reason our brotherhood exists. To keep that knowledge safe through time.'

'But now you have decided to share it with us,' said Khalil.

'Yes,' replied Zaki. 'The time has come for us to work together.'

'Could I ask you some questions, please?' said Fiona, looking intently at Doctor Zaki.

Zaki nodded. 'Of course.'

'Firstly,' said Fiona. 'When did the meteorite fall, and what happened to it between then and when the Israelites took a piece with them out of Egypt?'

'Well,' said Zaki. 'We do not know for certain when the meteorite hit. All we know is that it happened at some point during the reign of Pharaoh Khufu, so probably around 2570 BCE. The priesthood at that time recovered it, and swiftly covered up what had happened. As you can imagine, such an event, which caused devastation and horrific effects on human beings, was perceived to have the risk of undermining the divine omnipotence of the pharaoh. It is also quite likely that the priesthood was investigating ways to weaponize it, but they never succeeded. So, they hid it and kept the secret so well guarded that it almost disappeared from memory. It wasn't until the Hebrews re-discovered it, with the help of Joseph and his tribe, that a piece was successfully cut from it, and then brought out of Egypt as a weapon.'

'And the Hebrew mercenaries who found it on Elephantine Island then built a temple above the cave where it was hidden?" asked Fiona.

'Exactly,' replied Zaki. 'In fact, some of our brothers from that time were embedded with the Hebrew mercenaries, to ensure that only a small tight-knit group of people knew what was really hidden under the temple.'

'Are you saying that the Jewish temple on Elephantine Island never held the Ark of the Covenant?' asked Andrew.

'It only ever held a replica,' replied Zaki.

'The replica first brought from Jerusalem by Menelik I?' said Fiona.

'Correct,' nodded Zaki.

'What happened to the replica then?' asked Khalil.

'It was destroyed by our brothers along with the temple around 400 BCE when the Persians withdrew from the area, and the Jewish mercenaries were forced to flee.'

'The brotherhood destroyed the replica of the Ark?' asked Fiona perplexed. 'Why would they do that?'

'Yes,' replied Zaki. 'They had to vacate the island quickly once it became clear that the Persians were defeated, and that the Egyptian dynasties were reasserting control over the area. Rather than let a replica of the Ark be captured, and held up as war bounty by the Egyptians, our brothers decided to erase it from history. They knew that the real Ark was hidden safely inside Mount Horeb. And there it has remained ever since, unseen by human eyes. Until today.'

Fiona looked first at Andrew and then at Khalil, and then she bowed her head.

'I somehow feel the urge to apologize for the way we forced our way into the final resting place of the Ark,' she said. 'We had no right to do that.'

'We simply did what we felt we needed to do to try to unravel this mystery,' said Andrew. 'And we also thought it might give us a chance at saving Doctor Mansour.'

'We only spent a few minutes in the cave,' said Fiona. 'And I was about to take pictures of the Ark, but then I just could not bring myself to do it.'

'Why not?' asked Zaki empathetically.

'Because I am just me,' said Fiona, looking up at Doctor Zaki, her eyes welling up. 'It felt way too big for just one person to decide. The implications are too enormous. Who am I to make a decision like that? A decision that will impact billions of people all over this planet? And what possible good would it bring to reveal its location? It would almost certainly create even more strife and division between different religious groups.'

Doctor Zaki nodded. 'You are a wise person, Fiona,' he smiled. 'And I thank you for making the decision you did.'

'I almost wish you had arrived earlier to stop us from going in there,' she smiled.

'Well,' smiled Doctor Zaki. 'We would have stopped you if we had known you were on your way there. We clearly underestimated your abilities, and we were frankly caught off guard by how quickly you were able to connect the dots.'

Fiona nodded. 'We connected the dots, but I am not sure we thought it through.'

'I am at peace with what you did,' continued Doctor Zaki, and leaned forward to look Fiona in the eyes. 'I have discussed this issue many times with my *Malpannah*, my teacher, over the past couple of weeks, and what we have realised is that we here are all on the same side.'

'Which side is that?' asked Andrew.

Doctor Zaki's keen eyes looked at Andrew. 'The side that wants the power of the Ark, and the source of that power, to remain hidden from people who would use it to do ill.'

'I guess you're right, said Andrew and nodded. 'We're on the same team here.'

'Could you perhaps help clear something else up for me,' asked Fiona.

'Certainly, replied Doctor Zaki.

'I would like to ask you about Pharaoh Shishak, or Shoshenq I as he is known, and Jeroboam of the tribe of Ephraim,' said Fiona, taking out her notes from a bag.

Doctor Zaki nodded. 'I thought you might ask me about that,' he said and smiled knowingly. 'As you may have worked out by now, both Shoshenq I and Jeroboam, to whom he provided refuge during the reign of Solomon, were Jewish.'

'Yes,' said Fiona. 'We suspected as much. But were they also part of the Brotherhood of Horeb?'

'They were indeed,' nodded Zaki.

'And Shoshenq was part of the brotherhood because Shoshenq's mother was Hebrew,' said Fiona, her keen eyes looking expectantly at Doctor Zaki.

'That is correct,' replied Zaki. 'And she was also of the House of Joseph, so her family was enmeshed in priestly knowledge, rituals and secrets, and would have had at least some knowledge of the meteorite.'

'Presumably, that knowledge was handed down from her to Shoshenq,' said Fiona. 'And he then hatched the plan with Jeroboam, to retrieve the Ark and the piece of the meteorite that it held, from Jerusalem. It all makes sense now.'

'I must admit to being impressed quite with what you have uncovered,' said Zaki.

Fiona smiled. 'We have had quite a lot of help from Omran's notebook. I think he might have been working on this for years, possibly decades.'

'He is not the first,' said Zaki. 'But he managed to uncover more than we expected.'

'And that is why you decided to reveal yourselves to us at this time,' asked Andrew.

'As I said earlier,' replied Zaki. 'We have come to the conclusion that we need each other now. The brotherhood of Horeb was initially founded to protect the Ark of the Covenant and the secret of its power. The Ark may be the property of the descendants of the Israelites, who now reside in their own nation of Israel, but the Ark itself is of this land. It belongs here in Egypt, where it was made 3000 years ago.'

'And the meteorite?' asked Fiona.

'It is our duty to do the same for the meteorite, replied Zaki. 'We both have the same goal of keeping it safe from people with evil intent. The Ark of the Covenant used to be an insurance policy of sorts for the Israelites, and the Brotherhood was there to make sure that insurance policy was kept safe and available. But those days are long gone now. Times have changed, and the world does not look the way it did all those years ago. All we can do now is try to keep people away from the Ark, and keep the meteorite away from people.'

'We will do whatever we can to assist you,' said Fiona. 'It is the least we can do after what happened inside Mount Horeb.'

'Do you have any idea who is holding Doctor Mansour?' asked Zaki. 'Those people are without a doubt the same people who are looking for the meteorite, and I can guarantee you their intentions are not benign.'

Andrew shook his head. 'None so far,' he replied. 'I have been in regular contact with my people in London, and the British intelligence services are chasing down every lead they have. Still no luck though.'

'I fear that Mansour's kidnappers have been able to piece together more or less as much as you have,' said Zaki, looking concerned. 'Perhaps even a lot more, since they now have both the notebook and Doctor Mansour.'

'Are you saying they might have uncovered the location of the meteorite?' asked Andrew.

'Yes,' replied Zaki. 'May I see the copy of the notebook you made?'

Fiona flicked through the pages and handed Doctor Zaki the page containing the sketch of what she and Khalil believed to be a tomb complex.

'We thought this looked similar to the tombs found in the Valley of Kings near Luxor,' said Khalil.

'But there is a circular chamber at the rear,' said Fiona, 'It does not seem like it is part of the actual complex, and we have never seen a circular chamber in any of the ancient tombs anywhere in Egypt.'

'Do you know what this is?' asked Khalil.

'That,' said Doctor Zaki, 'is the inside of the temple of Queen Nefertari at Abu Simbel, where we are headed right now. And this circular chamber is the location of the meteorite.'

The three others sat stunned for a few seconds, staring at Doctor Zaki.

'Could someone please explain to me what Abu Simbel is?' asked Andrew sounding frustrated, and looking first at Doctor Zaki, then at Khalil and finally at Fiona.

Fiona smiled and looked at him. 'Abu Simbel is one of the most famous sites in Egypt. It is a huge tourist attraction, and it sits on the western bank of the Nile less than thirty kilometres from Sudan in the far south of Egypt. It has two huge temples cut directly into the rock, originally built to demonstrate the power of the pharaoh to the Nubian people right there on the very edge of the Egyptian kingdom.'

'Which pharaoh was that?' asked Andrew.

'Ramesses II, whose temple we visited in Luxor,' replied Fiona. 'He is also quite aptly called Ramesses the Great. As king of the 19th dynasty, he was one of the most prolific builders in the history of ancient Egypt, and he constructed a number of impressive temples across the kingdom from the Nile delta all the way down to Nubia, almost a thousand kilometres to the south.'

'Impressive,' said Andrew. 'So, when exactly were these Abu Simbel temples built?'

'Our best guess is that construction started in 1264 BCE, and lasted around twenty years,' said Doctor Zaki. 'But these are all estimates. They could be off by several years.'

'But that is pretty much exactly during the period when the Israelites were supposed to have been enslaved,' said Andrew. 'Just before Exodus.'

'Indeed,' said Doctor Zaki. 'So, they would almost certainly have had intimate knowledge of the interior of the temples.'

'Are you suggesting that the Israelites built a secret circular chamber at the back of the temple of Nefertari?' asked Fiona.

'According to our legends, yes,' said Doctor Zaki. 'It is no longer clear if the chamber was originally intended for the meteorite, but it is a possibility.'

'So, is this where the meteorite is hidden now?' asked Andrew, placing a finger on the circular shape on the sketch, and looking at Doctor Zaki.

'Yes,' nodded Zaki. 'It was eventually placed there by the brotherhood to keep it safe.'

'Wait a minute,' said Fiona. 'Are you saying this extremely dangerous highly radioactive meteorite is inside a temple that has hundreds of visitors every day? That is madness!'

'No,' smiled Doctor Zaki. 'The meteorite is inside a secret chamber at the back of the *original* temple, which is now sixty-five meters below the surface of the Nile.'

Once again, Andrew and Fiona glanced at each other, both of them looking decidedly perplexed. But Khalil smiled and nodded.

'Oh,' he said. 'I understand now. The dam.'

'What on earth are you talking about?' said Fiona. 'Where is the meteorite?'

'Let me explain,' said Doctor Zaki. 'Before the construction of the Aswan High Dam was even initiated in 1960, it was clear that the temples of Abu Simbel would eventually end up being flooded by tens of meters of water, once the soon to be created Lake Nasser had been filled. As a result, UNESCO set up an international consortium to relocate the temples to higher ground.'

'They moved the temples?' asked Fiona. 'I had no idea. Even I thought they had been there for millennia.'

Doctor Zaki smiled. 'Almost everyone does. It is not really something Egyptian tourism authorities tend to talk about. But yes, the temples were moved some seventy meters up onto the mountainside facing the Nile at that location. It was a major operation that took several years. The many fifteen-meter-high statues of Ramesses II and Nefertari were cut into pieces, relocated and then reassembled again. The same was true for the temple interiors. Everything was dismantled, logged, and then faithfully put back together much higher on the mountain.'

'That is amazing,' said Andrew. 'So, the original temple sites are now underwater?'

'That is correct,' said Doctor Zaki. 'The Lake Nasser reservoir was only completely filled by 1976, but Abu Simbel has been flooded ever since the late

1960s when the rising water table caused by the dam had finally reached the entire two hundred kilometres south along the Nile to the Abu Simbel site. So, over the course of roughly a decade, the old temple site containing the meteorite ended up deeper and deeper underneath lake Nasser.'

'And the meteorite was moved inside its chamber before the water rose?' asked Fiona. 'How? And why was it moved from Elephantine Island to Abu Simbel?'

'For the same reason we are sitting here today,' replied Doctor Zaki. 'Elephantine Island is just on the other side of the Aswan High Dam, and at the time it was not clear what effect the dam might have on the Nile river further to the north. They could not rule out that Elephantine Island would be at least partially flooded, potentially resulting in massive radioactive contamination of the Nile river, which would probably have killed thousands of people along the towns and cities along its banks. So out of an abundance of caution, the brotherhood decided to relocate the meteorite to a place where it could never again pose a threat to humans, and where it would be impossible to retrieve it.'

'Under sixty-five meters of water in a hidden chamber inside a mountain,' said Fiona.

'Precisely,' nodded Doctor Zaki. 'My own father and uncle were part of that precarious operation. My father was an engineer and my uncle was a surveyor, and they had managed to insert themselves into the huge UNESCO team responsible for the relocation of the temples at Abu Simbel. This allowed them to arrange for the relocation of the meteorite to the secret chamber inside Queen Nefertari's temple. The operation was carried out at night towards the very end of the project, and was only made possible because they had access to all the heavy equipment that had been used to transport the disassembled pieces of the statues, which weighed up to thirty tonnes each.'

'That's an incredible tale,' said Fiona. 'I can't believe they were able to pull that off. Presumably, they sealed the meteorite safely inside the chamber before the water rose?'

'They did,' said Doctor Zaki. 'The chamber at the back of the temple was closed off and completely sealed using modern construction techniques, including a waterproof resin used as a coating on the concrete that was inserted to block the water from reaching the chamber. If that were ever to happen, the radioactive contamination would eventually make its way to the cities of Aswan, Luxor, Cairo and every other populated area along the Nile. It would represent to Egypt what blood poisoning would mean for the human body.'

'So why are we here then?' asked Andrew. 'If the meteorite is safely locked away behind granite, concrete and millions of tonnes of water, how could our adversaries possibly get to it?'

'Because of an oversight during the operation to relocate the meteorite,' replied Doctor Zaki, looking uncomfortable with what he was about to say.

'An oversight?' asked Khalil. 'What kind of oversight?'

'After we had sealed the chamber in 1967, we needed to be able to resin-coat both sides of the concrete wall built to hold back the water. That meant we had to have someone on the inside after the wall was built.'

'Oh,' said Khalil. 'I see. And you had to create a way to get that person out again.'

'Zaki nodded. 'Actually, it was a team of people with various types of equipment. So, we had to drill a borehole from the surface sixty-five meters down into the bedrock, until it reached the chamber.'

'Are you saying that borehole is still there?' asked Andrew.

'Yes,' nodded Zaki. 'It was sealed with a huge granite slab at the top, but in hindsight, we should have filled up the entire thing with cement and closed it off for good. But our brothers at that time never imagined that anyone would find the borehole and actually try to access the chamber, not least because as far as they knew, no one else outside of the brotherhood even knew it existed.'

'So how big is this borehole,' asked Andrew.

'It is roughly one-and-a-half meters across,' replied Zaki.

'But sixty-five meters deep?' asked Fiona. 'And at the bottom of it is a chamber containing an absolutely lethal radioactive source. Sounds utterly terrifying. You're not suggesting that we have to go down there, are you?'

'It depends on what we find when we get there,' replied Zaki. 'Our adversaries, terrorists or whatever they are, might have got there before us. When you said that they now have Omran's notebook, I immediately began to worry that they were already ahead of us. We have to try to prevent them from accessing that chamber. We must do this at any cost, and fast.'

Andrew, Fiona and Khalil sat in their seats in silence for a few moments, trying to process what they had been told.

Fiona then glanced at Zaki. 'Doctor Zaki,' she said. 'May I ask you a personal question?'

Doctor Zaki looked up at her. 'Of course.'

'Do you consider yourself a man of faith?' asked Fiona.

'Well,' smiled Doctor Zaki, leaning back in his seat and looking up at the ceiling of the cabin. 'The honest answer is no. But that has no bearing on the responsibility that has been placed on me as a member of the brotherhood. My responsibility is to the protection of the secret of the meteorite and its lethal powers. And that has nothing to do with faith. What I do in that capacity, I do for the history and legacy of the Jewish people, my forefathers, who lived in ancient Egypt all those years ago.'

'I understand,' nodded Fiona. 'I was just wondering about it, since in some respects the mystery of the Ark is no longer a mystery to you and your brothers. And any notion of divinity must surely be removed from this picture, as far as you are concerned.'

'You are right in some ways,' replied Zaki. 'I do not believe in deities, and I do not believe that Moses brought anything down from Mount Horeb, except perhaps his thoughts about what was needed from the Israelites if they were to stand a chance of making it through the long trip back to Canaan.'

'You're talking about laws,' said Fiona.

'Laws, ethics, morals, a sense of community and common purpose,' replied Khalil. 'All the things that such a disparate group of exiles would have needed in order to survive as a people, possibly under extreme pressure from the environment and whatever other threats that might have faced them on their journey.'

'So, the Ten Commandments could have been a real thing, as far as you're concerned?' asked Fiona.

'They could very well have been,' nodded Zaki. 'In fact, it is very likely that something like the Ten Commandments were produced by Moses, or someone like him, probably based on existing ancient Egyptian laws.'

'But you don't think there was any divine intervention in their creation?' asked Fiona.

'No. Not at all,' replied Zaki. 'They represent some of the best but also most universal rules that any society could apply, in order to maintain moral unity, cohesion, and law and order, irrespective of time and place. In those laws are embedded truths about what it means to be a group of humans here on this planet, and trying to make a society function in a way that works and that also feels right and fair to all its members.'

'And the meteorite?' asked Fiona. 'How do you see that in this context?'

Doctor Zaki smiled. 'It was just a meteorite. A very unusual meteorite of course, but still. It was just a collection of atoms created somewhere in this universe, in the same way that this earth was created. They were ultimately made in the same way that the atoms that constitute your body and mine were made. Everything comes from the same beginning, whether it be rocks or water or plants or human beings. We are all made of the same things, and we come from the same place. And one day when we die, in some sense we return to that place.'

'That is a beautiful way of looking at it,' smiled Fiona.

'But trust me,' smiled Doctor Zaki. 'Divine power or not. The notion of the meteorite representing the power of the Heavens over the Earth is not lost on me. And I am not at all surprised that it was perceived as a divine power five thousand years ago.'

'But you seem to be saying that the Brotherhood of Horeb has moved on from this notion?' said Fiona.

'Yes,' nodded Zaki. 'You could say that. The brotherhood of today understands only too well that this is no divine power, and that we are charged with protecting a very explainable, but still extremely powerful and dangerous phenomenon. Our duty to protect it and keep it safe from people who would use it against others is no less important now than it was when the acolytes of Moses first discovered it and founded our brotherhood.'

'Well,' said Fiona and nodded sagely. 'I guess there is nothing we can do except get to the borehole and try to make sure it stays shut forever.'

'I am glad to have you on our side,' smiled Doctor Zaki. 'I wish I could have been more open with you when we first met, but I am sure you understand why that was not possible.'

'Of course,' smiled Fiona. 'The important thing is that we're on the same team now.'

'I might be able to call in assistance from London,' said Andrew. 'Depending on what we find there.'

'Ok,' said Zaki. 'Let's just hope we won't need it,'

Thirty-Two

The sun was setting as the aircraft began its descent just over fifty kilometres out from Abu Simbel Airport. The airport sits on a large flat rocky promontory on the western bank of the Nile. The promontory used to be the top of a plateau high above the Nile valley, but it is now only a few meters above Lake Nasser. The airport itself is surrounded by the town of Abu Simbel, and is connected to the rest of Egypt by Highway 75 which runs north through the desert to Aswan almost three hundred kilometres downstream.

The aircraft was heading almost due south over Lake Nasser, and then performed a long right turn to come in towards the runway in a north-westerly direction. As it banked, its passengers could see the Abu Simbel temples out of the windows on their right. The temples sit on the eastern side of what is now an artificial island in Lake Nasser, connected by a dual carriageway to the mainland and Abu Simbel town.

As soon as the aircraft had come to a stop on its parking apron and its engines had begun spinning down, the door swung open and a ladder came down to let the four passengers disembark.

'I have taken the liberty of arranging for a car,' said Doctor Zaki, and gestured towards a light brown Jeep Wrangler. It had large wide tyres and a winch mounted over the front bumper, and on its side were written the words *Abu Simbel Maintenance*.

He walked over to the powerful looking vehicle and opened the rear door.

'Please put these on,' he said and retrieved a box of clothes, placing it on the tarmac next to the car. 'We are going to a maintenance building next to the temple complex, and we need to look like we have a legitimate reason to be at the site. I hope the sizes fit well enough.'

Andrew pulled out a one-piece boiler suit the same colour as the Jeep, held it out in front of him and turned it over to look at the text on the back of it.

'Abu Simbel Maintenance Crew,' he read aloud. Then he shrugged and began putting it on. 'I guess that will work.'

After a couple of minutes, they had all donned their boiler suits and got ready to enter the Jeep.

'Mine is a bit baggy,' smiled Fiona.

'It will be fine,' said Doctor Zaki. 'As long as no one gets too close, we are going to be fine. The temple site is just about to close for today, so people will be focussing on getting their last photos before they have to leave.'

'Will we be able to access the site after dark?' asked Khalil.

'Whenever we like,' said Doctor Zaki, and held up an official-looking badge. 'Remember, we were involved in this project since 1960, and we still have several people working on the inside, to help monitor the site.'

Doctor Zaki got into the driver's seat, and the rest followed him, with Khalil next to him, and Andrew and Fiona in the rear passenger seats. Just in case they got held up, it would be better to have two people who look like locals sitting in the front seats. Andrew and Fiona donned their light brown caps and pulled them down as far as possible in front of their faces.

Then they set off and drove out of the airport complex, turning left for the short two-kilometre drive down to the temples.

'Doctor Zaki,' said Fiona. 'Can I ask you if your presence as a researcher at the Nuclear Research Center at Inshas is part of your work for the Brotherhood of Horeb?'

'Very much so,' replied Zaki and nodded. 'In fact, it is more or less the only reason I am there. I never planned for it during my studies, but when the opportunity arose, it was an obvious choice. It allows me to be close to nuclear research in Egypt, whether for military or civilian purposes, and it gives the brotherhood a way of monitoring and staying current on these issues.'

Khalil turned to look at Zaki. 'I can't quite believe that all of these things have been going on in our country for this long, he said. 'I would never have guessed that this sort of thing was real. While I was taking my exams at Cairo University as a young man, you were probably being introduced to the brotherhood and the history of your family. And probably at a young age too, I would imagine.'

Doctor Zaki smiled. 'I know. It must seem surreal to discover this, but it is and always has been very real to us. For me personally, it has always just been the way things were. My father was in the brotherhood, although I did not know this until I was a young man, and so was my grandfather and his father before him.'

'It must give you a certain perspective on life,' said Fiona intrigued. 'Being part of something so important that is stretching over such a long period of time, while the rest of us are squabbling about who said what last week, and who ended up getting upset.'

Doctor Zaki smiled and tilted his head slightly to one side. 'When you put it like that, yes. It is a different kind of existence, that is true. But there is also a certain loneliness to it. We carry this burden, but often we are not permitted to reveal it or share it with important people in our lives.'

'I understand, said Fiona. 'I would find it near impossible to keep something like that to myself.'

'Well,' said Zaki. 'As much as we have worked to keep our existence a secret, I am glad to have all three of you with us now when it really counts.'

Khalil placed a hand on Doctor Zaki's shoulder. 'I am sure I speak for all of us when I say, we won't let you down.'

The Jeep zoomed over the short land bridge to the artificial island where the temples are located and headed past the hotels, restaurant and shops towards the side gate to the temple complex.

'Khalil is right.' said Andrew. 'We will do whatever it takes to assist you.'

'Thank you,' replied Doctor Zaki.

'The people who are holding Doctor Mansour,' said Fiona. 'What could they do with the meteorite if they got their hands on it?'

'It is difficult to guess what their intention might be,' replied Zaki, as he brought the car to a stop in front of the large metal gate. 'But I for one do not feel like putting that to the test.'

He rolled down the driver's side window and reached out to present the access badge to the scanner.

There was a short beep, and then the heavy gates parted in the middle and slid back to allow their vehicle to enter the large flat open area to the north of the temple complex. Doctor Zaki put the Wrangler back into gear and drove through the gates, which then closed behind them.

'It is important to understand this,' said Zaki. 'The radioactive material inside the meteorite is not in itself anywhere near enough to use in a nuclear bomb. It is not nearly concentrated enough. It would have to be separated out and enriched many times over to reach a level of purity where it could be used as fissile material.'

'You mean in the same way that uranium is centrifuged to purify it for weaponisation,' said Andrew.

'Exactly,' replied Zaki. 'But it is possible that it could be used in what is called a *dirty bomb*, which is a conventional explosion, laced with radioactive material. Or it could perhaps be used to contaminate the water supply of major cities or even an entire country.'

'Either way,' said Khalil. 'We need to make sure that never happens.'

Doctor Zaki drove the Jeep along a narrow track, that had the rocky hills that the temples had been cut into on the right, and the Nile River just a couple of meters away on the left. The track curved round to the right, to an open area with a couple of trees and a small number of non-descript windowless service buildings.

The sun was setting beyond the hills of the western bank of the Nile, when Zaki parked the Jeep between two trees next to the shed around thirty meters from the river bank.

'Here we are,' said Zaki, and stopped the Jeep next to what looked like a prefab concrete maintenance shed located just off the temple site to the south. 'It doesn't look like anyone else has been here.'

It was still very warm, and the air felt heavy as they exited the vehicle. As they stepped out, they looked to any casual observer like just another maintenance crew, but the few people who were still on the temple site were all making their way towards the exit on the west side of the complex and were not paying them any attention.

To the south, they could see both of the enormous temples appearing to have been cut into the fifty-meter tall rockface. At the far end of the site, around one hundred and fifty meters away, was the temple of Ramesses II, with its four giant statues of the pharaoh lining the outside, and the entrance to the temple interior through a tall doorway in the middle.

Less than fifty meters from the shed was Queen Nefertari's temple, similarly designed with statues of her in all her glory on the outside and an entrance in the middle. Both temples towered some thirty meters above the ground, and all the statues were easily twenty meters tall.

'Spectacular,' said Fiona. 'I can't believe this isn't the location they were built in. They look so at home here.'

'Great care was taken to recreate both the temples and their surroundings,' said Zaki. 'What you see there are not actually real hills and rockface. They are artificial hills, with giant concrete domes inside them. They were designed to hold the weight of the hills above, and to create a space inside where the reconstructed temple interiors could be housed.'

'That is an incredible feat of engineering,' said Fiona.

'Where were they located before?' asked Andrew and looked towards the river bank.

'Down there,' said Doctor Zaki, pointing down to the ground at roughly a forty-five-degree angle towards the water's edge. 'Sixty-five meters below the surface of the Nile is where the original temple site was for more than three thousand years. It's hard to believe standing here, even for me, but we are standing almost directly above the sealed-off circular chamber at the back of the original temple of Nefertari.'

'And where is the borehole?' asked Andrew.

'In there,' said Zaki and pointed at the concrete shed next to them.

The shed had no windows and was approximately four by six meters. It had a single access point through a large set of double doors made of metal and painted dark grey. Across the doors was written in large capital letters, *DANGER. HIGH VOLTAGE.*

Zaki walked over to the doors and reached into his pocket for a large key.

'Shit,' he said suddenly, in a hushed voice. 'We've had visitors.'

Andrew immediately reached inside his boiler suit on his left side and pulled out his gun. In one quick seamless move, he checked the chamber and pulled back the slide to load a bullet from the magazine. Khalil also pulled out his gun.

Zaki turned to the other three and spoke in a hushed voice. 'The lock has been cut through. Looks like some sort of blowtorch or metal cutter. It is completely cold, so it happened a while ago.'

Andrew and Khalil knelt down in front of the shed and trained their weapons on the large red doors, while Fiona took cover behind the Jeep.

'On three,' said Andrew.

Zaki got out his own gun, nodded and whispered. 'One... Two... Three!'

He then pulled open the double doors and threw himself to the side on the ground. The rusty hinges gave a loud drawn-out metallic creak as they swung open.

The shed was almost completely empty, except for some ceramic high voltage electrical insulator coils hanging in a rack on one of the walls.

Andrew and Khalil lowered their guns.

'Clear,' said Andrew. 'I guess they're gone.'

'Yes, but where to?' said Khalil.

'No idea,' replied Andrew and looked at Zaki who was dusting himself down. 'Was this a power substation?' he asked. 'There's nothing in here.'

'That's what we would like people to believe,' said Zaki and walked to the far end of the building.

He then knelt down to a small hinged metal plate in the concrete floor. It had a heavy padlock on it.

'This one has also been cut,' said Zaki.

He then flicked open the metal plate, to reveal a very thick rusty looking metal ring, embedded into the concrete. He stood up, took a couple of steps back, whilst looking around on the floor.

'I think they might have been able to open this already,' said Zaki.

'Open what?' asked Fiona who had joined them inside the shed.

Doctor Zaki motioned to the back third of the floor in the shed. 'This whole section of the floor has an angled side facing the doors, so with the use of a winch, it can be slid up and over onto the section next to it. The borehole is underneath there.'

Andrew knelt down next to the metal ring embedded into the concrete slab.

'It looks like there has been a cable attached to it,' said Andrew. 'I can see clean shiny metal on the inside of the ring where the rust has been scraped off.'

'This is bad,' said Zaki. 'That means they have almost certainly already been down there. But there is no way of knowing when. It could have been several days ago, or it could have been this morning.'

'Could they still be down there?' asked Fiona, looking decidedly nervous.

'No,' replied Zaki and shook his head. 'They would never have pulled the slab back into place whilst any of their men were down there. The question is whether they have already managed to extract all or part of the meteorite through the borehole.'

'Would that even be possible?' asked Andrew.

'With enough men, the right equipment for cutting, and sufficient radiation shielding, it could probably be done in a day or so,' replied Zaki.

'We have to go down there then,' said Andrew resolutely. 'It's the only way to be sure. And we have to do it right now. If they haven't yet extracted any material from the meteorite, they will be coming back soon to do so.'

Zaki nodded with a grim look on his face. 'Yes. There's no other way. But someone has to stay up here to operate the winch.'

'Khalil, I think it should be you,' said Andrew.

Khalil nodded. 'Ok,' he said, sounding surprisingly calm and focused.

'We need someone up top who can handle a gun,' continued Andrew. 'So, Zaki and I will go down first to make sure it is clear, and we might need Fiona to come down too.'

'Me?' said Fiona, looking worried and sounding increasingly nervous. 'Is it even safe? I mean, there's a huge lethally dangerous radioactive meteorite down there, for God's sake.'

'It is safe,' said Zaki. 'Provided they haven't removed the radiation shielding. When the meteorite was placed there in 1967, it was encased in a steel box, with thick plates of lead mounted on the outside. The lead plates are ten centimetres thick, so they will absorb any gamma radiation coming from the meteorite.'

Fiona swallowed nervously. 'I will have to take your word for it, I guess.'

'Good,' said Andrew. 'Everyone ready?'

They all nodded their agreement, and then Zaki started to walk towards the Jeep. He got in, started the engine and repositioned the car so that its front was almost inside the shed. Then he locked the large wheels to prevent the car from moving when operating the winch. He then jumped out and walked round to the winch. Here he grabbed the hook that was attached to the steel wire and walked over to the metal ring embedded in the concrete, and then he attached the hook.

Less than a minute later, the heavy concrete slab had been pulled free and was lying on top of the one next to it. The slab probably weighed several hundred kilos, but the Wrangler was more than capable of pulling it up and onto the slab next to it.

Where the slab had been, the borehole was covered by an old wooden grate, which looked like it had seen better days.

'Careful now,' said Zaki. 'These pieces of wood are the only thing between you and a sixty-five-meter drop.'

He carefully lifted the grate off the borehole, to reveal a black pit just over two meters wide.

'We will need these when we get down there,' he said and took out a handful of green military issue glow sticks.

He handed one to each of the other three and then bent his own glow stick until it cracked with the sound of a handful of spaghetti being broken in half.

They all stood around the borehole when Zaki held the glow stick out towards the centre of it, and then let go.

The green glow appeared to get brighter as soon as the glow stick fell down into the darkness, and as it tumbled end over end on its way down, it lit up the sides of the borehole in its eerie green light.

The glow stick seemed to fall for an eternity until it suddenly seemed to jerk to one side and then come to an abrupt stop.

'Twenty-two seconds,' said Andrew. 'That fits with around sixty-five meters. If one of us falls in there, they'll be going over a hundred kilometres per hour by the time they hit the bottom.'

'That is an awfully long way down,' said Fiona looking anxious.

Doctor Zaki placed a hand gently on her shoulder. 'Perhaps you should go down first with Andrew. The winch can easily handle the weight of the two of you. Then I can join you afterwards.'

Fiona nodded, looking hopeful. 'I really would prefer that,' she said.

'Alright,' said Andrew. 'Let's do it that way.'

Zaki unhooked the winch wire from the concrete slab and brought it over to the borehole. He then placed a heavy steel beam across the centre of the hole and arranged the steel wire to run over it in the centre of the hole. This would allow them to descend down through the middle of the borehole.

'I need someone to get ready to extend the winch,' he said. 'The wire is easily long enough to reach the bottom.'

'I will do it,' said Khalil and walked over to the front of the Jeep.

'There are a set of harnesses in the back of the Jeep,' said Zaki. 'Please strap them on.'

Andrew and Fiona did as he asked, and then handed Zaki a harness of his own. They spent a couple of minutes checking the straps and latches on each other's harnesses.

Then Andrew and Fiona sat down next to each other by the steel beam, their lower legs over the edge and hanging into the borehole.

'We will use our torches to signal to each other,' said Zaki and looked at Andrew. 'I am assuming both you and Khalil know Morse code?'

Both men nodded. 'Affirmative,' replied Andrew.

'Also,' continued Zaki. 'The borehole comes down into a small ante-chamber, which then connects to the large circular main chamber where the meteorite is kept. Make sure to use your Geiger counter before entering the main chamber. We can't rule out our adversaries having been down there already, and who knows what they are up to. Better safe than sorry.'

'Ok,' nodded Andrew. Then he looked Fiona in the eyes. 'Ready?' he asked.

Fiona took a deep breath and exhaled slowly. 'Ok,' she finally said, seeming to steel herself against what was about to unfold. 'I am ready. Let's do this.'

Both of their harnesses were hooked onto the steel wire, but Fiona still held on tightly to Andrew, as they gently lowered themselves down, let go of the edge and ended up dangling in the middle of the borehole just under the steel beam. They kept swaying back and forth a few times like a pendulum until they lost the initial momentum. Andrew steadied them further by grabbing onto the steel beam above them.

'Final check,' said Zaki. 'All set?'

'All set,' replied Andrew, and looked at Khalil. 'Let's go.'

Khalil engaged the winch at its slowest setting, and the wire extended from the turning wheel at the front of the Jeep, Andrew and Fiona started to descend into the borehole.

'All good?' called Zaki to them after the first five meters.'

'Yep,' replied Andrew loud enough for Zaki to hear. 'We can go a bit faster.'

Zaki nodded at Khalil, who nudged up the speed of the winch slightly.

'Good luck,' called Zaki. 'I will join you as soon as you are down.'

From then on, Andrew and Fiona were on their own. The glow from their glow sticks and the light from their torches lit up a small area around them as they descended. After twenty seconds, Fiona made the mistake of looking up. By then, the top of the borehole was a tiny bright circle of light high above them. She suddenly felt very claustrophobic.

'Andy,' she whispered. 'I really don't think I am cut out for this.'

'You'll be fine,' said Andrew calmly. 'This wire could hold the weight of fifty people, and we are in the safe hands of Khalil and Zaki. Just breathe calmly, and we'll be down in no time at all.'

As it turned out, it took them almost a minute to reach the bottom of the borehole. It felt a lot longer than that, and by the time Fiona noticed the green glow from the glow stick lying at the bottom of the borehole, she was almost ready to unhook her harness from the wire, just so that it could be over with.

As they came down the final few meters, Andrew brought out his gun, pointing it in the direction of the floor below them and then at the doorway leading into the circular main chamber. There was no sign of anyone else, so Andrew brought out his torch and signalled to Doctor Zaki to stop the winch. Then they unhooked themselves and signalled for the winch to be pulled back up. Khalil now clearly let the winch run as fast as it could, because the hook and the wire went flying up through the borehole towards the top.

Andrew then motioned for Fiona to take cover next to one of the walls adjacent to the main chamber, while he brought out his Geiger counter. As he swept the room, the device picked up radiation levels that were clearly higher than background radiation levels, but they were nowhere close to dangerous.

'All clear,' he said to Fiona. 'The readings are within safe limits.'

Andrew had shone his torch onto his body whilst unfastening the hook from his harness, so it took his eyes a few seconds to readjust to the darkness. When they finally did, he spotted it immediately. Inside the circular room, less than five meters away, was what looked like a large metal box with reinforced corners and edges, and an intricate pattern of smaller square plates covering the entire outside of it all the way around.

'This is it,' breathed Andrew amazed. 'This is the actual meteorite, and all those small plates must be the lead pieces making up the radiation shielding.'

Fiona poked her head around the corner to have a look for herself. 'It looks ominous to me. Are you sure that thing is working correctly?' she said and pointed at the Geiger counter.

'If it wasn't, we would probably be dead already,' said Andrew matter-of-factly.

'Great,' said Fiona sarcastically. 'You really know how to cheer me up.'

Andrew did a quick but careful sweep of the perimeter of the circular chamber, and then returned to Fiona near the doorway.

'There is nothing in here except that box,' he said and gestured towards the large dark grey cuboid in the centre of the room.

It was approximately four meters long and three meters wide, with a height of around two meters.

'This thing is huge,' said Fiona. 'Does it look like anyone has tried to tamper with it?'

'Not as far as I can see,' replied Andrew. 'We should wait for Zaki though. He will be able to tell.'

Just then, several small pebbles smacked into the sand on the floor of the antechamber, producing short hard thuds. Someone was coming down the borehole.

Andrew stepped just inside the antechamber and quickly leaned in so that he could look up towards the top of the hole. He could see the silhouette of a person coming down towards them. The person had a green glow stick attached to his belt.

'It's Zaki,' said Andrew. 'He's almost down.'

A few moments later, Zaki was able to place his feet on the ground inside the antechamber, and then unhook himself from the steel wire.

He stepped through the doorway to the main chamber, holding out his own Geiger counter in front of him.

'Mine is showing very little radiation,' said Andrew. 'Yours?'

'The same,' replied Zaki and slipped the device back into his pocket. 'There has been no contamination, and the shielding looks intact. I don't think anyone has been down here yet, but we need to check.'

'What do you mean?' asked Fiona. 'You are not going to open the box, are you?'

'No,' said Zaki. 'The box is constructed by four large lead-covered steel sections, and those sections are held together by clasps on the corners. But if you look closely, there is a small hatch on the top of the lid, which was included in the design in order for us to at least have the ability to monitor the radiation levels inside the box without taking it apart.'

'But the half-lives of these radioactive isotopes are hundreds of thousands of years, aren't they?' asked Andrew. 'That would make it meaningless to monitor this thing on any normal human time scale.'

'That is true for some of the isotopes, but not all of them,' replied Zaki. 'Some of them have much shorter half-lives, so their radiation output changes measurably over say a decade. These changes over time allow us to guess at the composition of the meteorite, which in turn allows us to produce educated guesses about how long it might remain a threat to life.'

'It is still in the region of many thousands of years, right?' asked Fiona.

'Yes,' replied Zaki. 'This thing is extremely old, yet still highly radioactive, so it will remain dangerous for thousands of generations to come. All the more reason for us to understand it better.'

'I am starting to understand the time scales you in the brotherhood are operating on,' said Fiona.

'Anyway,' said Zaki and looked at Andrew. 'Do you see that mark on the ceiling above the hatch? Please point your Geiger counter at it. I am going to pull on this lever here on the side of the box, and the hatch will open. If the meteorite is still inside, we will be able to see it.'

'Wait,' exclaimed Fiona. 'Isn't this dangerous?'

'No,' said Zaki. 'Not at all. The radiation will only exit the box through that narrow hatch, and because it is directional, it will simply go vertically up and hit the ceiling. But if you point your Geiger counter at it, you should be able to see the reading jump on your display when it happens.'

'Alright,' said Andrew, and pointed his Geiger counter at the small mark above the box. 'I am ready.'

'I will only open it for a couple of seconds,' said Zaki. 'That will be more than enough for us to confirm whether the meteorite is still inside.'

'Okay,' said Andrew. 'I am ready.'

Thirty-Three

Doctor Zaki grabbed the small lever firmly with both hands, and then pulled it towards him.

As the small hatch snapped open, a distinct blue glow instantly emanated from the hole in the huge lead-covered steel box. It shone directly up onto the mark on the ceiling. As the blue light shone from the hatch hole, Fiona could have sworn that she heard a faint cracking or popping sound coming from somewhere. Less than two seconds later, Zaki pushed the lever forward again, and the hatch closed.

'We have our answer,' said Doctor Zaki. 'The meteorite is definitely still there.'

'Bloody hell,' said Andrew. 'My readings just went wild. What the devil is that thing?'

'We are still not entirely sure,' said Doctor Zaki. 'Many of the metals in the meteorite are well-known isotopes, but there are several which we have never seen before here on Earth. Nothing we have found in nature fits the profile, and neither do isotopes created artificially in particle accelerators. They are genuinely unknown, which also means that we have no way of determining characteristics such as half-life. Except of course to wait and observe.

'What about the blue light?' asked Andrew.

'The blue glow is the radioactive isotopes ionising the air, thereby making it glow. It is the same principle that applies to numbers on a wristwatch that glows in the dark. That happens because of the isotope called radium. But in the case of this meteorite, it is obviously on a scale that is orders of magnitude more powerful.'

'So, what do we do now?' asked Fiona. 'The meteorite is still here, but this location is clearly compromised. Whoever has both Doctor Mansour and Omran's notebook, have clearly been able to force Mansour to work out this location. They will definitely be back.'

'Yes,' replied Doctor Zaki. 'There is only one thing to do, and that is to seal the borehole once and for all. If I had a fleet of cement trucks ready, I would be doing it right now. We need to come up with a different solution fast.'

'Explosives might do the trick,' said Andrew. 'Set off a series of them all along the length of the borehole, and the entire thing should come crashing down.'

'That might be our best option,' replied Zaki. 'Even if it would create an enormous amount of noise and attention.'

At that moment, a pebble landed with a loud thud on the floor in the antechamber. Then another, and then several more.

'What the hell?' said Andrew. 'Is Khalil coming down?'

'No,' said Zaki. 'It can't be him. Someone has to hold the buttons down on the winch controls in order to make it work.'

Andrew yanked out his gun and moved swiftly and purposefully towards the antechamber with the gun gripped in both hands and pointing down towards the ground in front of him. He quickly stepped into the antechamber, swung his gun up and pointed it towards the top of the hole. He immediately spotted two men wearing what looked like tactical combat gear being lowered down through the borehole. In that instant, several shots were fired from what sounded like submachine guns. The bullets smacked into the ground right next to Andrew's feet, and he immediately threw himself backwards inside the main chamber.

'Take cover,' he yelled and sprinted towards the back of the cave behind the steel box.

Fiona and Zaki were already behind the box, and Andrew had just managed to throw himself down behind it when the first flashbang went off. The non-lethal grenade was designed to produce an extremely loud noise along with a blinding flash of light, in order to disorientate opponents. It exploded just as it hit the ground in the antechamber. A couple of seconds later another one went off, momentarily lighting up the cave in brilliant white light.

Andrew knew to keep his eyes closed and hold his hands over his ears, but both Fiona and Zaki had been caught out by it. They both yelled in pain and fell to the ground, pressing their eyes closed and holding their hands over their ears. But it was too late. In most cases flashbangs simply cause disorientation, but the sheer sensory overload they can produce can also result in nausea and vomiting. Both Fiona and Zaki were now effectively incapacitated.

The men seemed to be highly trained soldiers from the way they had moved and fired, and Andrew knew he had to act fast. Just as he removed his hands from his ears, he heard the sound of heavy boots landing on the ground in the antechamber. He realised this was his chance to move, so he jumped up behind the steel box and aimed his gun towards the antechamber. He could only see one of the soldiers and immediately fired two shots at him. They both connected with the body armour on his torso and made him stagger backwards, but only for a couple of seconds. The soldier quickly regained his footing and returned fire. Bullets whizzed over Andrew's head and slammed into the wall behind him. Several of them were stopped by the lead on the box they were using as cover.

'Fuck,' said Andrew through gritted teeth. The soldiers were wearing heavy body armour, probably Kevlar.

As soon as the soldier stopped firing, Andrew jumped back up and fired several rounds in the direction of the antechamber. He did not have time to aim, but caught sight of the two soldiers and now a third coming down the steel wire to join his two comrades.

Doctor Zaki was regaining his ability to see and hear, and as soon as he did so, he rose from cover and fired several shots himself, all of which missed. Fiona was sitting on the ground, leaning against the steel box, holding her hands over her ears. She was terrified and completely overwhelmed by what was unfolding around her. Zaki ducked down again.

When Andrew stood back up to fire again, the three soldiers were moving through the doorway and into the main chamber. He fired several times, before having to take cover again as the three heavily armed soldiers returned fire.

'We need a plan fast,' shouted Andrew as he slammed a fresh magazine into his gun. 'If they have grenades, we are dead.'

Zaki was kneeling on the ground, holding his gun with both hands. He lowered his head and seemed to hesitate for a second, but then he looked up at Andrew with a determined look in his eyes.

'Cover me,' he said.

Andrew had no time to respond. Zaki whipped out his glowstick and tossed it over the steel box towards the antechamber, and then he ran past Andrew around the corner of the steel box and out in front of it where the soldiers would have a clear shot at him.

But his ruse worked, at least for a few moments. The green glowstick momentarily disorientated the soldiers, who must have thought it was a grenade, because they knelt down to take cover, and followed the glowstick with their guns as it sailed over them and landed inside the antechamber. One of them lost his footing and scrambled to move away from what he thought would be the blast of a grenade.

By that time Doctor Zaki had made it to one of the corners of the box which was facing the antechamber and the soldiers. He reached up and pulled hard on first one, then another of the handles on the large clasps that held the steel box together.

Andrew was now back up and firing at the soldiers. He had virtually no time to aim properly, but several of his shots connected with the soldiers as he emptied his magazine. He was pretty sure he had managed to get past the body armour of at least one of them, but most of the bullets missed or slammed into the Kevlar pieces. When his gun clicked empty, he dropped back down behind the steel box.

The soldiers realised they had been tricked, and while two of them trained their guns at Doctor Zaki who was scrambling towards the second corner of the box, the third was reaching for a hand grenade attached to his tactical vest.

At that moment a strange sound was coming from the borehole. At first, it sounded like a rustling, but it was very quickly becoming much louder, and mixed into it was the voice of a man. It sounded like a terrified scream.

Then a black-clad soldier slammed into the ground just under the borehole with a loud sharp thud, along with the sickening crunching sound of bones breaking. In the middle of a cloud of dust, lay a soldier, dressed like the other three in the chamber. His body was contorted in an unnatural position, with his feet close to his head and one of his arms bent backwards and sticking up in the air.

The shock of the three other soldiers was the last bit of help Zaki needed. While they recomposed themselves and turned back towards Zaki, the doctor was reaching for the top clasp on the second corner.

Andrew heard the sound of the shots from the submachine guns, and the helpless yelp as the bullets slammed into Doctor Zaki. One went through his thigh, another shattered his right elbow, and another smacked into his shoulder and exploded out the other side, spraying blood onto the steel box.

But Zaki had managed to release both of the clasps on the second corner of the box. With a final effort, he tried to make it back towards the rear of the box, where Andrew and Fiona were taking cover. He was only a few seconds away from safety when a bullet struck him in the lower back, and he fell forward onto the ground with a thud. His head made a sickening sound as it slammed into the ground.

There were a couple of seconds of silence, but then the front of the steel box that was facing the antechamber and the three soldiers began to move. Slowly at first, but then faster as it went, the steel section began tipping forward and out towards the soldiers. As soon as it started moving, a faint blue light shone out from the box, and the light became brighter and brighter, the more the section fell away from the box to reveal the meteorite inside.

The three soldiers, who were just about to rush to the rear of the cave to kill Andrew and Fiona, stood dumbfounded as it happened. The whole thing took only a couple of seconds, but to them, it seemed like an eternity. When the steel section finally slammed onto the floor in front of them with a loud crash, they were bathed in a blue light that made two of them hold up their arms, close their eyes and turn away. The third, who Andrew had hit with two bullets in the leg, immediately turned and began to crawl back towards the antechamber.

After only a few short seconds, the lethal effects of the barrage of gamma radiation coming at them began to set in. It started with one of the two soldiers nearest the box suddenly producing a single short cough. Then he coughed again, and within a few seconds, he was on his hands and knees retching and spitting blood.

The other soldier was already disorientated, and he was in the middle of taking off his helmet when he was suddenly robbed of his vision. Blood was seeping into his eyeballs as small fissures in his blood vessels began to develop, and as he rubbed his eyes furiously to try to regain his sight, he only managed to rupture his left eyeball. He let out a terrified scream as the full horror of what was happening started to dawn on him.

The soldier crawling towards the antechamber was struggling to breathe, and he was leaving a thick trail of blood from the gunshot wounds to his leg. As he clawed his way towards what he hoped would be safety, his legs and arms suddenly started to disobey his commands, and instead seized up in excruciating muscle cramps. He let out a drawn-out moan from the pain and then doubled up on the ground, unable to move.

The soldier who had been coughing and spitting, was now in a writhing heap on the ground, vomiting blood and heaving. He tore his helmet off and clawed at his throat, but this only resulted in bloody gashes around his neck as his tissue began to decompose and liquify from the hellish torrent of radiation ripping through every cell in his body.

A strange liquid was running down the cheek of the soldier who had been rubbing his eyes, as he attempted to crawl on his hands and knees towards the side of the main chamber. His legs were not working properly anymore and muscle spasms made it impossible for him to make headway. With sweat pouring off his face and in near delirium, he tried to use his elbows to crawl forward, but it was no use. In a final desperate attempt to get out of the wide cone of blue light coming from the meteorite, he tucked his arms close to his body and attempted to roll out of reach of the lethal flood of gamma rays coming at him. He managed two rolls before he could no longer control his body. He flopped onto his back, heaving and trying desperately to get air into his lungs, which were now filling up with blood and other bodily fluids. He only managed a few slow laboured breaths, before he finally exhaled for the final time.

Momentarily stunned by the horrific sounds of the dying soldiers, it took Andrew and Fiona a few moments to realise what had happened. When they did, they moved to the rear corner of the box, from where they could see the limb body of Doctor Zaki lying face down on the ground. Andrew instantly leapt out from behind cover, grabbed his hand, and then dragged him to safety behind the steel box.

By then, the grisly noises from the soldiers had ceased. They were dead.

'He sacrificed himself for us,' whispered Fiona, and leaned in over the motionless Doctor Zaki, who was bleeding profusely from his shoulder. She brought her ear down to his mouth.

'He's still alive,' she exclaimed, suddenly sounding agitated. 'We need to get him to a hospital.'

'I know,' said Andrew tensely. 'But we have to find a way out first. We can't get to the antechamber without being fried by the gamma rays.'

'What the hell are we going to do?' shouted Fiona, now in a full panic. 'We need to get out of here now!'

Andrew knelt on the ground next to Fiona and Doctor Zaki, shaking his head slowly.

'Doctor Zaki would not have done this unless there was a way for us to escape this chamber,' he said. 'There has to be a way.'

'The front of the box is on the ground,' yelled Fiona. 'There is no way for us to lift it back up without ending up like those three psychos out there.'

'I know,' said Andrew, trying to stay calm. 'Which means, there has to be another way.'

He looked up towards the top of the steel box. 'The lid,' he said. 'We can use the lid.'

'How?' said Fiona. 'It is way too heavy to lift. It is covered in lead, remember?'

'We don't need to lift it,' said Andrew. 'We just need to slide it forward and down in front of the meteorite. That will shield us on our way to the antechamber.'

Fiona looked at him for a moment. Then she swallowed hard and tried to compose herself.

'Alright,' she said. 'This had better work. But first, we have to look after Doctor Zaki. We need to stop the bleeding.'

They both took off their harnesses and boiler suits, and quickly tore the fabrics into long strips that could be used as bandages. After a couple of minutes, they had stemmed the bleeding as much as they could with the tools they had.

'His breathing is very shallow,' said Fiona. 'We don't have much time.'

'Ok,' said Andrew. 'We're going to need all our strength for this one. Grab the edge of the lid down at that end,' he said and pointed. 'I will take this end. On three, we try to slide it along and onto the ground. And whatever you do, do not get your hands over the sides of the box.'

'I am aware of the danger, thanks,' said Fiona, and nodded towards the three dead soldiers. 'I don't want to end up like those guys.'

'One... Two... Three!'

They both put all their strength into dragging the lid of the box along, and it immediately started to shift, slowly sliding towards the open side of the box. As they did so, a gap at the back opened up and blue light spilt up and onto the ceiling of the chamber.

'Keep going,' groaned Andrew. 'It's working.'

Fiona produced a long, drawn-out moan as her muscles were screaming at her to stop doing whatever it was she was doing. But she kept going, ignoring the pain, and within ten seconds the lid of the steel box tipped over and slammed one of its sides onto the ground in front of what had been the exposed side of the meteorite. For a terrifying moment, it looked as if its forward momentum would make it tip all the way over and onto the ground, but it slowly rocked back to lean firmly against the steel box.

The lid was now almost vertical and leaning against the remaining sides of the box, thus shielding the area in front of it from radiation. However, the ceiling of the chamber was now bathed in blue light, and the radiation was barrelling upwards from the meteorite.

'I don't like the look of that,' said Fiona and peered up at the ceiling. 'There is no way that is harmless. We need to leave right now.'

'There are still two small gaps on either side of the lid where radiation can come through,' said Andrew. 'We have to cross through it. It will only take a fraction of a second, so we might be ok.'

'Might be?' asked Fiona.

'We don't have a choice,' replied Andrew tersely. 'The longer we stay here, the more the radiation is going to permeate the bedrock around us, and eventually bleed back into the room. We have to go now. Help me grab Doctor Zaki.'

They each slung one of his arms around their necks, and then rushed as fast as they could towards the antechamber. Andrew could have sworn he experienced a brief moment of seeing stars as they ran past the narrow gap between the side of the box and its lid. But that could simply have been a momentary lack of oxygen as they rose and started carrying Doctor Zaki along with them.

'Just a bit further,' groaned Andrew as they shuffled along as fast as they could. 'Almost there.'

As they dragged Doctor Zaki the final distance inside the antechamber, the popping noise that Fiona had heard earlier returned.

Andrew looked up towards the borehole above them. 'Those were gunshots,' he said. 'Shit. What now?'

They lowered Doctor Zaki gently against the wall inside the antechamber and looked up. At the top of the borehole, they could just make out someone's head sticking out over the edge of the hole. Then a torch started flashing.

'It's Khalil,' exclaimed Fiona relieved. 'He's ok!'

'Alright,' said Andrew. 'Harnesses back on. We need to hook all three of us onto the wire.'

They quickly arranged themselves, the two of them sitting down facing each other, and both of them holding on to an unconscious Doctor Zaki, whose body was like a heavy ragdoll. Andrew yanked hard at Zaki's harness and managed to attach it to the wire. After that, he and Fiona hooked themselves up, and a few seconds later Andrew signalled to Khalil to start the winch.

The trip to the surface seemed to take much longer than the trip down, and several times along the way, Fiona placed her hand on Doctor Zaki's neck to check for a pulse. It was faint, but it was there.

After what seemed like an eternity, they finally made it to the top of the borehole. They could not have prepared themselves for the sight that met them.

Khalil was sitting on the ground next to the Jeep, leaning against its bumper and reaching up to operate the controls with his right hand. His hair and his boiler suit were completely drenched in water, and the boiler suit was soaked in blood around his abdomen. His face had lost most of its natural colour, he was panting, and his eyes were staring into empty space in front of him.

Next to the borehole lay the dead body of another soldier dressed in the same black tactical gear that the soldiers down in the chamber had been wearing.

As Khalil let go of the button on the winch controls, and let his arm fall down limp beside him, Andrew reached up to grab the steel beam that Doctor Zaki had placed across the borehole only an hour earlier. He quickly pulled himself up onto the edge of the hole, and then grabbed Doctor Zaki and hauled him onto the ground beside him. Then he helped Fiona join him, and they both released themselves from the hook on the steel wire and took their harnesses off.

'What the hell happened here?' asked Andrew, without expecting an answer.

The sound of his voice seemed to wake Khalil from his stupor. He looked at Andrew and blinked a few times.

'I think I need a hospital,' he whispered.

'Already on it,' said Andrew and lifted Doctor Zaki up and into one of the rear passenger seats of the Jeep.

As he strapped the unconscious doctor in, Fiona helped Khalil into the other passenger seat.

'The hospital is only a couple of hundred meters from here, just before the land bridge,' winced Khalil. 'Just head back towards the airport. I will guide you. Is Doctor Zaki going to make it?'

'He might if we hurry,' said Andrew.

He and Fiona bolted into the front seats, and the doors had barely closed before Andrew slammed the Jeep into first gear and it leapt forward, wheels spinning in the dry dirt. Less than five minutes later, the car came to a screeching stop outside Abu Simbel General Hospital on Ramsis Road.

Thirty-Four

Andrew and Fiona were surprised to see Khalil sitting in the chair next to Doctor Zaki's bed when they entered the room in the hospital. He was leaning back in the chair next to the bed, looking much better than when they had handed him over to the hospital's Accident & Emergency staff only three hours earlier.

Fiona walked over to him and knelt beside him, placing one hand on his, and the other on the arm of the chair.

'Are you alright?' she asked. 'I thought you would be in your own hospital bed by now.'

Khalil smiled and sat up, but then winced at the pain in the side of his lower torso.

'It probably looked worse than it was,' he said. 'I received a knife wound in the side of my chest. There was a lot of blood, but there was no damage to any organs. The doctors here say I am lucky to be alive.'

'I'll say,' smiled Fiona and rose. 'We were afraid we were going to lose both of you.

'How is Doctor Zaki?' asked Andrew.

There were several pieces of medical equipment next to his bed on the other side, several of them producing soft beeps to indicate his heart rate and other vital stats.

'He will live,' said Khalil. 'But he has suffered major injuries to his shoulder and two vertebrae in his lower back. They are hopeful he will be able to walk again, but it will require a long period of rehabilitation. It will be a long road for him.'

Fiona looked pained, pressing her lips together and wringing her hands. 'Poor man,' she said. 'Without him, we would all be dead right now.'

Fiona went on to recount to Khalil what had transpired in the circular chamber deep inside the bedrock of Abu Simbel.

'Those soldiers got what they deserved,' grimaced Khalil, shifting slightly in his chair. 'They almost got me too.'

'What happened up there?' asked Andrew. 'We heard the sound of gunfire. Fiona says she heard it twice.'

'It was crazy,' said Khalil. 'It was like something out of a Hollywood movie. I didn't realise it at the time, but as I was lowering Zaki down through the borehole, five soldiers were approaching the complex from the river. They came in a dingy, as I later found out. I was standing next to the winch when I saw the shadow of two of them coming from the other side of the shed. Zaki had just reached the bottom of the borehole, so I knelt down behind the car and pulled my gun out. As soon as I saw them, I knew we were in deep trouble. They looked like Navy Seals, with their submachine guns, tactical vests and body armour.'

'Yes,' nodded Andrew grimly. 'Those guys were definitely pros. Probably serving members of the military. No badges or markings though.'

'No kidding,' said Khalil. 'As they came round the corner of the shed with their guns out, I was already aiming in their direction. As soon as the first one of them spotted me, he raised his machinegun and fired. How he missed I don't know, but I managed to shoot him twice, and he dropped to the ground. But at that point, I knew that I was going to lose that fight, so I just ran around to the other side of the shed which is facing the river, and then I sprinted towards the river bank. They spotted me just as I was reaching the water's edge, and I could hear the popping sound of suppressed weapons behind me as I leapt up and out over the edge. I am pretty sure some of the bullets whizzed past me or hit the water.'

'Must have been your lucky day,' said Andrew. 'Those guys are probably not in the habit of missing their shots.'

'I guess so,' said Khalil. 'Anyway, I managed to dive down and swim downstream, letting the current take me along underwater and away from them. And because of the way the water's edge curves around the temple complex towards the west, they were unable to follow me for more than a few meters when I was drifting away from them. I held my breath until my lungs felt like they were about to explode, and then I finally surfaced. At that point, I was really surprised at how far away from the temple I was, and as I looked back, I could see the soldiers running back towards the shed. I guess they gave up on me and decided their real objective was the meteorite.'

'Or they thought you were dead,' said Fiona.

'Possibly,' nodded Khalil pensively. 'Either way, I was then able to swim towards the shore around two hundred meters further downstream, where I crawled onto the riverbank and just lay there for a few seconds catching my breath.'

'But you came back?' said Fiona. 'You could have been killed.'

'I suppose,' said Khalil. 'But there was no way I was going to leave the three of you. I knew what those men were capable of, and I didn't think you stood a chance. I had to try to do something. So, I crouched down and began making my way back to the shed along the shore of the lake. I was very worried they would spot me, but I guess they didn't imagine I would be stupid enough to come back.'

'Sometimes stupid wins,' smiled Andrew.

Khalil grinned and then winced again. 'I was able to sneak right up next to the shed, and I could hear the winch running, so I figured at least two of them were on their way down. I figured it was the best chance I was going to get, so I found an old steel rod that must have been left over from when the concrete shed was built. Just as the winch stopped again, I decided that it was now or never. I raced around the corner of the building, hoping to surprise them, and luckily only two of them were still there. I used to play baseball in college, and as I ran towards the soldier next to the winch, I raised the steel rod and swung it with everything I had at the back of his head. He was wearing a helmet, but the rod hit the back of his neck, and I could actually hear the vertebrae shatter as it connected. I don't even think he ever realised what was happening. I can't say it felt good, but at that point, it was them or me.'

Fiona winced. 'And now he's dead. That sounded awful.'

'Yes, I guess it was,' said Khalil hesitantly. 'But when you are in that type of situation, you don't think about that. All you think about is survival, and those guys had to be stopped if we were going to have a chance.'

'Good man,' said Andrew. 'You have balls, I'll give you that. What about the other soldier?'

'He obviously saw the whole thing and out of the corner of my eye, I could see that he was bringing up his gun. To be honest, I am not sure what came over me then. Although I have basic military training, I have never been in hand-to-hand combat. But I always knew that I was physically stronger than most, so just as the dead soldier in front of me was dropping to the ground, I simply grabbed him, held him up in front of me and then charged the other soldier, who was probably about three metres away.'

'Holy crap,' said Andrew.

Khalil shook his head. 'I am still not sure how I avoided being hit by the bullets, but I guess the dead soldier's body armour stopped them. I heard them smack into him, and I could feel them hit him as well. I somehow managed to barge into the other soldier, and when I hit him, he must have let go of the gun because it went clattering onto the floor. He quickly reached for his knife and was able to reach around his dead colleague, and stab me once in the side, but then he tripped backwards and fell into the borehole. I only just managed to avoid falling into it myself.'

Fiona looked at him, open-mouthed and stunned into silence.

'I've heard a lot of war stories,' said Andrew, sounding amazed. 'But that probably takes the cake. You're a bloody machine.'

Khalil shook his head and winced. 'No, I am an archaeologist. But I did what I had to do to survive. I hope nothing like this ever happens to me again. I will have to find a way to live with having taken two lives. Even if they were bad people, they were human. That should never be taken lightly.'

'Well,' said Andrew. 'You're a better man than me then. I say they got what they deserved.'

'Khalil?' said Doctor Zaki in a weak voice, slowly opening his eyes. 'Is that you?'

'Doctor Zaki,' replied Khalil. 'I am here with Andrew and Fiona. You're in the hospital. You're alright, but you got beaten up pretty badly. It will take a while for you to get back to normal.'

'Are you all ok?' asked Zaki and looked bleary-eyed at the three of them in turn. 'What happened?'

'We're fine,' replied Fiona, and went on to relay the sequence of events that had resulted in the four of them being in a hospital room together.

'Someone will have to deal with the shed and the borehole,' said Andrew. 'The temple complex will open again in a few hours, and we don't want anyone to discover what went on there.'

'Let me take care of that,' said Doctor Zaki weakly, looking as if speaking caused him a lot of pain. 'I will need my phone. I am not the only one in the brotherhood who has access to the temple complex. We can send in a small team and stage some sort of issue with the electrical grid. They will cordon off the whole thing and clean everything up. They will also be able to set things right down in the chamber.'

'Good,' replied Andrew. 'That can only happen too slowly at this point.'

'We should probably also consider sealing the chamber once and for all,' continued Zaki. 'In hindsight, it was naïve to keep the borehole. But if we fill it up with concrete, that should be the end of it. It will take a few days, but after that, no one will ever lay eyes on that meteorite again.'

'Unless the Aswan High Dam breaks,' said Andrew. 'Or it is blown up, in which case all the water in Lake Nasser will drain away, exposing the old temple complex again.'

The three others turned their heads and looked at him in silence.

'What?' said Andrew. 'It could happen. This meteorite is going to remain extremely dangerous for hundreds of thousands of years, and I am pretty sure nothing we humans have built has ever lasted more than five or six thousand years.'

'You're probably right,' winced Doctor Zaki. 'But let's cross that bridge when we get to it.'

'Alright,' smiled Andrew.

Just then, the TV on the wall opposite Doctor Zaki switched to a news show. There was a report about unusual earthquake tremors in the southern Sinai Peninsula.

Zaki smiled weakly. 'No rest for the weary. We have people in several of the media outlets, including Egyptian state media. I am sure we can make that go away too.'

'We should let you rest,' said Fiona.

'Something just occurred to me, said Andrew. 'I am going to contact Major Elsayed and ask for armed security here at the hospital for as long as Doctor Zaki is here. You never know what those people might be planning to do next.'

'That is probably wise,' said Doctor Zaki. 'I feel pretty helpless lying here.'

'Let me do that right now,' said Andrew. 'You should get in touch with the brotherhood and take care of the Abu Simbel situation. The sooner that is dealt with the better.'

Andrew and Fiona said goodbye and left the room, but Khalil decided to stay behind until the armed guards arrived, which they figured might be several hours.

★ ★ ★

'Sir?'

'Yes. Speak! What happened?'

'We lost the team, sir.'

'What? What the hell do you mean?'

'We lost all five of them. They were meant to report in every thirty minutes, but they went dark just after insertion. We have to assume that they are either captured or dead.'

'Shit! Those men were Special Operations. Top-notch. Any idea what the hell happened?'

'None, sir. The final time they checked in, they were approaching the site in the dinghy. Nothing after that.'

'Any witnesses?'

'Still unclear at this stage. Our local contact tells us there has been no police or military presence near the temple site, so probably not.'

'Right. Evacuate the townhouse. Get them all out. Leave no trace. Burn it, if you have to. We must assume that we are compromised. Bring the prisoner. We will have to decide what to do with him later. He might be useful as leverage. Everyone relocates to the compound immediately.'

'Yes, sir. Understood.'

'Maximum alert level. If they track us, we need to be ready. I will be there in three hours.'

'I will make the necessary preparations, sir.'

'And when you get there, prep the suit.'

'Yes sir. Consider it done.'

★ ★ ★

Doctor Mansour had lost all track of time when the door to his underground confinement cell suddenly burst open. Bright lights were switched on and several people rushed in. Two of them came round behind him, blindfolded him, unbuckled his restraints and then yanked him up to a standing position. Then they manhandled him towards the door to the stair leading up.

Desperately trying to make his legs obey him after so many days strapped to a chair, he stumbled several times as he was hauled up the stairs to the ground floor of the house. Even though he was blindfolded, he was able to see through a small gap underneath the blindfold. He was able to make out what looked like a kitchen floor, then a hallway and then a garage. He was then bungled violently into the rear passenger seat of a black car, and immediately thereafter the two men, who he guessed were the twins, entered on either side of him.

Soon after that, he heard the sound of the carport opening. The driver revved the engine a couple of times, and then the car leapt forward and out into the road, turned hard left and accelerated down the road.

* * *

Fiona was sitting in the hospital's small cafeteria downstairs when Andrew returned. He had been outside to try to make a couple of phone calls.

His first call had been to Colonel Strickland at SAS headquarters in London, in order to update him on the situation, and also to see whether British intelligence had managed to have any luck identifying either Doctor Mansour's captors.

He had also tried to reach Major Elsayed of Egyptian Military Intelligence in Cairo, but the major was unreachable. His deputy had then asked for a point of contact in London, and had then gone through the proper channels to provide armed guards for Doctor Zaki. According to Zaki, he had been attacked by armed thugs just after arriving on a holiday excursion in Abu Simbel. Given his status as a high-profile nuclear researcher at the nation's main research lab, the armed guards had not been difficult to arrange.

'What did Strickland say?' asked Fiona.

Andrew sat down next to her, folded his hands in front of him and looked down onto the floor.

'Some disturbing news,' replied Andrew and looked up at Fiona. 'The people who are holding Doctor Mansour, are without a doubt the same people that attacked us on Elephantine Island, and the same people who tried to kill us here at Abu Simbel.'

'Well,' said Fiona. 'We had sort of already worked that out, right?'

'Yes,' said Andrew. 'But what I don't think any of us ever imagined, is that those people are all serving military personnel, and they are led by a Major Bahman Elsayed from Egypt's Military Intelligence apparatus.'

'What?' exclaimed Fiona. 'Are you serious?'

'Sadly, yes,' replied Andrew.

'I can't believe it,' said Fiona, stunned. 'But he has helped us on more than one occasion.'

'Probably just to keep tabs on us,' said Andrew. 'And in order to be able to follow us in our search for the meteorite.'

'Why? What does he want it for?' asked Fiona.

'We're not sure,' replied Andrew. 'But definitely nothing good.'

'How on earth did our people in London discover this?' asked Fiona.

'Well,' replied Andrew. 'Ever since we first made contact with Major Elsayed after arriving here in

Egypt, British intelligence have been monitoring his movements and his contacts. You can imagine their shock when they realised that he was meeting regularly with several unsavoury characters from the Egyptian underworld, several of whom had known terrorist sympathies. The final proof came when he informed his office that he was taking several days off to attend to a family emergency. MI6 were then able to track him to a large townhouse in Zamalek in central Cairo, and checking the CCTV cameras of nearby residences, it became evident that he had frequented that house on a very regular basis over the past several weeks.'

'How did we get access to that CCTV?' asked Fiona.

'There are ways of doing that without anyone knowing,' replied Andrew. 'The dark arts of hacking, I guess you could call it. All well over my head and paygrade. But it is amazing what someone in an office at MI6 can make happen, just by using a computer with an internet connection.'

Fiona seemed lost in her thoughts for a moment.

'Anyway,' continued Andrew. 'They were able to identify several cars that came and went at that address, and one of them was the one we had a small run-in with at the Egyptian Museum.'

'Oh,' said Fiona. 'That one.'

'Yes,' said Andrew. 'That one. And working our way back, we discovered that it was the same vehicle that was used in the kidnapping of Doctor Mansour. He was being held at that townhouse.'

'Was?' asked Fiona. 'So, where is he now?'

'We believe he has been moved, along with his captors, to a compound several hundred kilometres out into the desert west of Cairo, not far from the Libyan border.'

'Any help from Egyptian authorities?' asked Fiona.

'No,' replied Andrew. 'And we haven't asked for it either. At this point, we don't know who we can trust and who has been compromised. This also means that we are going to have to handle the solution to this problem ourselves, without the Egyptian authorities knowing about it. At least not until it is over.'

'What do you mean by *solution*?' asked Fiona.

'We are going to send in McGregor and his team to extract Doctor Mansour and take out his captors. No prisoners. We can't afford for any of this to get out.'

'Crikey,' said Fiona nervously. 'I guess we should leave then. I mean, we should leave Egypt.'

'Yes,' nodded Andrew. 'It is best if we are not in the country when this goes down. It could get messy, and we do not want to be on Egyptian soil when the inevitable fallout comes.'

'So, you are expecting some sort of diplomatic incident on the back of this?' asked Fiona.

'Most likely,' replied Andrew. 'But I am sure it will be handled pragmatically in the end. Both of our countries have too many other things at stake here to let something like that sour the relationship.'

'So, I guess this is it then,' said Fiona thoughtfully. 'It's over, isn't it? The Ark is safe inside Mount Horeb, and the meteorite will soon be sealed sixty-five meters down in the bedrock of Abu Simbel.'

Well,' replied Andrew. 'The SAS still needs to tidy up a few loose ends. But as far as our part in this is concerned, I think it is safe to say that our role has ended. We should get back to London as soon as possible.'

'The sooner the better,' said Fiona. 'I have had quite enough adventure for a while.'

Andrew smiled. 'Alright. Let's go then.'

The two of them walked back to Doctor Zaki's room again to say their final farewells to him and Khalil. Khalil was overjoyed to hear that his old friend was alive, but equally worried that he might be hurt in the rescue mission being planned by the SAS. Andrew reassured him that the SAS team would do everything they could to prevent any harm coming to Doctor Mansour, and that they would be bringing him with them to the UK once the mission was over. After that, Mansour would be free to choose what to do, and until he did, he would be under the protection of the British government.

Andrew and Fiona then made their way back to Abu Simbel Airport and boarded the BAe 146-200 aircraft back to RAF Northolt in West London. They were both exhausted and quickly fell asleep during the flight. Had they stayed awake, they would have been able to go to the cockpit of the aircraft and look at an LCD display on the controls. The display showed nearby air traffic, with other planes indicated by small yellow plane-shaped markers. Somewhere over the Adriatic coast of Croatia, their aircraft passed another plane travelling in the opposite direction. It also had an RAF designation but was otherwise unidentified. Inside it sat Colin McGregor and his squad, having a short rest before their final pre-jump checks.

Thirty-Five

The co-pilot of the Lockheed Martin C-130JSOF unbuckled his seat belt, left his seat and walked back towards the cargo hold. The four powerful Allison T56 turboprop engines were growling loudly outside the fuselage, making the entire aircraft vibrate ever so slightly as it made its way towards the drop zone. The flight plan would take it to the western tip of Crete, where it would turn almost due south and continue into Libyan airspace, crossing over the coastline just east of Tobruk, and then follow the border with Egypt as far as the town of Al-Jagbub. Here, the aircraft would turn south-east towards the border, in the direction of the oasis of Siwa. Their designated target was in the desert, around six kilometres due south of there.

The co-pilot knelt down next to Colin McGregor and showed him a tablet with updated mission information.

McGregor pulled his earplug out of his ear so he could hear the co-pilot.

'We just got this from your guys in London,' shouted the co-pilot over the noise of the aircraft. 'I have been told to ask you to read it. You do read, right?'

McGregor turned his head slowly, to see the co-pilot grinning at him. He clearly thought himself a comedian.

'Cute,' smiled McGregor and shook his head. Then he gave the co-pilot a thumbs-up and plugged his earplug back in.

The co-pilot rose and tapped McGregor on the helmet. 'Good luck,' he shouted.

McGregor nodded and looked at the tablet. It showed the latest intel update from Colonel Strickland. Extensive up-to-date satellite imagery had been acquired since they took off from RAF Northolt. There was also a couple of pages of text laying out additional information that the teams back in London had been working on, while his squad had been getting ready to board the aircraft.

Initially, the mission had been a simple kill mission, but just a couple of hours before take-off, it had changed to also include a hostage rescue and extraction objective.

The hostage was a fifty-two-year-old male of stocky build, one point six meters tall and weighing approximately 75 kilos. He was an employee of a museum in Cairo and had been missing for just under two weeks. His condition was unknown, but the squad had been told to prepare for a medical emergency. His exact location inside the compound was unknown.

The compound itself was located at the end of a long dirt road leading south through the desert from the Siwa Oasis. It consisted of two main buildings, and what looked from the satellite imagery to be a large warehouse.

The final and most recent section in the intelligence briefing made McGregor sit up. A chill ran down his spine when he read it. It was a brief and somewhat speculative report, based on initial intel from US intelligence sources. The CIA had covertly accessed the Egyptian Military's central computer servers located in Cairo, and retrieved an internal alert about missing weapons. It indicated that a batch of thirty-eight SS-26 Iskander short-range ballistic missiles from the Russian arms manufacturer JSC Tactical Missiles Corporation, were unaccounted for. They had been delivered the year before and had gone missing shortly after arriving from the production facility in Votkinsk in Russia. They had apparently been received at their intended destination, but when military inspectors had arrived, they were nowhere to be found. They seemed to have vanished without a trace, and Egyptian Military Intelligence had turned up nothing so far. The team in London speculated that Major Elsayed was involved somehow, but they had no hard evidence.

McGregor lowered the tablet and stared into empty space ahead of him with a grim expression on his face. This mission had suddenly got a lot more complicated.

Wilks, the squad's sniper and second in command, who was sitting next to McGregor, leaned over.

'Everything alright, boss?' he asked.

'All fine,' replied the Scotsman. 'Slight change of plans. There's a small complication in the form of a bunch of tactical ballistic missiles, which might be at our target location.'

Wilks looked at McGregor's face. 'Nuclear?'

'Unlikely,' said McGregor. 'But we need to search the compound and secure them if they are actually there. They went missing from a military storage facility a few months ago, and they have the potential to cause absolute mayhem in the region if launched.'

'Alright,' said Wilks calmly, and unbuckled his seatbelt. 'I will brief the men.'

★ ★ ★

Just under two hours later, the C-130 had made it deep into Libyan territory and was heading due south and flying parallel to the Egyptian border. The route through Libya had been chosen because Libyan radar and missile capabilities were significantly inferior to those of Egypt. Because the mission needed to be covert, neither the Libyan nor the Egyptian governments had been informed.

The engines had been fitted with special-purpose propeller blades that would allow it to climb to forty-five thousand feet, much higher than a regular passenger airliner. The aircraft made a slow turn to the east, heading straight for the Egyptian border. The sun was about to come up over the horizon, but on the ground far below them, dawn was still around half an hour away.

The red lights in the pressurised cabin came on, and the team rose, adjusted their weapons and equipment which was strapped tightly to their chests. They also carried out a final check of each other's parachutes. They then donned their oxygen masks, getting ready for the HALO jump. High Altitude Low Opening was a useful way to insert a small team of special forces behind enemy lines. Not only could the aircraft fly above the effective range of most surface to air missiles, but the high altitude also means that the targets on the ground would never see or hear the aircraft overhead. An additional advantage, which the team would employ today, was the ability to glide long distances towards targets.

The C-130 was now less than five kilometres from the Egyptian border and made another left turn to fly back towards the north. At no point would it cross into Egyptian territory.

McGregor prompted every member of his team for their readiness and got an affirmative response from all five. In addition to Wilks, the team consisted of Logan also known as *Ghost* who was a recon specialist, Dunn the team's 'sapper' or explosives expert, and Grant and Thompson were fire support. Grant was carrying the same silenced MP5 as McGregor and Logan, as well as their satellite communications equipment, and Thompson was armed with an L7A2 heavy machine gun.

McGregor opened the channel to the co-pilot, and a few seconds later the loading hatch at the back of the aircraft began to open. Ice cold air immediately rushed in and filled the cargo hold, and as the team waddled slowly towards the hatch, each member grabbing onto the shoulder of the man in front of him, the air tore at their clothes.

After another twenty seconds, the green light came on, and McGregor started his slow run towards the edge of the hatch. The rest of the team followed him and soon they were all moving towards the opening.

McGregor reached the edge and continued forward, leaning over and out into the void. There was an initial rush of air as the turbulence of the aircraft wrapped itself around him, but after a couple of seconds, he was dropping below the slipstream of the aircraft. From then on he was in freefall, picking up more and more vertical speed as he fell towards the ground.

The rest of the team filed out of the back of the aircraft, and as they dropped away the aircraft seemed to disappear faster and faster high above them in the crisp icy morning air.

They quickly accelerated towards terminal velocity, which is around two hundred kilometres per hour, but then they spread their arms and legs out, which exposed small wing-like sections built into their suits under their arms and between their legs. These would increase drag, and would also have the effect of allowing them to glide horizontally at high speed towards their targets as they dropped. At this altitude, this technique would potentially allow them to travel up to fifty kilometres from their drop location. The Siwa oasis was around thirty kilometres from the border, so they could comfortably reach it from inside

Libya. Total time in free fall would be just over four minutes.

Initially, the ground did not seem to be coming much closer, as they continued to fall whilst shooting through the air towards the east. However, after a couple of minutes, they had descended to around twenty-thousand feet, and the pale yellow desert below them was now approaching at appreciable speed. Hundreds of sand dunes stretched away in all directions as far as the eye could see. Their forward momentum kept carrying them closer to the Oasis, and they could now just make out their designated landing site about half a kilometre from the compound. The air was screaming past their helmets, and it was becoming noticeably thicker and warmer.

When they dropped below three thousand feet, McGregor signalled for the team, who were dovetailing behind him, to deploy their parachutes.

The light grey chutes came out and yanked the team members hard as it slowed them down violently for the first few seconds. Soon thereafter, their vertical speed had dropped to around thirty kilometres per hour. The difference between the air rushing loudly past their helmets and the sudden calm as they descended the final distance down to Earth was stark. They quickly made their way down towards their landing site and circled around a couple of times to bleed off more speed.

As their boots hit the dusty ground, and their parachutes deflated gently in the light breeze, the sun was about to come up over the horizon. The landing site was behind a small hill and therefore not visible from the compound.

The squad assembled quickly around McGregor, each of them rolling up their parachutes. They dug a small hole in the sand and buried them all inside it.

'Wilks, and Logan,' said McGregor. 'Let's get eyes on.'

'Yes, sir,' responded Logan and started jogging towards the small hill. Wilks followed him with his sniper rifle strapped to his back.

As they reached the top of it, they crouched down. Wilks took off his sniper rifle, and they both moved carefully towards the crest of the hill. There they lay down next to a couple of rocks. The squad was wearing desert camo, which matched their surroundings perfectly, so as long as they lay still, they would be virtually impossible to spot from the compound.

Wilks pushed the butt of the rifle into his shoulder and tilted his head to look through the optics. He immediately recognised all the buildings and the layout of the compound from their briefing back at RAF Northolt. As he slowly moved the rifle from left to right, he spotted only two guards sitting in two chairs outside the entrance to the building. They appeared to be sipping coffee and talking. Next to that was the larger main building, and behind it was the warehouse. Next to the warehouse were two large cylindrical storage tanks, probably containing fuel oil for the compound's generators.

Through his high-powered binoculars, Logan could see an entrance with an elevated loading bay, and next to it was what appeared to be a ramp leading down to some sort of underground facility. At the very back of the compound was a guard tower with one person atop it. He was leaning lazily on the railing, smoking a cigarette, and did not seem to be paying much attention to the area around the compound.

Wilks pressed the small button on the side of his helmet that activated his microphone. 'Two guards by the small structure. Hostage possibly inside. No guards around the main building as far as I can see. One in a guard tower behind the main building.'

'Copy that,' replied McGregor. 'Any sign of the missiles or their launcher vehicles?'

'Negative, sir,' replied Wilks. 'They might be in the warehouse. There's also a ramp leading down below it. The gate is closed though, so I can't see anything.'

'Roger,' said McGregor. 'We are moving out now. We will be circling around to the north and approaching via the irrigation ditch along the road. Cover us and keep us updated on any movement.'

'Roger that, sir,' said Wilks. 'I've got you.'

'Logan,' make your way around to the south. We need eyes on from the other side too.'

'Roger,' said Logan. 'Moving.'

He then moved back down the hill, out of sight of the compound, and then started sneaking around the hill to the south and then behind a low wall made of rocks that stretched away towards the east.

McGregor and the rest of the team proceeded in a wide arc to the north and around the hill until they reached the irrigation ditch that they knew from the satellite imagery was leading back south past the compound on its western side. This approach meant that they would be able to get within fifty meters of the compound without being spotted and that Wilks would be able to see both them and the compound at all times.

As they approached, Wilks would occasionally ask them to halt and crouch down low, whenever the guard in the tower was turning to face in their direction. They would then continue moving forward again after he had called in the all-clear.

'You are going to need to drop the guard in the tower,' said McGregor in a hushed voice when they reached the point where the irrigation ditch was closest to the small building with the two guards. 'We can't get close to the hostage without being spotted.'

'Just say the word,' replied Wilks.

'Dunn,' whispered McGregor and turned back to face the explosives expert. 'Make your way behind the warehouse and rig up charges on the oil tank. We might need to create a distraction.'

'Got it,' replied Dunn and nodded.

He then started crawling out of the ditch and towards the warehouse, making sure to keep as much cover between himself and the guard in the tower. He quickly made it behind the warehouse where the guard no longer had line-of-sight on him, and then he got to his feet and moved swiftly and crouched over to the oil tank where he placed a high-explosive charge in its side. Then he slipped down a small incline and made his way to a group of large boulders thirty meters away, where he got his submachine gun out and took cover.

'Charges are set, sir,' he whispered quietly into his microphone. 'Just say the word.'

'Copy,' said McGregor. 'Logan, are you seeing anything?'

'Negative, sir,' replied Logan. 'There is no one on this side of the compound. They must be inside the main building or the warehouse.'

'Copy,' replied McGregor. 'Wilks. Drop the guard in the tower.'

'Roger. Taking down the guard,' replied Wilks and repositioned himself, aiming his silenced Heckler & Kock PSG1 sniper rifle at the guard tower.

The guard was lighting a new cigarette, a big puff of smoke leaving his mouth and drifting off in the breeze. Wilks carefully placed the cross-hairs on the guard's head, and then took two long deep breaths, exhaling calmly each time. He then adjusted his aim slightly higher and to the left to take bullet drop and wind direction into account. Then he took another half breath, held it in, and gently squeezed the trigger.

There was a muffled pop, and the recoil made the rifle jump back into his shoulder, as the 7.62 standard NATO round left the muzzle at more than three thousand kilometres per hour, or almost two-and-a-half times the speed of sound. It travelled the roughly six hundred meters in just under a second, and the guard never knew what hit him.

The bullet struck the side of his head and blasted right through. As his legs buckled and his body slumped down like a ragdoll, the cigarette went tumbling end over end towards the ground below. The top of the guard tower was out of sight of the two guards sitting outside the smaller of the two buildings, so none of them saw what happened.

A fraction of a second later, the muffled sound of the sniper rifle firing made it to the small building, and the head of one of the guards snapped to the right in the direction of the sound. The silencer had absorbed most of the noise from the rifle, but it was a still morning out in the desert with virtually no ambient sounds, so the distant pop was just about audible to someone trained to notice sounds like that.

The guard rose and unshouldered his submachine gun. Wilks could see him quickly turning to his comrade and saying a few words. He then also got out of his chair and readied his own gun. The two of them moved quickly in a crouched position towards the corner of the building. It was clear from the way they moved that they were not just goons. These two had obviously had military training. What was also obvious, was that they did not know exactly where the noise had come from. They made their way to the corner of the small building, peeking around it. They were in full view of Wilks as he was lying on top of the hill in the distance, but there was not a chance of them spotting him.

'Tower guard down,' said Wilks quietly into his microphone. 'The two guards outside the small building heard it. They are investigating.'

'Roger that,' said McGregor, and signalled to the rest of the team to form up on him and get ready to advance.

As Wilks watched the two guards, he noticed one of them reaching inside a pocket in his armoured vest and pull out what looked like a small walkie-talkie. He spoke a few words into it, waited, and then turned towards his comrade, shaking his head.

'I think they just tried to raise the tower guard,' said Wilks. 'They might be on to us. We need to shut this down asap.'

'Copy,' said McGregor. 'We're moving. Cover us. Logan, make your way to the back of the main building.'

'Copy,' replied Logan and started moving stealthily towards the compound's main building, out of sight of the two guards.

McGregor and the rest of the squad crawled carefully up the incline from the ditch towards the compound. They were out of view of the two guards, since their line of sight was blocked by two vehicles that looked like Humvees, painted a pale sandy colour.

'Safety off,' whispered McGregor to Grant as the three of them crouched down behind the nearest Humvee.

'Thompson, get ready to lay down suppressing fire,' whispered McGregor.

'Yes sir,' said the big man, and checked his heavy machine gun.

McGregor looked at Grant, who nodded to indicate that he was ready, and then the two of them rose above the hood of the vehicle, aiming their suppressed MP5s at the two guards.

One of the guards spotted them out of the corner of his eye, but as he turned to bring up his gun, both McGregor and Grant fired two rounds in quick succession. Their silencers absorbed virtually all the noise, and their submachine guns only produced small clicks as they fired.

The guard dropped down into a heap on the ground, and his comrade immediately ducked down and scrambled around the corner of the building, more concerned with getting out of the line of fire than trying to return fire. This would have been the right choice, if it had not been for Logan who was approaching from the rear of the compound in a crouched position but with his MP5 up in front of him.

As soon as Logan saw the guard coming round the corner of the building, he came to a gentle halt, aimed down the sight and fired twice. The bullets struck the guard in the torso, and he dropped to the ground in a small cloud of dust.

Logan knelt down, still aiming at the guard.

'Guard down,' he whispered into his microphone.

'Roger,' replied McGregor. 'We got the other one. Make your way to the opposite corner of the main building from where we are.'

'Roger,' replied Logan.

'Dunn, are you seeing any movement?'

'Negative sir,' replied Dunn. 'All quiet here.'

'Alright,' said McGregor. 'Thompson, you stay here and cover Grant and I as we move up to the small building. We'll breach and extract the hostage. Anyone comes out of the main building, you lay down suppressing fire, got it?'

'Yes sir,' nodded Thomson affirmatively. He then moved to the other side of the Humvee and lay down just under the rear of it, from where he would be able to see both buildings and the warehouse, as well as have partial cover from the parked vehicles. He unfolded the support legs on the machine gun, and then pulled back firmly on the hand cocking lever to chamber the first round.

McGregor and Grant then quickly and silently moved up past the first dead guard to the door of the small building, and stood on either side of the door, McGregor on the right, Grant on the left.

McGregor nodded at Grant, who reached out and grabbed the door handle. He twisted it slowly, and to their surprise, it turned out not to be locked. He pushed the door, and as it swung open McGregor knelt down and trained his MP5 inside. There was no sign of anyone there. He signalled to Grant, and the two of them moved briskly inside while sweeping the first room with their guns up. The inside looked like a metal workshop, and on one of its walls was a door to an adjoining room. The door was partially open, and the two of them moved quietly towards it.

It was a small office with a desk and a PC, as well as a filing cabinet behind it. On the wall was a picture of former president Gamal Abdel Nasser in military uniform. The president had died in 1970, but someone here clearly still revered him.

'Clear,' said McGregor into the microphone. 'No hostage. He must be in the main building. Let's move out.'

★   ★   ★

Inside the basement under the warehouse, a serving soldier from the Egyptian military's special operations task force called *Unit 777*, was readying his suit. It had been brought out to the compound the day before in one of the two Humvees now parked outside the warehouse. He was one of only a handful of people in the special forces who had been trained in the use of this weapons system. Initially conceived for use in urban close-quarter combat against heavily fortified positions, it was able to withstand almost any ballistic weapons, including all small arms. The only thing it could not deal with effectively was fire, but then very few combat units carried a flame thrower around with them.

Weighing close to seventy kilos, the suit was currently mounted on a special rig from where it could be strapped on by a soldier. But not all soldiers would be able to use it. Its weight alone meant that it could only be used effectively by someone at least two meters tall and with a lot of raw physical strength.

He had always been tall, but he had bulked out with the help of anabolic steroids, precisely in order to be able to operate this system, and the military's doctors had been more than accommodating in supplying him and the other soldiers in his small team with enough steroids for him to put on a huge amount of muscle mass.

The mounting rig was placed in the facility underneath the warehouse. Next to it were the four S-26 mobile launcher vehicles, as well as the service vehicle carrying additional missiles that could be mounted and fired from the launchers in just a couple of minutes.

He walked up the steps to the platform and flicked a switch to bring the weapons system online. Its servo motors whirred into action, and it opened up to allow him to enter. The suit closed around him, and he could not help smiling as it did so, feeling intoxicated by the power that was about to be at his disposal.

Thirty-Six

The sun was slowly revealing itself over the sand dunes to the east as McGregor and Grant headed out of the smaller of the two buildings, and proceeded to the nearest corner of the main building. McGregor was about to ask Logan to sweep around the back of it when its door opened and two men stepped out. They were wearing civilian clothes, but they very obviously had body armour underneath.

As they came out, they did not initially notice the two crouching camouflaged figures off to their left and started heading towards the warehouse. Then one of them spotted the body of one of the guards outside the small building. He immediately brought up his gun, and almost at the same time, his comrade spotted McGregor and Grant by the corner of the main building. They both yelled and started firing at them.

McGregor and Grant scrambled around the corner of the building, just as Thompson opened up with his L7A2 heavy machine gun. It sent a hail of bullets towards the two guards, and one of them was hit immediately in the leg. He fell over, but incredibly, rather than turn tail and run for cover, both he and his comrade managed to return fire towards Thompson, who had to roll away and into cover behind the wheels of the Humvee.

The two men scrambled back inside the building and shut the door as McGregor and Grant peeked around the corner.

'Logan, see if you can make it up to the top of the guard tower,' said McGregor. 'We could do with some more cover fire.'

'Affirmative,' replied Logan and ran for the tower.

Within a few seconds, he had climbed the roughly ten meters to the top, where he found the dead guard with half of his head missing. Logan grabbed his Kevlar vest and dragged him to the edge of the platform, and then hauled him over the side. The body hit the ground below with a thud.

Just as it did, there was a loud noise from the direction of the warehouse. At first, McGregor could not see where it came from, but then he noticed the grey metal roller door at the bottom of the ramp opening up. From where he was, he could only see the top of the roller door. Logan was behind the warehouse, so he had no view of the front of the building, and because Thompson was lying on the ground, he also could not see what was happening.

The only one who had a clear view was Wilks, but he was just over five hundred meters away on top of the hill.

'Wilks, we need eyes on,' called McGregor with an urgent tone to his voice.

Wilks shifted his rifle slightly to the right and looked through his high-powered Hensoldt ZF 6×42 scope.

Just then, McGregor and Grant heard slow and heavy thudding footsteps on the concrete ramp leading up from the underground facility of the warehouse.

Then Wilks came on the radio.

'What the actual fuck,' he exclaimed.

'Wilks?' said McGregor sternly. 'I need to know what you're seeing.'

'Uhm. Well,' said Wilks. 'I am not sure. It looks like something out of a Sci-Fi movie. There's a guy coming up the ramp wearing super heavy body armour. He has a helmet on with full face cover, and he is completely covered in armour plating. It looks like some sort of armoured exoskeleton. But that's not all. It looks like he is carrying a Gatling Gun.'

'Shit,' said McGregor. 'This is bad.'

The M134 GAU-17 'Vulcan' Gatling Gun, is a six-barrelled machinegun used mainly for providing suppressing fire from the air. It is most often mounted on aircraft and helicopters, providing close air support to troops on the ground. With a length of around one meter and weighing almost forty kilos, its rotating barrels can fire as much as six-thousand rounds per minute, making it one of the most fearsome machineguns on the battlefield.

'We're going to need a new plan,' said McGregor. 'Wilks, try to take him out.'

'Will do,' said Wilks. 'Not sure if my ammo can penetrate his armour though. If I had my 0.50 Calibre I could have taken him out easy enough, but these NATO rounds are not made for this.'

'I know,' said McGregor. 'You have to try. Our MP5s won't even tickle him. Thompson, get yourself ready. You might be able to do something with your machine gun.'

'Roger,' said Thompson and crawled back into position behind the Humvee.

'Logan, stay where you are for now.'

'Roger that,' replied Logan, who was kneeling behind the barrier atop the guard tower.

McGregor could now see the helmet of the heavily armoured soldier as he lumbered up the incline of the ramp. He could also hear the sound of the electric motors and actuators that helped the soldier inside it control its actions. Soon the armoured soldier was near the top, turning his upper body from side to side in order to scan the area in front of him. He was fully covered in a layer of small thick hexagonal armour plates the size of small beer coasters all over his body, and his knees, shoulders and elbows had reinforced but flexible joints to allow him to move and operate weapons. His boots were large and heavy, and they sounded like they were made of metal when they made contact with the concrete.

In his massive armoured gloves, he held the Vulcan, whose six barrels were already spinning slowly, ready to be revved up to full speed for firing.

Wilks aimed at his head, held his breath and fired. The bullet slammed into the front of the helmet where the soldier's forehead would be, but it ricocheted off with a loud whine as the deformed bullet spun away into the desert.

The soldier staggered back half a step from the impact, but then pressed on as if nothing had happened. As soon as he did, Thompson opened up with his L7A2 heavy machine gun. It can fire up to one thousand rounds per minute, and as it produced its characteristic dry coughing noise, a hail of bullets flew towards the soldier in the suit.

As McGregor and Grant watched, they could hardly believe their eyes. Thompson's bullets were hitting and jerking the armoured figure slightly as they impacted, but he kept walking as if pushing through a strong headwind. And then they heard the noise of the six barrels of the Vulcan begin to spin up in preparations for firing.

'Thompson, get out of there,' yelled McGregor.

Thompson had heard the noise too and was already moving. He knew he did not stand a chance against the Vulcan, and the Humvees would provide virtually no cover. He left the machine gun lying on the ground and sprinted for the incline leading back down to the ditch they had entered the compound from. Just as he launched himself forward and into the air, diving the final distance into the ditch, the soldier opened up.

Amid a deafening noise, a hellish torrent of lead and sparks ripped through the air and tore through the bodywork of the Humvee, completely shredding the interior and punching out the other side. The soldier fired for less than ten seconds, but that was enough time for the Vulcan to spit out close to a thousand bullets, many of which smacked into the dry ground, creating a huge cloud of dust around the two vehicles. One of them had caught fire, sending black smoke into the air.

'Thompson, talk to me,' shouted McGregor into his microphone.

'I'm alright,' panted Thompson. 'Just keep him off me.'

At that moment, the soldier spotted McGregor poking his head out from the side of the building, and since the six barrels on the Vulcan were already spun up, he simply turned his upper body, sweeping his aim across the small building to the corner of the main building where McGregor and Grant were taking cover. As he pressed the trigger, sending a burst of metal tearing through the air towards the two men, they dove back into cover behind the building. The hail of bullets pelted the corner, ripping small chunks out of the masonry and creating a small cloud of grey cement dust.

'Wilks, try again,' shouted McGregor.

Wilks already had a bead on the soldier and fired almost instantly. The bullet slammed into his chest but pinged off like hail on a window.

This time the soldier saw the muzzle flash in the distance and spun up his gun again sending a short burst towards the top of the hill. The Vulcan is designed for close to medium range combat, and it is virtually impossible to aim when held by a person, so there was no way he was ever going to hit anything at that distance, but Wilks got the distinct impression that the soldier in the suit was simply taunting him.

'No joy,' said Wilks. 'He's playing with me.'

'Dunn,' shouted McGregor. 'It's all on you. Detonate the charge.'

'What about the missiles?' asked Dunn. 'What if they are inside the warehouse?'

'It's a chance we have to take,' replied McGregor. 'Detonate.'

'Roger,' said Dunn and lay down flat behind the handful of large boulders he was hiding behind. 'Detonating in three seconds.'

The blast was bigger than any of them had expected. There was a bright flash, and then a giant orange fireball exploded out from where the oil tank had been. The shockwave hit the side of the warehouse and the entire left side of the building was blown in, as part of the steel structure buckled. A fraction of a second later the shockwave slammed into the armoured soldier, lifting him up and sending him in a short arc through the air and then onto his front on the gravel.

McGregor and Grant were safely behind the main building, which had just had its windows blown in. Logan felt the guard tower swaying disconcertingly for a couple of seconds after the shockwave hit, but then it stabilised.

From Wilk's perspective, it looked like a small tactical nuclear warhead had gone off. There was a small mushroom of fire and smoke rising from where the oil tank had been. The fire burned dark orange with huge amounts of sot from the oil mixed into it. A couple of seconds later, the shockwave reached the top of the hill where he was lying prone. He could see it as it approached him, and he bowed his head and closed his eyes as it hit. As it struck, it sent dust flying around him and made his clothes flap around briefly.

The compound looked like a warzone, and when he reacquired the armoured figure through his scope, he could see him slowly getting to his feet and grabbing the Vulcan in his hands once again.

'He's back up,' said Wilks sounding stunned. 'Whatever this guy is wearing, I want one.'

At that moment, Logan stood up on the tower platform and hurled first one, then two grenades at the armoured soldier. The grenades were still in the air when he rushed to the ladder, and then let himself slide down rapidly towards the ground.

The soldier in the suit must have spotted Logan in his peripheral vision, because he immediately turned towards him, spinning up the Vulcan again. Logan hit the ground and just as he started running for cover, the two grenades rolled to a stop a couple of meters in front of the soldier. They went off almost simultaneously and produced two powerful explosions, accompanied by clouds of dust and dirt blown into the air.

As Logan ran the final few meters to take cover behind another low stone wall, the soldier opened fire, seemingly unharmed by the grenades. Logan narrowly missed being hit by the bullets as he disappeared behind the stone wall and rolled over a couple of times to stop his own momentum.

'That's me out of ideas,' he shouted into the microphone.

On the hill, Wilks had watched the soldier get pushed over by the shockwave from the explosion, and had watched as he got back up and turned to fire at Logan. He could not believe what he was seeing when the two grenades went off right in front of the soldier, and he had simply started firing at Logan as if nothing had happened.

But that was when Wilks finally spotted his opportunity. As the armoured soldier turned around to fire at Logan, he had also turned his back towards Wilks, and the sniper was sure he could see a gap between the helmet and the armour suit at the base of his neck.

Wilks knew he would probably only get one chance to end this, as he placed the crosshair on top of the soldier's head and slightly to the left. He took a deep breath, exhaled partly and then squeezed the trigger.

The bullet exploded out of the barrel of the Heckler & Kock PSG1, closed the distance to its target and went right through the gap in the soldier's otherwise impenetrable armour.

The soldier instantly let go of the Vulcan which fell clattering to the ground and took half a step forward due to the force of the bullet's impact. He reached up towards his neck, even as his legs gave way under him, and he fell to his knees. He sat there for a brief moment, with both hands around his neck under his helmet and crimson blood pouring out. Then he toppled forward, his heavy helmet slamming into the ground. He did not move again.

'Target down,' said Wilks into his microphone. Then he let out a long breath and bowed his head in relief.

'I bloody well hope they don't have any more of those,' said Logan. 'That was too close.'

'Listen up chaps,' said McGregor. 'We've taken out five of them. We need to clear the main building. Thompson, get your weapon and reposition to cover the entrance to the warehouse. Anything that comes out of there needs to be taken down. Wilks, you too. Dunn, join Logan to form up with me and Grant at the door.'

A couple of minutes later they were ready to breach. They formed up on McGregor on one side of the door as Dunn placed a breach charge near the door handle.

When the explosion came, it shattered the door, ripped it off its hinges and sent it flying into the room on the other side. As soon as the door had stopped moving, a hail of bullets came from the inside. It sounded like at least three shooters.

McGregor's team were surprisingly calm as they took cover, readying themselves for entry. This was something they had done in several previous firefights and something they had trained for countless times. McGregor signalled for Dunn to throw two flashbangs inside, and as soon as they went off producing two brilliant white flashes of light along with very loud bangs, the team stormed through the door, taking down two soldiers caught out by the flashbangs and temporarily disorientated.

The squad immediately took defensive positions inside the room, covering the next doorway whose door had been blown open. Keeping the momentum up, they proceeded through the next two rooms which were empty, and into the back of the building which appeared to be some sort of make-shift barracks with twelve beds.

McGregor signalled towards another open door at the back of the barracks room, which seemed to lead to a recreational room with a TV and a billiard table. As they moved up towards it, a grenade rolled out into the middle of the floor.

McGregor barely had time to react, before Dunn came sprinting past him. Just as he passed him, McGregor heard the click as Dunn unclasped his helmet. As the explosives expert launched himself through the air towards the grenade, he ripped off his helmet and just had time to hold it underneath himself as he landed, covering the grenade with the helmet.

In that same instant the grenade went off, and the sound was deafening in the confined space of the make-shift barracks. Dunn, still clutching his helmet, was jolted off the floor, but the ballistic steel and Kevlar helmet managed to remain intact and direct the blast down into the floor. Luckily, the floor was covered in wooden floorboards, which absorbed a significant portion of the blast. Had it been a concrete floor, the energy would have been deflected back up into the helmet, and Dunn might not have survived.

No sooner had the grenade gone off, than two soldiers peeked around the doorframes on either side of the door to the recreational room, both holding submachine guns.

Both they and McGregor's team opened fire immediately, and the room instantly turned into a hailstorm of bullets flying in every direction. McGregor managed to take out one of the soldiers almost immediately, and his body dropped onto the floor in the doorway. Grant was hit in the chest and the left arm and toppled backwards onto the floor. One of the bullets was stopped by his body armour, but the other tore through his lower arm.

Logan immediately pulled the pin on a grenade and threw it through the doorway. The remaining soldier in the room attempted to dash behind cover, but as he did so he ended up running out into the room, which allowed Logan to fire at him. Several bullets struck him in the back, and he fell hard on his face like a ragdoll. A second later, the grenade went off with a deafening crack inside the recreational room. Nothing in there would have survived.

'Clear,' called out McGregor while still aiming through the doorway. 'Logan, check on Dunn.'

The sapper was lying on the floor, his clothes still smoking from the explosion. As Logan made sure Dunn had no serious injuries, McGregor moved sideways towards Grant, never taking his eyes off the doorway. When he got to him, Grant was swearing under his breath.

'I'm alright,' he grimaced. 'It went straight through. I need a bandage.'

'Cover the doorway,' said McGregor, and put down his submachine gun to tie a bandage around Grant's arm to stop the bleeding.

Grant was holding his submachine gun and aiming at the doorway while McGregor worked on his arm, and Logan was helping Dunn to his feet.

'I smell like a bloody barbecue,' grinned Dunn.

'Focus people,' ordered McGregor. 'Form up on the door. The hostage might be in the last room there,' he said and nodded towards the recreation room.

Soon they were all up and moving again, Grant now at the back, covering them in case anyone came in after them from the outside.

McGregor, Logan and Dunn filed into the recreation room where the grenade had exploded less than a minute earlier. Smoke and dust were still hanging in the air, the walls and ceiling were peppered with tiny holes from the grenade fragments, and the body of the soldier who had run for cover was lying curled up next to a wall. A small pool of blood surrounded his dead body.

On the right was another door, and McGregor was about to order another breaching charge when a baritone voice shouted from inside the room on the other side of the door.

'I have Doctor Mansour. If you want him alive, you will put down your weapons and let us leave.'

'Who is speaking?' shouted McGregor. 'Identify yourself.'

'I am Major Bahman Elsayed of Egyptian Military Intelligence,' said the authoritative voice. 'And you are trespassing on Egyptian soil. Your presence here is illegal.'

'That is not my concern,' replied McGregor calmly. 'We are here for Doctor Mansour. And you had better hope we don't find any of those S-26 missiles in that warehouse of yours.'

There was a short pause as if the mention of the missiles had caught Elsayed off guard.

McGregor looked at Logan and nodded. Logan then gently grabbed the door handle, twisted it, and pushed the door open.

'Hold your fire,' shouted McGregor. 'I'm coming in.'

There was no reply, but McGregor decided to roll the dice. He did not think that the major had a death wish, and if he were to open fire now, he would have known that he would not survive.

The room was a small office, and as McGregor stepped into it, he was met by the sight of Mansour hunched over in a chair, with Major Elsayed standing behind him, pointing a handgun at the doctor's head.

'The game is up,' said McGregor. 'Your men are all dead. And your little mech warrior toy has been decommissioned. Put the gun down.'

'You have no idea what your doing,' spat the major, and pressed the gun harder into the temple of Doctor Mansour.

'We already know about your missiles,' replied McGregor.

'You don't know anything,' sneered Elsayed.

'Really?' said McGregor. 'We know you hijacked them on the way to their storage facility last year. What are they for anyway?'

'Justice!' shouted the major angrily. 'Justice for the Jews.'

'I am not sure what you are talking about,' said McGregor, making sure he spoke as calmly as possible whilst his eyes examined Elsayed's face. The major looked unhinged.

'They are vermin,' shouted Elsayed. 'Parasites. Locusts, that have settled on Arab land. And you English helped them do it.'

'Well, I'm Scottish,' said McGregor, trying to throw the major off guard. 'And I am not too interested in politics.'

'You fool,' shouted the major, practically frothing at the mouth. 'It's happening in your country too. You should be on *our* side. The Jews are taking over everything. Give them enough time, and they will take over governments, businesses, the banks, everything. Even the military.'

As he spoke, he removed the gun from Doctor Mansour's head and took a couple of steps towards McGregor, as if trying to persuade him to see sense.

'Let me guess,' said McGregor, momentarily playing along. 'You think they took Arab land when the state of Israel was created?'

'It is not something I think,' retorted Elsayed dismissively. 'It is a fact. Arabs lived on that land before the Jews came from all over the world and settled there. It is not their land, and if the world will not set this right, then I will make sure the land of Israel is uninhabitable for the next ten thousand years.'

McGregor stared at him for a couple of seconds, and then the pieces fell into place. 'The meteorite,' he said, as the full implications of the crazed major began to dawn on him. 'You were going to load those missiles with radioactive material.'

Major Elsayed produced a devilish smile. 'Well, look who's the clever one,' he said sarcastically.

'That sounds impossible,' said McGregor. 'How were you going to do it?' he continued, trying to appeal to the major's ego and vanity.

'It was destiny,' replied the major. 'That meteorite fell on this land eons ago, and it did so for a reason. It came down here to allow us, the descendants of the ancients, to protect the land of Egypt from foreigners like the Jews. Ground down to a powder, and spread over the entire area of Israel, it will force the Jews to leave Israel and never come back.'

'That's what the missiles were for,' said McGregor. 'Detonations at altitude. Airbursts with massive amounts of highly radioactive materials falling like rain everywhere.'

'That's right,' said Elsayed menacingly, clearly taking pleasure in imagining his plan playing out. 'Every last square kilometre of Israel would be irradiated and left uninhabitable for thousands of generations. From one day to the next, the Jews would be stripped of the land they stole from us. Like I said. It is simply justice.'

While Elsayed had been speaking, Doctor Mansour had been shifting slightly in his chair, and McGregor noticed how he had managed to free one of his hands. Mansour looked up and made eye contact with McGregor. The Scotsman quickly returned his gaze to major Elsayed, and did not react to what he was seeing behind him.

'The only justice that is going to play out here, is you ending up in a jail cell for the rest of your life,' said McGregor. 'Or perhaps I am mistaken,' he continued, feigning puzzlement. 'Does high treason carry the death penalty in Egypt?'

Major Elsayed's face turned red. 'I am no traitor,' he spluttered. 'I am protecting the Arabs from the toxic influence that you British laid at our door all those years ago. I am putting things right.'

As Elsayed shouted and gesticulated, Mansour, sitting behind him, had untied the restraints on his other hand and on his feet. McGregor could see the bandaged stump where the doctor seemed to have lost several fingers. The bandages were dirty with grime and coagulated blood, and they looked like they had not been changed for several days.

'The Jews need to be stopped once and for all,' continued the enraged major, stepping directly in front of Doctor Mansour and glowering at McGregor. 'The only question you need to ask yourself is whether you are going to help us do it, or whether you are going to roll over and let them take over the world. Make your decision and stop wasting my time.'

'What I am going to do,' said McGregor calmly, 'is take you back to the UK. And then I imagine the UK government will hand you over to the International Court of Justice for plotting to carry out acts of terrorism and crimes against humanity.'

As McGregor spoke, Doctor Mansour rose silently behind Elsayed.

The major produced a short, almost maniacal laugh. 'You pathetic little snake,' he spat. 'I would rather die than...'

At that moment, Doctor Mansour took a step forward, bringing his right arm up and out to his side. McGregor could see that he was gripping a pen in a white-knuckled fist. Mansour then produced a roar as he rammed the pen into Elsayed's neck. He immediately pulled it out again, and blood spurted violently from the right side of the major's neck. Mansour then rammed it back in again, as Elsayed instinctively dropped his gun and both of his hands reached up to his neck to try to stop the bleeding.

He produced a short gurgling sound as his throat filled with blood, and it started running out of his mouth and onto his military uniform. As he fell to his knees, probably knowing that he was dying, he looked up at McGregor with a look of both surprise and a plea for help. Perhaps he thought McGregor might have been persuaded to be on his side.

McGregor just stood there along with the rest of the team, watching as the major slumped onto the floor and bled out.

'Are you alright,' asked Logan, stepping around McGregor and Elsayed to help steady Mansour, whose legs were wobbling.

'The pen,' whispered Doctor Mansour with a trembling voice.

'Sorry?' said Logan. 'What did you say?'

'The pen,' repeated Doctor Mansour, in an exhausted tone of voice that was tinged with a sense of shock, as he stood there staring down at Major Elsayed. 'The pen is mightier than the sword.'

Logan glanced at McGregor with a perplexed look on his face.

'We need to get out of here,' said McGregor. 'Dunn, get back outside and radio central command for extraction. Grant, you stay here and look after the Doctor. Logan, you're with me. We are going to have a look at those missiles, and make sure there are no more nasty surprises under that warehouse.'

McGregor radioed Thompson and Wilks that they were coming back out, and then he asked Thompson to join him and Logan as they headed down the ramp under the warehouse. As expected, the missiles and their mobile launchers all seemed to be there.

'Shall we blow it?' asked Thompson.

'Negative,' said McGregor. 'This is still the property of the Egyptian state. We've removed the threat from those nationalist fanatics, so we should hand the missiles back to the Egyptian military. It might also make them more forgiving of our intrusion into their sovereign territory.'

Two hours later, their extraction arrived in the form of a chinook transport helicopter, accompanied by two F-22s circling just inside Libyan airspace some thirty kilometres away, from where they would easily be able to provide air cover with their long-range air-to-air missiles.

The Chinook was on the ground for less than a minute, after which everyone was safely inside and strapped into their seats. The crew included two field medics, who immediately attended to Grant's wound and Doctor Mansour's hands. After another ninety minutes, they landed safely at RAF Akrotiri on the southern tip of Malta in the eastern Mediterranean. From there, they caught a flight back to RAF Northolt the next morning.

Doctor Mansour had agreed to come along to assist in the debrief of the mission since he had significant insight into Major Elsayed's group of fanatics. After that, it would be up to the diplomatic services to iron out the ruffles that their mission would inevitably have caused.

Thirty-Seven

A week later, Andrew and Fiona were sitting on a bench in St James's Park after an evening dining out at a Greek restaurant. Sitting there next to each other, Andrew with his arm around Fiona, and her snuggled into his embrace, they looked for all the world to see just like any other couple. No one would have guessed that just a few days earlier, they had laid eyes on the Ark of the Covenant, as the first people to do so in more than two-and-a-half millennia.

'I am glad we agreed not to tell anyone about what happened inside Mount Horeb,' said Fiona. 'That would just not have been right.'

Andrew pressed his lips together and tilted his head to one side.

'I must admit,' he said. 'I have never lied in an official debrief before, but I felt that I had to do it this time. If for no other reason than simply out of respect to Doctor Zaki and the Brotherhood of Horeb. He quite literally saved our lives.'

'Probably twice,' said Fiona. 'I am not sure how we would have gotten out of the well without his help. Have you spoken to Khalil?'

'Yes,' replied Andrew. 'I had a brief conversation with him last week. He is almost fully recovered from his knife wound. What he did at Abu Simbel was nothing short of legendary. I would welcome him into my squad any day of the week.'

'Yes,' said Fiona. 'Without him, we might still be stuck down in that chamber, slowly being roasted by radiation. I got my results from my second scan today. Seems like none of us suffered any damage from the radiation. They estimate that the dosage we received was roughly equivalent to a CT scan, so we were very lucky.'

'We certainly were,' said Andrew. 'I was sure I could feel the radiation going through my body as we raced out of that place. But perhaps that was just my imagination.'

'What happened with the whole Elsayed situation?' asked Fiona.

'Well,' said Andrew. 'It was obviously an extremely embarrassing incident for the Egyptian military intelligence, and they were only too happy to play down the whole thing diplomatically. The loss of thirty-eight state-of-the-art ballistic missiles was bad enough, but a renegade major with nuclear weapons ambitions was a nasty shock to the higher-ups.'

'Could it have worked?' asked Fiona. 'I mean, could Elsayed and his men really have pulled their plan off and irradiated Israeli territory so no one could live there for thousands of years?'

'Doctor Zaki's assessment was that the plan could have worked if he and his group of nationalist fanatics had managed to get their hands on the meteorite. From then on, it would apparently have been straightforward to grind the metal into powder and convert the ballistic missiles to perform airbursts with the powder as payload.'

'That is terrifying,' said Fiona. 'I am glad McGregor and his team got in there. Real heroes, if you ask me.'

'They sure are,' replied Andrew. 'But they will never be recognised publicly for it. That's just the nature of these things.'

'Has anyone been able to piece together what the motivation for Elsayed was in putting together this insane plan?' asked Fiona.

'In the end, it was all depressingly trivial,' replied Andrew. 'It turned out that Major Elsayed's father had served in the Egyptian army, and had died in the Six-Day War in 1967. This probably sowed the seed of his hatred of the Jews, and of his frankly delusional ideas about the role they have played in that region.'

'Yes, that all sounded deeply paranoid,' said Fiona. 'It is true that the state of Israel was created by the British, but it is not true that the Arabs alone owned what is now Israeli territory. As we now know better than most, the ancient history of the southern Levant is much more complicated than that. It was held and occupied by dozens of different tribes and ethnic groups in a hugely complicated tapestry of humanity, spanning many millennia. So, trying to decide who it originally belonged to is just futile. And pretending to know the answer to that question is irresponsible and dangerous.'

'Well said,' smiled Andrew.

'And Doctor Zaki?' said Fiona. 'How is he? Is he recovering?'

'He is well, all things considered,' replied Andrew. 'He managed to make the incident at Abu Simbel go away, as far as public attention was concerned. The official story in the news media was that an electrical substation in the Abu Simbel power grid had malfunctioned, requiring the area to be sealed off until workers could fix the situation. Of course, the "workers" were Zaki's brothers, and they managed to seal off the underground chamber by filling the entire borehole with concrete. It took a whole day, but there is no way anyone is getting close to that meteorite again.'

'What about loose ends? Are we sure there aren't people somewhere who know about the meteorite?'

'As far as we know, that information died with Major Elsayed and his group of fanatics. The only ones who know about it, are the brotherhood of Horeb, and Khalil and Zaki. And of course, Doctor Mansour. I don't think we need to worry about any of them ever talking about it to anyone.'

'I hope so,' said Fiona. 'Nothing good can come of that.'

It was a clear evening, and even with all the lights of central London shining up into the sky, they could see hundreds of stars in the black night sky above them.

'Do you see those three stars up there,' said Fiona and pointed. 'That is the belt of Orion, in the constellation of Orion.'

Andrew followed where her finger was pointing to, and he could make out three stars sitting next to each other in the night sky.

'Isn't it amazing?' said Fiona. 'The pyramids of Giza are arranged exactly like those three stars relative to each other.'

'Yes,' smiled Andrew. 'Those ancient Egyptians knew a lot more about the heavens than most people realise.'

'Look closely at the Orion constellation,' said Fiona. 'Just north-west of it is the Taurus constellation, and in between the horns of the bull, is what looks like another star. We can barely see it with the naked eye because it is so far away, but that is the Crab Nebula. When the ancient Egyptians looked up at their night sky, that blob of light was not there. Right now, when we look at it through modern telescopes, we can see that it is a beautiful nebula, made up of gigantic veils of gas and the remnants of an exploding star. But back in 1054 CE, the star that was there before suddenly went supernova. Apparently, the explosion was so bright and released so much energy that it could be seen even during the day for more than three weeks.'

'Wow,' said Andrew. 'That is astounding.'

'Considering that it is more than six thousand light-years away, you can begin to appreciate the absolutely huge amounts of energy that would have had to be released for it to be so visible here on Earth.'

'It is quite amazing,' said Andrew, gazing up at the night sky.

'What is more amazing,' said Fiona. 'is that by the time people saw it here on earth, it had already happened more than six thousand years earlier, because that is obviously how long it took the light to get here.'

'So, what we're looking at right now is ancient history too,' said Andrew.

'That's right,' said Fiona. 'The photons that are hitting our eyes right now as we look at it actually left the Crab Nebula back when the very first people were just beginning to settle in the Nile delta during the pre-dynastic period.'

'That is enough to make my head spin,' chuckled Andrew. 'I am just glad to have you around.'

'Yes,' smiled Fiona knowingly. 'Lucky you.'

THE END

NOTE FROM THE AUTHOR.

Thank you very much for reading this book. I really hope you enjoyed it.

I am always trying to improve my writing, and the best way to do that is to get feedback from readers. Therefore, I would be very grateful if you would write a review of it on Amazon. I read all the reviews I get, and they are a great way for me to understand the reader's experience. This will help me write better books in the future. Thank you again.

Lex Faulkner.

Printed in Great Britain
by Amazon